Copyright © 2014 Lindy Zart

All rights reserved

The characters and events portrayed in this book are fictitious. Any similarity to real persons, living or dead, is coincidental and not intended by the author.

No part of this book may be reproduced, or stored in a retrieval system, or transmitted in any form or by any means, electronic, mechanical, photocopying, recording, or otherwise, without express written permission of the publisher.

Cover design by: Mae I Design
Printed in the United States of America

Thanks to Kyle and Judith Frazee for pointing out my star errors —and if my information is incorrect, I solely blame them.

To Regina Wamba—thank you for the perfect cover.

I am much obliged to Wendi Stitzer—your set of eyes helps mine.

Thank you to Crystal Ferrill Morris for the name suggestion of Delilah.

For the beta readers this run—Tawnya Peltonen, Judith Frazee, Kendra Gaither, Jen Andrews, Tiffany Dodson, April StinsonScott, Desiree Wallin, Megan Stietz, and Tiffany Alfson —your words made my words better.

This is for Michael and Diane Mecikalski. I even used a line of yours, Dr. Mike—something about telling kids to get off the lawn.

I'll be sure to send you a royalty check.

In fact, it's in the mail right now.

UNLIT STAR

USA Today **Bestselling Author**
Lindy Zart

ONE

WHEN I WAS YOUNGER, I didn't understand that life was focused on what you had, what you looked like, and what others thought of you. The seventh grade showed me what reality was, and it was ugly. As I watch Rivers Young sit in his chair by the pool, I think maybe reality finally caught up to him as well. There is a slump to his broad shoulders I never thought I'd witness. Even with the distance between us, I can see that he looks broken. At least I learned at a fairly young age how cruel life can be—it took eighteen years for it to slap him upside the head.

What does it all mean?

It's a general question, but if you ask yourself it, you will already have the answer. You just know, because to you, it's whatever is prevalent in your thoughts at the time. To me, the question is about life. What does it all mean? What's the point of it? Why do we endure this journey of perpetual heartache and loss? And pain—there is always so much pain.

It changes us. The duration of our mortality is spent having instances transform us, whether we want them to or not. We're molded into some form of us only to have another moment morph us into another variation of us. It is endless. When someone asks what made someone change, I always think, *what didn't?*

Sitting across the deck from me is the perfect example of that.

I wipe sweat dampened bangs from my eyes and shove my aviator sunglasses back up my nose. Turning 'Dark Horse' by Katy Perry up on my Samsung, I sing along while watering the plants lining the wood deck around the pool. Swirls of pinks, purples, and whites make me think of cotton candy formed into the shape of flowers. The deck wraps around the shimmering white-blue of the water like a glove, hugging it as though to keep it warm. The yard beyond is lush with emerald strands of meadow and shrubbery. I think the only thing missing from it being a perfect retreat is a large Willow tree with its thin branches hanging down in perpetual sorrow—or not.

There's enough of that around this place.

Willow trees have a place in my heart and I am not exactly sure why. I guess because they remind me of my early childhood, but also because they look so woebegone. Their straggly green branches hang down like they are crying with their very being—I suppose that's where they get their name, Weeping Willow. A neighbor of ours has one in his backyard that my brother and I used to swing from the branches of many years ago. I haven't been near that tree in a long time. That was a time far in the past; a time I sometimes wish I could return to.

For most, life isn't just simple when you are young—it's innocent as well.

I make my way around the deck, dancing as I go. There's no worry about Rivers listening or watching me—he's in his own world most of the time. As far as he is concerned, I don't exist. I suppose I could feel bad for him, and a small part of me does. He was in a boating accident a few months ago that mangled his legs to the point where he is only recently using them again, and with difficulty. He'll always have a limp. He'll always be scarred.

The reason I do not feel worse for him than I do, is the fact that, yeah, okay, everything pretty much sucks for him right now, but *he is alive*. He is alive and every day that I see him sitting in that stupid chair with his dead eyes, I just want to shake him and slap some life back into him. I want to yell, *What do you have to feel sorry about? At least you're still breathing!*

Of course, I don't. I'm just the hired help. Plus, I don't think it would register in his thick skull anyway. When his eyes touch on me, it is as though I am not there. There is no recognition, no acknowledgment. There is nothing. I think he is so lost inside himself that nothing and no one can reach him.

The scent of flowers and candy float over to me and I grimace as I recognize the smell, glancing over my shoulder. Riley Moss hovers near Rivers, her blue eyes large and troubled. *She* tries to reach him. According to his mom, after his accident she was over here daily, crying and fawning over him. Now it's more of a two times a week visit. Soon it will be one, then it will be every few weeks, and finally it won't be at all. I know Riley. When she cuts her ties with someone, she doesn't just *cut* them—she severs them to the point of being irreparable.

Where Riley is concerned, I think of cruel laughter, taunting words, and the flipping of long brown hair—all the things I remember about her from school. And I think of anger heating my skin, my retorts, and wondering how two beings could get to the place we were. Her tongue was an arrow, I was the target, and my heart was the bullseye. Did she ever miss? Not usually.

Even now, as I look at her, I am shot through with her verbal ammunition. I glance down, expecting to find holes in my chest.

"Did you get your clothes from a secondhand store? Or, wait...did you make them?"

"Your eyes are so weird."

"The only reason you get such good grades is because you have no friends to hang out with. Of course, you study all the time—you have nothing better to do."

If I was a smaller person, I would hate her. Part of me does anyway, but the majority of me cannot. I can't hate something I understand. It would be like hating a bully that you know goes home and gets abused by their parent—it's impossible. In Riley's case, though, she's the only bully she goes home to. Her life, her world, her view of herself—she created it all. No one else had to tell her she wasn't good enough the way she was because she had already decided it on her own. She hates herself. I don't know if anyone else has realized that, but I have.

I decide it's time to water the plants near them—not because I am being nosy, although, okay, I sort of am. I casually stroll their way, careful not to look at Riley. I hum 'Timber' by Pitbull and Ke$ha as I pass by, my eyes sliding to her. Damn! Why did I look at her? When I see the pain and fear in her face, my chest tightens. And that pisses me off.

How many times did she make fun of me without caring about how her words affected *me*? How many times did she say or do something just to see how I would react? I guess if I had never seen the nice side of her, maybe seeing the horrible side of her wouldn't have pierced me so deeply. It's hard to face a monster staring back at you when you remember they once had good in them.

I think the cruelest thing she ever did, all her many spiteful words aside, was when she pushed someone in front of me so that I tripped over them. It was one thing to go after me, but to be mean to an innocent to get to me was going too far. I helped the boy to his feet, gave him his books, and walked away without looking at her.

The next day, there were flyers all over the school stating what she had done. I might have been the one to make them—I can't be sure. The boy was George Nelson; a sophomore with a minor form of autism. The kicker is, I don't think she realized who it was when she did it, but it didn't matter. No one likes people picking on disabled kids. For one solid week she walked the halls of the school in shame. Too bad it didn't last.

My goal for this summer was to be positively perky to the point of nauseating. I need to. I *have* to. Her proximity sort of messes with that, as does Rivers', to be honest. Rivers is easier to ignore, because, well, he ignores me too. And he was never outright cruel to me during school—he just acted like I wasn't there, even when I was right beside him. In school, it was Riley against me on a daily basis. I know why. I get it. But it's all so pointless.

"Hey, Del," she says in a small voice.

"Yo," I respond, glancing at Rivers.

His eyes are trained on the clear water of the pool. I wonder what he thinks as he watches it. Does he remember falling into the river water—how it wrapped around him and pulled him under? Does he think about his lower limbs being caught in the propeller? Does he wish he would have sunk into the dark abyss of the Mississippi River and forever remained there?

People have to be careful on the river—the currents can be treacherous and people can get sucked under the water and never be seen again. It's taken children, dogs, and adults alike. The Mississippi River is greedy in its quest to acquire lives. Why did he think he was above all of that, that he couldn't be injured in those angry, unforgivable waters?

Because he thinks he's unconquerable.

Or he *did*.

"How long have you worked here?" she continues. I think the only reason she is talking to me is because there is no one else to hold a conversation with. It's clear Rivers isn't up for nonsensical chitchat, or even meaningful.

"A few weeks. You were here last week when I was working."

"Oh. Yeah. My mind...sorry."

I set the watering can down and narrow my eyes at her. Is she for real? "Did you just say you're sorry?"

I mean, after everything we've been through, *this* is what she apologizes for?

A flush creeps up her neck, brightening her eyes. Pushing a lock of wavy brown hair behind her ear, she looks away as her small white teeth bite into her lower lip. "I..." Riley shakes her head and crouches next to Rivers. "I have to go out for dinner with Mom and Dad tonight. I just wanted to stop by quick and say hi."

I pick up the watering can and walk away, but not before I see her rest her forehead against the side of his short black hair and hear her whisper, "*Please*, Rivers. Please talk to me."

In an attempt to escape the empathy that slashes through me, I quickly slide open the glass doors that lead into the spacious white kitchen, and find Monica at the counter gazing at papers. I don't want to feel bad for Riley; she doesn't deserve it. And yet...

I set the watering can on the floor beside the door and walk over to Monica. When I first met Rivers' mother, I had a hard time linking her to him. With her pale blonde hair and gray eyes, her coloring is nothing like her son's—and neither is her personality. She is kind and generous. From what I've seen, Rivers—yeah, not so much.

I'm not really sure if she has a job or not. I know she goes to the gym in the mornings and does a lot of community-based meetings and fundraising meals, but whether or not she has an actual income is something I have yet to dis- cover. As her husband is an accountant for some big business across the bridge in Iowa, I don't think she needs one. I mean, they have a *pool*. A lot of people in Prairie du Chien do *not*. The closest we ever came to having one was a blue plastic contraption big enough for me to sit in—and that was all I could do in it. I had to splash water on my upper body to pretend I was in water of any substantial depth.

She looks up with a smile. "Want to trade bills?"

"What bills? I have all of one. For my baby." I pat my smart phone that holds an endless source of music and in- formation. And okay, distractions. My favorite line: Google it. Anything, everything. You have to google it.

"Exactly." Straightening on the bar stool, she nods toward the deck. "I'm grateful she continues to stop by, but…" She pierces me with her intelligent eyes. "I almost want to tell her to quit coming over."

I grab an apple from the bowl on the counter and take a healthy bite, juice squirting out as I chomp down. I wouldn't normally just help myself to the food around me, but Monica tries to force it on me every chance she gets. It's as if she thinks I am constantly starving and thirsty. I may be slight of form, but it isn't due to lack of proper nutrition.

I chew slowly to bide myself some time before answering her, because I know she expects a response. She always does, even when there is no actual question.

"Why would you want to do that?"

She looks at the back of her son and the sorrow on her face takes over until that is all she is—a throbbing mass of bleakness. My heart twinges in response and I swallow with difficulty. I can't handle this kind of serious, sad, emotion- al stuff. I just want to smile and laugh and forget there are any bad things in this world. I know—not very sensible

"It isn't helping her any, seeing him like this, being treated this way. She needs to move on. This Rivers isn't the Rivers she knows. He just—he doesn't *see* anyone. He hardly talks at all. Nothing anyone says or does gets any kind of reaction out of him other than belligerence. It's been almost two months since the accident. He should be recovering faster. It's mental more than physical. The doctors say there is nothing keeping him from healing but himself. I keep waiting for the day when he wakes up out of whatever world he's stuck in, but I'm afraid that day might not come.

"College is starting in the fall. I understand why he's depressed. He's supposed to be going to University of Texas on a football scholarship. Obviously, that isn't going to happen. I don't even know if he'll be able to run again. I know it's selfish, but I am okay with that, because at least he's *alive*. I am *so thankful* for his life, but I think all he sees is what he's lost, not what he still has. All he sees is a dream taken from him."

She pauses, and in that frozen instant, pain takes over her features, pinching them. It is the look of a mother who would give anything to help their child, but is unable to reach them. "Riley is going to Texas. They had it all planned out. She said she would stay here for him, but I forbade her.

"Her life can't stop because of what happened, and she needs to think of herself and not just Rivers. I didn't say it, but I don't think there is anything left for her here any- more. I just wish...I just wish my son would somehow let me know he's okay. He doesn't have to be the person he used to be; he just has to be *someone*. That's all. That's all I want."

"Hmm. Maybe some therapy would work?"

She snorts as she leans her palms against the glass of the

sliding doors and it looks like she is trying to reach her son through the window panes. "He is in therapy. He doesn't talk."

Turning from the door, she says, "I feel like I'm paying you to listen to me moan and groan more than I'm paying you to do stuff around the house."

"You're right. You are. I should get a raise."

Soft laughter falls from her lips. "You're a good kid, Delilah."

It's my turn to snort.

"Did you get everything done for the day?"

"I have Rivers' room left to clean and then I'm done."

"Okay. I won't keep you. Riley's leaving anyway, so I'm going to go sit with Rivers for a while. Let me know when you're heading out."

I nod, making sure I am not facing the backyard as I finish my apple. This whole place is enshrouded in sadness, making it hard to breathe at times. Watching Monica with Rivers is too much—the grief she feels rolls off her in waves of discontent, and I am constantly trying to duck out of its way. I chuck the apple into the garbage as my eyes trail over the stainless-steel appliances, creamy white walls, and hardwood floors. Nothing in this room is out of place nor requires my non-professional professional touch.

The lines of my actual job duties are blurred. I was hired to do daily cleaning around the house, but I've sort of entered the role of errand-runner, babysitter, and confidant as well. I am saving up for a post-summer trip, so I need the money, and there are far worse ways to spend my summer days than in the Young house, mopey scene and all.

There is a reason I always leave Rivers' room as my last clean of the day. Now, standing in the middle of the room darkened by drawn curtains and tragedy, a chill goes through me. My brain has an enormously hard time replacing the Rivers I went to school with, with the Rivers sitting outside. And this room doesn't help anyone, least of all him. It's like a shrine to his previous existence.

The room is as big as my kitchen at home and has a high

ceiling with two picture windows, milk chocolate walls, and gray curtains and bedding.

The scent I associate with Rivers—sunshine and something sweet—lingers in the room. A flat screen television takes up a good portion of the wall facing the bed, and awards line the shelves on the other walls. Most of them are athletic, but even Solo Ensemble and Forensics are in the mix. The guy was sickeningly talented throughout his school career.

At one point, there was nothing Rivers couldn't do.

When I think of the boy I went to school with, I see dark eyes lit up with confidence and the easy-going manner of someone who knew anything they wanted, they would get. Did I ever see him frown? Did I ever see any hint of seriousness to his stance? He was floating on the conviction that he would never fail. It must have been something, going through school like that.

School was something I had to excel at so that I could have better things once it was over. It was about getting good grades so I had a set future. I endured it—I didn't *enjoy* it. I wasn't timid, but I was quiet, keeping to myself unless I felt the need to state my opinion. I was a contradiction in a way—I didn't mind public speaking, but I also didn't go out of my way to interact with my classmates.

Framed pictures take over the remaining wall space. Riley and Rivers' smiling faces stare back at me and I turn away. With her fresh-faced good looks and his dark handsomeness, they were breathtaking to watch together. Their relationship is legend throughout the Prairie du Chien school walls. They started dating freshman year and have regularly been on and off since then. In fact, I think they may have been in an off stage at the time of his accident.

I wonder if Rivers, instead of Riley, is going to be the one to tear down whatever bridge of shared history is be- tween them, allowing Riley to fall down and away into the past. She's supposed to be the heartless one—the one that snips the ties that bind one being to another, but when it comes to him, it seems like her heart is an overachiever, and *his* is nowhere to be seen.

The thought doesn't really brighten my day like I thought it would.

Rumors of cheating, physical violence on Riley's part, and Rivers' insensitivity have been whispered in their wake. Riley supposedly cheated, who knows why—insecurities, revenge, to make him jealous?

I saw her slap him once, in the dark corner of a hallway after school had let out. I'd forgotten a homework assignment in my locker and was walking down the dimly lit hallway when I saw it, the sound of it like a piece of something beautiful being ripped away in a bandage of vileness, the sight of it enough to make the air freeze in my lungs. And what did Rivers do? He walked away; a perfect display of indifference.

I guess if no one ever cares about what you do, you keep doing more and more bad things in the hope that *something* will matter to them. At least, I think that's how Riley's mind works. If someone doesn't care about anything you do, then they don't really care about you. So maybe Rivers was the worse of the two —acting like he cared, not caring enough, and yet stringing her along.

They were in a bubble of implied perfection, and that bubble popped—or maybe it exploded. The majority of the kids in school acted like they were something special. *I* knew they weren't, but then, I didn't exactly have people running up to me asking my opinion on the subject of them either. Determination straightens my spine as I pick up a shirt from the floor and toss it into the laundry basket by the door. It probably hurts Rivers to sit in this room and see what his world used to be like. I don't even like seeing it all, and I have never been a fan of his. In fact, the first thing I would do is take down all of their pictures, which my fingers itch to do anyway. I hate looking at them, particularly *her*.

I go about straightening the room, careful not to look at anything for too long. I feel like I am spying on a life I have not been invited to see. For the duration of my employment here, I have spoken nil to Rivers and that's okay with me. Although, had

I immediately known it was *his* house I would be cleaning over summer break, I would have hesitated to accept the job.

I still would have taken the job, but I would have pondered it for a brief moment. I'd already had plans that, strangely enough, coincided with him. Funny how that stuff tends to work out. The despair and hopelessness in Monica Young pulled at my heart and I wanted to help her. I can't stand to see others in pain. Not her, and not even Rivers. I blow out a noisy breath, wishing my stinking inclination to heal everything wasn't so profound. Life would be so much easier if I didn't want to fix every broken thing I come across.

When I was a kid, I found an injured dove in the park near my home. It was in the grass beside a tree, just lying there. I knew something was wrong when it didn't try to fly away as I approached. It was pale gray with white—so exquisitely beautiful. It lay on its side, its eyes blinking, one of its wings broken. I couldn't leave it there, all alone.

With tears running down my face, I gathered grass and leaves, placing them in a notched-out part in the base of a tree. I gently picked up the dove. It was still, quiet, and so trusting of me. I knew it was dying and my heart was beating so fast, it was as if it was trying to pump enough life force for me as well as the bird. I held it close to me, wanting to heal it and knowing I couldn't.

I sat against the tree, keeping it warm, waiting. The sky darkened, its chest barely moving with its breathing. "I'm sorry," I whispered. When dusk fell and I knew my mom would be worried about me if I didn't get home soon, I placed it in the bed of green foliage, giving it back to the earth as the earth once gave to it. I turned to go, not wanting to leave it and knowing I had to. Looking back once to see its chest no longer rising and falling, and with grief heavy in my steps, I walked home.

The next day, I went back and the bird was gone. At the time, I told myself it was lifted into the sky by the hands of God, taken back home to live in a dream-like world full of endless blue skies. Now I know it was probably eaten by an animal, but at the time, thinking what I did gave me peace.

Not that I can compare Rivers to a bird, but even so, my impulse to help him comes from the same part of me that wanted to protect that dying creature. In his case, he makes it simple to keep my distance with his silent glares and dismissive nature. His muteness is almost less welcome than his arrogant personality had once been, but at the same time it is a relief to not have to interact with him. I've always been a little nervous in his presence, which aggravated me in school and yet continued all four years anyway. He was just *so much*—his presence took up the school.

I tug the charcoal-toned sheets from the bed and find clean ones in the closet, remaking the bed as quickly and efficiently as I can. Even though he is not here, I can feel his dark eyes watching me from this room that embodies him. The pictures that line the walls, the awards that boast his talents, even in the framed painting of an ocean above his bed—they all remind me of eyes that are dark and layered in ice, as though winter has encompassed his whole being. I hurriedly finish up like the very air is singeing me the longer I am in the vicinity.

I leave my final touch on the room by opening the curtains and allowing sunshine in. It coats the room in streaks of gold, its fire glittering on the frozen banks of a barren climate. I know the curtains will be closed again tomorrow. They always are.

THE STARS FILL THE SKY with their light as I stare up at them, feeling small and insignificant. I lie on an old itchy blanket I found in the garage, ignoring how the rough fabric abrades my sensitive skin. This is what most of my nights consist of, but I like to do this. My mom has asked me repeatedly why I so often lie on the ground and watch the sky. I never have a real answer. It's peaceful, in a way, but it also reminds me of how majestic the world truly is, and how what happens to me and those around me doesn't alter anything in the sky. One day we will all be gone from this world, but the stars will still be here, no matter what.

They are imperishable, even while we are not.

The tree limbs overhead sway with a gentle breeze, and around me are innumerable flowers in every shade imaginable. I love our backyard. It's my haven from the rest of the world. True, there are houses on either side of it, and even one farther behind it, but in the middle of it is a little piece of floral perfection. The uneven lines of trees and flowering bushes form a semblance of a natural gate around the yard, offering seclusion.

Not that I need it—the neighbors are used to my oddities and barely pay attention to me anymore. I don't think I could surprise them, with any of what they most likely perceive as shenanigans, if I tried. We live in an older community. I think the youngest neighbor we have is Mrs. Hendrickson, and she just turned sixty last week. I know because my mom had us take her a potted plant as a birthday present.

I close my eyes as a smile captures my lips. Focusing on my breathing, I draw air in and out of my lungs as my body melts into the lumpy ground beneath the blanket. Memories come to me in the sound of laughter, a feeling of contentment, and the scent of flowers on the breeze. That is what my childhood consisted of, and I miss it.

I may keep my distance from others, but I am in no way shy. I keep my distance because I've found that I am a better person when I have no one looking at me, making me feel like I need to prove something to them, like I need to show them I have worth. I know my worth and the only person I need to prove anything to is myself. I like to dance. I like to sing. I like to talk to birds and squirrels. And I don't care who sees it. I'm not saying I never cared, because when I was younger, yes, I cared. I cared too much and I was hurt because of it, but not anymore. In recent years, I embrace me, exactly as I am, and the rest of the world can screw off.

And isn't it weird that no one wants to change who they are, yet they aren't even trying to be themselves? Just a thought. We're all so focused on being somebody, and it's usually never the real us.

On the wind comes the crisp scent of growing vegetables. If green had a smell to describe it, that's what it would be—a garden of fruits and vegetables coming to life. It amazes me that a seed or a little piece of root can turn into something that keeps us alive. My mom likes that even vegetables and fruits produce flowers. Every summer we plant a garden. I watch it grow, nursing it, caring for it, and am reminded again and again how even something tiny can be needed to live. It's never about how much you have—it's about how much what you have means to you.

I suppose in answer to my mother's question about why I find myself lying under the stars whenever I am able to, surrounded by earthy beauty, my response would be simple. I fist my hands around silky strands of grass and close my eyes. It's so obvious, to me at least. Only within the arms of nature, am I truly free.

ANOTHER DAY, ANOTHER SET OF closed curtains to open. Monica is out on errands, Thomas is wherever Thomas works, I'm assuming, and Rivers is glaring at me from the doorway of his bedroom. It's not as much fun opening his curtains when he's watching me do it. I do it anyway, revealing the fiery light, the green of the trees that brag of life, and the calming, motionless blue sky. Why would he want to keep all of that beauty out of his room.

I pretend I don't notice him, humming to myself as I grab the laundry basket of clean clothes by the dresser. It's not my job to fold and put his clothes away, nor would I feel comfortable doing it if it were. The thought of touching Rivers' boxer briefs—I only know he wears those because there's a pair of white and black striped ones staring at me from the top of the basket—makes my face warm and my breaths come a little faster.

Weird.

I set the basket on the chest next to the dresser so he doesn't have to lean down so far to get the clothes out of it. Not that he'll appreciate it or anything. Maybe his mom will just do it for him anyway. I think everything he's ever had was either handed to him or came effortlessly to him—good grades, sports, good looks, girlfriends—he never had to work really hard at any of those things and yet he always excelled.

Or so it seemed.

The hand that clutches the door frame is white and there is stiffness to his body from the strain of trying to stand straight with uncooperative limbs. He wants so badly to be normal. I can tell. I see it every time he struggles to walk a short distance. I see it every time his eyes look through me and into the person he used to be. That's all he's seeing—his past he can never get back to. There is so much pain in his face, a lot of it physical, a lot of it mental.

I open my mouth to say something—I don't know what—but the look he slices my way halts any words from coming out. It was dismissive, cold, and vague at the same time. It was sort of eerie, and the chill that sweeps over my spine supports that assessment. Rivers is lost. I walk by him, my face forward, my eyes on the stairs in the foyer beyond, and I wonder how someone as lost as he is, can ever get back to themselves. And then I think, maybe it isn't about getting back to himself, but about moving forward and finding a new version of himself. I wonder who is going to help him out with that and then I get a mental image of me raising my hand.

Muttering to myself, I grab my tote bag and walk out the front door. I think it was settled the first time I saw him after his accident, actually. Me, the girl with no friends, yet who has the heart that wants to save everyone. Makes a lot of sense. The sunshine targets my pale skin and the hot air heats me as I hook a leg over my bike and pedal away. A warm breeze, scented with lilacs, caresses my face, and the strong brown limbs of trees sway with it. I smile, taking it all in.

Some compulsion has me turn my head to see if the curtains of Rivers' room will once again be closed like I figure they will be, and my breath hiccups when I find they are not only open, but also that Rivers is standing on the other side of the window. It's creepy how intensely he's watching me, or something near me anyway. What has finally caught his attention enough to give him a small tug back into this world?

ICE CREAM SHOPPE IS THE place to be for ice cream lovers in the summer. I may have an addiction, but I am not admitting it to anyone. All flavors appeal to me, but as peanut butter is my first love—above ice cream even—I usually get a 'Peanut Butter and Chocolate Chunk Frozen Avalanche'. I fight the sunshine as I inhale my large melting cup of euphoria, eyes trained on the railroad tracks across the road. I could watch trains all day and night.

Although faint and faraway, I can even hear them from my house and they lull me to sleep at night. It has been ten minutes since the last one blared its way across the tracks. Most towns no longer use them as a prominent source of transporting goods, but Prairie du Chien seems to cling to that bit of the country's past. I find the town all the more appealing because of it.

The umbrella hovering over the table I am sitting at offers minimal shade and I am melting along with my ice cream. Perpetually paleskinned, I have to lather myself in a layer of sunscreen every time I'm outside, or I burn. It gets to be quite tedious slathering the lotion on whenever I have the urge to go outside—which is often. I carry a bottle with me at all times 'cause I'm cool like that.

Chunks of choppy red hair have fallen out of my short ponytail and frame my face. The white tank top I'm wearing is damp with perspiration and my legs are sticking to the bench in an uncomfortably intimate way.

"You love summer," I remind myself.

"Look, she's talking to herself. Probably because she doesn't have any friends."

I roll my eyes at the familiar voice and turn to face the Evil Duo.

"You're exactly right. The selection around here is pretty

poor."

Avery is a shorter, curvier clone of Riley. They both have wavy brown hair, blue eyes, small features, and dress in clothes at prices unavailable in Prairie du Chien, Wisconsin. I don't understand why they would want to pay more for clothes, but then, I was never part of their crowd, so I don't know these things. Today Avery is dressed in a red sundress and Riley is in a white one. Whereas Riley looks slim and ethereal in hers, Avery looks plump and dolllike.

Eyes narrowing, she starts to say something else when Riley interrupts in a soft voice, "Leave her alone, Av."

Confusion pulls her mouth down, and I have to think I have a similar look on my face.

"Come on, let's go," Riley says, giving her friend's arm a tug.

I take a deep breath once they are speeding off in Riley's black Jeep with their hair floating behind them in ripples of silky brown. Something cold drips onto my knee and I realize it's my ice cream, forgotten in my raised spoon. I do not understand what just happened and that bothers me. The lines are supposed to be clear: Riley is a cruel bitch and I dislike her in a thoroughly therapeutic way. What does she think she's doing, melding black and white together like she is? And *why*? Maybe the whole Rivers scenario has softened her.

Right. No one *ever* really changes, do they? Not if they don't want to and not if they can help it. I'm no different. I *like* me. I like that I voice my opinions and I like that I am honest. I like that I know who I am and I am confident with that person. I like my funky hair and my mismatched clothes. I don't care what others think and I don't care if people like me or not. I will not change, not for anyone. I suppose that makes me as bullheaded as the rest of the world, and an easy target for ridicule. So be it.

At least I'm not a heartless wench.

I drop my empty cup in a garbage can, wipe my sticky hands on a napkin, and pop my ear buds in, beginning my mile-long trek home. 'Love Don't Die' by The Fray thumps through the wires. I have determined that music makes everything better, even this walk through air so humid that each time I breathe in it feels like I am inhaling steam. My feet crisscross and I slide to the right, a smile on my face as I dance my way home. Vehicles speed by on the highway and I only hope I make someone else smile as I bust a move.

I feel the ground vibrate before I hear or see it, and I pause on the sidewalk beside the massive locomotive. It shoots by in greens and oranges, graffiti and logos flashing by. The horn is loud and vibrates through my teeth. I whoop and pump my fist in the air, grinning as the monster machine roars by. It's impossibly strong, and looks indestructible. I wonder if I could be sucked under it if

I stood too close, the wind pulling at me even as I gaze at it.

An image of Rivers being sucked under his dad's boat clouds my brain and I frown, shaking the mental picture away. It follows me, though, and I keep thinking about how scared he must have been, and how much it had to have hurt. I rub the chilled flesh of my arms and hurry my pace.

Something tugs at me as I pass by the road that leads to the Young house—probably that stupid bleeding heart of mine that makes me care about others, even if they don't deserve it. The list is long and includes everyone, really, that has ever had something bad happen to them. Whether I like them or not, I empathize with them. One word: Riley. It's ridiculous.

As I am thinking it's too bad I can't just listen to my brain instead of the beating organ inside my chest, I veer to the right and head down Winne Court. Most of the houses are large and newer on this street; a collage of whites, reds, browns, and blues. Everyone knows just by looking at them that the owners have money. The exteriors are pristine and the lawns are well-kept —no patches of dirt are allowed in these yards. Each tree and shrub are strategically placed for optimal visual enhancement. It's sterile, unnatural. I prefer a disorganized lawn of flowers, trees, and bushes to add character.

I'm all about character.

I live in one of the poorer sections of town, more in the lower middle class instead of upper, like here. Not that the flowers around my home can't compete with any shown here—they so can. Flowers are my mother's life and even if there is no other beauty found on our street, there is the majesty of her blossoms to pretty it up. But whereas the yards around here are perfect and orderly, ours is like a super-sized floral bouquet. Janet Bana's motto is this: Flowers make everything beautiful. In keeping with that belief, she plants perennials in the yards of those who will allow her to, and she sets flower baskets on the doorsteps of those who will not.

I agree that flowers are pretty and everything, but I think they hide what is ugly more than make everything beautiful, if that makes sense. The ugliness is still there, merely muted. Sort of like laughter to hide tears, kisses to snuff out doubt, holding something close to make yourself believe it will never go away—you know, *delusions*. And I know why she's planted so much recurring life into the lawn surrounding our house. She's not just trying to cover up the ugliness—she's trying to pretend it doesn't exist.

My footsteps slow as the two-story white house with plum accents comes into view. It has a colonial feel to it, strong and simple with pillars that frame a small porch. Red, pink, and white flowers that I water five days a week line the sidewalk up to the house, and green bushes reside before the house. So far, I haven't killed any of the plants or flowers inside or outside of the house, so I consider that a plus.

In the two weeks that I have worked for the Young family, I have seen Mr. Young a total of one time. I usually get to the house around eight in the morning and stay until four. I realize some working people wouldn't be home during those hours of the day, but I get the sense that he is gone a lot more than he is around. Call it the disillusioned look in Monica's eyes as she speaks about her husband, or the emptiness of his touch on any part of the house. I see pieces of Rivers and Monica in her sweatshirt tossed over the back of a couch, a book I've witnessed Rivers reading left out on an end table, the scent of his deodorant or the smell of her perfume, but Thomas Young? Where is he?

Thinking these things, it makes sense that he is the one that answers the door at my knock. Tall and rangy in build, his hair is black and thick, his eyes dark, and the slant of his mouth is thin, showing how often he *doesn't* smile. Rivers is a slightly shorter, more muscular version of him, though his lips are fuller like his mom's and the shape of his eyes are reminiscent of hers as well. He also doesn't make me apprehensive like his father does. I'm not sure why I am so uncomfortable around him—maybe it's the unfriendly, I-am-better-than-you, angle of his face.

His Native American heritage is plain to see in his features and coloring; which I know because his son did a re- port on it in eighth grade. I remember this mostly because I was jealous that he was one half Native American, and one-half German—whereas I, on the other hand, am a mixed breed of who knows what. My report was inconclusive due to the fact that I stopped at four nationalities instead of continuing on—which are Irish, Norwegian, German, and English. Apparently, I am snobbish while drinking, tell Ole and Lena jokes, and have a bad temper.

Who knew?

"Hello." There is a quizzical cast to his face, like he cannot fathom what one such as I am doing on his front step. Dressed in red swimming trunks and a sleeveless gray shirt, it's a good guess he is either about to get into some kind of body of water or just got out.

"Hey." I nod.

"Can I help you?"

"I clean your house."

"It's Saturday."

"Yep." I rock back on my heels. "Hence why I am not cleaning your house today. So...is your wife home?"

He opens the door farther as he turns away, but I catch the suspicious cast to his eyes before they are hidden from me. He is wondering what I am up to, and he is positive I *am* up to something. "Yes. I was on my way out. She's in the sunroom. I'm assuming you know where that is."

"I clean it."

"So, you know where it is."

My eyelids lower a little as I say slowly, "Yeah."

That was implied when I said I clean the room. If I didn't clean it, I wouldn't know where it is.

"Go on in," he says, sounding exasperated.

"Got it." I slide around him and into the entryway.

I pretty much love every part of this structure, but the foyer is my second favorite room of the house. It's spacious and has a bay window with plants resting along the ledge of it. The walls are alive with memories of the Young family and a well-preserved antique desk rests against one of them. Vibrant plants are scattered throughout the room. It has a sense of class and serenity, like the person who decorated it took a lot of care to make it soothing and appealing. It wasn't just an entryway to this person—it was the start of a haven. I imagine that person was Monica.

A partially open stairwell in white leads to the second floor, and directly across from where I stand is a level of the house, somewhat lower than the rest, that is made up of one massive entertainment room. It has a movie projector screen, gray leather furniture, a bar, a universal gym, and a pool table. I think it's technically Thomas' place to hang out because the interior is darker and more masculine than I imagine Monica would pick, based on the rest of the house. Whenever I want to find her, I always check the sunroom first. She spends a lot of time in there, and I noticed Rivers does as well.

At first, I found that odd because I figured the guys would band together to watch football and adjust themselves in the manly man room, but if I go by physical proximity alone, it seems like Rivers is closer to his mom than his father. It isn't like he really talks to anyone all that much. Although, I've at least seen him with his mother, whereas I don't recall ever seeing Thomas and Rivers near one another—not that I see much of Thomas anyway.

Throughout the house, the walls are painted in creams, grays, and whites, and there is an astounding number of windows in every room to allow heaping doses of sunshine in, not to mention all the floors are wood. Putting all of that together, it has an open, sunny feel that has to fight with the melancholy seeping through the house in the form of beings. I still say the cheerfulness of the interior outweighs the dreariness of suffocating emotions.

A turn to the right is the living room and off of that is a small sanctuary—otherwise known as the sunroom, and my most favorite room out of the whole place. I kick off my silver flip flops near the door and head in that direction.

Monica is curled up on a rust-colored couch with a book in her hands. She looks up as I approach, a smile taking over her mouth. "Delilah! What are you doing here? Isn't today your day off?"

"I'm a workaholic." I sink into the recliner. "What are you reading?"

Pink floods her cheeks. "It's a book."

"Got that part. What's it about?"

She tosses it across the room and I catch it.

"'How To Get Your Child to Cope with Grief'." I grimace. "You need a book to tell you how to do that? Can't you just, you know, hug him or something? Tell him everything will be all right? Make him soup?"

Sighing, she rubs her face. "No. Yes. Apparently. He isn't a complete mute, but he barely says a word to anyone. I don't know how to get through to him. You went to school with him, right? Maybe you could try talking to him."

I hate to dash the hopeful gleam in her eyes, but I have to be upfront about this. I get to my feet as I say, "No. I can't talk to him. We weren't friends and we didn't talk in school. I don't think he even knows who I am."

"But you're a friendly face at least. He has to remember you. Maybe it would work?"

"I'm really not a friendly face."

"Oh." Her shoulders slump. She picks at the couch with her

head lowered. The hopelessness swirling around her is thick and potent. I unconsciously take a step back as though to keep from catching it.

When she looks up, she asks, "Was he unkind to you?"

Her eyes beg me to say no.

I am instantly and one hundred percent uncomfortable. I get an image of Rivers strolling down the hallway of the school with his posse, one arm carelessly slung around Riley's shoulders. She's smirking like she has something everyone wants and she isn't going to let it go. I hate walking so close to them, but the hallway is crowded and I just happened to fall into the mass of adolescent bodies after they passed my locker.

Their scents of money and popularity waft over me like a toxic ailment, the sound of their voices loud and boisterous. He looks over his shoulder, glancing at me and away as though I don't exist, and says something to Kent McPherson. They both laugh and keep walking down the hall as my footsteps slow and I realize how truly non-existent I am.

I take a calming breath and shake the memory away. Just months ago, that was my life. Now this is. The only attention I got was when I opened my mouth, and I didn't like to do that unless I felt it necessary, mostly as a form of defense—so any attention I got was of the negative variety. High school is recently in the past and that is where I want it to stay, although the fact that I am in this house, thinking that, seems ironic, and a little stupid. Plus, talking about the way I was or wasn't treated by a fellow student isn't really something I want to discuss with that student's mom.

"Um…" I blow out a noisy breath. "He wasn't exactly, no, but the people he hung out with weren't the nicest."

"And he never made them stop?" she guesses.

"Nope. But I honestly don't even think he was aware of it. Look, it's not a big deal," I hurry to reassure her. "You know how high school is. People make fun of people. It's just the way it is."

"It shouldn't be that way. Did you make fun of people?"

I fiddle with my ponytail. "No."

Nodding, she says quietly, "I tried to teach him about respect and manners, but somehow that all got lost when he began to listen to his friends more than me. And his father..." she trails off.

She shakes her head; the clouds clear from her face. "Anyway, since you're here, would you like some iced tea? I was just about to make some."

I accept, following her into the kitchen. Along with the lines of my job duties blurring, so have our roles as employee and employer. We almost seem like friends, but that can't be. If anything, I think she is lonely and worried and doesn't have anyone to reach out to, so I fill the hole the lack of companionship has formed inside her. I don't mind. I like Monica.

"Where is Rivers?" I ask as I watch her mix water and instant lemon iced tea together in a pitcher.

"Outside."

I glance out the glass doors, but all I see is the chair he usually sits in—empty. "Are you sure? I don't see him."

She turns to the door, a strange stillness to her. "I'm sure he was out there. Maybe he took a nap?" Even as she is saying this, she is striding from the room.

I have no such compulsion to search the inside of the house for him. I'm pretty sure I know where he is. I don't know how I know, but I do. Call it intuition. Call it understanding the workings of a person's broken mind. When you allow helplessness to take over your thoughts, you find yourself contemplating things you normally wouldn't, maybe even acting on them.

I sprint for the door and fling it open, racing toward the edge of the pool. The sun is instant fire on my skin, the air stolen from my lungs as the heat works away at me, instantly wilting me. I have time to think a single word—*No*—and then I am diving into the cool water. It's shockingly cold after being under the burning star in the sky. I find his form near the bottom of the deep end and my arms cut through the liquid in fast strokes.

He isn't moving and I wonder how he is keeping himself weighted down. Then I see his fingers digging into a grate in the floor of the pool. Anger and sorrow rise within me, clashing against one another as I swim toward him. The water isn't that deep, but deep enough. Doesn't it only take two inches of water to drown? This is six feet of it.

Rivers vehemently shakes his head as I reach him. I grab his arm and tug, and even though he is compromised, he is still stronger than me, easily eluding my efforts to rescue him. One hand shoves me away and the other refuses to let go of his possible form of demise. My lungs are struggling to expand and the chlorine is burning my eyes like liquid fire. I have always been a good swimmer, but my ability has never been tested like this before.

I jab my finger up with my free hand, the nails of my other hand digging into his forearm. He jerks away and panic propels me closer to him. I wrap my legs around his and squeeze as hard as I can, knowing this is a low blow, but I am desperate. My leg muscles are lean and strong from all the walking and biking I do and I use them in this moment without remorse.

He spasms in pain, no longer resisting me. His fingers release the grate and I take advantage of his temporary incapacitation to wrap myself around him, and shove us up with only the muscles in my arms. They want to resist, feeling heavy and noodle-like, but I will not give up. It isn't even an option.

I navigate us through the water until we break the surface. I draw in a ragged breath of air, my chest heaving as I doggie paddle us to the shallow end of the pool. Rivers' heart thunders against my forearm. He is quiet and still against me. He's given up. Completely. Knowing that puts a sharp pain in my chest. I blink my eyes and refuse to think about it right now. My ears are plugged and it takes a moment for the shouts to sink in. Monica is wading into the pool, her arms outstretched.

She pulls her son from my arms. "What happened?" she cries. "What happened, Rivers? Are you okay? Is he okay?"

She trains panicked eyes on me.

He tries to stand, but sways on his weak legs. I reach for him, firmly gripping his bicep within my hand. His eyes, usually so lifeless, are blazing with heat as they connect with mine.

Not breaking the visual connection, I tell his mom, "He fell."

His black eyes narrow, but otherwise there is no reaction to my words. I don't lie. Why did I just lie for him? Or was it for his mother? Maybe I lied for both of them.

"What? How? How do you know? How did this happen? I called the ambulance. I'm sorry. I didn't know. I was so scared."

I blink water from my eyes and keep my tone even. One of us needs to be calm about this—my pounding heart tells me I am a better actress than I realized I was. "It's okay. It's good that you called the ambulance. They can check him out and make sure he's okay."

Rivers' arm stiffens beneath my touch and I squeeze it hard. He will endure a physical examination so his mother can be confident he is truly all right—physically anyway. With the stunt he just pulled, he owes her that. It is also obvious that mentally he is not all right.

"Let's get out of the water. I think I hear the sirens. Why don't you meet them at the door, Monica, and explain the situation?"

She hesitates, her eyes locked on her son.

"It's okay," I tell her soothingly. "I'll stay with Rivers."

We manage to get Rivers onto the deck, and from there he struggles to a bench, each step slow and painful for him. Seeing his bare legs for the first time is shocking and I fight to not look away. I knew it must be bad, but I didn't know what to expect. He usually has them covered with a blanket, or wears lounge pants. Chunks of muscle are missing from the back of his left calf —jagged, mismatched areas of pink flesh the result of doctors patching his skin back up as best as they could.

The backside of his right leg has similar gashes of pale, angry flesh the length of his thigh with the skin around it puckered up in protestation of being sewn up in such a way. The consequences of being at the mercy of merciless boat blades is a collection of gouged-out flesh and scars that line almost every surface of his legs. The propeller made mincemeat out of his lower limbs.

He falls onto the bench and winces, maneuvering his body around so he can sit. That sympathetic part of me that I can't seem to shut off around him wants to help him and I clench my fingers against the urge. I know he wouldn't appreciate it anyway. I hate seeing people in pain and I finally have to look away from him. It literally makes me feel sick—my stomach gets all jumbled up and the urge to heave hits me, like now. It's like I can feel their pain with an empathetic knife into my very heart. I suck air through my lungs with jerky, shaky breaths.

Monica gently touches my shoulder, our eyes connecting, and then she walks toward the house to admit the EMTs. Her look was a silent thank you. I want to tell her I don't deserve a thank you for saving someone who doesn't want to be saved, for someone who won't even appreciate it because he doesn't appreciate his life. I want to tell her I didn't do anything to be thanked for. But she is already gone and my time is up.

I look at Rivers. His legs are straightened out in front of him and his features are twisted in pain, but even without the grimace on his face, it is contorted in ways it never used to be. He must have hit his head against something sharp as he fought for his life, maybe the underside of the boat or even a river rock —possibly an edge of a propeller blade.

The left side of his face has a pink scar that starts under his eye and ends near the corner of his mouth. It's thick and angry looking, like the river was upset it didn't get more of him than it did, though it still managed to leave its mark. He's lucky. Two inches higher and it would have been his eye. Another healing gash goes from his left temple up to the crown of his head.

He isn't pretty anymore.

It has to bother him. The crowd he hung around with in school was all about looks. They had the right hairstyles, the right brand of clothes, the right faces and bodies. I'm surprised Riley even came to visit him with his body and face marred the way they are. Maybe she really does care about him. The thought causes me to blink and I shrug it off, turning my attention back to him.

I wonder if he realizes how fortunate he is. I wonder if he cares. I sort of think he doesn't, what with tossing himself into the pool to drown and everything. And how shallow is that? To think your life is over because you don't look like you think you should. I wonder how I would be, in the same situation. Then I think of my current situation and I know I wouldn't be the way he is. I realize that is where we differ the most—I'm glad for every day I get, and he wishes the promise of a new dawn would fade into oblivion.

I lower my face so that we are at eye level. "The next time you decide to end your unwanted life, swallow some pills. Make it easier on all of us. Only make sure you do it when I'm not around so I don't have to try to save your ass again."

I stomp away, water trailing down my head to my legs as I move, leaving puddles in my wake.

I don't expect him to answer and his low words halt my footsteps. Not just his words, but the fact that he's actually speaking to me. Shock goes through me at the sound of his rough voice. It is the uneven timbre of a voice grainy with disuse.

"No one asked you to save me."

Anger spins me around and I stare at him for a long time. I think about the gift he has; the gift he is willing to throw away, and the unfairness of it burns through me in shades of black. There are so many people who have no choice in whether or not they live—he was given another chance when he was pulled from the destructive clutches of the river, and yet here he is, not grateful for it. That sickens me in ways that make my stomach roil.

"I didn't do it for you," I finally say.

His dark eyebrows lower and he looks away.

I pass by EMTs and a harried-looking Thomas as I decide my best exit route so that I do not get water all over the floors of their home. I can just imagine what nice things he'll have to say to his son—any time I've witnessed him talking to Rivers his words were clipped, his expression something close to disgust.

The thought that maybe I'm supposed to hang around and give a statement or something goes through my mind, but no one stops me, so I keep moving, intent on getting out of here while I still have some form of control over my mouth. I'm thinking if I suddenly went on a screaming binge, I might worry some of the people within the near vicinity and get hauled off instead of possibly Rivers. I hop from the deck and head for the gate of the wooden fence that surrounds the backyard.

"Delilah, wait!" Monica calls.

As I turn back around, I notice Rivers is staring at me, a flash of something in his eyes before he looks away. It almost looked like longing. For what? I know it wasn't for me personally. Maybe it was for my ability to walk without limits, or maybe it was for my ability to walk away from here.

Thomas stops beside him and Rivers immediately freezes, all expression wiped from his face. It is like witnessing a flower wither away to nothing as I watch. He looks down as his father says words I cannot hear; words I am sure I do not want to hear.

I turn to Monica. "I'm going to head home. You two should rest."

She looks away from her husband and son, wrapping her arms around herself as she shivers. Her face tells me she is worried about their exchange, but the smoothing of her features says she will pretend that isn't so. With her hair slicked back she looks young and vulnerable. Not surprisingly, her makeup is still in place. She must buy the good kind.

She says, "Thank you. If you hadn't asked about him...if you hadn't been here..."

"Lots of ifs there, Monica. I try not to think about those too often. It's the equivalent of giving power to some- thing that you shouldn't. Doubts suck ass enough on their own without tossing ifs into the mix."

A wobbly smile takes over her mouth. "You're right. How did you get to be so sensible?"

I shrug. "I grew up fast."

With a small wave, I open the gate and resume my walk home.

I've lived in the same house my whole life. It's dark blue with white shutters and a small porch—nothing outstanding about it, nothing to make it shine any more than the houses surrounding it. Well, except for the flowers. They abound in all colors and varieties, lining the structure and haphazardly sprouting up throughout the yard like a minefield of blossoms. The house is worn down, but the natural beauty of the flowers pretties it up. I don't understand my aversion to it. Maybe it isn't so much the actual structure as the memories inside it.

I just know that, as I stare at it now, I don't want to enter it. My chest is tight and I am finding it hard to breathe. Once I cross the threshold it isn't so bad. It's just getting there. Quite possibly it is due to the image of a smiling dark-haired boy with golden eyes playing with trucks on the porch that freezes me in place, piercing my heart with over-whelming sorrow. A memory, but potent enough to shred my insides with loss. It doesn't happen all the time; these memories I want to forget at the same time that I never want to forget. I wonder how my mother does it, day after day.

If I were her, I don't think I could.

My mom isn't home, but I didn't expect her to be, and I am actually glad for it. Things are more tense when she's home—I'm more tense. Not because of anything she says or does; Janet Bana is so purely sweet and I love her with every fiber that makes me who I am. I just, I don't know, put up so many invisible walls between us when I was younger that it seems impossible to tear them down now. And I don't understand that. How can something you can't even see, have the power to stop your tongue, turn your eyes away, and keep you from reaching out to the one person you should?

She's at her floral shop most waking hours. My mother lives and breathes her flowers, and I get why. They remind her that even in a world of pain and ugliness, cruelty and loss, there are still amazing things to cling to, to tell us not to give up, not to lose hope, and continue on to another day. There is life in death, always.

Sometimes I hang out with her there, cleaning and whatnot. Other times, like now, I want to be alone. I make myself a peanut butter, jelly, and honey sandwich and pour a large glass of milk. Sitting at the kitchen table with my snack, the sun heats my back through the window, drying my damp clothes. I tug the ponytail holder from my short locks and mess them up so they don't dry flat against my head.

I pull my sandwich apart as I eat, popping chunks in my mouth and chewing. The kitchen is painted a light shade of teal with yellows and creams added in the form of cabinets, furniture, and framed pictures. The trim along the windows and walls is white, as are the cabinets and appliances. My mother loves to decorate with light colors, as do I. They are like the sun shining in the form of hues, brightening the world, giving it a softer look. Green ivy plants hang from the ceiling by hooks, their vines trailing down in a waterfall of leaves. The room is smallish, and yet endless in its serenity.

I helped renovate it last year. We repainted the walls and furniture, added and removed decorative pieces, and rearranged where things sat. It was our summer project. It was also the first time in a long time that we worked side by side with nothing but the present in the room with us. I miss last summer in a way I do not feel comfortable examining. Lately, I long for it. Last summer was the final one spent untouchable by the past or the future. This summer I am suffocating in it. Everything is about time, and what I need to do with it.

The refrigerator hums and I focus on that as I eat my comfort food, feeling my body unwind and relax. I don't think about anything, because thinking about things makes me feels things, and right now, I want to be numb.

TWO

"WHAT?" I GRUMBLE INTO THE phone. My eyes are closed and I'm lying on my back, pretending I am still sleeping like I want to be.

"Delilah?"

I sit up and squint at the name and number on the phone. "Monica?"

"Yes. I'm sorry to call you so early and also on your day off, but..." She pauses and then says the rest in a rush. "Thomas' mother is ill. She has terminal cancer. She's been diagnosed for a while now, but it's rapidly progressing and they don't know if she's going to make it through the week. I have no one else to ask and, well, I would feel more comfortable leaving knowing you're around. I'm sure he'd be okay on his own, but just in case, I mean, with what happened yesterday—it should only be for a day or two and—"

"What is it?" I interrupt.

"Can you stay at the house with Rivers?"

"*What?*" I tell myself I misheard her, but then she continues and I know I didn't.

"We're trying to catch a plane immediately and Rivers can't travel like he is. I mean, he could, but it would be difficult. I need someone to watch over him, especially with the pool incident yesterday. I would feel better knowing he isn't alone."

"I'm sure Rivers is all for that."

"It doesn't matter what he wants," she says sharply. Apparently, they've already had a conversation regarding this. "It's for his best interest that someone be around while we're away and I trust you. All of our family is in California. We have some friends in town, but no one we consider close. I don't have anyone else to ask." Her voice has taken on a pleading note and I am not immune to it.

In fact, I already see myself weakening and saying yes.

"What about his girlfriend?" I ask in a last effort to keep from agreeing to her proposition.

"Rivers and Riley broke up before his accident. I think she was hoping he would want to date again, but...she came by yesterday and...it didn't go well. He finally talked to her. What he said..." She inhales deeply. "I don't think she'll be visiting anymore."

"Oh." Not really sure how I feel about this. Sort of sorry for Riley, but sort of indifferent as well.

"I'll pay you."

The selfish part of me wants to ask how much, but I can't do that without guilt eating at me, so I tell her, "I'll do it. For free. Well, I mean, I'll still be doing my normal job, so count it as part of that."

"Of course. Help yourself to whatever you want. The fridge is fully stocked. The couch in the sunroom pulls out into a bed, if that's comfortable for you. There is a spare bedroom upstairs too, but I would feel better if you were on the same floor as Rivers. Can you come over now?"

"Yeah. How long should I plan on being there?"

She pauses. "I'm not sure. A few days, at least, maybe a week. You can use the washer and dryer while you're here and anything else you want or need. If you need to go home, of course you can. I don't want you to think I expect you to be caged in here while we're gone. I appreciate this so much, Delilah.

I know this isn't part of your job description, but I am grateful. Thank you."

I end the phone call after telling her I'll be over in twenty minutes and flop onto my back to stare at the room enshrouded in the shadows of sunrise. I think I *should* have made a list of what my job duties were and were not, but I know it wouldn't have mattered. I would still be here, just like I am, saying yes all over again. The sun isn't even fully up yet. It is just wrong to be up before the sun says hello. Sighing, I blink my tired eyes and sit on the edge of the bed. There is no point wasting time grumbling about things. I could have said no. I didn't.

I heave myself from the bed and find my hot pink tote bag in the back of my closet. My bedroom always looks like a tornado has recently been through. I keep the butter-toned room clean with sweeping and dusting, but for whatever reason, I have a hard time keeping my clothes in the dresser drawers and hung up. I have piles of folded clothes on the wood floor, in laundry baskets, and on the foot of my cream and black swirled bedspread. It seems like such a waste of time to put all the many articles of clothing in their proper spots when there are better ways to spend the same amount of time.

Or it could be I simply have too many clothes—or I'm lazy. I quickly toss that description away.

As I dig through my dresser drawers, the coolness of the wood seeps into my knees where I kneel. I think about spending multiple days and nights in the same house as Rivers. I'm sure we will talk so much we'll run out of things to say. We can discuss in great detail his total shun of me throughout the history of our association. It'll be fun. And him smiling at me all the time? I'll probably faint from the sheer wattage of it. I toss my lime green two-piece in the bag and grab random articles of clothing to shove in the bag as well. I decide I don't need to bring makeup or jewelry because there will be no reason to get glammed up while babysitting the former football star of Prairie du Chien High.

After a quick stop in the bathroom to take care of necessities and grab what I'll need for the duration of my stay at the Young residence, I follow the scent of coffee into the kitchen. My mom is standing at the counter near the coffee pot with her back to me. I take in her light pink top and white lounge pants and the way her long hair is pulled up in a perfectly symmetrical ponytail.

I'm five and a half feet tall, but my mom is closer to five feet eight inches. I'm naturally a brunette where my mom's hair is blonde—so blonde it seems silver in certain lighting. Her eyes are large and blue while mine are some strange mix between yellow and gold. In the summertime her skin bronzes to an attractive shade of creamy tan—I burn and go back to white. There is an overall kindness to my mother that is harder to find in me. Sure, I have a big heart, but I keep it hidden. Hers is bright enough for all to see.

"Janet," I greet when she turns in surprise. I started the first name basis bit when I was six. Life happened and I thought I needed to act and think like an adult from that moment on, so in my mind she went from mom to Janet. At first, she was upset, but she learned to adapt. I know it bothers her though, and yet, I cannot get that three-lettered—or six-lettered—word to form on my lips.

"You're up early." Her voice is soft and lyrical, as is everything about her. My mom makes me think of a humming-bird—dainty, beautiful, and fragile. She's taller than me, so that brand doesn't really fit, except she is fineboned and seems smaller than she really is. I think it's because of her bearing more than her physical appearance. And no one can argue that she is visually breathtaking.

"Yeah. You know me—early to bed, early to rise." Except I wish I was still in bed.

I swipe hair behind my ear and reach for a mug above her head. She moves out of the way and sits down at the cream-painted table with its mismatched chairs of blue and green. My mother's decorating sense leans toward the antiquated, worn look. Nothing has to match; it just has to have character. My tastes tend to go the same way. I like the serene, vintage feel of it, almost like we are in another era where life was simpler and less hectic.

I pour steaming black coffee into the white mug with red lips on it. "Monica asked me to stay at the house for a few days or so. They have a family emergency and she doesn't want to leave Rivers alone."

Her coffee cup thumps against the table. "You aren't trained to take care of an invalid."

"He's not an invalid. He's just...semi-restricted." I sit down at the table and blow on the coffee.

"Still. Why don't they hire a nurse? And how well do you know him?"

"He doesn't need a nurse. He just needs someone to keep an eye on him—a babysitter."

Two pale eyebrows lift at this.

"I went to school with him. It isn't like we were friends or anything, but there's nothing to worry about. He's harmless."

"Bring your can of mace."

"No."

"Then carry Raid around with you. It's just as effective."

I take a sip of strong coffee, feeling my brainwaves accelerate. I don't particularly like coffee, but on my tired days, I give in to the pull of its caffeine. Otherwise, I'm more of a juice and water kind of girl.

"I would look pretty dumb with a can of Raid clipped to my waist on a hip holster."

She blinks. "That's a great idea! Easy access."

"No," I repeat.

The sigh that leaves her is the sound of her giving in. "You're an adult. I can't tell you what to do. But please be safe. And please call me every day, okay?"

She probably could tell me what to do, adult or not. This is her house, her rules. I am grateful to her for not pushing the issue.

I grab an orange from the chipped white bowl in the middle of the table and toss it from hand to hand, not sure if I should ask the question foremost on my mind. I do anyway, because I have to prepare her. She has to be ready.

A chill goes through me at the thought of the future, but I keep my tone merely curious as I ask, "What are you going to do when I'm not here?"

"What do you mean?"

I shrug, keeping my gaze averted. "You know, move out...pretend to be an adult, stuff like that."

She stiffens, her knuckles turning white around the mug she clutches within her calloused hands. True, wrinkles don't even think of marring her skin, but callouses do not have the same view. I think the rough patches of skin only make her more beautiful, really.

"You don't have to move out."

"Right. I get that." I knew she was going to say that. I set the orange down and stand up, dumping the remainder of the coffee down the sink and setting the mug on the counter. I turn to face her with my hands on the edge of the counter top behind me. "But I am, hopefully by this fall."

"There's no hurry, Del. Really. I like having you here. I mean, do you have any plans once summer's over? I know you aren't interested in college right now. Are you going to keep cleaning the Young family's house indefinitely?"

"It's just a summer job. They have a full-time cleaning lady, but she stays with her family in North Carolina for the summer. She'll be back in a few months. After that..." I shrug. "I don't know yet."

"You can stay here for as long as you like. This is your home. It wouldn't feel the same with you gone. I realize you're eighteen and impatient to start life on your own, but you don't have to rush it. Life, adulthood, and responsibilities will still be waiting for you in a few months."

She doesn't know that, not for a fact. No one knows that.

I study my mom's pinched features and the strain around her mouth. I'm trying to help her here, but of course she doesn't see it that way. She sees it as her last child abandoning her. The thought of me not being in the same home as her really upsets her, but I am me, not the ghost of someone, and because of that, I *need* to not be in this house for any longer than is necessary.

But on the other hand, how can I leave her, knowing what I now know? My insides twist up thinking about it all. I face the sink and quickly wash the cup, setting it in the strainer to dry.

"I'll be in touch."

I grab the orange, hoist the tote bag to my shoulder, and offer a weak smile. Hers is just as listless.

With a small wave, I head outside.

My mood brightens considerably when the sun and warm June air greet me. I watch tree limbs and leaves move with the force of the wind, hear the chirping of birds, and smell the sweet fragrance of blossoms around me. I smile. Even nature is saying good morning and that today will be a good day, no matter what. I tip my head back at the cloudless sky and close my eyes, inhaling deeply. The sun tries to burn my eyelids and I cover them with sunglasses, striding toward the small garage with chipping white paint and an uneven door. I unchain my orange and cream-colored Huffy from a pole in the cool interior of the building and swing a leg over the bicycle.

It's time to ride.

PRAIRIE DU CHIEN IS THE second oldest city in Wisconsin. Its name is French and means "Prairie of the Dog". I'm really not sure why it was called that, but I suppose the settlers who deemed it as such had their reasons for it. Maybe they brought a lot of dogs with them and let them run loose? When it was first settled in the late seventeenth century, it was known to be a trading post for fur trades. The city didn't become fully American until after the War of 1812.

The population is presently around six thousand, but the city is constantly expanding and growing as new businesses come in—something that saddens me but is necessary for it to survive. Without change, there is no advancement. The city is also well-known for the Mississippi River that hugs it and the fishing and hunting that comes along with the wooded areas surrounding it.

In 2001, Prairie du Chien gained brief national attention for its first annual New Year's Eve celebration, during which a carp from the Mississippi River was dropped from a crane over the downtown area at midnight. The "Drop- pin' of the Carp" celebration has been held every New Year's Eve since. I think all of the citizens have been to it at least once. My mother and I haven't missed a single year, no matter how cold it was or how much snow was on the ground at the time. Pain sweeps through me as I wonder if we will have the chance to watch it together this year, so I pedal my feet faster, trying to outrun what I cannot change.

I love this city. I love the large body of water that lines one side of it, the trains that blast through it and startle those unprepared for its booming horn, the beauty in the trees and flowers throughout it, and the history of it. I cut across the street that leads to the Young residence, the wind flitting over me like the brush of a warm hand. I hop off my bicycle and pull it up to the garage, kicking the stand down.

I hear Rivers' raised voice as I enter the house after knocking once on the screen door. It noisily swings shut behind me, effectively cutting him off. He and his mother are standing in the foyer, their stances stiff and the tension in the room overpowering. His head swings toward me, eyes dark with intense dislike. I smile brightly in return until he looks away. Monica looks flustered, her hands outstretched and entreating toward her unreachable son.

"Hello!" I set my tote bag down and walk farther into the room. I pretend I didn't hear Rivers saying he didn't need a babysitter, especially not me, just before I walked inside. I pretend I don't feel their discord in the air like a trap of negativity. I pretend I want to be here and am happy that I get to watch over a spoiled brat who can't even be glad he is taking oxygen into his lungs even now. "All set for the trip?"

Monica's hands drop to her sides. Her hair is pull backed in a messy bun and she is wearing jeans and a thin purple jacket. The expression on her face is a mixture of frustration and sorrow. "Yes. We need to leave in ten minutes in order to make the flight. Thomas is finishing packing." Her voice is weary.

"Awesome! Just keep us updated on everything." My voice is falsely bright and grating even to me, but I have to keep upbeat so I don't walk right back out the door.

Monica gives me a strange look I ignore and takes a deep

breath.

"I'm going to check on Thomas." Her eyes flicker to Rivers and away as she trudges up the stairs.

His hair is sticking up in black spikes only a restless sleep could create. One hand balances against the wall to relieve pressure on the worst of his two legs, though he is trying to be nonchalant about it. A white tee with the arms cut out frames his muscular upper body and black lounge pants cover his legs. The strength of his arms is evident in the way they bulge and contract as he shifts his stance, the detestation he has for his legs is evident in the way he keeps them hidden. I'm surprised his vanity doesn't insist he wear a mask as well, or at least a baseball cap, to try to cloak the scars of his face.

"I don't need someone watching over me," he growls, his face forward so that I can see the clenching of his jaw.

"I heard that. Don't worry, I agree. What you really need is a psychiatrist, maybe some meds—no, definitely some meds. But you got me instead." I raise my hands apologetically. Then I smile sweetly as I say, "I'll take good care of you. Promise."

Well, I'll keep him alive anyway.

His eyes land on me and quickly lose interest in what they see. Nothing new there with Rivers. "You're so weird, Bana."

I laugh. "You say that like I should be offended. I'd rather be weird than a clone of everyone else."

It was a jab and he recognized it as such. He doesn't respond, but I notice the stiffening in his perfectly proportioned body. It's still a remarkable creation. His body may be filled with imperfect fissures, but all I see is something made more beautiful by tragedy. Like an ocean formed from a meteor. Something remarkable can always be the result of something devastating, if you choose to find that one positive in a nest of negatives.

And what is your positive? a little voice whispers in my head.

Shut it, I tell myself, not really inclined to examine all my positives and negatives at the moment.

I remove the orange I brought from my tote bag and raise it to my face, inhaling its sweetly citrus scent as I walk from the room. I'll eat it in a cheerier atmosphere. I used to wonder about names. Like, why is an orange called an orange? And why is the color orange called that?

Of course, I never got any answers, but it didn't stop me from wondering. Why is anything named what it is? When I was nine, I asked my mom why she chose the name she did for me and she said because she thought it sounded pretty.

I looked up the meaning of my name once and I wasn't really impressed. I was either some jezebel who did horrible things to the man who loved her, *or* I was something gentle. The two definitions completely contradict one an- other. Out of the two, I prefer the latter, although neither are particularly complimentary. I don't want my name to mean *gentle*. I want my name to mean something cool, like driven by fire, or something to that effect. Who was that first person, or people, who chose the names to mean what they did and why did they think they were appropriate?

I guess I think a lot about unimportant things.

I just popped the last of the juicy citrus fruit into my mouth when Monica appears in the kitchen. I straighten from the counter as she approaches. Without speaking, she hugs me. Too stunned to pull away, I awkwardly pat her back. She smells like lavender, which makes me think of my mom with all of her flowers, herbs, and vegetables. There is a tremble to her body that causes a pang in me.

Pulling away, she offers a wan smile. "Thank you. I know he's going to be difficult. Just…you can handle him. I know you can. If anything happens, call me, no matter the time. I'll have my cell phone. Maybe…" She hesitates. "Maybe you could try to get him to open up about some things? No one else has been able to, not even me."

"If you can't get him to respond, why do you think I would be able to?"

She tilts her head as she studies me. "I don't know," she answers slowly. "I just think you might be able to think up some method I haven't been able to. Call it intuition."

Monica smiles, brushing bangs from my eyes. "I'm really grateful to have you here this summer, Delilah."

I move back, shifting my eyes from hers. Those words warm me at the same time they cause me to go cold. Apparently, my body is conflicted. "What do you want me to do?"

"I don't know. Even if he worked on walking more, it would help him. *Anything*. Or talking. You're so easy to talk to. I bet he would talk to you more than he is willing to with anyone else." She pauses, chagrin flushing her features. "I'm sorry. I'm asking a lot of you and I feel like I'm being extremely demanding."

"A little bit." I smile.

"I'll make it up to you," she promises, squeezing my arm. "I'll be in touch once we're settled in California. There's a credit card in a dish on top of the refrigerator. Use it for whatever you need or want. And thank you. You truly are a blessing."

I salute her, following her from the room and into the foyer. Rivers and his dad are in the room, the span of it between them. I don't think that's all that stands between them, from what I've seen. I wouldn't call it animosity, but there is certainly discord among them. It's in the way they stand when next to each other, the way they avoid one another's eyes. The way they don't talk to each other unless they have to.

Mr. Young's lips lift and lower in what I'm assuming he thinks is a smile. I give a flash of my own. He looks at his son. "Stay away from the pool while we're gone—since you've apparently forgotten how to swim."

Rivers' mouth tightens, but he says nothing as he looks down. Two things hit me. The first being that his dad must know his endeavor into the pool yesterday wasn't an accident. A glance at his mom's face shows she believes it as well, though she looks saddened by it instead of revolted like his dad. The second thing is, why would his dad say such a jackass thing to him? He was in a terrible accident while on the river—was that in reference to *that* and not the pool? My unease where Thomas Young is concerned turns to immense dislike.

The enmity in the room lessens astronomically once they are

gone, but it is still here.

I exhale slowly and look at him. "I know you don't want me here, but I am. This will go a lot smoother if I don't have to watch you every second of the day." I pause. "Do I need to be worried about anything?"

What I really mean is, is he going to be stupid again and put his life in danger.

His stoic silence is the only response I get, which isn't a response at all, but I think we understand each other. I'll leave him alone if he doesn't give me any reason not to. I decide to ignore Rivers like he normally ignores me and go about my usual stuff.

"Shout if you need me," is all I say and start up the stairs.

It hasn't escaped me that being a maid for one of the most popular boys in my grade should be beneath me. It really is too. Only I didn't take the job for him, although, in a way, I guess I did. That and my post-summer trip. The reasoning for why I do the things I do is something I cannot fully explain, so most days I try not to.

My subconscious knows, and that will have to be enough.

The young man I left below is a mystery. He in no way resembles the laughing, smiling jock from school. All I can associate with the Rivers from school and the Rivers downstairs is the obvious disdain he has for those not as physically and athletically gifted as he—meaning me. Other than my bright, and sometimes clashing, clothes and hair, I am pretty plain in appearance and I didn't play sports in school—I hated them, actually. They are too competitive.

People get fanatical about them. Come on, they're *games*. I mean, playing sports for fun is one thing—that I get—but when people go nuts because you miss a shot or are not perfect in your pitch, well, that is ridiculous.

And why do there have to be winners and losers? Why can't everyone be winners, or at least *tied*? Why must the game go on until one team outscores the other? Telling someone they have to win is putting a lot of pressure on them, and then when they don't win, they feel bad about themselves. Losing is apparently supposed to make you feel so terrible about yourself that you won't give up until you win. It is an obsession.

Anything less than first place isn't acceptable. What does thinking that way do to your self-esteem? I mean, it's good to strive to do well at something and we all need goals, but to think you're worthless because you aren't perfect is wrong, and to teach children to think that way is wrong as well.

I guess it's a good thing I never went out for any sports because it really doesn't make sense to me. I would have spent the whole time trying to get everyone to believe we can all be winners. I can just see myself; a lone figure on my campaign for equality in sports. I imagine I would have been sent to the dugout indefinitely for thinking like that. It probably was never even an issue for Rivers. I've seen him in action. I never understood all the plays that go along with football, but I could see the ease with which he moved, the fluidity of his limbs, the speed he ran with. Watching him was like watching art come to life.

Even I can mourn the loss of his graceful limbs, though I do not share the view that he is less than he used to be.

A small voice asks: *What if that was Rivers' life? What if nothing he ever did was good enough? What if winning was the only way he knew how to get approval?*

I don't think Monica would ever put that kind of pressure on him growing up, but I could so see Thomas doing it. Again, an emotion I'd rather not feel scorches my insides, telling me the detachment I pretend to have toward him is a lie.

I'm wiping the master bedroom windows with a Windex-doused cloth when I hear a crash. I freeze, listening but hearing only the thumping of my heart, and then I scramble into motion. My first thought is that Rivers decided to break our silent agreement and tried to harm himself again. Anger and fear war within me.

I race down the stairs, stubbing my left big toe in the process, and follow the sound of rushing water. I stop in the doorway of the white and cream bathroom and stare. Rivers is on the floor beside the tub, clad only in red boxer briefs. A mix of pain and shame has captured his features.

I give myself a shake and enter the room, careful to keep my eyes averted from his body as I say, "What exactly were you attempting to do? Take a nap? I suppose the bathroom floor is as good a place as any. The sound of the water is soothing too, if you like that sort of thing."

I lean over him, groping for the knob in the garden tub, and turn the water off while trying not to think about my chest being inappropriately close to his face.

He doesn't answer and I sigh, turning to look at him, struggling to keep my eyes on his and above his neck. My face has to be red because it abruptly feels like it is sunburned. "Well, let's get you up, shall we? Nap time is over."

I don't know why I'm acting like I don't know that he fell. I guess to spare him the embarrassment of me stating the obvious. Although, I don't think he appreciates my attempts, which is glaringly blatant when he talks.

"I can get up on my own," he snaps as I reach for him, jerking his arm away.

"Yeah?" I step back and put my hands on my hips. "Be my guest."

Something happens to me as the seconds tick by, turning into minutes as I watch him try again and again to maneuver his body into a standing position. He struggles to get up, but every time either his hand slips or his legs won't cooperate or he loses his balance. Over and over, it goes.

It isn't pity I feel, although I know he wouldn't want me feeling *anything* toward him—it's more like respect. He isn't getting anywhere. Sweat lines his face and he's panting, but he *won't give up*. I wonder how long he'll do this before admitting defeat. I almost think he won't give up until he is on his feet. Then I notice the trickle of blood starting to run down his forehead and I know it's time to end this. He can prove he isn't helpless another day.

I move for him, stating, "You're bleeding."

"I don't need your help!"

"And I don't need your shit!"

He blinks at the heat in my voice.

I sit back on my heels and take a ragged breath. "Look, it's obvious you're struggling to get up, and your head is bleeding. You might have reopened a wound. Just let me help you up and look at your head, and then I'll leave you alone again, all right?"

"Fine," he grinds out.

I put my hands under his armpits and haul him up with difficulty, his hands reaching for the wall behind him to help get him to his feet. He's heavy, especially when most of his weight is leaning on me. It is awkward and takes a prolonged number of attempts, but between the two of us, we finally get him standing.

"Did you hit your head when you fell?"

When he doesn't answer, I pull back to glare at him.

"I don't know. I guess," he mumbles.

"How did you fall?"

"Moved too fast, leg spasmed."

He's against the wall, one hand on the top of the toilet, the other on my shoulder. Tired, we momentarily rest this way with my head lowered between us. My muscles are shaking from effort and a sheen of perspiration covers my skin. I wonder if this is going to turn into a routine thing—me, rescuing him.

The longer we stand this way, the more I begin to notice things. He smells like sunshine and vanilla, which is sort of different for a guy to smell like, but I like it on him. It reminds me of a beach—sunscreen, the sun, waves. His skin warms my hands where they touch him and I can hear his heart pounding near my ear. When I realize I'm staring at his defined abdomen, I jerk my head up and clip his chin.

He curses.

"I'm sorry!" I cry, feeling bad for further injuring him.

"You can let go of me now." Annoyance forms crinkles in the corners of his eyes. I wonder if creases ever form there anymore from smiling.

I drop my hands and move back. "What were you trying to do?"

"Isn't it obvious?"

I cross my arms. "What? That you're rude and belligerent? Yep. That's pretty obvious."

"I was trying to take a bath."

"Do you normally do that on your own?"

"Take a bath? Yeah. I usually manage that on my own. Are you offering to join me?"

I press my lips together as heat whooshes through me. "I *meant* get it ready on your own. You know, I think I liked it better when you *didn't* talk to me."

"I aim to please."

"Next time you fall, don't call for me," I declare, stomping out of the room.

"I didn't call for you *this* time!" he hollers after me.

"Maybe you should have!"

Grumbling to myself as I finish making the upstairs squeaky clean, it occurs to me that I am seriously irritated. That doesn't happen very often. I take slow, deep breaths as I work, finding my happy place once again as I focus on the sun streaming through the windows, the calming colors of gray, cream, white, and pale yellow that make up the upstairs decor, and the lingering scent of lavender. It takes a while, but my heartbeat returns to normal and the glaze of anger melts away.

When I get back downstairs, it's after one o'clock in the afternoon and my stomach is growling for food. On my way to the kitchen, I realize I forgot to check his head injury. How could I have let that slip my mind? I blame his belligerent behavior for my brain malfunction and yet, that doesn't relieve the guilt I feel. I'm supposed to be looking out for him and he's already injured himself within hours of my presence. Maybe Monica will fire me.

Shoulders slumping, I backtrack to his bedroom. The door is closed and low music sounds from within. I knock on the door and the volume of the music escalates. Glaring at the door, I contemplate whether or not I recall ever meeting such a childish person. I don't think so. I check the doorknob and when it turns, I shove the door open. Rivers is lying on the top of his made bed —the bed *I* made—with his hands behind his head and his eyes on the ceiling.

Without looking at me, he mutes the music with a remote control long enough to say, "Go away."

I note the closed curtains and stomp over to them, grabbing an end in each hand and throwing my arms open wide. Sunlight filters into the room and lands directly on him—light and darkness colliding to form a beautiful monster.

"Close the curtains."

His tone is extremely arrogant and I want to punch him.

Instead, I put a hand to my ear and look at him with my eyebrows raised. "What? Can't hear you above the music. Too loud." I shrug.

His jaw bunches as he sits up. He turns the music off. "Close the curtains."

"Get up and close them yourself."

"Isn't that part of your *job*?"

"To be your slave? No. I don't think so." Although, technically, has it ever really been discussed? Either way, he doesn't need to know.

"I didn't realize you were such a pain in the ass in school."

The fact that he even knows we went to school together stumps me for a second. I figured I was one in a mass of insignificant people not noteworthy enough to matter to him.

"That's the difference between you and me—I *did* realize you were."

He clamps his lips together.

"Silent treatment time again? I'm cool with that. It'll make checking your head easier without you being a loud-mouthed brat the whole time."

I walk toward the bed, watching him stiffen as I get closer. "Did you take a bath then?"

I don't wait for him to not answer me, continuing with, "You must have. You don't stink anymore."

Not that he ever did. I can tell he bathed, though, because his hair isn't sticking up everywhere like it was this morning and the vanilla sunshine scent is intensified.

Surprisingly enough, he doesn't pull away or complain when I hover over him. I pause, staring down at his lowered head. Maybe he is finally resigned to me. Good. It'll make life easier for the next few days if he just accepts the situation.

Once again, I am aware of the closeness of my body to his face, and my pulse picks up because of it. I gently touch the gash on the top of his head, his hair thick and soft against my fingers. The wound is scabbed over with freshly dried blood evident only in a small area of it.

Without thinking about what I am doing, I brush my fingers across the silken locks of short black hair, an unconscious part of me wanting to comfort him like I would anyone hurting. He is torn into a million different parts; none of them resembling who he used to be, and I do understand that, even if he is a pretty unlikable person.

I've been lost before. I've lost myself; I've lost those I love. I think we all have. Tingles start at my fingertips and move up my arm as time freezes and spins by at the same time. I glance down and notice how still he is—only his chest moves in time to his breathing.

Snatching my hand away, I hurry to put space between us. I refuse to look in his direction because I don't want to know the expression on his face. "It, uh, it looks fine. Are you hungry? I'm going to make food. I'll be...in the kitchen."

I turn my mind toward filling my stomach with something, because that is something I *do* understand, and grab random things out of the fridge. I take in my stash—an onion, deli sliced turkey, garlic and herb-flavored wraps, spinach, and cranberries.

One thing is missing. I open the freezer and search in vain.

I am about to give up hope when a voice says from behind, "She puts it behind a wall of frozen vegetables. She figures if she doesn't see it all the time, she'll be less likely to eat it."

Without glancing over my shoulder, I ask, "Does it work?"

"Not really."

I demolish the barricade made out of bags of frozen vegetables, uncovering a tub of mint chocolate chip ice cream. I swear I hear the heavens rejoicing. Mint chocolate chip wouldn't be my first choice, but I'll take what I can get.

I pull it out, the container cold and covered in a layer of frost, and set it on the counter. Finally looking up, I meet Rivers' gaze. It isn't exactly unfriendly, but it isn't open either—it's more of a guarded, wary look. He's lingering by the door-way like he isn't sure if he's welcome in his own kitchen.

I look down, finding it hard to swallow. "Want some?"

I make a sound of exasperation when he doesn't say anything and go about making us each a wrap.

His gait is methodical as he makes his way over, getting bowls, spoons, and an ice cream scoop out. The time it takes him to do this is drawn out to the point of being difficult to watch. I have two wraps made and two glasses of lemon iced tea ready by the time he procures the ice cream necessities. When that is done, he leans against the counter with his hands clenching it, his shoulders hunched and his head lowered.

I turn away; it pains my heart to witness him struggling to make the broken pieces of his body work as a whole.

"Why don't you sit down and eat?" I suggest, focusing on keeping my voice even.

"I'm...fine," he answers slowly.

"You look it," I say with a nod.

A scowl is his response, but it's better than nothing.

I don't really want to torture him further, but the thought of the two of us sitting on bar stools side by side is a little too farfetched, so I take the plates and glasses over to the table near the sliding glass doors. I scoop ice cream into the melon-colored bowls as I wait for him to make his way to the table, careful to keep my eyes down so he doesn't think I'm staring if he happens to look my way.

When he is seated, I head over, sitting across from him.

The silence is awkward as we eat, neither of us looking at each other for long. I search my mind for conversation topics, deciding on the future. It's either that or the weather and that seems a little too overused. Everyone talks about the weather when there is nothing else easily thought of to talk about. I do it all the time when I'm at the shop and customers approach me. It's safe, non-invasive.

"Are you going to college in the fall?"

It hits me that this was a poorly chosen question at the same time his shoulders tense. Should have gone with the weather.

"No."

It's my turn to not reply for once, swirling my melting ice cream around with my spoon. I know why he isn't going, though his reasons are illogical to me. Just because he can't go to college on a football scholarship doesn't mean he shouldn't go at all. He could use his brain or something to get through it. He's smart. Even if the plaques in his room weren't evidence of that, I remember from school.

"I didn't graduate, not that I would have been able to use my football scholarship even if I had. I suppose I'll have to use my good looks to get by in life now," he says, sarcasm lacing his words.

"You didn't get your diploma?"

"I was in the hospital or at the doctor most of the last month and a half of school."

I frown. "Why aren't you in summer school then or working on getting your GED?"

He drops his spoon, it clattering against the side of the bowl. "What's the point?"

Anger builds inside my core. "Meaning?"

Leaning back in his chair, he replies, "Meaning I'm deformed. I can barely walk. I'm ugly to look at. What am I supposed to do with the rest of my life? Sit at some desk job and talk to people over a phone?"

I jump to my feet and begin to clean off the table.

"I'm not done," he tells me.

"I think you need to go practice up for your future career as a nobody. Go sit in your room and hold a phone in your hand or something."

I take his bowl and plate away, dumping the food and tossing the dishes into the sink hard enough to cause a burst of noise, but not break anything. I put the stopper in the sink and begin to fill it with hot, soapy water that smells like synthetic lemons. I count to thirty before I turn around, not surprised to see his back as he makes his way out of the room.

Probably going back to his bedroom so he can mope some more and feel bad about his poor, pathetic, worthless life.

I grab a dishrag and take my frustration out on the dishes. "Deformed," I scoff. "Ugly. *Stupid*. He acts like his whole life is over just because he has a few scars and a limp."

I toss the rag into the water and suds fly up to coat my face. I absently wipe them away with my arm, staring out the window at the fence and yellow house beyond it. It seems far away, a different world from where I stand.

"Fine. Whatever. That's his prerogative, I guess. It's none of my business." I talk myself into a better mood and finish the dishes with less animosity.

THREE

BY THE TIME I HAVE all of my daily chores done, it is close to four in the afternoon. I haven't seen or heard any- thing from Rivers since the lunchtime fiasco, and that's okay. He messes up my good vibe. I purse my lips as I shake my head, not understanding his way of thinking.

Quickly changing out of my clothes, I slip on my two-piece, the neon green of it clashing with my dyed red hair as I study myself in the full-length mirror. The overhead light catches the silver stud in my nose, causing it to shine for an instant. My skin is ghastly pale, but there is nothing to be done about it. I touch the spattering of freckles on my nose and turn away, folding my clothes and putting them on top of my tote bag. Phone, sunglasses, sunscreen, and yellow beach towel in hand, I head to my form of liquid heaven.

The sun is relentless under the cloudless sky and I squint against it, thinking of an upside-down ocean of calm waters. The humidity isn't bad today and a warm breeze rustles my hair. From my position, I can see the surrounding houses, trees, and parts of varying streets, and yet I feel separate from it all—untouchable. Summer makes me feel free, like there are endless possibilities and the future can hold anything I want it to. Tomorrow is a whole new chance to do something great. I feel the curve of my lips and know a smirk of contentment covers them.

Setting my stuff down on the bench at the far end of the deck, I walk to the edge of the pool and raise my hands above my head. I bend my knees, and push off into a dive, the water sluicing on either side of me in smooth lines. My arms stroke the lukewarm liquid as I balance my breathing with my movements. Time escapes me as I become part of the water, the laps melding into a dizzying line of back and forth.

An awareness tickles the back of my neck and I shoot to a standing position, my heart pounding as I work on steadying my breathing. I look to the chair normally occupied by Rivers, surprised to find it empty. Instead, he sits on the bench with his hands clasped together and his arms resting on his knees. The intensity of his gaze singes me, but it only lasts a brief moment before it is replaced by nothingness. How can he so effectively wipe all emotion from his eyes within the span of an instant?

Practice, a voice tells me.

I wonder if I should say something, but I am kind of tired of never being acknowledged, so I don't. I go back to swimming, feeling his eyes on me the whole time. It's strange that I find it comforting in a way and I wonder if he gathers comfort from watching me as well. Ludicrous, and yet the brand of his eyes is unwavering the entirety of my swim.

Hours later I am freshly showered and clad in a neon yellow with pink stars tank top and gray shorts, ready for some lounging. I like to be active, but I also like to do absolutely nothing and vegetate just as much. I designated the sunroom as my bedroom for the duration of my stay. One, because the couch is comfy. Two, because Monica asked me to. And three, because this room is alive with the sun.

Odd that there are two of us in this house and we are both acting like there is only one—Rivers keeping to his room and me letting him. I wonder if that's how he usually spends his days, just listening to music and watching tele- vision, segregated from others by his choice. How boring. I mean, yeah, I keep to myself, but I'm not brooding as I do it.

I'm flipping through the channels on the television when my phone rings with 'Man on The Moon' by R.E.M. I pick it up, asking, "How's everything going?"

The sigh is heavy. "As well as expected. How are things

there?"

"Perfect."

"Don't exaggerate, Delilah. I know my son."

I twirl a lock of hair around my finger. "I was trying to make you feel better. Not too bad, actually. Rivers has been in his room most of the day."

"I'm not surprised." Monica pauses. "He called a little bit ago."

"Oh?" I can just imagine all the nice things he had to say about me.

"Yeah." Her tone sounds perplexed as she continues, "He brought up the ice cream."

I drop my hand. "Oh. Was that off limits?"

"No, no, of course not. It's just...did he eat some of it?"

"Yes," I answer with furrowed brows. The amount of attention presently being placed on the ice cream consumption is definitely puzzling to me.

"That's so odd," she mutters to herself.

"That he brought it up to you or that he ate it? It seems kind of strange that that was his reasoning for calling you, definitely. Is he worried about calories or something? Maybe he wanted you to tell him to build the ice fort back up so he stays out of it. It was totally his idea to eat it," I hurriedly add.

"Rivers doesn't like ice cream."

I search my brain to remember whether I did, in fact, actually see him raise a spoon of ice cream to his mouth and swallow it. Yes. I did. Why didn't he tell me he doesn't like ice cream? Why did he get himself a bowl and a spoon? Why did he eat it? It isn't like he's sensitive to my feelings or anything. What purpose did any of that have?

"He must have decided he does."

Her response is slow and not completely confident. "Right. I'll call again tomorrow. And Delilah?"

"Yes?"

"Whatever you're doing, keep doing it."

I don't want to take credit for something I haven't even done, but I say, "Yeah, okay."

After getting off the phone with Monica, I give my mom a quick call to assure her I am still alive and unharmed, then find a movie on the television to watch. As the minutes turn into hours and night descends upon the sky outside like a dark blanket with specs of light in the form of stars, my brain continually tries to wrap around what Monica told me. It doesn't make any sense. Why would he eat something he doesn't even like, and why would he tell his mother about it too?

Obviously, he didn't bring up his fall in the bathroom or what I am sure he considers bullying. Why would he do that? Bring up the ice cream and not the other stuff? I get him not bringing up his fall, because he probably views that as a sign of weakness, but me forcing the curtains open in his room, what about that? That's the first thing I would have thought he'd bring up to his mom as a reason to get rid of me. He has a growing list of ammunition to use against me and he hasn't used any of it.

Why?

MY EYELIDS FLY OPEN AND I stare at a ceiling blackened by night as I fight to remember where I am and what woke me up. I sit up and look out the windows, realizing I am in the Young house instead of my own. The moon is bathing the night with a faint glow. I hold still, waiting.

Nothing moves outside other than bushes and tree leaves in the wind. The only sound in the room is the ticking of a clock, marking off the seconds of time, but I know that isn't what forced me from sleep. I'm about to lie back down when I hear the sound again.

I vault to my feet and from the room, thinking, *What now?*

Without hesitating, I fling open Rivers' bedroom door. He's writhing on the bed, his back raised as he cries out. The sound is harsh, broken. I flip the light switch up to see if he is in actual pain or in the grasp of a nightmare, my eyes stinging from the sudden light. His eyes are closed, his features twisted in a grimace, and a layer of sweat is covering his face and chest.

I watch him struggle, feeling helpless. I don't know what to do. I don't want to make it worse by trying to drag him from a world only he can see, but I also can't leave him like this.

I step back from the bed and bite my lip. "Rivers? *Rivers. Rivers, wake up.*"

I know it's probably not the best idea because he could unintentionally and unknowingly hit me in his sleep, but I can't stand to see him like this any longer, so I step closer.

I scan his taut body and rest my eyes on his hands bunched around the blankets of his bed, minutely reassured that they aren't swinging in the air. I'm thinking a punch received from him would be painful, even while in the clutches of slumber.

Placing my cool palm against his hot forehead, I lean close to his ear and speak soothingly, "Rivers, you're okay. You're okay now. I'm here and you're okay. It's just a dream. It can't hurt you. Wake up, Rivers. It's okay to wake up."

For a moment I don't think it's doing any good, but as I continue to talk to him, my words slowly reach him through the blackness of his mind and he settles down.

I give nonsensical details about myself as I kneel beside the bed, taking in the loosening of his muscles, the way his fingers begin to unclench, his breathing evening out.

"Have you ever noticed how many different colors of green are in a single strand of grass? There are all these lighter greens that meld into darker ones, even hints of yellow within them. It's amazing. The most beautiful things in the world are right in front of us in the beauty of the actual world. If I had any form of creativity with a paintbrush, I'd try to paint a field of grass and flowers. Sadly, I cannot even draw stick figures."

His fingers relax against the bed.

"My favorite color is a rainbow. In the fifth grade, Mrs. Williams asked us all to come to the front of the room and state what our favorite color was and why. You were in her class too. Do you remember that day? I got up there and said what my favorite color was. She told me not to be silly, that I had to pick *one* color, and I told her I couldn't, and I wouldn't, because I loved all the colors, and I especially loved all of the colors found in a rainbow.

"She sent me to the principal's office for being insubordinate. I painted my hair in stripes of yellow, orange, red, green, purple, and blue the next day. She hated me from that moment on. Also, my mom threw a fit when she tried to clean it from my hair. It took weeks for all the colors to be completely gone.

"I thought about trying out for choir freshman year. I love to sing. I'm not saying I'm good at it, but I love it. I didn't try out, and not because I was nervous or scared, but because singing is something I treasure, and I didn't want it to somehow be used against me in a negative way. What if I wasn't good enough?

"What if I was mediocre compared to everyone else? What if people made fun of me just to make fun of me? I didn't want the joy of it to get lost in sharing it with others, or to have it taken away from me by knowing I'm not any good at it. I don't even know if that makes sense. Probably not.

"I feel bad for bugs. I mean, I don't want them swarming me or biting me or anything, but I understand them. I understand how they're judged a lot of the time on the way they look. People don't like ugly things. People don't like things they don't understand. I know what that's like.

"I've been disliked just because of how I look for a long time—because I chose to dress differently from everyone else. Because I like stuff that doesn't necessarily match or go together, because I didn't want to be like all the other kids. Why try to be like someone else when our individuality is what makes us, us.

"I could have let myself get bitter over it, but I really just feel sorry for people like that. I suppose it used to upset me, but the longer it went on, the more immune to it I became. I decided I was above all of that petty shit, although at times, I did lower myself down to respond to situations when I probably should have ignored them.

"The whole high school scene is bizarre, if you really think about it. Kids are mean, everyone is struggling to find their identity, social status is your *life*. If you aren't good at sports, you suck. If you aren't popular, you might as well fade into the woodwork. People..." I trail off as I notice how still he is.

I look up and meet his unflinching gaze. It's black, unfathomable. I feel like I could get sucked into his dark eyes and become wrapped in him.

"People like I used to be," he says in a rough voice.

I lean back on my heels, letting my hand fall away from his face. "I didn't say that."

"You didn't have to."

Slowly standing, I push down wayward strands of my hair as I become aware of what I must look like. My hair is a wreck on a good day and I can't imagine what it looks like now. I catch his eyes going up and down my body and face like a warm touch. I self-consciously cross my arms.

"Are you okay now?"

He doesn't answer, turning his face forward.

All right then."

I head for the door.

"Stay."

Softly spoken, raw with emotion—this one word has the power to halt my steps.

"What?" I turn around to face him, but he won't meet my gaze. I think I must have heard him wrong.

Even with his face partially turned away, I can see the confusion and need warring in his expression. I think he astounded even himself when he said it.

"Will you...stay?"

A long minute ticks by, the weight of my decision heavy in the room. Will I stay? What will it mean if I do? What does he expect from me if I do? I glance at him, knowing there was nothing seductive about that request. It was brought on by vulnerability in a hurting young man.

I don't think I can leave, not after he said that. Walking away would be a pretty nasty thing to do after he ignored his pride to voice that word, and I am a lot of things, but cruel is not one of them. He needs someone. It probably isn't really even me, but just *someone*. I can be that someone for the night.

"Yeah," I whisper, flicking the light switch off before we can gauge each other's reaction to his surprising question and my just as surprising answer.

In the dark I make my way to the large bed, aware of him scooting over to make room for me. The rapid beat of my pulse is proof that this is insane and completely unexpected. We're practically strangers, we are from different worlds, and we don't exactly bring out the best in one another. Yet, here we are, together because of night terrors.

I know what nightmares are like. Sometimes they are there whether we are sleeping or awake, unavoidable and inescapable. I suppose Rivers feels like he is in the middle of one, even when his eyes are open. I exhale slowly, knowing exactly how that feels.

I lie on the bed with my hands clasped together over my midsection, my body tense. His body heat seeps into my side, as does his sweet smell that makes me homesick for a home I've never had. It's more of a *sense* than an actual place—a feeling of wholeness. Where I am and what I am doing sinks in the longer I am in his bed. Me, lying next to Rivers Young. Crazy. This summer has been a collision of disbelief upon disbelief. Strangely enough, this one I don't mind so much.

"What did you dream about?"

"Water," is his gruff response.

I close my eyes against the dark only to see more dark. I wonder if this is what Rivers feels like he is in—waves of unending darkness, never knowing how to get back to who he used to be, unable to tread forward through them, constantly sucked under them, struggling to breathe. Stuck. Lost.

His arm relaxes against mine and he instantly moves it away. I pretend I didn't notice, asking, "Do you have nightmares often?"

The silence is drawn out to the point where I don't think he is going to answer me, but then he says softly, "Every night."

No words are really appropriate after that admission and I

focus on the steadiness of his breathing instead. In and out. Slow and deep. I feel him sinking back into the nothingness of slumber. How do you break through the black and into the light? How does a boy who used to have everything decide he has something to fight for when he's lost all he's known? What will be strong enough to pull him from the waters of his dark abyss of reality? I think he has to do it himself, but he has to want to. I also think it's the scars of his heart that need to be mended, not the superficial outside ones.

It is true that no one can save you, no one but yourself. And sometimes...even *you* cannot save you, no matter how much you wish it was untrue. Sadly, some things are not meant to be saved.

My limbs melt into the mattress as I fade away.

THE FIRST RAYS OF SUNLIGHT awaken me, warming me from the direction of an uncovered window. I almost smile when I realize he left the curtains open. Then I remember I can only know that because I am lying in his bed with him sleeping next to me, and the compulsion to do so disappears.

I lie still for a moment, convincing myself last night really happened and it wasn't just a dream. It was completely innocent—the only time we touched by accident. I guess he just needed to not be alone in order to sleep. I'm sure any warm body would have sufficed.

Slowly turning my head, I take in the body lying next to me. It's long and tanned, the muscles defined in a way only someone naturally athletic and constantly moving can acquire. Studying the olive-toned features, I note the boyishness not normally seen on Rivers' face, the long, black eyelashes that kiss his cheeks, and the slight part between his lips.

He looks so young without the lines around his mouth and the frown between his eyebrows he habitually has while awake. A shadow of stubble frames his jaw, adding a roughness to his otherwise youthful features. Rivers is a perfect mix of clouds and sunshine, openness and hardness. He's an impeccable, yet inconsistent being of all that is good and all that is not. And I am in his bed.

If I had a list of things least likely to happen, this could be on it. No—this *would* be on it. Maybe even number one on the list.

It takes another moment for me to realize there is a heavy weight on my stomach. His arm is across my torso with his hand around my waist, keeping me exactly where I am. My fingers slide down the tendons, muscles, and bones of his arm, stopping on his hand. I know I shouldn't enjoy the feel of him so much, but I do. He's made so differently from me. I may be active on a regular basis, but I don't have the hardness to my muscles that he does.

A fine dusting of hair covers his arm, glints of blond catching my eye. I am paler and my hand is smaller than his. Everything about him is *more*, larger, harder—extraordinary. I squeeze my fingers around his for just a touch longer than is necessary and carefully move his hand away, able to breathe only when we are no longer touching.

The process of getting myself out of the bed is methodical, but once on my feet, I run from the room as if I can run from last night. *You didn't do anything wrong. You didn't do anything but sleep beside him.* Still, there was an intimacy to it that I am unsure how to feel about.

The only boy I've ever fallen asleep beside is my brother, and that was so long ago that I only know it happened from photographs I've seen. Of course, there is no way to compare the two as they are on completely different levels of understandability.

I shower and get myself ready for the day, deciding pancakes sound good. Homemade pancakes are better than from the box, and I resolve to have it be my mission to make the mouthwatering thought of them a reality. I get out the flour, eggs, milk, and vanilla, placing everything on the counter. Finding a recipe book proves harder than it should. After futilely searching through all the drawers and cupboards, I lean against the counter top and sulk.

Minutes later I hear the precise footsteps of Rivers. I straighten as I wait, heat crashing over me in unrelenting waves as an image of his sleeping form shoots through me. *Don't think about it.* I decided earlier to pretend like last night never happened, for both of our benefits. We'll see how good I am at pulling it off.

The first thing I say to Rivers when he appears is, "Does your mother not cook?"

He's wiping sleep from his eyes and drops his hand to blink at me. The shirt he's wearing is teal with a silver surf- board on it and his shorts are black and loose—quite a change from his usual camouflaging pants.

I wonder if he's even been surfboarding before. I answer myself with, *of course he has*. He is one with the water, which makes his accident all the more baffling. I mean, even his *name* is a connection to water.

"Why were you named Rivers?"

"What?" he asks around the lingering fog of sleep.

I decide to go back to my first question, most likely confusing him, but deciding it's the lesser of difficult questions for him to answer. "Your mom. Does she cook? I can't find a recipe book."

"Why do you need a recipe book?"

"So I can cook?" I raise my eyebrows.

A frown twists his lips. "Pretty sure my mom isn't paying you to cook."

"Pretty sure your mom isn't paying me to sleep with you either." As soon as I say it, I bite down hard on my tongue, tasting blood. So much for my idea to pretend last night never happened.

Shutters close over his face and he turns away.

I make my voice bright as I say, "Forget cooking. Let's go out to eat."

Rivers pauses long enough to say, "I am not going out to eat with you."

"Oh? Scared to be seen with me in public?" I ask curiously. It doesn't bother me if he is—that's his problem. I just like to know these things.

He mutters to himself.

"What did you say?"

"I *said*, you don't get it."

I reach into the bowl above the fridge and find the rectangular piece of plastic. I also find a set of car keys. I take both. "Well, I'm going out for pancakes. You can stay here. 'Bye!" My arm grazes his as I fit by him to get to the front door.

Clouds obscure the sun as I walk from the house to the detached white garage. The four-car garage is bigger than the whole downstairs of my house, a fact that has me shaking my head. The inside of it is cool and bare except for two cars, a gleaming white Ford truck, and a small stack of totes along the far wall.

One of the cars is a reproduction of an original Volkswagen Beetle in pastel green and the other is an older model, gun metal gray Dodge Charger. I stare at the two-door vehicle with something close to awe swirling through me. I don't even care whose car it is; I just really hope I have the right set of keys.

I push a button on the wall and the garage door rambles up. I get in the Charger and put the key in the ignition. Joy abounds within me as it fits, and a wide smile cracks my face. I don't know a lot about cars, but I know I like fast ones. I'm hoping this is one of them, but if not, at least it looks cool.

It reminds me of the car used in the television show 'The Dukes of Hazzard', a show my mom used to watch reruns of on a regular basis. I never understood that. As I gaze at the shiny leather interior of the car, I decide it had to have been because of the car.

I roll down the windows as a voice says, "That's my car."

I just shrug.

Rivers stands in indecision beside the passenger door before wrenching it open and getting in as quickly as his body allows. "If anything happens to this car, Bana, it's your ass."

"Psssh." I look in the rearview mirror. "Hold on."

I hit the accelerator, laughing as Rivers shouts an obscenity next to me.

I find a classic rock station and The Doors play as we zip along the back streets of Prairie du Chien. The car handles a lot more easily than my mom's Ford Taurus. I almost want to say it's touchy. It's sleek and slim-framed, everything inside it formed with a touch of daintiness to it.

If I told Rivers that, I'm thinking he wouldn't like it too much. Rivers Young and muscle cars? Never would have thought it. He seems too polished for such a thing. Cars like this make me think of boys covered in dirt who smoke cigarettes and slack off in school.

I know—people and their misconceptions. And I among them.

"How come you never drove this car to school? You always drove that white truck I saw in the garage."

He gives me a look. "Right. And have someone bash into it?"

"You're like one of those people with the flashy cars that park all alone in the Wal-Mart parking lot so no one is by their car. They never seem to realize that parking like that just calls even *more* attention to it."

When he doesn't respond, I say, "It's so sad you keep it hidden away so no one can enjoy it."

"Looks like *you're* enjoying it," he mutters.

I laugh. "Well, yeah, but that's because I commandeered it."

"Is that what it's called?"

Smiling, I ignore that and ask, "How can you afford a truck and a car? And nice ones, at that. Or did you parents buy them for you?"

"I've worked every summer for as long as I could as a lifeguard. Didn't you ever go to the pool?"

Once. Riley and her friends made fun of my ghost skin the whole time. It got old. I didn't return.

"Nope. And that's still not enough money to be able to afford something like this."

Out of the corner of my eye, I catch his shrug. "I worked at the grocery store during the school year, in between and around sports. And I got this at an auction for a lot less than it was worth. It was a heap. Some friends and I worked on it every weekend for months. The truck is technically my parents. I just drive it."

Knowing that Rivers worked to get this, that he paid for it and made it what it now is with manual labor and not just green paper, makes me soften toward him. It wasn't just given to him and I like that. He *earned* it.

"What about you? How come you don't have a car?"

"I like my bike, and when I have to, I take my mom's car. I don't need a car for myself." I add, "I'm practical."

"Practical," he murmurs quietly, his tone saying he doesn't understand why anyone would want to be that.

"Where do you want to eat?"

"Whatever is closest," is his immediate response.

I look over at him and laugh again. Rivers is sitting against the door, one hand gripping the armrest with the other over his eyes.

"I'm a safe driver," I call over the wind and music. After I get the initial zeal for speed out of me, I slow down and pull over, putting the car in park. "Want to drive?"

He just looks at me.

"What? You like me chauffeuring you around?"

"I can't drive."

"Why not?"

"Didn't you get really good grades in school?"

"Valedictorian," I supply quietly.

"How can someone so smart not have any common sense? My legs are ruined. I *can't drive*," he says harshly.

I fist my hand and thump him on the shoulder. "Are your legs gone?"

"No."

"Can you walk?"

"Barely."

"Can you walk?" I insist.

He mutters, "Yeah."

"Okay. Your legs *are not* ruined. You just have to figure out how to use them differently, that's all. And you can drive. Unless a doctor told you, you couldn't?"

He shakes his head, a scowl on his face.

I open the car door and get out.

"What are you doing?"

I walk over to the passenger side.

"I'm not driving, Bana!"

I reach for the door and he locks it. Shrugging, I sprawl out on my back on the crinkly green grass beside the road and close my eyes, my arms out wide. Luckily, we are in the business part of town and not residential.

I suppose people may have an issue with me camping out in their front yard, but the fabric shop probably won't be so quick to notice my prone form in the grass on the other side of their parking lot. Well, hopefully anyway. I have nothing but time right now.

Shadows and light play over my eyelids as the clouds catch and release the sun. I'm wrapped in sunshine and warmth. A stillness comes over me, an awareness of the earth around me, and peacefulness with it. I enjoy it for as long as I can, tranquility taking over and turning my limbs languid.

The shadow suddenly holds, though, and I slowly open my eyes. Rivers is glaring down at me, standing in his uneven way.

"Let me guess, you want to drive now?"

"You are unbelievable," he tells me.

I hop to my feet and bestow my sunniest smile upon him. He blinks, swallows, and walks to the car. The seat has to be moved back to allow room for his six-foot two frame and once he's in the seat, he sits unmoving with his hands around the steering wheel. I catch the tremble in his arms as he struggles with his fear.

"Are your legs bothering you right now?"

He glances at me. "There's never a time they aren't."

"What do you do about it?"

Resting his head against the seat, he closes his eyes. "Endure."

"You don't take pain meds?"

"No," he bites out.

"Why not?"

"Because I don't like them. Ibuprofen is the strongest thing I'll take, when I have a choice. Obviously, I didn't for part of the time in the hospital because I was unconscious and out of it. I couldn't stand that feeling."

"What feeling?"

"Of not really being me. I was just some shadow of myself."

I digest that bit of information before moving on. "Do you *want* to be able to drive?"

A gruff nod is his response.

"So, drive. You don't have to go fast. You don't have to go far. Just prove to yourself that you still can. And whenever it gets to be too much, you pull over and I'll take over," I tell him softly. "There's no shame in needing a break. What's most important is that you do it again after your break.

"That's what life and living is about, Rivers. Second chances. Every day is one more blessing we don't know whether we're going to get or not from day to day, so we should make the most of them as they come, right? We should *drive*."

He slowly turns his dark head and watches me, his expression neutral. I think maybe he catches a glimpse of something he hasn't seen before, or didn't realize is there until this moment. I think he sees a bit of me for the first time—the real me, not the version he perceived me to be.

I study him back, taking in the short ebony locks, the angled jaw with the shadow along its sharp edges—the eyes that are so dark, yet so full of light when they choose to be. The air around us is still as I wait for his perusal to end. When he finally looks away, I hide a smile, feeling a tug in the center of me.

"Where are you going to college at in the fall?" he asks as he angles the car toward a little diner on the outskirts of town.

The smile falls from my face. "I'm not."

He brakes abruptly and I put a hand out on the dash. "Sorry," he mumbles, putting the car in park and shutting it off. "Why aren't you?"

I unhook my seat belt and open the door. "It seems like a waste."

He limps around the side of the car and meets me near the hood. "You're not serious. You were the smartest kid in our class. The *valedictorian*. And you think college is a *waste*? What are you going to do, clean houses for the rest of your life?" His tone is incredulous.

I cross my arms. "I wasn't the *smartest*. I just studied the hardest. It almost seems like you *care*, for some reason, but that can't be. I sort of thought your life revolved around feeling sorry for yourself. How did you find the time to squeeze the details of *my* future into your brain?"

Anger tightens his mouth. "I *don't* care."

"Great!" I head for the door of the pink and white building. It makes me think of pink frosting over vanilla ice cream. A sign above the door reads 'A Dash of Delicious'.

I turn to him and say, "I'm related to Eric Bana."

Confusion filters through his eyes. "No, you aren't."

"You're right. I'm not. But you had to think about it for a second, didn't you?"

"Weird, Bana, really weird," he mutters behind me as we walk inside.

The scents of coffee, bacon, and cinnamon tumble over me as I head toward the booths. The restaurant has six of them, four tables, and a counter for people to sit at as well. It's a small, but popular establishment.

The walls are lined in framed black and white photographs of Prairie du Chien throughout the years, complete with the historical Villa Louis and dozens of years' worth of rendezvouses. I like coming in here. It reminds me of sitting back in time, observing what once was and meshing it with what is.

I pause as I feel Rivers hesitate behind me. I wonder if this is his first social outing since the accident. I decide to pretend I don't notice his faltering steps, focusing on the Eric Bana discussion instead.

"It *would* be weird if I was related to him. And unfortunate. He's really hot. Sigh."

"Did you just say sigh?"

I stop beside a booth. "I really did."

"No one says sigh. They just...you just *sigh*, okay? You don't *say* you're sighing. That completely defeats the purpose of sighing."

I stare at him. "*Sigh*."

Rivers looks torn between finding me hilarious and super annoying. He settles for sighing as he angles his body into the booth and I burst out laughing. He rubs his mouth and I think it's to hide the smile he wants to unleash.

"What happens if you smile? Do you turn to stone?"

He grimaces. "No. But you might."

I grab a pink and white laminated menu and flip it open. I don't understand why he thinks his scars detract from his good looks in any way. Or why he cares so much about how he looks. How you look does not define you as a person.

I set the menu down and place my chin in my hand as I study him. He's all dark smoldering looks that attracts one like a moth to a flame. Pretty to look at—deadly to get too close to. He scowls back the longer I stare.

"What?" he finally snaps.

"You're conceited, shallow." I pause. "Vain."

Rivers blinks.

"I mean, sure, you're not perfect anymore. You have an uneven, gougedout line that goes from under your eye to your mouth and you have a smaller one that slants down your forehead with a little patch of hair missing around it. And, yeah, your legs are a mess, but at least they still work. Do you think anyone really cares about a few imperfections on your face and legs? *Big deal*. You're still living. You still have your eye. You still have your mouth in one piece. You still have your legs and you can *walk*. Be thankful instead of resentful.

"So you have a few scars. You're good-looking regardless,

more goodlooking than most. No one cares about how you look as much as *you* do. And anyway, perfect is boring. At least now you have some character to you. Who wants to look at something perfect all the time? It just makes the rest of us feel that much more *im*perfect. So, really, you're doing everyone else less fortunate in the looks department a *huge* favor. You should look at it that way." I suck in a lungful of air and catch my breath.

"I should be glad for the boating accident then, is that what you're saying?" he says with narrowed eyes.

I shrug, turning my attention back to the menu. "I think I'll have pancakes."

I slap the menu down and give him a smile.

His response is a stare.

I raise my eyebrows.

Shaking his head, Rivers takes my menu and looks it over.

The waitress, a sixty-ish woman with pale blonde hair, glasses, and black painted on eyebrows, shows up to take our drink orders. I get orange juice and Rivers orders coffee and water. I kick my feet in beat to 'Son of A Preacher Man' by Dusty Springfield playing from a radio somewhere in the restaurant, and when that isn't satisfactory, I hop to my feet.

"What are you doing?" Rivers asks worriedly, looking around us.

"I'm dancing." I spin around and strike a pose, grinning at him over my shoulder.

With a groan, he covers his face. "I swear you have it out for me."

I shake my shoulders and bend over to bump one against his. "Want to join me?"

"I don't, no." He leans over and hisses, "Sit down. You're embarrassing me."

"Maybe *you're* embarrassing *me*," I say close to his face.

I admire the lush fan of his eyelashes around his eyes, noting the line of chocolate brown around his pupils. His brows furrow as he returns the stare, his eyes shifting over my features.

"You look different without all your makeup on. You're sort

of pretty," he says in a hoarse voice, clearly stunned by this knowledge, or maybe by saying it out loud.

I grin, my stomach clenching and releasing. "You're sort of talking a lot." I straighten as the waitress stops by our table with our drinks.

I sit down and place my hands on the table top, eyes on Rivers. He won't look at me, which is okay. I think he shocked himself with his halfway compliment.

I order pancakes and so does he.

"Have you had the pancakes here before?"

"Who hasn't?" he says after a pause.

I almost sigh, or say the word. I guess it's back to him being all moody and non-responsive. I sit back and look out the window, wondering when the next train will come. I feel his gaze on me and wait for him to ask whatever is on his mind.

"How'd you get hired to clean our house anyway?"

"Your mom apparently thought I was qualified." I hear the faint roar of an engine, my eyes glued to the window as I wait.

"Why? How? She just saw you on the street and asked you to clean our house? And why would you want to anyway?"

"I need the money."

"For?"

I glance at him. "I'm going on a trip."

"You're going on a trip," he repeats slowly. Leaning back, he crosses his arms over his chest. "What kind of a trip?"

"One that requires money." The train appears in green and black. I avidly watch it, the sound and speed of it breathtaking.

"Most trips do. You didn't answer me. How did you come to work at my house?"

I turn from the window, the vibration of the locomotive faint from this distance but still noticeable. "We were at the grocery store, in the checkout lane by each other. The line was long and we started talking. She looked frazzled, said the regular cleaning lady who also did the grocery shopping had just gone on vacation and with everything the way it was, she hadn't had time to hire a temporary replacement.

"She said she had planned on not hiring anyone for the summer and doing it all herself, but realized she didn't have the time because of situations at home. I think she was desperate."

It isn't the full truth, but a close variation of it. Everything I said is true on his mother's part. I just left some details out.

"And you volunteered." His tone says he doubts this.

I nod. "I did."

"Again, why?"

I jut my jaw forward, fighting to keep irritation at bay. "I told you why. I needed the money."

"Did you know it was *my* house when you offered? Did you know you were talking to my mom?"

I shift my eyes from his and cross my fingers under the table. "No. Not at first."

A partial truth again. Another jolt of annoyance sparks through me. I promised myself this would be a peaceful summer, but there are times—most of the time, I should say—in Rivers' presence that I forget this.

"Why are you asking me all of these questions anyway? What does any of it matter?"

"I'm just trying to figure it all out."

"Well, you have. Now you know the mystery behind my employment. Bully for you."

"Right. You wanted to work at my house so you can get enough money to go on a trip where the destination and activities of it are apparently top secret." The expression on his face is dubious.

"I like trains."

He gives me a look. "Okay."

"I've never been on one before and I've always wanted to go on some kind of trip on one. I'm planning on going on a six-day Amtrak trip to Memphis and New Orleans. It's called 'Blues and the Bayou'. Both are places I've always wanted to see."

"Oh." His look tells me he doesn't understand why I would want to do such a thing.

"Have you ever been on a train ride before?"

Rivers shakes his head, his attention captured by those around us. He seems to shrink in size, as though he is trying to make himself as uninteresting as he can. Such a complete reversal of how he used to be. He used to shine when others paid attention to him; now he seems to deflate. Rivers' eyes shift over the other patrons and he looks down, clenching his jaw.

"What is it?"

"People are staring at me. This was a bad idea. We should go."

I lean against the table top and crane my neck back to look over him. There are five other customers in the diner; all older, and not a single person is looking in our direction. "Who?"

"I don't know. People."

"Mmm-hmm." I sit back. "Do you know any of the people in here right now?"

"No."

"Okay. So, they have no reason to be staring at you then. You're imagining it."

I thank the waitress as she sets the white plate of fluffy round pancakes before me.

"And if you don't stop thinking everyone is obsessed with your looks as much as you are, I'm going to punch you," I tell him pleasantly.

He snorts. "Try it."

Rivers smears butter on his pancakes with a knife, his eyes down.

"You always thought you were so important," I say, carefully setting my fork down.

His eyes lift to mine.

"I don't think you ever realized how *un*important high school and your role in it really was. High school is what happens *before* your life begins. You can be the top dog in that big brown building and a nobody outside it. You and your friends thought everyone wanted to be like you, because you were so self-absorbed you thought everyone else loved you as much as you loved yourself. You were wrong."

I pop a straw in my orange juice and sip, the tangy citrus

bursting over my tongue.

He puts his knife down and straightens. "That's it? I was wrong? You make this big speech and that's your summary of it? I was wrong?"

"Yep." I pour a generous amount of maple syrup on my pancakes and dig into them.

"What did people really think about me then?" He takes a sip of his coffee. "What did *you* really think?"

I pop a forkful of pancakes into my mouth and chew. Swallowing, I say, "You completely missed the point of what I just said."

Frustration flashes in his eyes. "What was the purpose of putting me down then?"

Sitting up in my seat, I look at him. "You missed the point again. I didn't put you down. You care too much what others think."

"Maybe you don't care enough," he retorts.

"I don't care at all," I answer evenly. "I was making an observation. It wasn't intended to hurt you or make you feel inferior. The point of it was, it doesn't matter. None of it matters. High school is over. So whatever anyone thought of you, whatever I thought of you, you shouldn't care."

"It's not that easy," he mutters.

"It really is."

His fork clanks to his plate as he shoves it away. "You know, maybe for you it is. It's easy not to care when you don't have anything worth losing, when you don't have anyone to disappoint or anyone looking up to you, depending on you to be a certain way."

I flinch, my appetite dispersing like leaves falling away from a tree. And then the headache starts. I drop my head to my hands, aware of Rivers asking me if I'm okay, but it's background noise to the sharp twinges forming in my temples and progressing all the way to the back of my head.

Not now. Don't do this now.

My brain is wrapped in throbbing pain. I'm sure he thinks I'm crying or something because he hurt my feelings. He did hurt my feelings, I'm annoyed to realize, but that is minor compared to the agony flashing through my brain like bolts of lightning. I swear I even see streaks of light behind my closed eyelids.

A presence is next to me, a hand strong and warm against my shoulder.

"It's okay," I mumble, massaging my temples. "It's just a headache." My voice is weak and faraway at the same time it's unusually loud to me.

"Just give me a minute," I continue when he says something else.

I inhale and exhale slowly, counting to sixty. The pain lessens, but doesn't fully go away. I am aware that all kinds of attention is being drawn our way because of me and not Rivers, something he should be grateful for, but will probably be irritated by because attention to me brings attention to him.

A glass is pressed into my hand along with two pills. I carefully raise my head, the scene coming at me in jagged pieces. I focus on the face before me until all the faces of Rivers morph into one, seeing the concern drawing his eyebrows down. I concentrate on him, watching him watching me, until I am able to swallow the pills. They will dull the headache, but only sleep will take it away for good.

Until it comes back.

I didn't want this to happen in front of anyone, especially him. In fact, I wanted to pretend it hasn't happened at all. Part of me was hoping it *wouldn't* happen again—that the headaches and what they mean was all a mistake. I *do* feel like crying, but not because of Rivers and what he said to me.

Bravado waning, I stiffen my shoulders and force it back into me by will alone. *Be positive. Enjoy the rest of the day. Even try to enjoy Rivers' presence.* That last thought eases some of the tension from me and I almost smile. I would, if the pounding in my head would allow me to.

"Are you okay?" he asks in a low voice, his hand dropping from my shoulder.

"Yes."

I'm not, but I am well enough. I thank the waitress for the pain pills and she nods, turning away to help another customer.

"I'm sorry I ruined the meal."

"I think I can take most of the credit for that," he says, moving to stand. "Do you want to stay and finish or leave?"

"Leave. Pancakes don't really sound good anymore." I touch my head. "If that's okay?"

"Somehow, I'll manage to return to the solitude of my home." A ghost of a smile captures his lips and even that semblance of one is enough to make his features turn from handsome to inconceivably exceptional.

I ease into a standing position, dizziness hitting me. I grip the top of the booth until the diner stops moving.

"Is this..." I take a deep breath, directing my mind to concentrate on walking in a straight line. I feel drunk. I might not mind it so much if I'd actually consumed alcoholic beverages.

One foot in front of the other, Delilah. Distract yourself. Keep talking. Maybe he'll even talk back.

"Is this the first time you've gone anywhere since the accident?"

"Anywhere other than various doctors, yes."

"Was it so bad?" We're almost to the door. I glance behind me, my eyesight in slow motion with my movement, and note his hand hovering by my elbow in case I need assistance.

"Well, it wasn't excruciating, so it was a little better than I had estimated. Your obvious need for attention and melodramatic acting sort of trumped my disfigurement."

I want to glare at him, but the motion would cause me pain. I settle for mumbling, "Jerk."

He snorts.

For once, I am thankful for the clouds that have taken over the sky and hidden the sun. Even the gray is sensitive to my eyes. I look down as I walk, feeling incompetent and loathing the fact that I do. Understanding for Rivers scorches me, hot and complete in its burn.

He must hate people looking after him all the time, watching over him, trying to help him. I just want this helpless feeling to go away and never return. At least in his case, he will slowly get better, if he lets himself.

That isn't an option for me.

When he opens the passenger car door for me, I tell him, "We make quite the pair right now."

I don't think he is going to respond, but then he says, "We do, don't we?"

FOUR

I AWAKE TO THE CRASH of thunder, my eyes opening just as lightning flares to life outside. Rain pours down, pinging against the glass doors and windows. There is only the light of the thunderstorm to offer visual assistance. I check my phone to see how long I've been asleep and note the missing calls from Monica and my mom. I slept five hours. My head is free of pain and I am grateful for it, though my mouth feels dry and there is a languidness in my limbs that makes it hard for me to get them moving.

I call my mother first and let her know everything is okay, not mentioning my mega headache that put me out for over five hours. I know I need to tell her, but I just can't bring myself to, not yet. Soon, I silently promise her and myself. Monica informs me Rivers called her a few hours ago, that she knows about my headache, and refers to it as a migraine, telling me rest is the best thing for them. I agree with the assessment, but not the term she uses.

I don't have migraines. I have something much, much worse.

She sounds tired, but her tone is also lighter than usual, and if I had to guess as to why, I would say it's because her son is reaching out to her, if only through the phone. The phone is better than nothing. Thomas' mom is the same and she tells me they may have to stay longer. I tell her that's fine and hang up.

And it is fine.

I'm not really sure what I'm thinking or doing or why the thought of going home makes me even more uneasy than usual, but it's almost like when I am here, I can tell myself this is my reality. It won't last, I know, but it's like a little joy in the midst of tragedy. I watch the tree limbs shudder under the force of the strong winds, taking comfort that even in the middle of nature's wrath, I am safe.

For now.

I find Rivers outside, sitting in his chair just under the roof ledge. Strangely shy after my unfortunate ordeal earlier, I take hesitant steps toward him. For the first time that I can remember, he speaks first.

"Do you get them often?"

I wait until a large rumbling of thunder is over before answering. "Recently, about weekly."

"Before that?"

"I don't know. Rarely." I bite my lip, hoping he finds a different subject to discuss. Anything would be better, really, even a conversation about ingrown toenails.

He looks up at me, a frown turning his lips down. "And have you gone to the doctor?"

I rub my arms and look into the black depths of the pool. The temperature has dropped considerably with the appearance of the storm.

"You sound concerned." My tone is flippant and I can tell he doesn't appreciate it when he continues to wait for me to answer. I sigh. "Yes. They're just headaches."

Lying is becoming increasingly easy for me lately. Or telling partial truths, I should say.

"Migraines?" he guesses.

I shrug noncommittally and he doesn't press.

I pull over a chair and sit down beside him, taking in the rain, the occasional clap of thunder, the way the sky lights up to daytime from atmospheric electricity. We sit in silence, but it isn't tense. There is peacefulness to it, the sound of raindrops pummeling the house and ground calming. I have so many questions I could ask him, but none of them seem important right now. Sitting here like this is more therapeutic than any conversation could be.

Minutes tick by and I jump when he says, "I'm sorry. About earlier."

He glances at me, his eyes glowing in the near dark. "I shouldn't have said what I did. It was mean."

I pick at an uneven edge of my thumbnail. "Honestly, it doesn't really phase me anymore. I'm used to it."

"But not from me," he tells me roughly.

I meet his gaze. "What does it matter if you're the one saying the words or the one standing there saying nothing to refute them?"

He winces, facing forward. "I thought being popular made me fearless. None of it was real. I'm not courageous. And clearly, I wasn't as well-liked as I'd assumed either."

His eyes flicker to me and away.

"Oh, loads of people liked you. Envied you." I pause. "But then there were the rest of us."

The laugh is gruff and cuts off short, but that he laughed at all freezes me in place. It's a deep, rich sound that has a melodious cast to it. It reminds me of a cool breeze to break the unrelenting heat of a smoldering sun—unexpected but appreciated.

"I don't...I don't really remember too much about you. I mean, I remember seeing you, but most of the time, you were just...*there*," he says slowly, clearly embarrassed to admit such a thing. "Was I that bad?"

I blow out a noisy breath and focus on the puddle of water my feet are resting in. "Do you really want to get into this? You have a clean slate, you know. School is over. However you choose to be from now on has no correlation to how you used to be. Why bring it up? Why wonder?"

Something I said must have irked him because Rivers is up and glaring at me before I finish my words. "You know what? Never mind. You act like you're so superior, and even though I don't remember a lot about you, I *do* remember your mouth. Sure, you got a lot of shit tossed your way, but you gave it back just as harshly. Or did you forget about *that*?"

He's already stalking away when I whisper, "Clean slate."

I don't know how long I stay outside, the numbness inside me seeping to my exterior as the coldness of night wraps around me. He's right. I didn't really have any friends in school, and part of it was because of how Riley and Crew treated me—no one wanted to be picked on by association with me, but some of it was how I acted as well.

I made it hard for others to approach me when I wore a chronic scowl on my face and talked back to anyone who said something I could take offensively. I thought that was the way I wanted to be, that making my individuality prominent was a way of showing strength, but now, I realize maybe I was trying *too* hard to be different.

You need to be yourself, but you also shouldn't feel like you have to fight everyone, even yourself, to be it.

I didn't want to get hurt, so I didn't open myself up to anyone to even allow for the potential of being hurt. I assumed anyone talking to me had an ulterior agenda and responded in kind. Did that mean I was a backwards bully? Maybe. I never thought about it before. I don't mind solitude, but I guess once in a while it would have been nice to have someone to talk to, had I felt the need to. I had a group of classmates I loosely hung around, but were any of them friends? I don't think so. And the reason for that falls on my shoulders.

Apparently, Rivers is not the only one who needs to take a look at his younger years and analyze how he was compared to how he should have been. I sort of have. That's why I am choosing to be positive instead of negative, why I want to smile instead of frown, why I decided to not care about anything other than just being me.

This summer is supposed to be my last chance do-over on so many levels.

The chattering of my teeth tells me it's time to go inside. I do, the silence echoing behind me with enormity. I head to the sunroom, tugging a book from my tote to settle in for an evening of reading. I don't want to be around Rivers right now, and I am sure the feeling is reciprocated. We both have said things the other didn't appreciate hearing.

Hours pass, my eyelids growing so heavy I can no longer keep them open. I sink into the abyss that is slumber, awakening during the night to a noise that tugged at my consciousness even as I rested.

I already know it was Rivers.

I don't turn on the light. I don't speak. I walk to the bed and touch his clammy brow, his body almost immediately relaxing. I climb into the bed, halfway sitting up, and wrap my arms around his trembling form, holding him. I don't know if he is awake or sleeping, but eventually his breathing evens out and his arms slowly move to lock around my waist, his head of dark hair resting against my stomach. Something weaves its way through me, coming to rest in my heart. I don't put a name to it. It isn't that I don't think I can—it's more that I am not ready.

We sit like this, my fingers gently tracing the lines of the scars that start at the crown of his head and end near his temple, moving on to the short locks of his silky hair. I tighten my hold on him, feeling the hardness of his muscled body, wondering how someone so physically strong can be so emotionally vulnerable, knowing we never truly understand another until we have been in the same place they are at. Maybe that's why I care for a boy I don't want to care for, and deny that I do every other thought.

As I hold Rivers in my arms for the duration of the night, I decide I will fight his demons for him if he can't fight them on his own. It isn't a matter of whether or not he'll allow me to, because I think just being here with him is enough most of the time.

Something in him needs something in me. I saw it today and I saw it the first day I saw him after his injury. Rivers needs to know someone cares about him. I can be that person. After all, that is why I originally came here.

WE ARE IN SOME SORT of routine, but it is a strange one. At

night we sleep wrapped around one another and during the day, we barely speak. I can't say the sleeping arrangement is all for Rivers' benefit anymore because I sleep so soundly when I am with him, more peaceful than I recall ever sleeping before. I want to rest beside him. I want to close my eyes at night knowing he is next to me. I want to hear his breathing, feel his arms, smell his scent, and get lost in him so that I forget me.

There isn't anything sexual about our sleeping arrangements—although, yes, I should admit I am attracted to him which is absolutely crazy because I'm not even sure I really like him—but it's about the safety I feel near him. I keep his nightmares at bay and he keeps my world at a distance.

It's strange, but even though there is darkness and quiet and little touching between us at night, it is as though the nighttime hours are stitching us together, making us into something we are not consciously aware of. I feel closer to him. I feel like I am starting to know him. We seem to unknowingly gravitate toward one another during the day. He finds me or I find him. Maybe words aren't necessary—maybe that's why we hardly speak. I just need to look up and see him or he just needs to enter a room and feel me.

I take him to his physical therapy sessions two times the first week and a counselor once. His body is exhausted from the first and his mind from the second. He doesn't speak at all after the counseling session for the remainder of the day. I want to ask him what makes him close up the way he does, but I assume it's from the horror of the accident. Doubt trickles through my mind, asking, *What if it's more than that?*

Monica and Thomas decide to stay in California until his mother passes on—the doctors say it won't be longer than a week or two more before the cancer irrevocably claims her. According to Monica, any time Thomas mentioned returning home, his mother broke down and cried. It's hard to leave someone you know is dying, when they weep at the thought of your departure. Sometimes I think it would be better for everyone if no one knew when they are dying. Too bad that isn't an option for some.

Each time I talk to Monica, guilt eats away at me. She thinks I'm doing some great thing for her son, but am I really? Sure, he's engaging his mother in conversation and finally acting more like a human being than a robot, but what happens at the end of the summer, when all of this is over? I'll go back to my life and Rivers will go back to his, and these few months spent together will be a piece of the past.

Do they have to be?

I answer myself with a resounding, *yes*.

It's nice to pretend for a while, but the truth always catches up to you. Always.

I'm swimming laps like I do just about every evening. I feel his eyes on me and heat goes through the length of my body. There is nothing predatory or seductive about his gaze; it's more of a studious observance, but knowing he is examining all the dips and curves of my body as I swim makes me self-conscious. The intensity with which Rivers watches the world makes my pulse skip.

He doesn't just *look* at things—he *sees* things. I don't know how I never noticed this about him. I think I saw all his flaws and didn't even look for his good points. I guess I did exactly what I accused him of doing. I also think I need to admit to myself that I wasn't any better than those around me that I thought were so terrible.

Maybe he never gave me a chance, but did I ever give him one?

I tread water as I face him. "Want to come in?"

Indecision shadows his features.

"Oh, come on. You sit there and watch me almost every day. It's obvious you want to be in here too. What's stopping you?"

"I like watching you," he confesses.

I brush water from my face because I am suddenly nervous and don't know what to do with my hands. "Why?"

Broad shoulders lift and lower. "You're like a fish. A natural in the water. It's soothing to watch."

"I'm sure you're a much better swimmer. Haven't you been

in some form of body of water most of your life? I've seen the pictures—swimming, jet skiing, surfing, water skiing, boating—you've done it all."

His face darkens, but it's too late, there's no going back now.

I trudge onward. "What happened, Rivers? What happened out on the river?"

You shouldn't have gotten hurt, is the unspoken sentence I bite back. Not with his natural prowess on the water. True, accidents can happen to anyone—no matter their level of adequacy, but what if it was something more? Negligence comes to mind.

Who was driving the boat? Who was out on the water with him that day? Was he drinking or was he sober? If he was drinking, that would at least make it a little more understandable. Maybe he was intoxicated and misjudged the distance between the boat and the water, or maybe he slipped. Maybe.

The real question is: How did he fall into the water and get injured *that* bad?

"I don't want to talk about it."

I open my mouth to push the conversation and then decide against it. With a shrug I return to my laps. I know the exact moment he goes inside. My body cools without the burn of his gaze on me and I feel strangely empty and lonely. I've always sort of been alone, but I've never really felt *lonely*. Unease creeps through me as I get to my feet in the water.

It feels like everything is backfiring on me. I had it all figured out; all the details were sound, unbreakable. I knew what I was going to do. It was a simple plan.

Only nothing is happening the way I thought it would.

THE DOORBELL CHIMES THREE TIMES before I toss my book aside with a sigh and get up to answer it. It's Friday night, and I do realize how lame it is of me to be reading on a Friday night, but I haven't read a book for pleasure since I was twelve. The person at the door is totally interrupting my reading time, and I know Rivers had to have heard the doorbell because his bedroom is closer to the front door than the sunroom is. He may be physically compromised, but he isn't deaf. And it isn't like whoever is at the door is here for me. I don't live here—he does. It's a given they've come to see Rivers. So why am I the one answering the door?

It's ridiculous to get upset over this, but I am finding that pretty much everything about Rivers aggravates me on some level. I haven't fully analyzed why just yet. I'll save that self-discovery for another rainy day. I try to calm myself down by saying maybe he has his music loud and can't hear the doorbell, but when I pass by the closed bedroom door, I hear silence.

Ear buds. He could have in ear buds. He so doesn't, I know it. He's simply being his moody and difficult self again, like he is prone to be.

I draw my hand toward me when it fists and raises to pound on his door, instead moving on to the front door.

Mentally groaning at the sight that greets me, I feign nonchalance as I nod. "Riley."

To say she is surprised might be an understatement. Her chestnut locks are all wild around her pretty face, her slim body is clothed in a black halter dress, and her eyes continually blink as her mouth slowly closes when only seconds before it was hanging open. And then, of course, there's the scent of her perfume—candy and flowers—in all its cloying enormity to further agitate me.

"Um..." She looks around like she thinks maybe she got the wrong house, finally fixing her blue eyes on me. "What are you doing here?"

I cross my arms. "I work here."

My action draws her eyes down and her brows furrow as she takes in my purple tank top and black shorts. They're skimpy, I guess, but I am ready for bed. I wasn't expecting a social visit at nine in the evening, but I should have known there was a chance Rivers would have one. My bad. I guess he should have answered the door then.

"At night?"

"Temporarily."

"I don't understand."

She really doesn't. I kind of feel bad for her. She is so prettily confused. Then I remember how viperous she can be and stiffen my spine.

"Monica and Thomas had to leave the state for a week or so and asked me to babysit."

"Babysit? Where's Rivers?" She looks past me.

"I don't know." The irony of not knowing where my charge is or what he is up to hits me and I clear my throat. "So... did you need something?"

Face reddening, her mouth pulls in. "Yes. I'd like to see Rivers."

"I thought you broke up."

Whoa. There was a snarky undertone there. Where did that come from?

Her eyes narrow. "Is it any of your business what goes on between the two of us?"

"The two of you," I repeat slowly, "as in you're a couple...even though you aren't."

Riley's mouth thins as she takes a step closer. "Are you going to get him or not?"

"Does he want to see you?"

I know I'm being a bitch, but I have to embrace these little moments of perfection as they come along. Riley, deferring to me as though I am her superior, is classic—and about time.

Plus, I don't know why, but I sort of want to rip her apart right now, solely on the basis of her wanting to see Rivers. Not cool for me, not at all.

"Look, Delilah," she begins in an icy tone, her voice faltering as she looks up and beyond me.

I glance over my shoulder and connect gazes with one of black storms. My stomach swoops and I quickly look back to Riley.

"Here he is. Have fun."

I leave the room, my feet not moving fast enough. They could never move fast enough. I feel like my body is encased in lead and is moving as such. Have fun? Really? Like I want them to be having any kind of fun together—ugh times infinity.

What was that swirly feeling in my gut when he looked at me? Nothing. It was nothing. Absolutely nothing. The denial seems lame, even to me. It was something. It was something and that something is not a good idea. Do feelings ever care whether it's a good idea or not to have them? Nope.

Reading has lost its appeal, so I spend the next few minutes pacing the length of the sunroom, gnawing on my thumbnail as I wait—for what, I don't know. I guess for Rivers. Or maybe for Riley to leave. And then what?

And then the careening of my pulse and the pounding of my heart will relax. I wonder what they're saying to each other. I wonder what Rivers is thinking as he looks at his ex-girlfriend. He has to have lingering feelings, right? I mean, she is amazing to look at, so there is that.

I freeze in the middle of the room. What the hell am I thinking? Since when do I care about Rivers or anything that involves him? I want to say since we started sleeping together at night, and oh, how innocent does that not sound? But it really is. There has never been a moment where the thought of taking it further than actual sleeping has reached me.

Well, I mean, it's maybe in the back of my head, but I would never act on it. It's more of a curiosity thing, like wondering what it would feel like to be kissed by Rivers Young. But then, why do I seem almost...jealous? This is insane.

Because Rivers and me? No.

A car door slams and an engine purrs, fading into the distance along with headlights I spot out the window. Riley is leaving. It isn't relief that hits me as I fall onto the couch because there's no reason for it, or any other emotion, to sneak up on me. And I do sort of feel like I am being sporadically pummeled by things when I least expect to be.

But really, how can you prepare for something you don't see

coming? I rub my face, dropping my hands at a thought. Maybe Riley didn't leave, but took Rivers somewhere with her. Maybe they went off on a date, or to reconcile, or...have sex.

I gasp from the discomfort that shoots through me, angry with myself for thinking what Rivers does or doesn't do has anything to do with me or that it should affect me in any way. Wanting to distract myself, I decide stuffing myself with ice cream is a good way to go about it. I do not pause when I reach Rivers' closed door and I do not hold my breath in hopes of catching a sound from within the room. And I do not falter in my steps when his dark visage is the first thing I focus on as I enter the kitchen.

"The jig is up," I tell him, nodding to his bowl. "I know you don't like ice cream."

He wordlessly grabs another bowl and spoon, scooping chocolate chip cookie dough ice cream into it. The mint chocolate chip was gone days ago. He pushes it across the counter top toward me, one eyebrow lifted as he looks at me.

"Thanks." I scoop some of the cold deliciousness onto my tongue and swallow.

"I have no idea why I ate the ice cream," he murmurs. He looks up, a small smile on his face. "I guess I didn't want to put all your effort to waste."

"Effort? I took apart a wall of frozen peas. It didn't entail a lot of muscle work."

He shrugs. "Maybe I wanted your company so I suffered through eating the ice cream in silence."

I laugh. "Why would you want my company? I mean, *I* know I'm fascinating, but you seem a little slower to have that inevitable epiphany."

His eyebrows lift. "Big words."

"What can I say? I'm super smart." I'm not, but it sounded good.

"Humble as well."

I wink. "It comes with the territory." We both become silent until I pipe up with, "So eating ice cream is considered suffering to you? Clearly you have been spoiled."

He looks down.

I realize maybe he thinks I'm minimizing his accident. I set the spoon down in my bowl. "Sorry. I mean, I know you haven't had it exactly easy lately. I didn't mean anything by my comment."

"I know. But you're right." Rivers' eyes take me in and I feel like he is sucking me into him with those dark, dark eyes. "I *was* pretty spoiled. It isn't that I didn't have to work at what I got, because I did, but a lot of it also came easy to me. Most of what you say angers me, but once I decided to think about it, I realized *why* it bothers me so much. Because you're right."

"I'm right that you secretly love ice cream? I knew it."

"I don't love it or hate it. I can do with, or without." He shrugs again.

I widen my eyes at him. "You're not normal."

He glances at me before walking to the table with his bowl. "And you know a lot about that, right?"

"Enough." I take my ice cream and sit across the table from him.

River asks, "What's up with you and Riley?"

I quickly swallow a mound of cookie dough and wait for it to dislodge from my throat. "What's up with *you* and Riley?"

"We dated for a long time. It didn't work out. She won't let go. And now that I'm partially helpless, she thinks I need her to baby me, which only makes me even more glad that I am no longer dating her."

The intensity of his gaze singes me. "And you? She's always been particularly nasty to you, more than to anyone else. I never stopped to think there might be a reason for it."

"Do you even realize how sad that is?"

He ignores that, asking, "What happened with you two?"

"Why did you two break up?" I shoot back.

He won't look at me as he answers, "We grew apart. I realized I didn't like a lot of things about her, or how I was when I was with her, or even why I continued to be with her. I guess maybe

I matured. Why did she shove you into the lockers sophomore year?"

"You saw that?" My voice is faint. I can't believe he remembers that. It was over two years ago. And there's the whole idea that I thought I was invisible to him.

Rivers nods, his eyes down as he mashes his ice cream into a melting blob. "Yeah. Saw it, didn't do anything about it, didn't care." His tone almost sounds remorseful but that can't be.

"She called me a freak, so I called her a slut. Her reaction was to shove me and I landed against the lockers. The principal decided to make an appearance right after that so I couldn't retaliate." Even now, my fingers tighten with the memory of humiliation and anger.

He squints his eyes at me. "Her tire was flat that day after school. Was that you?"

My bowl of ice cream becomes mesmerizing.

A gruff laugh escapes him. "What else?"

"Freshman year she wrote on the bathroom wall in the girls' locker room that I would screw anything that walked. I wrote back that she already had."

"Not bad. I mean, not exactly great for me, but not bad."

A smile slowly curves my lips and Rivers returns it. This moment, right now, is going to end up being a bad thing. I can already tell it will mean something to me. I will look back on this moment and I will remember how I feel as he smiles at me and I will miss it. But for now, I just enjoy it. I shove another mouthful of ice cream into my mouth so I don't have to talk.

"You wanted to know why I was named Rivers," he begins, his gaze scorching as it connects with mine.

I nod, waiting.

"My legal name was Benjamin until I was ten months old. Now it's my middle name."

"What?" I scrunch up my face in confusion. "Why would they name you something and then name you something else?"

A faraway look enters his eyes—a touch of sadness with it. "I was born in California and spent the first years of my life there.

I guess I was obsessed with water. I wanted to be in it every day and I screamed when my mom or dad took me out of it. I was swimming before I was walking. They didn't want to name me Lake or Ocean or Sea, because those aren't really names, so they settled with Rivers. Most rivers either begin or end with other bodies of water anyway. I was supposed to be a merging of all things watery."

"They could have called you Bathwater," I tell him.

He shakes his head, the hint of a smile softening his face. "That's two words."

"Okay. First name Bath, second name Water. It totally would have worked. They were being selfish, really, taking that possibility away from you. You would have been famous for that name ingenuity. And I like Lake. Lake could be your name. Can I call you Benji?"

"Don't even try it," he warns.

I laugh and shove another spoonful of ice cream into my mouth.

"I wouldn't. You're definitely a Rivers. Tumultuous, consuming."

"What about peaceful and calm?"

I snort. "Yeah. You're that all right."

He watches me, his head tilted, a curious gleam in his eyes.

"I don't know if I deserve you," he suddenly murmurs.

I go still. I am frozen and he is frozen, our eyes locked.

"I mean, we—I don't know if we deserve you. You do a better job than the normal cleaning lady," he quickly corrects. Rivers' face lowers as though he wants to hide himself from me.

I hastily change the subject, my heart pounding in a frighteningly fast way. "We used to be friends. Riley and me," I specify when confusion enters his gaze. "We grew apart too."

He puts his chin on his hand, studying me. "I think there's more to it than that."

"Isn't there always?" I ask lightly, standing up. "I'm done. Are you done?"

"You're going to ask this time, huh?"

"Last time your behavior didn't warrant you being asked."

Rivers walks over to where I am standing, quietly taking a dish towel and drying the dishes as I wash them. After a while, he says, "We have a dishwasher."

"I don't like dishwashers. They're lazy."

He smiles.

I tell myself I can't get used them. They are magical and I slowly unravel a little more each time he graces me with one of them.

"The dishwashers are lazy or the people running them are?" he questions.

"Either."

"Are you...do you..." He closes his eyes, shaking his head. Rivers takes a deep breath and starts over. "Want to watch a movie together?"

If I didn't know better, I would think he is apprehensive, but that is ludicrous and I quickly chuck the thought aside. "Sure. What kind of movies do you like to watch?"

Lowering his voice, he says sinisterly, "Scary ones."

I drain the water from the sink and turn around, crossing my arms as I meet his gaze. "I can handle scary."

"I'm counting on it." He walks from the room, his movements a touch closer to smooth than unsteady. He is healing, getting better—emotionally and physically. I won't be needed here much longer, not for him anyway.

I look out the glass panes that lead to the deck and pool, searching for the nightlights in the sky and finding none. For the first time in months, I feel the weight of an unknown future pressing down on me. I have to balance the future with the present. I have to take what I can of the happy moments because, eventually, they will become less and less.

I have to remember instances like this, right now, when a broken boy found something in me to smile at, when I went from being just me to him to someone who can make him smile —someone he wants to smile at.

And that is why I skip from the room and sing 'Free Fallin" by

Tom Petty as I spin in a circle in the foyer, laughing when Rivers pops his head around the corner to give me a strange look. I don't mind. He doesn't join me, but he also doesn't leave. He quietly watches me in that smoldering way of his. I can read his eyes and what they are saying is that he is trying to figure me out, that he finds me interesting enough to *want* to figure out.

The wink I aim at him tells him he'll never solve the complex being that is Delilah Bana so he should just enjoy me while I am here. When he grins at me, I grin back. All we are given as a guarantee, are instances of perfect freedom to say and do exactly what we want. I've realized this. I think Rivers is finally realizing this.

Why let them pass us by?

FIVE

IT ISN'T EVEN A QUESTION. He stands and looks at me, waiting, and within seconds I am following him from the sunroom and into his bedroom. I wonder what his mother and father would think if they knew about our sleeping arrangement.

I wince.

We're not doing anything wrong. I continue to tell myself this, but I still feel guilty. With any luck, I won't have to worry about Monica's reaction to it. Because I'm hoping she doesn't find out, which also means we should stop before she does find out. And yet, still I follow him.

I wonder what this means to him. A small part of me wonders if he is using me because I am close in proximity, but if that was the case, I wouldn't be here and Riley would. He would be talking to Riley and not me. He would be opening up, smiling and laughing, with her instead of me. I don't think he simply needs someone. I think he needs me. I am seeing him in a different way than I used to—I have to think it is the same for him.

His eyes linger on mine longer than they should and when he touches my arm, my heart reacts by pumping extra hard. Every time he looks at me, I feel scorched from the emotions I see in his gaze. Something has changed. I don't know what. I don't know when it happened, but it has.

"Did the movie scare you?" he asks, moving around his room as he gets ready for bed.

My eyes trail after him. "'Saw' isn't scary. It's just gross."

"You wouldn't be scared if that stuff happened to you?"

I narrow my eyes. "That wasn't the original question."

He smirks and my eyes are drawn to his lips. Part of me wonders what it would be like—to be loved by him. Or even just desired. To be with a guy like Rivers has got to be unforgettable. Everything he does is done with such intensity that being loved by him couldn't be any less than overwhelming. I think it would be comparable to continually trying to catch your breath and failing.

We take turns brushing our teeth in the bathroom. When I return to the bedroom, he has the blanket pulled down and is idly watching television as he waits on the bed. It seems so domestic, like we're playing at being a married couple. Only there is no commitment, there is no love, there is no happily ever after—or some idea of it.

My eyes mold to the construction of his bare chest and I turn the light off to halt my staring. Ignoring his protestations about the sudden dark, I get into the bed. The television goes blank and the remote thumps as it falls to the floor. The silence is heavy, but this time it is not peaceful like it usually is. We need to talk about something, anything, so this tension abates, or at least dims.

"With your grandma the way she is...I'm surprised you didn't insist on going with your parents. Don't you want to be with your grandma right now?"

A full minute passes before he answers, "No."

My mouth pulls down. "Why not? She's dying. Why wouldn't you want to be with her right now? I mean, aren't you sad?"

"I don't know. I guess a little."

"Wow."

I can't believe his coldness. Where did it come from? What caused it?

"She's not my real grandma," he tells me. He shifts in the bed and our faces are now inches apart.

"Oh?" I ask, suddenly breathless.

"No. She's my step-grandma and Thomas is my step-dad. Other than when I was a baby, I've only been around her twice, I think—both times before the age of ten. She's basically like a stranger to me."

"But..." I sputter, my mind still stuck on the father revelation. "You look just like him."

"I look like my dad." Rivers' voice is ice as he faces the ceiling. "He's dead. Thomas is his first cousin."

"I... oh...wow," I say again, realizing how lame I sound.

"I didn't know him. I was a year old when he died. Freak accident at the factory he worked at. My mom's been with Thomas since I was three."

"How did your mom end up with your father's cousin?"

I feel him shrug next to me. "I don't know. Sometimes I think she wanted to replace my dad as best as she could and he fit in the looks department."

"But not in any other departments?"

"He's an ass. He won't exactly ever win any awards for best husband or father of the year. He..."

"He what?"

"Nothing. Never mind. What about your dad?" The topic was changed a little too hastily, proof that Rivers is upset.

"My dad...hmm...that's a good question. What about my dad," I muse. "I don't know my dad."

"What do you mean, you don't know your dad?"

I purse my lips. "Well...my mom didn't know my dad; hence I don't know my dad."

"Oh." I can hear the confusion in that one word.

"It was a one-night stand. I think she was grieving over her ex-husband or something. She's always been sort of vague about the details. She didn't know him, didn't know his name; he wasn't from the area. So, you know, a few months later she finds out she's pregnant. No dad."

So many questions could be answered if I knew him, but there is no point in thinking about it, because I don't. I take a deep breath, closing my eyes.

"Neither one of us knew our dads," he remarks.

"No."

"But at least I know my dad's name. You don't even have that part of yours. That really sucks. A lot. I don't know what to say—I'm not any good at comforting people, sorry."

I give a small lift of my shoulders. He can't see my movement and maybe he didn't even feel it. Maybe I am shrugging for no reason other than to shrug.

I reply, "You're really not fluent in making people feel better, I'll give you that."

Suddenly I am wrapped in strong, warm arms with my head resting on a solid chest. For the first time since we started our nightly sleepovers, *he* is consoling *me*. My heart sighs and I fight the impulse to hold him back.

Whatever we have, if we even really have anything, I don't want to tamper with it.

"I'm not sad about it," I reassure him.

His fingers stroke hair from my face, lingering near my lips before falling away. "You sound sad."

"I am, but not about that," I tell him truthfully.

Rivers moves so that he is partially leaning over me, his eyes shining in the night as he studies me, the glow of the moon reflected in them. "What are you sad about?"

I rise up and gently touch my lips to his. I figure the worst he can do is not kiss me. He goes still, his lips unresponsive against mine, and just as a trickle of disappoint weaves through my heart, he parts his lips and kisses me back. It's slow, hesitant, flooding me with sweetness I have never experienced before.

The kiss deepens, his body pressing against mine, and the poignancy of it is snatched away and replaced with heat. My veins, my core, every part of me is flooded with fire. I don't want him to stop. It is a dangerous path I have started on, but not going down it would have been even more detrimental.

Imagine if I had never kissed him, just once.

I break away first, knowing our relationship has morphed once more, and that the blame falls on me. Is this wrong? My intentions are purely innocent, but am I still at fault if someone ends up hurt? I'm stealing moments because I know none of this can last.

I'm not being fair to him. I'm not being fair to anyone, not even me. But when I look at him, when I touch him, and even when I just know he is near, I feel alive in a way that tells me life truly is infinite, in some aspect. I feel like there is nothing that can take me away from here, from him.

I feel like I have found my positive, and it is a doozy of one.

He stares down at me, his chest grazing mine each time he pulls and releases air from his lungs. My pulse is going haywire, and I shove him aside when I note the way I am clenching his thigh between my legs.

Apparently, my body was doing more than my brain was capable of deciphering. Neither of us speaks, the pounding of my heart loud enough to make words inessential. I wouldn't be able to hear myself talk anyway—I can barely make sense of my thoughts that are careening wildly out of control at the moment. Closing my eyes, I focus on breathing. That I can at least manage to do.

My body loosens up and my heartbeat slows. I tell myself I have to stop this, but the discomfort that comes with that thought calls me a liar. There is no stopping this. I don't think I could if I tried. Whatever this is, whatever we have, I am choosing to look at it as a gift. One I may have to return, but a gift all the same. I will treasure it while I can.

"I talk about Thomas—at the therapy sessions," he says in a low voice.

I close my eyes as my chest tightens; in joy that he is sharing this with someone, in sorrow that his step-dad can't be what he needs in a father figure, and in bittersweet pain that he has chosen me to confide in. It's all a jumbled-up mess of emotions.

"What do you talk about?"

"My earliest memories, my only memories, are of him telling me failure was not an option, that I wasn't anything unless I was something, and that second place was for quitters. One time, when I fell and skinned my knees, he told me to get up and not to cry—told me to be a man about it. I was four."

I want to reach out to him but fold my fingers into my palm

instead.

"I got second place in the fifth-grade spelling bee and he punished me by making me choose one word every day from the dictionary to write an essay on. I had to do it for a whole month."

I wince, his pain touching me in tendrils of discord, flowing through my limbs, into my veins, and pooling within the center of my being.

"He told me I had to be the best, at everything. He expected perfection from me, but you know what? He never gave it back. He failed at being a father and I want to tell him that, and every day I don't, it eats me up. I let it control my life, I let it determine the person I was going to be, and it wasn't someone I am proud of. I told myself it was who I needed to be, who I wanted to be, but...since my accident, I know it never was. I have all these awards, I had the girl, the popularity, everything—and all I felt was empty.

"Now it feels like I'm fighting to be me, and I am not just fighting myself, but the weight of his judgment as well, and it is so...heavy. And I keep losing. But..." he trails off, inhaling deeply. "But I also feel like maybe I can finally do it, and I don't know if it's because you're here, or just because I finally don't care what he thinks of me, and... anyway—I keep trying. No matter how many times I don't get it right or I mess up, I don't stop. And I guess that makes the power he has always held over me become nothing."

I don't speak, his words more dominant than any control Thomas ever tried to wield over him. Though we are merely inches apart, the space between us is wide and insurmountable. It's the doubt growing to slam up walls between us. It's the fear unraveling the bits of us that have come together. It's every insecurity we can possibly dream up shredding the magic created between a boy named Rivers and a girl named Delilah. And we're letting it win with our silence.

I refuse to let it.

I roll to my side, placing my hand over his heart, and feel the steady tempo of it beating against my palm. His hand covers mine, holding it there. "You're stronger than you think you are."

"Am I?" Doubt twists his voice and turns it disbelieving.

I turn my hand so that my palm is up, resting against his, and lock our fingers together. "Definitely stronger."

His chest rises in a deep inhalation of air, his fingers tightening around mine. We fall asleep like this—just the touching of our hands enough to wash away all the darkness of circumstances we have no say in. Sometimes we cannot control what happens to us, but we can decide how to go on from it.

OUT OF EVERYTHING I HAVE found out so far this summer—good and bad, I think realizing what I feel for Rivers scares me the most. How can emotions be more worrisome than all the rest of it? I roll my shoulders and sit back on my heels, dropping the rag into the tub of soapy water. Everything about Rivers terrifies me. There. I admitted it. But what scares me the most about him is that he makes me want more—more of everything. More than this life, more than what I am promised, more than I can ever truly have.

I see who he used to be, who he is now, and who he can be, and all of those meld together into what he is. Rivers is a scarred young man, but I am only now seeing that they run deeper than I imagined. What he told me last night closed the deal—I cannot go back to thinking I knew him. I am only starting to now. There is depth to him I wasn't expecting—there are so many layers of him to pull away and I want to be the one to do it, and that is *wrong* of me.

It doesn't matter. I can't turn off what I feel and I don't want to.

I finish scrubbing the walls of the upstairs bathroom. It is even bigger than the downstairs one and that is already impressive. My shoulders and arms ache and my fingers are wrinkly and prune-like. I've been hiding out in the upper half of the house all morning. It's silly to think that in staying away from Rivers, I can pretend I don't feel what I do. On a positive note, the upper level of the house is shining like it has never shone before. I've cleaned three bedrooms, an office, and now the bathroom, not to mention the hallway.

The stairs are difficult for Rivers to maneuver and I feel sort of evil about being in the one place he can't reach me, but I need to be alone to think. I am used to my solitude and sometimes the urge to return to it is unavoidable. I am sure I'm overthinking what the kiss meant to Rivers. It probably meant nothing. He probably just kissed me because I put my lips against his and I am a girl and he is a guy and that's all. I don't even think he likes me. But he didn't kiss me like he doesn't like me.

My heart twinges when I find a turkey sandwich waiting for me in the kitchen with a note that reads, *I figured it was my turn to show off the culinary skills. - R*

I eat half of the sandwich and carefully wrap the rest of it up and set it in the refrigerator. It was probably the best sandwich I ever ate, even better than my peanut butter, honey, and jelly ones. I turn in a circle, wondering what I should do now since my household chores are done for the day. I should have taken my time, but the restless energy I was carrying around made that an impossibility.

I spy Rivers' dark head in the grass beyond the deck. Curiosity, and something more, pulls me forth. He's sitting in the green foliage, his eyes lowered to his distorted legs. They are stiff and straight before him, unapologetic for their appearance—which is how Rivers needs to learn to be. He is what he is.

He shouldn't feel bad about it.

"Thanks for the sandwich."

He nods, flexing the fingers of his left hand.

I exhale, ignoring the overactive beating of my heart. "What are you doing?"

"Staring at my super-hot legs."

Rolling my eyes, I say, "Don't you already have enough admirers without being one yourself?"

"Funny."

"What are you thinking?" That's the real question I want

answered. What does Rivers think about the kiss we exchanged last night? I am not sure

I *want* to know, but I decided I couldn't hide out in the upstairs of his house indefinitely, so here I am.

"It shouldn't have happened." His eyes are downcast as he fiddles with the hem of his yellow shirt.

A crack forms somewhere inside me. I pretend it isn't there, forcing a lightness to my tone I do not feel. "What shouldn't have?"

He glances up, a scowl on his face. "You know what I'm talking about. The kiss."

I sit down in the grass beside him, partially turned away from him. "Are you sorry I kissed you?"

"Aren't you?"

"I instigated it, didn't I?"

"Yeah. About that. I don't get it. *Why* did you?" Our eyes meet, his dark and searching. I don't have time to answer before he says, "When you look at me, you have to be repulsed."

"By what?" I ask.

He gestures to the scars that line his face and then to his legs.

"I don't even see them," I say with all honesty.

His eyebrows lower and his eyes follow. I caught the blatant yearning in his gaze just before he hid it. He wants to believe me, but can't allow himself to.

My fingers curl into the palms of my hands to keep from reaching out to him. I blow out a noisy breath and look at a caterpillar ever so slowly creeping along the grass. I put my finger out and it carefully feels my skin before crawling over it, tickling my flesh as it goes.

I smile. "He's so slow, but you know what? He never gives up. He knows, one day, he'll be free," I say in a low voice. "He's ugly to most, but to those that matter, he's beautiful. They know his potential. They know where he started and where he'll end, and how long it will take for him to get there. It's something to be admired, not tossed aside."

"You're saying one day I'll be a butterfly," he says skeptically.

I look up. "I'm saying you've always been one."

Rivers stares at me for a long time, his eyes tracing the angles and curves of my face. "You say a lot of strange stuff, you know that?"

Nodding, I hide a smile. "I guess so."

His tone is thoughtful when he tells me, "I like it. I like being around you."

My pulse picks up. "Why?"

With a shrug, he states, "I don't feel so sorry for myself when you're around. I don't feel so ugly or worthless. I feel normal."

"You are neither of those things."

"Yeah." His voice says he doesn't believe me.

I run a finger along the soft grass as I say, "I kind of like being around you too."

"Why?" he shoots back.

I tilt my head, my hair falling to the side as I ponder this. "Well, aside from the fact that you make me look good—oddly enough, I think I like your personality."

"Hmm. You *think*? I'm usually wanted for my body and not my mind."

"Given the circumstances, we all have to make exceptions."

His mouth twitches. "What circumstances?"

"Your hideous disfigurement," I tell him airily.

"Thanks," he says dryly, a faint smile on his mouth.

"Sure. I'm all about looking on the bright side. Want to go for a walk? We'll go slow," I add when he hesitates.

His face darkens. "I hate that—that you even have to say that. I don't *want* you to have to go slow for me."

I get to my feet. "So I won't."

I walk to the fence gate, opening it and going through. A tendril of elation webs through me and spreads when he follows.

The walk takes twice as long as it normally would for me, but I don't mind. Being with Rivers is all I really focus on. Each smile of his opens a wound inside me at the same time it heals it. When he brushes a lock of hair from my eyes, I try to swallow and have to repeat the motion three times before having success.

I can tell the farther we walk that his legs are beginning to bother him. I wonder if each and every step he takes is painful to him or if his legs start to ache after a while. He doesn't say anything about stopping or going back, so I don't either. It isn't for me to decide when he's had enough.

Rivers will make that decision.

"Your mom owns a flower shop, right?"

I nod, the mention of my mom causing a hint of longing within me. I blink at the realization that I miss her. I always thought I wanted to be on my own, out of the house where the past lingers in much too fine detail, but now that I've been away, I want to see her, to sleep in the bed I have always slept in, in the house I have always lived in, knowing my mom is but a short walk away. I feel homesick, something I never expected to be.

"What's the name of it? 'Flower Appeal'?"

"How do you know the name of my mom's flower shop?" I can't help smiling that he would know such a thing. It seems too trivial a detail for him to remember.

Rivers shrugs. "My mom's sent me over there before to get flowers. And I've been in there for myself too," he adds.

"Really?" I wonder if his mother knows my mother. It's possible they've even had actual conversations, although I doubt they knew they were talking to one another. I can see Janet and Monica becoming friends. In fact, I hope one day soon I can arrange a meeting between them.

I also wonder if my mom talked to Rivers without knowing it. The thought of Rivers holding a discussion with my mom makes my cheeks heat up and I don't understand why. I think because it makes me think of a boyfriend talking his girlfriend's mom—totally *not* what I should be thinking, not with him. I don't think *anyone* I ever dated met my mom, not that I had a lot of boyfriends. I never dated anyone for long and I never felt inclined to introduce them, because I never cared about them. Rivers, I already care too much for.

"Why does your mom allow Thomas to treat you the way he does?"

He squints at the sun, his body unconsciously tensing. "She can't exactly make him stop."

"But she could say something. She could...leave."

He shakes his head. "She did once. He cried and begged her to come back. She went back. I think they love each other, in some way. He isn't a bad person, he just...isn't the greatest either."

The wind is cool and the sun occasionally peeks out from behind gray and white swirled clouds. It's always windier in Prairie du Chien than it is in surrounding towns. I'm assuming it's because it is at a higher elevation plus the river is nearby, but I do not know that for a fact. I was book smart in school, but that is because I worked my butt off. My academic glory didn't come naturally to me. I had to work for it. Some people have brains that just seem to *know* stuff. Mine isn't one of them.

"Sometimes, I think it's a jealousy thing. Like, I remind him of his cousin, the man my mom first loved, still loves, and would be with if he hadn't died, the man who is my real father. He's the replacement. Maybe he realizes it. In me he sees what he can never be." He shrugs.

"That's terrible to put that blame on you."

Half of his mouth quirks in a sardonic semblance of a smile. "Is blame ever logical?"

Traffic is heavy as we cross the highway, my feet unconsciously taking me to St. Feriole Island and the Mississippi river. I don't realize where we're at until Rivers mentions it.

"I don't want to go there."

I blink, lost in the floral beauty around us. There are flower beds along the sidewalk, alive in the hues of red, yellow, pink, and orange. It makes me think of sunsets and fire. "Where?"

He nods toward the vastness of the moving waters farther down the path.

The Mississippi is still far off in the distance from where we stand, but I don't think that little tidbit matters too much to Rivers right now.

"Okay. Where do you want to go?"

"Might as well see if the Villa Louis really is haunted."

The silence is heavy between us as we make our way toward the historical building that was once a house and is now used for reminiscent tours of years long passed. In 1843, Hercules L. Dousman—a wealthy man well-known as a fur trader, lumberman, and land sculptor—built a Greek Revival style brick home directly on an Indian mound. Apparently, he wasn't worried about cursed land.

He was the first millionaire in Wisconsin. After his death, his son, Louis, tore down the House on the Mound, as it was called, and built what currently is known as the Villa Louis estate; a large Victorian Italianate-styled structure. The building is now a museum, open for scheduled tours, and holds the title of being the first state-operated historic site. It's reputed to be haunted, but then, most old structures are. There is an ambivalence to them that is old and heavy with years gone by.

The building is a sprawling mansion of window upon window, pillars and multiple levels; surrounded by colorful flowers and greenery. As I look at it, I am struggling to aptly describe what I am seeing and feeling. Just standing near it fills me with nostalgia. It seems like I am trespassing upon history. It is eerie, almost surreal, like we have stepped into the past and are not exactly allowed. We walk along the outskirts of the lawn, neither of us anxious to get too close to the beautiful, untouchable house.

"Thomas was driving the boat."

I keep my face forward and my pace even, waiting. What he is about to tell me is big, and I don't want to screw it up by talking and having him clam up in return.

He draws in a lungful of air before continuing. "It was the twenty-seventh of April, but we'd been having warmer weather and wanted to take advantage of it. Of course, on that day the weather was a little cooler, but the sun was shining, so we still went. It was Thomas and me and a friend of mine—Dustin Richter."

Rivers seems to struggle for words, his lips pressing together. He finally looks at me, his expression sad and tormented.

His voice is ragged as he says, "I don't know what happened. I got up to get a drink out of a cooler and I swear he chose that moment to jerk the wheel and aim us right at the waves. The river was already choppy and we hit hard. I lost my balance from him turning the wheel so sharply and when we hit the first wave, I fell into the water.

"I didn't even have time to react before I was already sucked under. And then...then I remember fighting to breathe...and the pain. I blacked out, woke up in the hospital. It was crazy. People were shouting and I didn't fully know what was going on. The pain was excruciating and I felt like I was in this fog..."

I suck in a sharp breath as I wonder how much he remembers about his arrival at the hospital, but Rivers doesn't notice, lost in the nightmare of the watery depths of the Mississippi River. He finally glances at me, silently gauging my reaction to his words. It takes me a moment to find my voice.

"Are you saying you think he *wanted* you to fall out and get hurt?"

"No. I don't know. I don't know what I'm saying. I mean, I'm sure he didn't really think I'd fall into the water or that he intended for me to get hurt, but he at least wanted to scare me. I would even feel better about the whole thing if he would just admit he did something wrong, but he won't.

"He acts like it was my fault I ended up in the water, which makes me think he doesn't give a shit about me. I don't want to care, but...he's the closest thing I have to a father, even if he's a sucky one, so I guess I do anyway. I know how stupid that sounds."

He pauses, reaching down to pick a dandelion. He twirls the stem between his fingers, releasing it to sway to the ground. "I've never told anyone else that—any of it."

"Why are you telling me?"

He shrugs. "You're easy to talk to. You seem like you understand a lot."

"Children love their parents, no matter how good or bad they are. They're forgiving, resilient, adaptable," I tell him softly.

"Children see the good in a being when others can't, maybe even when they shouldn't. Don't feel bad about wanting approval from him. That's natural. All children really want is to be loved, and most importantly, by their parents. What you *can f*eel bad about is that he is losing the chance at loving you, and it's a shame he doesn't realize what he's missing."

The unflinching way he studies me takes my breath away, but I cannot look away from him. I watch as his features transform from scowling to longing, certain aspects of his face darkening while others lighten. My heart hurts seeing that look on his face. Swallowing, he finally turns his face from mine, but not before I see a sheen of moisture over his eyes.

"You're killing me, Bana," he says after a long pause.

That is completely the opposite of what I am doing, and we both know it. He's living again. Not because I made him, but because he chose to. Maybe I am the one that gave him a shove back into consciousness, but he is the only one that can decide how he is going to be. He is choosing to live in the light instead of sleeping in the dark. We all must return to the dark at some point—why go there before we have to?

I sweep the fallen dandelion up into my hand and swipe it across his face, leaving a yellow streak in its wake. Rivers blinks at me before narrowing his eyes and grabbing a handful of the weedy flowers, striding for me with his weapons of mass flowery.

I sprint away, laughing. "Come on, Young, show me what you got. Terrify me."

"I don't need to terrify you. I'll just wait you out. You can run, but eventually you'll get tired. I'll be here, waiting," he promises.

"I'm counting on it," I taunt from under the reaching limbs of a Willow tree.

A stillness creeps over him as he watches me, and my eyes drink in all the dark, scarred beauty that is Rivers. The sun is at his back, creating a contrast between light, silhouettes, and shadows. He stands in a bed of grass, looking mythical or magical, and the placidity in him reaches out to me.

It's strange how our movements coincide; he moves for me at the same time I move for him, and I know, when we reach one another, nothing will be the same again. I could stop. I could hesitate. I could walk away. But I don't. I meet him in a field of flowers and sunshine and we kiss, arms locked around each other, bodies pressed together like two missing puzzle pieces finally fitting as one for the first time.

I feel whole wrapped around him. I feel invincible. I feel unbreakable. I feel like I could never die, never fade away, never become nothing, as long as we are together. As long as he keeps holding me, I will stay.

His eyes drink me in when the kiss ends, studying me like he is only now seeing an exceptional quality in some- thing he used to view as plain.

"Have you ever felt like you were searching for something, only you didn't know what it was until you found it?"

I run my finger down the length of his damaged cheek, brushing short black bangs back to touch the marred flesh of his temple.

"If you didn't know you were searching for something, how would you know when you find it?" A teasing smile takes over my mouth as our gazes collide.

"It's..." He swallows, briefly resting his forehead against mine. "I don't know how to explain it. It's a feeling of...fullness. Being centered. My heart, my head, every part of me, feels it. It's because of you, or maybe how I feel about you."

"And how do you feel about me?" I ask, holding my breath as I wait for his answer.

He steps back as he tilts his head, studying me. "I'm not sure."

I snort. "Thanks. Way to brighten my day."

"I feel better when I'm with you," is his simple response, and it is perfect.

But I have to ask, "How can you feel anything for me? We haven't been talking that long."

How can *I* already feel for him what I do? And what is it, exactly?

Rivers shrugs, looking toward the water. "When you know, you know. Does the amount of time really matter so much?"

A twinge of pain sweeps through me and I step away from him. "Yes," I whisper. "And no."

Time is an interesting thing—it takes time to love, it takes time to heal, it even takes time to die.

The warmth of his hand as he takes mine into his and holds it washes away the ache. "Are you thinking about the past? About how I was in school? That wasn't really me. I mean, I guess it was, but it isn't me anymore. The accident...it changed me. Does that make sense?"

I nod. "Yes. It does. But I wasn't thinking of you, I was thinking of me. How I used to be, how I'll be in the future. We're all allowed to change. You don't have to feel bad about who you used to be. You never have to feel bad about which version of yourself you are at any given moment. All the parts that make you up are a blessing."

"Do you really mean that?"

My voice is solemn as I say, "I do."

He watches me. "I know what you're doing."

Though my body goes still, my pulse races. "What do you mean?"

"I'm observant enough to realize you're slowly pulling me out of the depressing hell I was wallowing in. But I don't understand why. Why have you been so adamant about helping me? What do you get out of it? Why would you *want* to help me? I've never been particularly nice to you."

"You're asking me this after we've kissed? Twice?"

He shrugs. "I'd like to know why you even gave me a chance in the first place."

"Maybe I thought you were worth knowing."

"You've already said you didn't like me. Why even try to reach someone you don't like?"

"You didn't like me either. Why open up to someone you don't like? Why be nice to me now when you never were in school?"

I shouldn't have brought it up; no memories from the past are helpful to us now. But I guess since Rivers means something to me now, it hurts more than it did when we didn't interact. I *know* him now. I know him and that changes everything.

"It's funny...you say I was always mistakenly judging you, but weren't you doing the same? I was the jock, the prick, the guy who didn't care about anyone or anything but myself, right?"

I let out a deep sigh, knowing his words are true. I look down as I nod. "I was wrong."

"You were, in a way. In another way, you were entirely correct." He tips my chin up, forcing me to look at him. "Does any of it matter now?"

"No." And it doesn't. Because I won't let it.

He smiles, the sweetness of it like a knife to all of my convictions over what I should and should not allow to happen.

"Tell me...why did you want to help me?" His voice is soft, as is the kiss he presses to my brow.

I want to ask him what is happening between us. I want to ask what our kisses and touching—not to mention our sleeping arrangements—mean, but instead I answer his question. It seems the simpler option of the two.

"I don't like to see something usually so strong, broken. It's like watching someone fall and being unable to get to them in time. It *hurts* me to see others in pain. I want to fix them," I whisper.

"You can't fix me."

I look up and my eyes clash with his. "I know I can't fix you. I can't fix anyone, but maybe I can heal them somehow."

He leans down and scoops up gravel, watching it fall between his long, calloused fingers. "You had a brother, right?"

I blink my eyes as a wave of pain goes through me. "Yes."

He nods, his eyes still downcast. "I remember. He was a few years older than us. I was at the park that day."

A tremble forms in my lower lip and I press my lips together, turning so that my back is to him. An image of a smiling face with golden eyes and unruly brown hair flashes through my mind, but I shove it back into the darkness. The blackness is always near, hovering beyond the brink of consciousness, but I am not able to face it yet, and I don't know if I ever will be able to.

"You must have hated me at first."

I glance over my shoulder at him, but remain quiet.

"The first few weeks you worked for us. You must have hated me. Watching me act like my life was over just be- cause my life was changed from that point on. You know more about loss than I ever have. I was such an asshole."

"You lost your father," I remind him, facing him.

"That's different. I didn't really know him. I miss that part of my life and my heritage I'll never know, but I can't miss a person I never met. I mean, I miss the *idea* of him, but not the actual man."

My voice is soft as I say, "I think I would have missed you even if we'd never met."

I should have kept the thought to myself, but whether he likes it or not, it is true. Whatever I am feeling for him—it would have been a shame if I had never had the chance to feel it.

Rivers stares at me and I feel the heat of his eyes all the way into my chest, where it warms and spreads. He looks away as he mumbles, "You should have left me in the water."

"You wouldn't have drowned."

He cocks his head as he listens.

"There were two parts of you struggling. I watched them. Part of you wanted to give up and the other part of you didn't know how. You would have eventually come back up."

"Then why'd you jump in after me?"

I shrug. "I think maybe you needed to know someone wouldn't let you drown, even if it wasn't really a possibility."

A long moment passes before he speaks again. "You're different from school."

"*I'm* different? Maybe you're different."

He pauses and then narrows his eyes. "Nice try. No. You're different. But then, yeah, I suppose I am too. You know those flowers that close at night and open again during the day? I don't know what they're called—"

"Morning glory," I murmur.

He squints his eyes at me, slowly repeating, "Morning glory."

"There are other kinds, but that is the first that comes to mind. They close at night to conserve their fragrance and during the day they open, producing fragrance to attract bees and other pollinators."

I can see I've lost him by the faint glazing over of his eyes.

"Are you saying I'm seducing you with my alluring scent?" I tease, a grin in place.

"I'm saying during school you were closed up to the point that no one could see what an amazing person you are, and now you've opened up like a morning glory, and you're...breathtaking." He clamps his lips together, looking like he thinks he has said too much.

If I could put a feeling into a physical embodiment of something, I would say that right now, what I feel is like a warm, light rainfall.

The drink of cool water against a dry throat, or the gentle lapping of waves. Peaceful, calm, serene.

"You know what I see you as?"

Wariness creeps into his stance and expression. "What?"

I smile. "A moonflower. They close during the daytime light and open during the night. That's you—you shine in the dark."

He digests this, a small smile lifting his lips and entering his eyes to alter them from a dark brown to a warm chocolate. And there he is, the radiance that manages to hit me all the way into my core.

I *feel* that smile.

"What's happening between us?"

The directness of his question surprises me, but I like that he asked it. I like that he wonders—at least I am not the only one trying to figure out this unthinkable, yet totally workable association we have.

His eyes are steady on mine, his face a mix of curiosity and confusion as he waits for me to respond.

"I don't know," I tell him. I have not *one clue* what is going on with us, but I want to wrap myself around whatever it is so it can't escape.

Rivers reaches up and touches a lock of my hair, his fingers slowly sliding through the hair above my left ear, causing tingles to dance along the sensitive flesh of my skin. His other hand gently clasps my chin as he lowers his face to mine.

"I don't know either, but I do know I like kissing you. A lot. And I know you do too," he murmurs against my lips, his eyes black with emotion. I feel his mouth smile against mine, see the corners of his eyes crinkling up, and my stomach drops.

And he kisses me again.

SIX

"ARE YOU A VIRGIN?"

I frown at the pages of the book I am holding between my hands, glancing up. "Wow. Way to be tactful. No really, just blurt it out like that, out of nowhere."

"Sorry." Rivers taps his fingers against the wrought iron patio table, squinting against the sunlight hitting him, despite the umbrella above us. He doesn't sound sorry. He sounds and looks agitated. "I've been wondering for weeks and I didn't see any good way of asking it, so…are you?"

"No." His eyebrows furrow and I laugh, setting the book down. "Not the answer you were expecting?"

"Honestly, I think no matter if you had said yes or no, I would have been surprised."

"Why's that?"

He frowns as he ponders my words. "I don't know. I guess because in some ways you seem innocent and in other ways you seem worldly."

"Hmm." I turn to the crystal liquid of the pool. It looks tranquil, undisturbed.

"Who was it?"

"I am *not* answering that!" I lightly punch his shoulder and he grunts.

"Why not? I'll tell you who I slept with."

"*Everyone* knows who you slept with." Bitterness creeps into my tone, putting a sour taste in my mouth. I am annoyed that it upsets me more that Rivers was with Riley than it does that Riley was a bitch to me all through middle and high school. Where is the logic in *that*?

"Yeah, but they don't know she was the only one."

"Yeah, right," I scoff. Rivers only having sex with one female? Incomprehensible.

"Riley cheated on me. I never returned the favor. I never got serious enough with anyone else for it to come to that," he tells me softly.

The somber cast to his expression gives me pause and I know he is telling the truth. He has no reason to lie anyway.

"Why did you take her back, knowing she did that?"

Was it some great love others can only hope to have? Doubtful.

"I don't know. I guess because she needed me. I did care about her. I even loved her, in a way. Riley doesn't mean a lot of what she does. She can be horrible at times, but I understand her and why she is the way she is.

"She's scared. And when you're scared, you do things you wouldn't normally do. Sure, I didn't feel the same for her after that. How could I? But I didn't want her to think she was unforgivable."

His words make me hate Riley a little less, and at the same time, a little more.

I sigh, deciding I can be honest too. "It was Jeff Monroe. The whole experience was uncomfortable and forgettable."

"*Jeff Monroe?* That guy is a serious dumbass." Rivers shakes his head at me. "I mean, *really*? Jeff Monroe?"

"Yes. I realize that Jeff Monroe was not the best choice to have sex with. I was there. I remember how it all played out," I answer dryly.

"Why'd you do it then?" He sounds angry and I wonder if he is jealous.

Crazy. Of course, I'm jealous of the person he had sex with, so I guess we're equally insane.

I shrug, faking a nonchalance I do not feel. It's embarrassing, really. The first time is supposed to be special and with someone you love. Mine was with a guy I didn't really like or know all too well. The alcohol I'd consumed at the party that night didn't help with my decision-making skills. He was sitting there and I was sitting there and it just sort of happened.

I felt dirty and cheap for a long time after that. I feel it even more right now, thinking about it, especially compared to how I feel about Rivers and how it would feel with Rivers. It would mean something. It would mean everything, which means it would mean too much. I have not fully admitted my feelings for him to myself, although I have, at least, admitted I have them.

"That's your answer? To *shrug*?"

"Well, at least I didn't say *sigh*."

He moves away, situating himself in a patio chair farther away from me.

"You did not just physically shun me."

Rivers' response is to glare into the lapping water of the pool. I want to laugh at the same time I want to roll my eyes, but then I really look at him. He is actually upset over this, over who I had sex with, or maybe that I ever had sex with anyone, or maybe that it wasn't with him, or...isn't.

His body is tense, his lips pulled down and fire blazing in his eyes, but I can see beyond the anger. I can see into him and I can see he is angry because he cares about me, and oh, if that doesn't pull at something deep inside me.

Looking at him, taking in his stance and the pure energy that is him, I feel poignancy wash over me, but there is sweet- ness to it as well. And desire. Yeah, I want him. I admit it, and not just a little, but *a lot*. He is this beautiful, dark creature that is consuming me the longer I am around him.

"Why are you so mad?" I quietly ask, moving to stand near him.

"I honestly don't know," he admits, glancing up at me. He shakes his head and sighs, looking down at his clasped hands.

"You know what I think?"

"What?" he asks with hesitation clear in his voice.

"I think we should go shopping."

"For?"

"I don't know. Whatever we want."

"You know what I think?"

"What?"

He looks up at me. "I think you're terribly obvious when you're trying to change the subject."

"Duh." I grin.

Rivers gets to his feet. "Do you like steak?"

"Now who's changing the subject?"

"Steaks on the grill sound good." He puts his hands on his hips and studies the fancy stainless steel grill across the deck. "Do you think we can manage it without starting anything on fire?"

"I guess we won't know until we try."

He snorts. "I guess. We need to go to the store."

"We? As in you and me? In public again? Together? Are you sure you want to chance it? Someone might recognize us."

He looks up at the sky. "Why did my mom have to hire such a smartass to babysit me?" Glancing at me, he answers my question, "Depends on if you're going to put on a big show again or not."

"I'll try to contain my theatrical tendencies."

"And I'll try not to fall on my face while attempting to walk."

I thread my arm through his as we walk toward the house. "Do you know how unbelievably awesome we are?"

Rivers pauses as he glances down at me, secrets and emotions unable to be kept hidden floating in the depths of his eyes. "I do now."

We take the Charger. He lets me drive. I can tell he regrets that decision when I roll the windows down, crank the stereo up, and maneuver us through traffic like I am a race car driver. 'It's Tricky' by RUN-DMC is on the radio and I whoop, fist pumping the air.

"This song is amazing!" I shout to Rivers over the force of the wind, bopping in the seat as I drive.

"You are absolutely out of your mind!" he tells me, but he's laughing.

I pull into the parking lot of Market Fresh and cut the engine, grinning out the front window. Letting my head fall against the headrest, I laugh as my heart pounds from the exhilarating ride. "I love this car."

Rivers doesn't respond and I turn my head to look at him. He is watching me with a strange expression on his face. His eyes never leave mine as he ever so slowly brings his rough hand to my cheekbone and lets his fingers slide down the side of my face. My breathing becomes shallow, the rise and fall of my chest fast and deep.

"What are you thinking?"

His eyes fall to my mouth. He focuses on the dip and curve of my lips as he answers, "I'm thinking I'm glad I fell into the water that day."

He looks up, holding my eyes.

"You're thankful your legs are a mess, your face is scarred, and your life has been changed forever?" I keep my tone dubious, but I really, really want him to say yes. I guess that makes me selfish.

"You're here, aren't you?"

"Yes," I breathe.

"And you don't care about what I look like, do you?"

"No."

"In fact, you think I'm pretty hot." Half of his mouth lifts.

I roll my eyes. "Upon occasion. When your mouth is shut, usually."

He laughs, but immediately sobers. "Knowing that makes me think maybe I'm not so bad the way I am. I'm okay not being perfect."

"You were never perfect."

"But close," he tells me, his lips turning up at the corners.

There is this giddy, sick, swirly feeling starting in my stomach and bubbling up to my throat. I want to laugh. I want to toss my head back and shout from the pressure of it. What is it?

As I stare at Rivers, unable to keep a smile from my face, I think I know what it is. It's him. He makes me feel this way. He makes me look past all the crap that has the power to bring me to my knees if I let it, and he makes me strong enough to stand. I think that's what I do for him as well. I'm not even going to try to figure out why.

I turn in the seat to face him, reaching my hand forward and letting it caress the length of his marred flesh. Tenderness washes through me and I know it shows in my expression. "You should be proud of your scars, and you know why? Because your scars tell the world that you were stronger than whatever gave them to you."

"What about you? Where are your scars?"

I look away, my hand falling to my lap. "Mine are where you can't see them."

"So they run deeper than mine."

"Deeper? Maybe, maybe not. Are they any more significant than yours? No. We all have scars, Rivers, in some form or another. Yours are just more visible than some. Doesn't mean they hurt any less."

He tilts his head. "You know what I think I like the best about you?"

I squint my eyes at him. "What?"

"You make me think." He opens the door, carefully shifting his body out and up.

I meet him at the side of the car, unconsciously reaching for his hand. I don't realize what I have done until his hand is lifting to mine. Without hesitation, he threads his fingers through mine—naturally, without thought. I look down at our clasped hands and then up to his face.

Rivers has a faint smile on his mouth. He is unapologetic. That hits me hard, shattering through whatever lingering doubt I had about the popular boy falling for the loner girl. What we were in high school doesn't even matter to him. The emotions I have for him grow, deepen.

I hold his hand tightly, feeling the warmth of it move up my arm until it is like I am cocooned in all of his heat. I am ablaze with Rivers. I sing the lyrics to 'Piano Man' by Billy Joel as we walk to the store and he joins in, surprising me that he knows the song, and that his deep voice harmonizes so well with my higher one. I go to drop his hand when we get to the tan and brown building and he grips my hand harder, telling me without words that he refuses to let me go.

Our eyes meet, his fierce and determined, and I spontaneously kiss his nose. He does something really crazy then. He drops my hand long enough to cup my face and he kisses me, right in the entrance of Market Fresh, in public, for anyone and everyone to see. It isn't a quick kiss. It isn't a sweet kiss. It's deep and long and powerful. It makes my stomach swoop and my lips tingle as I get lost in Rivers, forgetting where we are, forgetting the world around us.

It's the whistling that finally reaches through the fog of my brain. We break apart, smiling at each other. How long we smile at one another, I do not know, but my face feels unusually warm and my mouth hurts from the wideness of it, so it must be for quite some time.

"We should probably go inside," Rivers finally tells me.

"Yeah."

I feel half-drugged as we walk up and down the aisles. It's chilly inside the store and my skin pebbles. Rivers shops one-handed, the other firmly locked around mine for the duration of our shopping experience.

"I wanted to fly planes when I was a kid," he tells me as we pick out T-bone steaks, placing them in the carrier I hold in my free hand.

"You don't anymore?"

He shrugs. "Seems a little farfetched. It was just a kid thing. What did you want to be?"

This is an unusually hard question for me. It shouldn't be. I try to simplify it as we stand in the checkout lane.

"Well," I begin, immediately faltering.

"Well, what? Why don't you want to tell me? I can tell from the expression on your face. It wasn't something bad, was it?" he teases. "Did you want to be a government assassin or what?"

"I liked to create things, but I wasn't artistic. I liked to sing, but not enough to want to pursue it as a career. I've always liked patterns, colors, and putting them together in unusual ways. I like to decorate. My mom and I redid the kitchen last summer. It was fun," I end with, waiting for the strange look to come.

But it doesn't.

He nods, a thoughtful expression on his face. "I remember in Home Economics junior year—you made a scarf. It was red and purple with these yellow dots on it. You designed it?"

"Yeah."

"It was hideous."

I laugh. "How is it that you don't remember much about me, but you always remember the negative things?"

He shrugs. "When you did something unexpected, I took notice."

Like this summer. Everything I have done has been unpredicted, most of all to me. And I am now realizing that Rivers paid more attention to me than I thought, and probably more than he knew too.

"You know, being a government assassin takes all kinds of creativity, in case you need something to fall back on. If you're decorating career doesn't work out."

I bump my arm to his, knocking him off-balance. Rivers' hold on my hand tightens as we both stumble back, him landing against an aisle of chips and me on top of him. The sound of whole chips becoming partial ones crackles around us and our eyes meet guiltily.

I laugh as we scramble to a standing position. Rivers grins and brushes bangs from my eyes. Every touch I receive from him sends a tingling through me.

He pays for the food and we walk back out into the hot day, his hand once more locked with mine.

"Why did you want to be a pilot?" I ask him.

"Because I wanted to be free, and the sky seemed limitless. Plus, there's the whole being able to fly thing. It's like being Superman without the cape." He grins.

"Free from what?"

He looks down at his feet, not speaking for a long time. He glances at me as he says, "Everything."

My throat tightens, sad for a young boy who disliked his world so much he wanted to be able to escape it.

"And now?" He frowns at me and I specify, "Do you still feel like you need to get away from your life?"

I am not entirely sure what I am asking, but the pounding of my heart lets me know how much his answer means to me.

"I already have," he says softly.

He smiles as I frown—a perfect balance of seriousness facing off lightheartedness, and draws me in for a quick hug.

I wonder, as I get into the passenger seat, if part of him knows this can't last as well, and that is why he is so adamant about having some part of him in constant contact with some part of me. He links his free hand with mine as he drives, further affirming my thoughts. Maybe he thinks he can keep me with him from a physical link alone. If only that were possible.

Is this his version of freedom, here, now, with me? It's funny that, with all his current restrictions, he appears happier than when he had none.

When we get back to his house, Rivers prepares the grill as I rub spices on the steaks. I cut up a yellow pepper, zucchini, sweet potatoes, and a red onion, tears burning my eyes and trailing down my cheeks as I do so. I toss them with oil and salt and pepper, turning to face Rivers as the patio door slides open.

He takes in my face and smiles, snapping the tongs together. "Crying every time I leave the room is getting to be redundant."

"I can't help it. Look." I show him the vegetables in the blue bowl. "They're so pretty."

He leans over the island, one eyebrow lifted. "It's like a vegetable rainbow."

"Exactly."

Grinning as he raises his face to mine, he places a kiss against my forehead. "The smallest things make you happy. It's endearing."

"I'll show you endearing," I mutter as I set the bowl down. "Are you going to eat any of these?"

"I can't promise that." He pauses. "But I can promise I'll try."

We go about grilling the steaks and vegetables, the scent of herbs surrounding us, the sound of sizzling meat filling my ears. I sit at the patio table and watch as he plays chef for me. I sip peach iced tea and eat celery with peanut butter and raisins. He occasionally glances back at me, shaking his head at my snack choice. I make sure to smile wide when my teeth are covered in peanut butter.

"I found a toad in our backyard when I was kid."

A smile curves his lips. "Oh yeah? And? Did you run away screaming?"

I laugh. "No. I decided to make it my pet. I named it Cha-Cha. I found a box and put grass, rocks, and a dish of water in it. I had no idea what I was doing. Anyway, it stayed around for a few hours, humoring me, I suppose, and then it jumped out. And that was the end of my pet toad."

"What possessed you to name it Cha-Cha?"

I squint my eyes as I think this over. "I don't know. I guess because it looked like it was dancing when it hopped around." I shrug. "Did you have any pets?"

"I had a kitten when I was seven." He looks down. "It got outside one day. I searched the house and yard for hours and couldn't find it. No one knew, but...it was under the car. My mom ran it over without knowing it."

"Well, that's depressing," I tell him dryly.

He flashes a quick, sad smile at me. "Yeah. I cried for weeks over that. Thomas got so annoyed with me moping around that he got me a stuffed cat."

"A *real* stuffed cat?" I widen my eyes at him, totally kidding.

His narrow-eyed look tells me he knows my tricks. "No. A toy one. He thought it would help."

"Did it?"

He shrugs, his attention locked on the food. "It didn't hurt."

"What did you name your kitten?" I ask softly, getting up and moving to stand beside him. I rest my arm against his, giving him silent support. I rub my cheek against the hardness of his upper arm, placing a light kiss against the warm flesh.

His smile turns to a laugh, flowing over me like the notes of an alluring melody. "He was orange and white and liked to play fetch."

"This was a *cat*, right?"

"Yeah." He glances at me. "I named him Fido."

"I guess that's on par with Cha-Cha."

"You could say that."

Low music plays from his phone, his diversified taste impressing me. He likes a lot of the same music I do—Cold- play, AWOLNATION, The Killers, The Fray, Imagine Dragons, as well as older music like The Rolling Stones, Aero- smith, Red Hot Chili Peppers, and Guns N' Roses.

I move away, studying him. The lines of his form are captivating, even as he stands off-center to favor his left leg. Each movement is with purpose and I think I could watch him do anything, or nothing, and still find him interesting.

He catches my eyes on him. "Food's ready."

I nod, feeling warmth pool in my chest. "I'll get the plates and bring everything out here."

I turn to leave and he grabs my wrist and tugs me back to him. I look up and his dark eyes sear mine. "Yes?"

"I feel like I should be asking that. What are you looking at?" He waits, staring back at me like he can find the answer he seeks in my face. Maybe he can.

"You."

"Why? Am I really so fascinating?"

"Oh, yes," I assure him. "You always have been."

He releases my wrist, lines forming around his eyes as he gauges whether I am being serious or not. In this, I am.

His expression clears as he says, "You too."

A shaky exhalation of air leaves me as I spin away. I truly think he meant that. I don't even know what just happened, but it felt like a shifting in the foundation of our relationship, or how we view one another.

The steak is delicious, and Rivers surprises me by not only trying the vegetables, but liking them enough to have two servings. We spend the afternoon in the sun; me with my layers of sunscreen on and him without. We talk about music, movies, and school, but we focus on the good and do not mention the bad. It's a lot of good-humored arguing over movies, and laughter over school.

I bring up the time Sandy Smith freaked out over a spider in History class and knocked herself out by running face-first into the wall. He talks about the pep rally for the first football game senior year when Melissa Mathison and Brent Stickler got caught making out behind the bleachers and the principal made them stand before the entire student body and apologize for their indecent behavior.

When he mentions my Halloween costume freshman year, the words I was about to say falter on my lips.

Noticing my look, he asks, "What?"

"I... I'm just surprised." I frown, looking at the hem of my orange cotton shorts. Why didn't I try to know him in school? True, Riley would have freaked out if I'd ever approached him, but I could have made an effort.

I gave up on the social aspect of high school before giving it a chance. I gave up on *him* before I ever talked to him.

"You won the school contest for funniest costume. You had rollers in your hair, crazy makeup all over your face, and you wore a robe over a nightgown with slippers. I couldn't believe it was you when I first saw you."

He looks down, taking my hand in his and squeezing it before letting it go. "I don't think you realize how much you were noticeable, at least at times. Usually, you kept to yourself and it was easy to forget you were there, but then you would do something totally out of character for you, or at least, how you were perceived to be, and... people noticed. *I* noticed."

"Huh," is my amazing comeback.

HE IS IN THE WATER with me. This truth makes my pulse trip and scatter. I feel like this is a monumental moment right now. Maybe it is, maybe it isn't. Rivers is on the far end of the pool, not even paying attention to me, and here I am, motionless, quiet, my eyes riveted to his lithe frame as it cuts through the water like a blade.

Night has fallen on us, but the air is thick with hot moisture, making the water around me feel like a blanket of cool relief. The moon casts its glow on the water and us, giving the black liquid a spotlight and making Rivers the focal point of the show. He barely makes a sound as he swims, his muscled form impressive to watch. I can tell he's missed the water.

With the warm, occasional winds, the scent of lilacs floats toward me from neighboring yards. I slowly move my legs back and forth through the water, propped up against the ledge of the pool with my elbows as I notice more than I probably should about Rivers.

He breaks the surface, his face shadows as he turns to me. He swims over to my end of the pool, stopping when inches are all that separate us. His eyes shine as they meet mine. "You finally get me in the water and all you do is watch? What's the fun in that?"

"Trust me, it's loads of fun."

Swiping a hand over his wet hair, he mutters, "Not even going to try to understand that one."

I switch the subject before he makes me explain what exactly I *did* mean by that comment. "How are your legs?"

"Not bad."

"Swimming is probably the best form of therapy for them. Low resistance."

"Mmm."

I can tell he doesn't want to talk about his legs or therapy for them, so I try to think of something else to talk about. "Peanut butter is my favorite food."

Rivers looks at me for a long time, finally shaking his head.

He moves to my side, reclining next to me. "Peanut butter is not food."

"Then what is it?"

"I don't know. A condiment. Like ketchup or mustard."

"Really, Rivers? Do you put peanut butter on a hamburger?"

"Do you eat it plain?" he shoots back.

"Yes."

"Okay, do *most* people eat it plain?"

"How would I know about most people? I know *I* eat it plain. I also like it with honey on bread, or with jelly on bread, or all three on bread. Have you ever had a grilled peanut butter and jelly sandwich?"

He slowly turns his head toward mine. Our noses are almost touching as he says, "Are you saying you grill peanut butter and jelly sandwiches like we grilled steaks tonight? On a *literal* grill? What's wrong with you?"

I laugh. "No. Like a grilled cheese. Although, I never understood why it's called a grilled cheese. You don't grill it, you fry it."

"Fried cheese just doesn't sound as appetizing."

I consider this. "I guess. I'll make you one tomorrow."

"No thanks."

I put my hands on his shoulders, feeling them tense beneath my touch. I lean close to him as I say, "You know what else is really good?"

"What?" he asks warily.

"Peanut butter and bacon on toast. I'll make that for you too."

"No. Really. Don't."

I scrunch my nose up at him. "You shouldn't think you don't like something before you even give it a try."

Rivers' hands find my waist beneath the water as he closes the distance between us. He stares down at me, his expression hard to determine masked as it is by night, but I can feel the scorching intensity of his eyes as they rove over my face. His fingers move around my waist to my back and slowly trail up it, causing goose bumps to break out in their wake.

Sliding his palms up my neck so that his forearms are flush with my back, he lowers his mouth to mine. The kiss is slow but short, and ends with him catching my lower lip between his before he pulls away. My stomach is doing crazy flips and my limbs feel too heavy to keep me upright.

"You're absolutely right," he murmurs. He straightens, a grin taking over his mouth. "Tired?"

My mouth opens and closes. Part of me is still back in the last moments locked in that seductive kiss. "Are—are you?"

"Extremely." The teasing glint to his eyes disappears as he watches me. His manner has shifted, become dark like the sky surrounding us.

I feel my heartbeat quicken, but I keep my tone light as I say, "You're just saying that. You really only want to get me into your bed so you can have your way with me."

"Oh, I'm planning on it." His voice is a purr.

I go still as I gaze at him. Okay, so I wasn't expecting that. Innuendoes and come-on lines make me blush and stammer out ridiculous comebacks because my brain doesn't know how to digest that kind of behavior. But with Rivers, I don't know, I want to be naughty. I want to flirt.

I want *him*.

I trail my fingers along his chest, feel the taut skin pebble beneath my touch, and say, "Don't blame me in the morning when you're irrevocably obsessed with me."

"I don't think I need to wait until morning for that to happen," he murmurs.

Damn. He did it again.

I laugh, but it sounds shaky. "Stop."

He smiles. "Never."

We leave the pool and enter the house, our hands locked together. As we lie down to sleep, I cannot keep the joy from my being. It seeps out into the smile that won't leave my face. It bursts forth in the laughter that falls from my lips. It even tendrils through my arms as I wrap them around Rivers' waist, resting my cheek on his warm chest.

This feeling, this joy, outshines anything that has ever hurt me. It heals all past wounds. This joy is a shield against the future. It is my strength to face another day not knowing what it will bring.

"You know how, when you get hurt, you feel it all the way to your stomach? It's not just felt in the place you actually hurt, but within your whole body?"

I kiss his bare shoulder. "I guess, yeah."

His arms tighten around me. "That's how I feel about you. I feel it everywhere, and it really isn't pain, but it isn't exactly pleasure either. It's an ache that sort of hurts, but also gives relief. Does that make sense?"

A smile forms to my lips as tears prick my eyes. "Yes."

It is the epitome of what I feel now with his words lingering in my head and heart.

"WHAT HAVE YOU DONE WITH my son?"

No form of greeting, just that.

I coat two slices of bread in peanut butter, glancing at the cell phone on the counter next to me. I put it on speaker phone, but now I wonder if I should have. I look up, glad Rivers isn't in the room in case I am about to get yelled at. Being yelled at in private sucks—being yelled at with a witness listening is excruciating.

"I think he's around here somewhere. Do you want me to get him?"

Monica laughs. "Delilah! I meant, where did the brooding, unhappy young man go? Not that I want him back. I'm just wondering how you managed to do in less than two weeks what I, and doctors of any kind, haven't been able to do in months."

I open my mouth to ask if any of them offered to make out with him, but decide she might not find that as humorous as I do.

"I got skills," is what I go with.

I finish with the jelly, place the buttered sides of bread in a frying pan, and place the twins on top. Making them makes me happy. The thought of watching Rivers try one makes me even happier.

"He's swimming."

"Yes," I answer.

"You're amazing, you really are."

"That's me." I twist a lock of hair around my finger and rest my backside against the counter, the scent of butter filling the room. "How is everything going over there?"

The line is silent, but somberness can somehow be felt through the phone.

"Not good. It shouldn't be too much longer now." She sighs. "It's all so horrible—waiting for someone to die, knowing they're about to, and being unable to do anything about it but watch."

My mouth goes dry and a sick feeling punches me in the stomach. "Right."

"Sorry. We don't need to talk about maudlin things. Cheer me up. Let's talk about you and Rivers."

The way she said that implies there is something to talk about.

"Oh, you know."

Rivers appears in the doorway, one eyebrow lifted. I turn the speaker phone off and pick up the phone, placing it to my ear. I flip the sandwiches in the pan and they sizzle as butter meets heat.

"Actually, you should know, Rivers ate all of your ice cream. He didn't want me to tell you, but I felt I should. I mean, you're my employer, not him, so my loyalties have to be to you."

His eyes narrow and I grin.

"I got more, but then he ate that too. I think he has a problem."

"Hmm. He's in the room, isn't he?"

"You could say that."

She chuckles. "I still have a hard time imagining him eating it at all."

"He loves it!" I hold a laugh in when he scowls at me, nudging me aside to eye the grilled peanut butter and jelly sandwiches. I flip the burner off and move the pan, bumping my hip into his side.

He gently bites my bare shoulder in retaliation and I have to fight for air for a moment. I push him away and he gives me a look saying he'll get me back for that.

"I think he's just trying to impress you."

"Most likely." I stick my tongue out at him.

"Tell Rivers hi and have fun. I'll be in touch."

"Got it." The call ends. "Also, he likes to kiss me, like, all the time. He even shoved his tongue in my mouth. And the groping…it's *endless*."

The phone is grabbed away from me. Rivers puts it to his ear, his eyes on me. "Funny."

He sets the phone down and brushes a finger across my lips. "Were you eating the peanut butter as you made the sandwiches?"

"No."

He shows me the peanut butter he removed from my lip.

"It fell…upward…somehow."

"And just happened to latch onto your lip? Who knew peanut butter was so gifted."

"Me." I point at myself and laugh when he rolls his eyes.

He moves around me and grabs two plates, sliding the sandwiches from the pan onto the plates. "Am I going to regret this?"

"No. You only regret the things you don't try," I tell him.

Grabbing a butter knife, he cuts the sandwiches into halves and offers me a plate. "That's one way to look at it. Although, that one time I went skinny-dipping and came out to a swarm of mosquitoes biting me in really bad places—totally regretted trying that. Let's eat."

I want to ask who he went skinny-dipping with, and then I realize that, no, I don't.

I wait to eat my own sandwich until he takes the first bite of his, laughter wanting to break forth at the cautious look in his eyes. He slowly chews, his eyes going to mine. With a shrug, he

takes another bite.
"It's good, right?"
"Not bad."
"I'll show you not bad."
"I'd rather you showed me bad."
Rivers = 1.
Delilah = 0.

I COULD TELL FROM THE phone call I received from my mom the night before that it is time to stop at home. She sounded unusually sad and I know the past ten days with me away is weighing on her. The longest we've gone without seeing each other is probably two days, max. When she asked me to bring Rivers over for supper, I couldn't say no. Hopefully he doesn't either. If he does, I'll just go by myself. For some reason, though, I feel that they need to meet. I guess because they are the two people in my life I care about the most.

The breath whooshes from my lungs when I admit it to myself. I'm not saying I love him, but I do care about him. I mean, yeah, I've known the idea of Rivers for a long time, but I have only really known him for close to a month. That isn't long enough to form feelings like that for someone. Of course, that doesn't stop me from thinking I have been given something I need to cherish and hang on to for as long as I can. So maybe I do love him, on some level. Why waste time trying to figure it out? I just need to embrace it while I can.

That settled, I grab clothes from my tote bag to change into. As I am kicking off my pajama bottoms, I hear a noise behind me and spin around. Rivers stands frozen in the doorway, a coffee cup in each hand. His hair gleams like the feathered wings of a raven from a recent shower and he's wearing a white tee shirt and khaki shorts. I can smell him and the coffee from across the room, both of which are welcome. His expression is sort of comical, as is the way he is standing like a mannequin. Great advertisement for coffee, though. I'd buy that brand.

When he continues to remain silent and unmoving, I sigh and head toward him. It's not like I am naked. I have a pink tank top and underwear on, although, yeah, okay, the tank top is tight and I don't have on a bra—and the underwear are red and skimpy, but still. I'm clothed.

He tenses as I advance, and I fear he may take off before I can reach the coffee that I would actually love to slurp down this morning. I didn't sleep well last night and ended up in the sunroom at some point, which made sleep ultimately impossible. I couldn't sleep with Rivers and I couldn't sleep without him. It was a long night of asking myself what the hell is going on. The answers remained unknown until this morning, when I just had that scary epiphany.

"Are you back to not speaking to me? Fine. I can get used to that again. Your comments are kind of annoying. You have this air of superiority every time you open your mouth that really gets on my nerves after a few hours." I take the mug from his limp fingers and blow on the steaming black liquid.

A deep inhalation of air is sucked into his lungs, breaking whatever trance he was under. "You weren't there when I woke up this morning."

I raise my eyebrows as I sip my coffee. "You are extremely observant."

With a scowl blackening his already dark looks, he sets his mug down on a window ledge and swipes a hand through his hair. It is clear he is agitated and my comments are not helping. "Why weren't you there?"

"Did you miss me?" I tease, although I am curious as to whether he really did. In fact, my pulse stutters a little as I wait for him to respond.

Rivers' eyes flicker up and down the length of me and immediate heat shoots through me. I forgot about my partially dressed state. Without saying a word, he takes the mug from me and sets it down next to his. His arm shoots out, his hand palming my waist, and he yanks me to him.

When our bodies touch, the heat turns to fire. Both hands

hold me now, his fingers dipping low and dangerously close to my rear. He's teasing me, I realize. His fingers inch down, then retract, again and again, until my breaths are leaving me in little spurts and I want to scream at him to just grab my ass already. And let me tell you, I do not think things like this. Apparently, with Rivers, I do.

He presses his lower half to me but leans back so that his eyes are locked on mine as he says, "Miss you? Yes. Long for you? Yes. I realized something last night, as I laid there without you next to me. All it took was one night."

He pauses. "I don't think there is a question as to whether or not I want you, because that is painfully blatant right now, but did I miss you? It was so much more than that. And do I need you? Yes. I need you. My heart needs you, Delilah. I don't want to wake up without you again, not until I have to. And even then—even then I will just barely tolerate it."

Oh...my...

Chills start at my scalp and make their way down to my toes at the sound of my name on his lips. I do believe it is the first time he's spoken my full first name in front of me since I started working here. My heartbeat picks up at the way he fits against me, and the conviction I see in his expression makes my stomach swoop over and over again. His words—his words just tossed away whatever reservations I had about trying to keep my distance. Keep my distance from the fire that keeps me warm in the face of the cold all around me? Impossible.

My heart needs you, Delilah.

"Why didn't you..." I falter as I struggle to breathe. "Why didn't you come get me then?"

"Obviously you wanted to be alone, but trust me, I contemplated it. In depth. Don't try it again, though. There *will* be repercussions." He scowls at me, but there is lightness to his eyes—lightness *I* put there.

I grab the front of his shirt and yank him toward me. I kiss him with all the passion inside me. He pushes against me, his fingers tangling in my hair, and we get lost in each other. His mouth sears mine, claims it as his, and tells me I will never get enough of this. The touching and kissing are going to reach a point where it is no longer enough. I think we are both dangerously close to that edge. Once we jump, there is no return to the pre-intimacy stage. I don't think I'll miss it.

I smile as he shudders against me, feeling empowered in the desire of Rivers. I feel beautiful, like I was never any- thing but. I feel like I am perfect as I am, and always have been. I feel like I never thought I would feel, *especially* with him.

When we finally tear ourselves away from one another, I put substantial distance between us so we don't end up all over each other again. His eyes are glazed over, his nostrils flared as he sucks ragged breaths in and out. He has never looked more appealing.

"We're eating at my house tonight. My mom demands it," I state.

Rivers blinks, some of the fog clearing from his eyes. "Bossy, aren't you?"

"You wouldn't like me as much as you do if I wasn't. And my mom's the bossy one. I'm just relaying the message."

"Hmm." He rubs his jaw and shrugs, dropping his hand to his side. "Sure. I need to thank your mother anyway."

"What for?" I grab clean clothes from my tote in preparation of showering.

"She sent me flowers in the hospital."

I go still, glancing over my shoulder at him. "How do you know they were from her?"

"Do not keep standing like that. I mean, you can. Just know that there will be consequences if you do."

I straighten, blushing as I become aware of the view I was giving him.

"There was no note on the card, but it had the name of her business on it. At first, I thought someone forgot to sign it, then I realized it was probably from the flower shop. Wait."

It is his turn to freeze. Rivers' eyes narrow as he studies me. "It was you?"

My face heats up as I look away, holding my clothes in front of me like a shield. I shrug, trying to appear nonchalant about the whole thing. It took me hours to find the perfect flowers, to arrange them just right, to have the courage to send it.

"They were the prettiest ones," he says quietly.

"They were plain."

I chose the ones that didn't stand out, but had the most character to them. I chose the ones I found the most beautiful, even with their uniqueness—because of their uniqueness. They were simple, imperfect, and strong.

"Do you know how many different colored roses I got?" He pauses. "You probably do, actually. Most of them came from your mother's shop. Is that why you chose the ones you did?"

Shrugging, I fiddle with the stud in my nose, uncomfortable heat coursing through my veins. "Roses are pretty and everything, but they're so generic. Everyone gets roses. They're the flower you can pick without really thinking about it."

"And you thought about it," he slowly confirms.

I wordlessly nod, thinking of the baby's breath, calla, delphinium, dahlia, snapdragon, and peony ensemble I put into a slim purple and black swirled vase. Each stem was precisely cut so that no two flowers were the same height, each painstakingly set in the perfect position to complement the others. It was the one time I truly enjoyed working with flowers. I guess because I knew I was making something beautiful for someone who needed to see it.

Maybe that's how it is for my mom every time. I never thought about it that way. With everything, I suppose, how you decide to look at something determines what you get out of it.

"I need to show you something." Rivers leaves the room.

I am not sure what I'm supposed to do, so I wait, feeling nervous and fidgety. I chew on the inside of my lower lip and stare out the window toward the green grass and blue sky. The thing about me is that, although I enjoy doing good deeds, I don't like attention brought to them. I just want to do them and have people appreciate them, leaving me in the shadows as an unknown.

He comes back with the most serious expression on his face, holding a folded paper towel. When he gets to me, he slowly lifts the top half off, showing dried, but whole flowers in varying colors of purple, blue, pink, and yellow. My chest painfully squeezes as I stare down at the remnants of the gift I thought would be dismissed without a glance and was instead revered.

"I watched them die."

I look up, catching his dark eyes on me.

"That sounds morbid, but it really wasn't. Something about them intrigued me. Maybe it was the different kinds of flowers, or the fact that no one else sent anything like them. Maybe it was because I was bored. All I know is, I watched them wither into the curled and shrunken pieces they now are, and I felt some of the helplessness fade along with them. It was...cathartic."

Rivers' eyes hold me in place. "I didn't even know they were from you, that you had touched them and constructed them into the form of art that stood in a crazy vase by my bedside, and yet I felt a connection to them."

He pauses, taking a deep breath. "Do you believe in fate?"

I look down at the flat pieces of what were once vibrant with life, and I say, "Fate? I'm not sure if I believe in that, but...something like it...yeah, I think I do."

SEVEN

WE WALK TO MY HOUSE. It was his idea to travel this way, and I wonder if he is trying to prove to himself that he can. I realize that sometimes we are our biggest critic, and that the person we have the hardest time gaining approval from is usually ourselves. I can see the strain on Rivers' face as we get closer to our destination, but he remains close-lipped about it. If it was anyone else with him, they might not even notice the tightness around his eyes or the way he faintly winces as he moves.

But I do.

I imagine he'll always have some form of soreness or discomfort in his legs. When muscle is damaged as badly as his was, it never fully recovers. But at least he's walking. That's what it's all about—continuing on even when it is hard. I glance at his sharp profile, all straight lines and geometrical angles constructed to form beauty.

He notices me watching him. "What?"

"I really hope you do everything in your life that you've ever wanted to do."

A frown line forms between his eyebrows. "Why are you saying this?"

I shrug and scratch a bug bite on my forearm. "Because you need to never give up, no matter how bad things get. There won't always be someone around to help you. Sometimes you have to do it all on your own. I want to make sure you remember that giving up is not an option. Not for you, not ever."

He stops walking. I want to keep moving but I know I will be going alone, so I sigh and stop as well, turning back to look at him.

He's staring at me in a way that makes me uncomfortable. The longer he studies me, the more my skin heats up. He finally breaks eye contact, his face angling up as he watches a group of birds fly overhead.

"You make it sound like you won't be around for it," he finally says, not looking away from the sky.

My answer is simple and true. "I want to be. I can't say I will be—no one knows that. But I know I want to be."

Rivers looks at me, a slow, sweet smile curving his lips. "I guess that has to be good enough then."

I smile back, a charge going up the hand that he clasps with his, continuing into my arm, and pooling around my heart. Warming it, warming me.

Maple and oak trees line the sidewalk in browns and greens —tall and strong. This residential part of town is less busy than Rivers' street. That could be because most of the people are elderly and don't get out much. The air is crisp with summer; a hint of fragrant blossoms, a touch of rain to come, and everything encased in sunshine. We come to my house and I pause, wondering what his reaction will be, and then I feel bad for thinking he would ever judge me based on the place I live. That was the old Delilah thinking she knew the old Rivers.

A buzzing sounds near my face and I swat a mosquito away, noticing Rivers looking at me with a knowing smile on his face. I ask him what he's staring at and his grin widens.

"I thought you liked bugs."

"Did I say I like them? I don't remember saying that, exactly."

"Bug killer."

"Only mosquitoes! They have no purpose other than to suck our blood. Little leeches," I grumble, itching at the swelling lump on my cheek.

"What about gnats? I'm sort of partial to them, actually. Swarming masses of tiny bugs that swallow up anything living. They're like teeny, tiny, zombie bugs."

"Ugh," is all I say.

He laughs, swiping the air around him as a cloud of gnats decide that's their cue to make an appearance.

"This is it." I gesture to the Victorian-era house of blue and white; bits of character showing through in the lines and curves of the house. I note the new flowers my mom planted within the last week or so. Two large pots rest on either side of the steps that lead to the porch, flowers of purple and white bursting from the soil and over the rim of the tin tubs. A trace of homesickness flutters through me and I blink against the sting of it.

"I like it," he tells me, glancing at me and grinning.

"Glad you approve." I secretly am.

"The flowers fit you."

"They really don't." I shift my feet and cross my arms. Flowers are my mom's thing, not mine.

He tilts his head. "But they do. Nature becomes you. I was trying to figure out where you fit—"

"Where I fit?" I interrupt. The thought of him trying to decide where I belong rubs me the wrong way. I guess because I thought he was beyond that sort of thing.

"Hear me out. Okay?" I nod and he continues, "I used to fit in with the athletes, right? If I didn't know anything else, I knew that. You never really fit anywhere. Now I know why. There is no way to put you into a category when there is no one way to define you. You're like..." He pauses as he looks at me, smiling when he says, "Sunshine. And rain. Flowers. You're everywhere, everything. The wind. The stars.

"Your eyes reminded me of something and I couldn't figure out what it was. I know now. They're like the sun set- ting, when the golds and oranges, and even hints of brown, can be seen. I don't understand the red hair dye, but even that seems to work for you. It's like fire. Everything about you is some form of a natural element. It's like...you're the complete embodiment of life. Your laugh, your sense of humor, your personality—you just—you put all of you into everything you do. You know? Even your heart..."

He inhales deeply. "You're a beautiful person, Delilah Bana."

Tears trickle down my face, but I don't try to remove them. He has to see them, he has to know how perfect his words are, how much they mean to me. Each tear I shed is a thank you.

I stare at Rivers, trying to burn his image into my mind so that I never forget it, no matter where I am or what happens in the days, or months, to come. I want to remember him looking at me like I could be his air, looking at me like I could be the one thing he cares about more than an image, or a role, or a category. He does, I know he does. In the fracturing of him, he found a better him. And that broken version of Rivers found me. I think I was waiting for him to, in some cosmic way.

My heart is full, so full it aches, but it is a good pain. It is the kind of hurt that comes with the pressure of indescribable emotions, building and building, until they become too much, and they have to be eased or your heart will crack from them all. I cry to alleviate the feelings I cannot put into words right now. I don't think there is a correct word, or words, for what I have in my heart for Rivers.

He uses his thumbs to caress my cheeks, effectively removing the wetness from them. "Are you crying because I ate the last of the ice cream? We'll get more, I promise."

I laugh shakily. "Yes. And because you refused the peanut butter and bacon on toast I offered to make for lunch."

"I can only take so much peanut butter."

"It's like I don't even know who you are," I tell him.

A door creaks, banging as it shuts. "Are you two going to stand out here all night or are you going to come in? The bugs are terrible."

I slowly look up and meet my mother's gaze. I suck in a sharp breath at the yearning that hits me. Sometimes, you don't realize how much you miss something until you see it once more. And sometimes—you don't get that chance. Why have I been wasting time? I feel like that's all I've been doing my whole life; wasting whatever days I get on things that don't even matter instead of focusing on the things that do.

She offers a small smile and I return it as she goes back inside.

An invisible cord pulls at me, telling me it is time to make things right with her, even if it is a slow, stumbling process. There comes a point when all the walls seem impossible to break down, when the person you see the most becomes a stranger. Between my mother and I, there is awkwardness where there should be familiarity. Maybe it's her fault for allowing it, but it is certainly my fault for instigating it.

Sometimes when someone tries to push you away, you have to push back.

She has loved me for eighteen years—even when I was in my most unlovable state. I didn't put this clear barrier between us because I don't love her back, or because I wanted to hurt her. Part of the reason I have shied from her over the years is because I was afraid if I got too close, I would see our unattainable past staring back at me. Or what she would see when she looked into my eyes was all that we cannot change nor forget.

But I also kept my distance to protect her. And me. I'm still trying to protect her and I don't know how much longer I can keep the truth from her. And when that day comes, I fear I will break, and everything I have strived to do this summer will wash away like most good intentions do.

Rivers nudges me. "Are we heading in or making a run for it?" he says close to my ear.

I break out of the spell of nostalgia and tug at his hand. "There is no running away from this."

I meant for my tone to be carefree, but even I can hear the ominous taint to it.

"You and your mom don't seem close," he notes as we walk toward the house.

"How can you tell?"

"I don't know. There's this...uneasiness between you. She looks at you and you look away and the reverse."

"You saw all of that within a minute?"

He shrugs.

"We're not," I answer his earlier question.

"Is there a reason for it?"

I glance over my shoulder at him. "Just one? No. There's a lot of them."

"You should have told me this before now."

"Why? Would you have decided not to come?"

His jaw juts forward. "No, but it would have been nice to be prepared."

"Being prepared for things is dull. Spontaneity is more entertaining." I reach behind me and pat his stomach. "You'll be fine. Just don't talk about politics or religion."

"Isn't that the rule for anywhere?"

"See? You're so knowledgeable."

"I get this feeling you're making fun of me."

I open the door and smile at him as we walk into the house. "Never."

The living room is directly ahead—a spacious room with walls the color of a stormy day, the trim looking as though blanketed in snow, and a ceiling high enough that when I was a child, I thought it reached the stars. The floors are hardwood and I used to pretend they were an ocean; the furniture was my refuge against the sea monsters. Maybe Rivers is right—I do tend to see nature in all things.

The small entryway we are standing in has a lower ceiling than the living room, but the trim around the floor and windows is still the shade of snow, though the walls are creamy yellow, like butter. Black and white photographs in chipped and faded white frames take over one whole wall, the wall I unconsciously turn away from whenever I enter the house.

Plants abound from corners and window ledges. With the sun streaming in through the large picture windows it almost seems like we are in some sort of tropical jungle, or a strange new world where we are the only existing humans. That would be okay with me.

"It smells good in here."

I look at Rivers. "I hope you like garlic."

One dark eyebrow lifts.

"My mom loves it. She puts it in everything, even cake."

His other eyebrow raises to meet the first when my mom appears, giving me a look. "I heard that. And it's not true. I don't put it in cake, although I might have to try that. Maybe for your next birthday," she tells me with a wink.

I try to smile, but my lips are frozen into a stiff line. My next birthday is seven months away. A lot can happen in seven months. My mom catches my reaction. I can tell from the frown on her face that she doesn't understand it, which is logical.

She opens her mouth to say something, but Rivers must have picked up on the tension because he says, "Remember what you told me about trying things? You really don't have a choice. If your mom makes it, you have to eat it."

I shake the blackness away and fight to brighten my tone when I counter with, "You're absolutely correct. I'll make sure you're there too."

I smile at my mom. "This is Rivers, Janet. Janet, Rivers. I'm not sure if you've been properly introduced yet."

She offers a genuine smile. "Hello. It's nice to meet you."

"And you. I've talked to you before at the flower shop."

Janet nods. "I thought you looked familiar."

She gestures in the direction of the kitchen. "Come on in. I'll get us something to drink."

When Rivers goes ahead of us, she looks at me and mouths, "He's cute."

Heat creeps up my neck, but I can't keep the grin from my face. "I know," I mouth back.

The scent of garlic gets stronger as we enter the kitchen, along with herbs, spices, and a hint of chocolate. I make a beeline for the counter where a cake pan sits. I'm about to pop the gob of chocolate frosting I acquired from the top of the cake into my mouth when Rivers catches my eyes. I grin and instead swipe my finger across his mouth. He pauses, his eyes going black as he slowly licks his lips without his gaze leaving mine. It's dark, smoldering, hot. My breath catches and I forget we're not alone.

Luckily, my mom clears her throat, effectively breaking through the magnetism of our gazes. It would be pretty embarrassing if I attacked him right in front of her. I offer to help with supper, Rivers agreeing almost immediately, and my mom sets us to work preparing a salad. The mood is light as we work and I feel not only connected to Rivers, but also to my mom. He and I tease each other, making my mom laugh, and she embarrasses me with stories about my younger years.

Rivers acts as a buffer between my mother and I, or a single point of continuity that pulls us together so that we take notice of one another and interact in a way we haven't in a long time. He is working the magic he used to in school and I don't even think he is aware of it—it's just a part of him.

He is like a focal point in the darkness of our existence—a beacon. How did the boy swathed in black become my shining light?

At one point, he murmurs close to my ear, "Why do you call your mom by her first name?"

I glance over my shoulder, but my mom isn't in the room. I set down the tomato I was slicing and look at him. "It's sort of a long story. Let's just say...I felt like I needed to grow up at a young age, and I thought calling my mom by her first name was part of that. It stuck."

"I'm surprised she allows it."

"Well, I don't think she particularly likes it, but what's she going to do?"

"Ground you."

I shake my head at him. "And what, take away my bike? Oooohhh." I roll my eyes, a smirk on my face. "Hey! Maybe she'll make me stay at home and then I won't get to sleep with you anymore. No more petting and fondling through the night—"

He slaps a hand over my mouth just as my mom enters the kitchen. When she pauses to take in the scene, he immediately drops his hand, red-faced. He's lucky. I was about to bite it. He gives me a warning look when she turns away and I give one right back.

"How's the salad coming?" is all she asks.

"It's ready." I dump the last of the tomatoes into a small

bowl and carry it to table to sit beside a dish of baked garlic honey chicken, cheesy garlic mashed potatoes, a fresh lettuce salad, and garlic butter rolls. I wasn't exaggerating about my mother's love of garlic—just about the cake part. The croutons accompanying the salad are even garlic and herb.

"I made lemonade. Do you like lemonade, Rivers?"

"Yes. Thank you."

He's being so polite that the urge to shake him up emboldens me.

Just as we sit down, I announce, "Rivers asked me to marry him."

He spits out the lemonade he just took a drink of. Luckily it doesn't hit any of the food. Unfortunately, it does hit my mom directly in the chest. A squeak leaves her as her arms raise and hover out at her sides.

"I'm so sorry," he says, lurching to his feet and then standing there awkwardly. It isn't like he can exactly wipe her down.

"You should get her a towel. There's one on the stove," I tell him, laughing when he glares at me.

My mom waves him away. "It's fine. Sit down. I'll just go change my top. Really, Del?" she asks in exasperation as she walks by.

"What are you doing?" he demands, eyeing me suspiciously.

"I'm having fun."

"At my expense."

"Well, yeah."

"Stop it."

"No."

"Stop it or I'll be forced to fight back."

My breath catches at the gleam that enters his eyes.

"That's what I'm waiting for."

The glint in his eyes turns dangerous and I know he is thinking about all the ways he could get me back, and I also think he is thinking of things that would make me blush—until I realize I already am. My face is on fire and it matches the way my body feels. I gulp down lemonade and tear my eyes away from his, instead focusing on the vines of a plant in a corner of the room.

"You're in so much trouble, and you don't even know it," he promises. "You can always dish it out, but you can never take it, can you?"

He rubs a finger over his lower lip just as I return my gaze to him and my pulse careens out of control. "What are you thinking about? Right now?"

Sex. That's what I'm thinking about. And it's his fault. I always innocently tease; he turns everything into an insinuation. I'm not complaining, I just get flustered by it. Let's just say I am not suave in the art of flirting, or anything sexual, really.

"Nothing," I answer quickly.

"Mmm-hmm," is his dubious reply.

As soon as she gets back into the room and sits down, I continue with the previous conversation, much to Rivers' annoyance. "I told him no. It's too soon. But, maybe, ya know, in a few more weeks."

She stabs a piece of chicken with her fork and plops it on her plate, offering the dish to Rivers. "Yes, that should be sufficient time." She glances up with a question in her eyes. "What's with you tonight?"

I shrug, taking a bite of mashed potatoes. They melt on my tongue in a perfect combination of butter, cheese, and garlic.

"I like teasing Rivers. Look at him. He doesn't know what to do."

"I know what to do, I just don't know if your mother would approve." There is a double meaning there, and his eyes confirm what it is when they meet mine.

My face flushes and I stare down at the salad, counting the dark flecks of seasoning in a crouton as I wait for my face to stop burning. I think I need to admit defeat. I am out of my league here.

I am not sure if my mother is truly aware of what is going on between us, but she chooses to say in response, "If I were you,

Rivers, I'd tease back. Delilah needs that once in a while."

And that's all the encouragement he needs.

"Your daughter is obsessed with me," he casually supplies as he cuts into a piece of poultry.

My mouth drops open and I quickly close it before a chunk of tomato falls out.+

A smile flits over my mother's lips. "Really? How can you tell?"

"She follows me around, taking indecent pictures of me at every opportunity." He shrugs, a smirk on his face as he looks at me. I promise retaliation with my expression and he laughs, turning back to my mom. "She even wrote me a love song. It's sweet, but sort of embarrassing as well, especially when she serenades me from outside my window at night."

"I can see her doing that. She wrote a song once when she was a child. How did that go?" She looks at me, her eyes alight with happiness.

"I don't remember," I state slowly and firmly, widening my eyes at her.

"It was about peanut butter; I do remember that."

I drop my face into my hands.

"Peanut butter?" Rivers sounds like he is choking.

"Yes. She really loves peanut butter."

"Trust me, I know."

I remove my hands from my face and divide a glare between the two of their smiling faces. "It was for school. I was eight! We had to write a song about something that brought us joy. Peanut butter was an easy answer. Lots of people love peanut butter!" I add when they start laughing.

Was it called 'Ode to Glorious Peanut Butter'?" he teases, and even I laugh at that, though I fight to keep a scowl on my face.

The meal continues on with Rivers and I tossing words back and forth and my mom being entertained by it. After the meal is finished, we clean up the kitchen. I want to show Rivers the backyard and go in search of a blanket to take with us.

My mom follows me into the closet near the living room.

I glance over my shoulder at her. "The both of us are not going to fit in here."

She fidgets with the hem of her top, nibbling on her lower lip. "I know we really don't talk about boys, but...what's going on with you two? I thought you were working there. It seems like you're...dating?"

Pulling a soft fleece blanket from the top of a pile, I back up, forcing her to move away, and face her. "I am working there."

I purposely avoid the dating question.

"You seem..." she trails off when she catches my eye, her face reddening.

"What? What do I seem?"

"You both seem really happy, that's all. Like you care about each other."

"I do care about him," I admit, shifting my stance.

Her smile is bright, but also bittersweet. "He seems like a nice kid. Just...what happens after summer?"

I sigh. "You ask me that a lot." I pause, deciding to be honest. "You know, I really have no idea, and I don't even want to think about it right now. I'm just going to enjoy the summer."

She nods. "I've dated a boy or two, if you ever need advice or anything."

"Thank you," I say after an inner debate upon how exactly I should respond to that offer.

"Let me know when you're leaving so I can say goodbye."

"I will."

"I'm going to stop over to Alice's for a bit, but I won't be too long. She found a new recipe and wants me to try it with her."

Alice is seventy-seven years old and lives across the street. The only recipes she ever looks at or makes are for alcoholic beverages. She used to babysit me when I was younger. I associate her with the scent of baby powder, chocolate chip cookies, and a raspy voice brought on by years of smoking. She's nosy and blunt, but also endearing.

My mother loves her. I suppose I do too.

"Okay. Tell her hi. Don't have too much fun boozing it up."

She smiles. "There is no such thing as too much fun."

"Or too much booze," I add and she laughs.

Rivers and I are camped outside on a blanket when my mom returns. I scoot over and she sits beside me, looking up at the black sky dotted with little blips of light.

"That was a good margarita," she supplies.

I laugh. "What kind was it?"

"Mango with frozen mangos in it. Delicious. I'll make you one when you're twenty-one." She bumps her shoulder to mine. That's over seven hundred days away—too far into the distance to consider.

"Only three years away. It can be your ultimate achievement," Rivers says.

I lift an eyebrow at him, the night hiding certain features of his face while illuminating others. "It's more like two years away. I'll be nineteen in less than a year…and you're saying my goal in life can be to have a mango margarita at the age of twenty-one?"

"You've got to start out small."

I turn my face upward, letting it be kissed by the moon. "I thought the saying was, go big or go home?" "No one likes a critic," he tells me.

"I wonder if critics even like critics?"

My mom shakes her head. "They probably criticize one another."

I snort. "I would *love* to see that. The entertainment possibilities are endless."

Touching my shoulder, my mom gets to her feet with popping knees. "I'm going to go in. I think my body is telling me I am older than I want to believe I am. It's past my bed time."

"You look great, Janet," Rivers says, and I shoot him a look. He shrugs with a grin in place.

"Thank you, Rivers."

I hop to my feet, tugging on the blanket before Rivers is off of it. "My babysitting hours start early and the child in question is extremely demanding, so we should be going." My tone is snippy and the gentle squeeze on my hand tells me Rivers caught it. I fold the blanket up and hand it to my mom, following her inside the house.

"Thanks for the grub, Janet. It was really good," I tell her.

Rivers shakes her hand. "I agree. Thank you for having me over."

My mom smiles. "You're welcome. It was nice to meet you. We'll have to do this again soon."

I wave and start down the sidewalk, but am abruptly halted when an arm slings around my waist.

"Hey. Stop for a minute."

I go still, scowling at nothing in particular. "What?"

"What just happened? You were awesome and then you were scary. Tell me why." His hold tightens on me before leaving altogether. "Are you—are you *jealous* that I told your mom that—about her looking good?"

I cross my arms. "No. Of course not."

He moves around me, stopping when he is before me. "What's going on?"

"I'm just...you know..."

He laughs. "I really don't. What are you trying to say?"

I exhale and rub my face, turning to stare at the house I grew up in. With its dark coloring and old architecture, it looks eerie and magical under the cover of night.

"My mom's beautiful. It isn't a jealousy thing, not at all. I love my mom and I love her beauty. I look at her in wonder all the time. I just...I just wish I was too."

I can't believe I admitted that, especially to him. I hold my breath, my pulse working at a crazy pace, and wait for the mortification that is sure to come with whatever he decides to say next.

His fingers tip my chin back so that I have nowhere to look but into his eyes. He smiles tenderly, looking like a damaged angel under the radiance of a nearby streetlamp. "Who are you to judge beauty based on how you view yourself? We all look at ourselves and see our flaws. Look at me. I have scars I cannot hide, scars I think make me ugly. Do *you* think I'm ugly?"

"No," I whisper, my voice like a caress of air.

The back of his hand slides down my cheek, and my breathing turns quicker while my insides warm. "Your eyes are like honey, your lips like the soft petals of a red rose, and your cheekbones are sharply designed to accentuate your unique features."

"Unique?" I repeat, my voice higher than I would like.

Half of his mouth lifts. "Yeah. Sure, you're not classically goodlooking, but you have your own form of beauty. It's your light, your heart. You *glow*."

"Rivers," I begin raggedly, my heart thundering inside me like a million drumsticks beating against a drum.

"Yes?"

"Stop or I'll be forced to write you a sonnet. For real."

Quiet laughter floats over me as he takes my hand in his. We begin to walk. "Don't pretend you haven't already started it. It probably begins with you rescinding your love of peanut butter for me."

"Don't push it."

THE SUN WARMS MY BACK with its blanket of fiery heat as I swim laps in the pool. I have learned recently to take joy in the smallest of things—like the sun shining, the rain, the wind, the colors all around us. I never paid enough attention before. Now every intricate detail is important to me.

Fingers dance along my spine and cause a tingling where they meet my flesh. I jerk away and up, finding Rivers standing beside me.

"Hey. You surprised me." I splash water at him, grinning when I get him directly in the face.

He wipes an arm across his face and my eyes are drawn to the muscled length of his arms and down to his chest. "Why do you splash water at me when I'm already wet? Doesn't that defeat the purpose?"

"Oh, Wise One, thank you for pointing that out to me."

He squints through the sunshine at me, water dripping down his face and chest like glistening teardrops. "Your back says Neil."

I blink, it taking a moment to make the connection between where he touched me in reference to his words. There is a black four-lettered word tattooed down my spine that I got on my eighteenth birthday, along with the nose piercing. It was my tribute to a little boy—my way of saying I will not forget him, not ever. Well, the tattoo was. The piercing was all for me.

It does, yes."

"Who's Neil? Was that your brother?"

I swallow and look down, trailing my fingers back and forth through the clear water. "Yes."

"I didn't know his name." He nudges my chin and I look up. Rivers smiles sweetly, his eyes warm. "I bet he thought you were pretty cool, didn't he?"

"Actually, he found me to be quite annoying." I laugh softly, remembering how I used to follow Neil around every- where, much to his chagrin. He couldn't even go to the bathroom without me on the other side of the door trying to talk to him.

"If he could see you now—he'd know the depth of your coolness."

"Maybe. Or maybe I'd still be just really annoying."

"Tell me about him."

I take a deep breath, the warm water swaying around me, and I sway in return. Or maybe my legs are wobbly from thinking about my older brother I have missed for twelve years. He would be twenty now, probably in college, in love with some girl and partying it up with his friends. I could see him as a version of Rivers in some ways—he loved sports so much he would have had to be good at them. My older brother that I have surpassed in age, making me the older sibling.

It's weird how once someone dies, they are forever frozen at the age they left this life. Everyone around them continues to grow older, but not them. They are forever preserved. It is an abnormality that shouldn't be. In my estimation, we should all have long, well-used lives; not half-lives, or quarter lives.

We all need our chance at life.

"He was on a jungle gym—"

"No," he interrupts. "I don't want to know about that. I was there that day. I remember. I want to know about *him*."

Rivers just gave me a gift without even knowing it. I feel my heart expand and fill as I gaze at him. No one asks me to talk about him, not even my mother—*especially* not my mother. The death of Neil is this big wall between us, unbreakable because we let it be. And here Rivers stands, asking me to scale it for him. I press my lips to his, tasting water, feeling the warmth of his life through his lips.

And I talk about my brother.

The sun goes higher in the sky as we do back floats, and I tell him about Neil trying to teach me about sports. He loved watching football, baseball, and basketball. He tried to explain the logistics of the games to me, but I was too young to understand. *He* should have been too young to know what he was talking about, but he seemed to under- stand the plays. I still don't understand sports.

I reapply sunscreen as I tell him how one summer Neil went an entire two months wearing the same shirt. He would let my mom wash it two times a week, but that was the longest he'd agree to go without it. She had to eventually wrestle it from him when he announced he was going to wear it to school too. The shirt magically disappeared that night. Neil cried. It was a SpiderMan shirt and he thought as long as he wore it, he had Spidey senses. I cried with him, thinking my mom had stolen his powers away.

Rivers watches me—not speaking, just listening. I tell him how my brother would play zombies with me and I always had to be the zombie. I got shot a lot with an imaginary gun. One day I squirted ketchup all over the front of a new dress to be a more effective zombie. Neil thought it was real blood and went screaming to our mom. She was not happy, mostly because she'd just gotten the dress and we were supposed to get family photographs taken that day. She rescheduled. He laughs, sweeping hair from my face as we make make a light lunch of roast beef sandwiches and fruit salad.

We eat on the deck under the shade of the umbrella. He steals my grapes and I take his banana slices. And still, I talk of my brother, never tiring, never running out of words. I needed this. Rivers somehow knew I needed this. The sky has turned from blue and cloudy to streaks of pinks, purples, and oranges by the time I finally go quiet.

I am exhausted, and not just my body, but my mind. I am also empty of some of the sorrow I normally carry around. I feel cleansed, relieved—not fully, but enough. I exhale slowly, turning my head to find his eyes still on me.

In fact, I don't think they strayed far from me all day.

"I've been thinking." he tells me.

"Oh?"

"I've been thinking a lot, actually." The intensity of his gaze is startling. "There are so many people out there, so many lives unknown because of stereotypes, or because someone doesn't fit in with the majority the way they are expected to. There are so many chances to know amazing people thrown away without people even realizing it."

I pick at my yellow nail polish. "You just now realized this?"

"Yeah. I guess I'm a little slow. I was always seeing life in one way when I should have been seeing it in another. Apparently getting injured turned out being a good thing for me. Who knew, right?"

A warm breeze caresses my face like a kiss from a loved one and I smile as I close my eyes. He is finally getting it. I lie back on the soft blanket we procured from inside. It's so serene here with the sun setting and our enclosed area behind the fence. I think I could lie here forever and be at peace.

"You're evolving. Be proud."

"You make me sound like a caveman."

"Well..."

"Funny." He lets out a deep sigh. "Anyway, I think...I think I know what I want to do."

"What's what?" I whisper.

He shifts beside me, lying down with his arm touching mine. "I want to be more like you."

I laugh. "No, you don't."

"I do. Teach me how."

I open my eyes and turn my face to look at him. Rivers is grinning. I push at his shoulder. "Well, let's focus on presentation first. You'll have to get your nose pierced. I mean, that's a given." He purses his lips, nodding.

"And dye your hair random colors. I would go with pink to start off, personally."

"Did you ever dye your hair pink?" he asks dubiously.

I give him a look.

Sighing, he closes his eyes, looking pained. "What else? Tell me. I can take it."

"You'll have to hang out with me on a daily basis so my goodness rubs off on you."

"Goodness?"

I elbow him.

"Okay, okay. I think I can do that."

I make my voice stern as I tell him, "It's a deal breaker. Either you can handle my awesomeness or you can't. And if you can't, you have no right trying to be as almighty as me. Got it?"

His eyes pop open. "Okay. But do I have to wear the green bikini? Because I don't want to outshine you in all your pale glory."

Laughing, I squint my eyes at him even though the sun has all but gone under the horizon. "We'll negotiate that later."

I close my eyes again, going still as his arm slides beneath my head. I am tugged closer to him, his heat seeping into my side, his scent assaulting my senses. The word *perfect* comes to mind.

"We should sleep out here."

"We could," he says. "But what about the bugs?"

"We can spray so much bug spray on us the fumes alone will kill them from a mile away."

"*Or...we could put a tent up and sleep in it.*"

I go up to my elbows and look down at him. "Really?"

Rivers laughs as he sits up. "Yeah. You act like you've never slept in a tent before."

"I haven't," I confess.

It's his turn to look shocked. "*Everyone* sleeps in a tent at least once in their childhood."

I point at myself and shake my head.

"I don't know what to say," he says with a mournful expression on his face that is totally fake. "We need to fix this. Stat."

"Do you have a tent?"

"Of course. It's in the garage. Come on." He stretches his hand out to me and I take it.

"Do you guys do a lot of camping?" I ask as we go through the house and into the garage.

"We did, yeah." He rummages through a stack of boxes, totes, and bags in a far corner of the room. "We did a lot of outdoors stuff when I was younger—camping, hiking, fishing, hunting. We still do once in a while, just...it isn't the same. It is more like an obligation now than a tradition. Here it is!" He pulls a dark green rectangular cloth bag from the pile, his expression close to gleeful as he holds it in the air.

I think I am not the only one reconnecting with a childhood missed as we struggle to get the dome-shaped contraption into a standing position in the backyard. We tease each other as we work, and when I trip over a stake and land face first in the half-constructed tent, Rivers just laughs as he pulls me to my feet.

The tent is caved in, so we start over, but it is of no consequence. It is full dark out by the time we finish. We grab blankets and pillows from his bed and the spare bedroom, throwing them in a disorderly pile in the center of the tent.

Then we look at each other.

I grin, he grins, and we start laughing. I am not even entirely sure why, but it feels good. It is like reaching into the past has swathed us in giddiness, and made us in this moment simpler, but happier. We put a tent together.

And it made us smile.

"You have dirt smeared across your nose," he tells me.

"And you have grass in your hair."

I reach for him as he reaches for me and we collide, which makes me laugh even harder. I tip my head back and let it leave me in a cascade of mirth. When I look at him again, he is staring at me in a way that makes me think he feels like if he doesn't memorize every single detail of my face, he will miss something he will later regret. I go still, wondering what he is thinking as he looks at me.

"Hey there, Delilah," he says softly, a slow smirk taking over his features.

"Don't even," I warn. I can tell what he is thinking of doing just by how he said that.

He does.

He sings 'Hey There Delilah' by The Plain White T's. Night holds us in its embrace, but he lights it up with his essence alone. His voice is steady, deep, and touches me in a way I cannot explain. This feeling I have for him, it has washed away anything that has fought to darken my heart and soul. I feel reborn in what he gives me with his mere presence.

Before he even finishes the song, I am springing myself at him, wrapping my arms around his neck and squeezing him to me. *Don't let go, don't let go*, I think. I don't know who I am telling that to—him or me. I guess both of us.

"Girls always fall for that," he says close to my ear.

"How many Delilahs have you sung that to?" I ask, never relinquishing my hold on him. It is always hard for me to pull away from him.

"Just one."

I inhale deeply and step away, emotions too deep to withstand trying to pull me under. I smile brightly. "Thanks for going with me to my house the other night. My mom liked having us over."

"No problem. I had fun too. We should get our moms

together. I think they'd like each other."

"I agree."

He reaches down and grabs the can of bug spray from the ground, putting a layer of it over his bare skin. "This stuff smells horrible," he says, coughing.

He hands the bottle to me and I do the same, the scent of it biting to my senses I study the can. "It says it's unscented."

"It lies. Think it'll work?"

"Only one way to find out." I crawl halfway into the tent and pull out a sleeping bag.

"You don't really want to sleep *outside*, do you?"

I unroll the thick sleeping bag. "I do."

Rivers gets another sleeping bag from the tent and opens it up. "Then what was the point of putting up the tent?"

"Practice?" He narrows his eyes at me and I laugh. "In case it gets too cold or the bugs are too bad. It's our back-up plan."

He tosses his sleeping bag back into the tent and looks mine over. "This is for two people."

My pulse picks up. "Oh?"

Glancing at me, he nods. "Yeah. And even if it wasn't, we should try to conserve heat."

I look around us, the air warm even though dusk has fallen. "Right. Because it's freezing out."

He gets this solemn look on his face. "And I'd hate for you to get frostbite." A flash of a grin transforms his face. "Who would clean my room then?"

I punch his arm and he grabs my outstretched hand, tugging me to him. He interlaces our fingers, staring down at me. I study him back, my gaze flitting over the jagged lines of his imperfect face. He goes still, allowing my scrutiny, watching me. His grip tightens on my fingers when I lean up to press a kiss to his temple and another to his cheek.

I whisper something into his ear and he cups my face, only inches between us.

"I don't even care about them anymore," he says softly.

His thumbs caress my cheeks, tenderness lightening his eyes.

Rivers smiles, causing crinkles to form around his eyes, and gently attaches his lips to my lower one, moving his mouth languidly over mine. He pushes into me, his body taut with repressed need as the kiss becomes deeper, more urgent.

The sleeping bag becomes our cushion against the hard ground, his body my blanket as he holds himself over me, putting his weight on his forearms as his lips trail down the side of my neck, each touch sending a spark through my nerve-endings. His hands mold to my upper body as he goes to his knees between my legs, becoming acquainted with me in a way I have not allowed another man.

His mouth replaces his hands, touching me with reverence as I arch into him. When his fingers slide up my stomach beneath my top, shivers follow in their wake. A graze here, a caress there. I am struggling to breathe, my limbs nothing but pulsating noodles. I want him. I exhale deeply. But it can't be now.

As though he knows my thoughts, he sighs, pressing a light kiss to my collarbone, and lies down beside me, both of us staring at a starlit sky.

"Didn't we just do this?" he asks after his breathing has evened out.

"Do what?" I ask, although I know exactly what he is referring to.

"Watch the stars."

I smile. "We did."

"I used to pretend each star was a spaceship, flying through the sky on some top-secret quest to keep peace with unknown aliens."

I turn my head toward him and find him watching me. "I used to pretend they were lightning bugs, lighting up the sky for us to be able to see at night. The imaginations of kids, right?"

"I like your imagination better."

"I like yours." I look back to the darkened atmosphere. "I know you love water, sports, and now camping, but what else do you love?"

A finger trails down my forehead, over my nose, and pauses

on my lips. I swallow thickly, focusing on my heart- beat as I wait. "Campfires, music, thunderstorms, the color red... being with you. What about you?"

My breathing stutters. "Sunshine, this summer, the sound of rain hitting pavement, and the different colors of fall leaves."

"Why this summer?"

"Oh, I don't know. I guess because it's been a warm one." I gently bump my head against his shoulder. "And maybe because of you."

"There's no *maybe* about it," he argues.

I smile into his arm, giving his upper arm a quick kiss. "You're right."

We become quiet once more, the stars our nightlight, the sounds of crickets our music, and the air our blanket. At some point he moves his arm underneath my head and I rest my arm across his stomach. His breathing evens out and I tighten my hold on him, closing my eyes as I listen to his heartbeat and feel his warmth. This man is becoming everything to me. I fall asleep with trepidation in my core, but it pales when compared to the bliss I feel in my heart.

Your scars are beautiful.

That's what I whispered to him.

I DECIDE TO FOCUS ON Rivers—putting all of my energy into knowing all the many facets of him. Maybe I subconsciously already was, because when I saw him on that day when he was fragmented and I was fragmented, it seemed like if I could somehow reach him, maybe I could heal myself in the process of rebuilding him.

To me, learning about him is like luminosity in the middle of a rayless abyss, warmth in the coldness, hope in the face of despair—a crack of light through the nothingness blackness brings.

"How come you don't hang out with your friends anymore?" I pose with the basketball in my hands and release it, watching as it soars into the neighbor's yard, not even close to hitting the basket.

He laughs and shakes his head. "You're terrible at this."

I scowl and retract the basketball from the ground, forcefully throwing it at him.

"Don't take your non-athletic aggression out on me." He dribbles the basketball a few times, pauses in a temporary sculpture of grace, and makes the basket. He hasn't missed a shot since we came out over an hour ago.

"You didn't answer me."

"My friends," he repeats slowly. Rivers flexes his fingers around the ball, squinting his eyes at the sun-filled sky.

"Need me to list them? Forgotten their names already, have you? So fickle."

He shoots me a look before shrugging. "I don't know. They came over at first after the accident, but I didn't want to talk to anyone. In fact, I couldn't stand the sight of anyone. After a while, they stopped coming over. I get an occasional call or text, but..." He shrugs again.

"But?"

He shoots again and again he makes it. "I don't have anything in common with them anymore. They're all going off to college in the fall and I'll still be here. I live in a different world from them."

"By choice," I point out.

With a sound of frustration, he grabs the ball. "Is there any sport you *are* good at?"

"You're changing the subject."

"I'm going back to the previous subject. I'm allowed to do that."

"No. I equally suck at all of them. I like to keep things balanced."

"For real?"

I hesitate, and then confess, "I've always been interested in baseball. I've never played it other than in gym class when it was required. I wouldn't mind trying it once for fun. I even think I might understand how the game works."

"You think?" One eyebrow lifts.

"Yes. I don't know for sure." I laugh at the confused look on his face.

It fades almost as quickly as it appeared. "Ever been to a Brewers game?"

I cock my head. "Hmm. Isn't that our state football team?"

"That...what..." he sputters.

"I'm kidding! And no, I haven't."

"You know they're our *baseball* team, right?"

I blink. "They *are*?"

Rivers groans, making another shot. "You need some culture. You're all earthy and eau de natural, but you know nothing about the real staples of living in the United States—like sports."

"Eau de natural?" I wrinkle my nose. "That makes me think of someone who refuses to wear deodorant.?

"We're going to a Brewers game. I'll even get us tickets today."

I shrug. "Okay. I'm in."

I steal the ball from him, kicking my leg up as I shoot. Miraculously, it makes it in and I whoop, jumping around in a circle and clapping my hands.

"I just needed the leg kick. You should try it!" I shout, laughing as Rivers shakes his head at me.

"Not in this lifetime," he informs me.

"So, there's a chance for the next?"

"Doubtful."

"HERE." I TOSS THE PAPERS onto the kitchen counter and stand back to observe.

Rivers sets his glass of water down, his eyebrows lowering as he studies the forms. "What is this?"

"Your future. If you choose to make it."

Glancing up at me, he says, "I'm getting a little 'Mission: Impossible' vibe going on right now."

"No idea why."

We watched the movie last night. Or rather, I did. He fell asleep halfway through it, blissfully snoring away on my shoulder. The music was the best part, and it was really hard to concentrate on it with him being so noisy beside me. I had to elbow him. I don't regret it.

"Why are you giving me informative technical college and high school forms?"

"You need to contact both places so you can study and take whatever tests you need to get your GED. They'll know what you need to do. Call them. You can be a loser for a summer, but any longer than that, and it's just not kosher anymore. And after you get your GED, you go off to college like the star pupil I know you are."

He stares at me for a long time, and then something shifts in his expression. "Let me get this straight," he begins slowly, and I immediately tense at the tone of his voice. I am not going to like his next words. "You're pushing me to go to college, a guy who didn't even graduate—"

"The only reason you didn't graduate is because you were in an accident that made you miss too much school. You could have been done with all of this by now, but instead you decided to mope around for a while instead of getting things taken care of," I say in a rush.

"Yet *you*, the valedictorian, are not supposed to do the same?" he continues like I never interrupted.

Damn. Should have seen that one coming.

He crosses his arms. "Tell you what, I'll go if you go."

"No."

"Why?"

Heat creeps into my cheeks. "Because."

"All right." He nods. "I'm not doing it either. Just because."

I grind my teeth together. "At least I graduated. You can't even say that."

"You know, I planned on doing this. In time, in my own way, when I was ready," he says heatedly. "But I want to know why *you* care so much about it, especially when you're not doing the same. And I want to know why you *aren't* planning on going to college."

"Because there's no point to it!" I blow up, startling him and myself with the force of my voice.

He rubs his jaw, a calculating gleam to his eyes. Then he shrugs. "No point for me either. I don't have any talent. The only thing I've ever really been good at is playing football. I won't be doing *that* anytime soon. We're at a stale-mate. We can be long-time losers together—drink, smoke, talk about how good we had it in high school, how smart we used to be, how good at sports I used to be. How good-looking *I* used to be. Good times."

I have this really strong urge to hit him. Not just because of his tone and the words he is saying—although his comment about him being good-looking, insinuating that I am clearly not when I already know he finds me attractive, is enough reason to smack him—but because he is purposely being obtuse and not caring enough about himself and his future. I have logical reasons for my decision. He is simply being bullheaded.

I storm from the kitchen, but not before giving him a lethal glare. I end up in his room, whirling around in a circle of fury, and aim my eyes on the many awards lining the walls and shelves of his room. There are so many they even had to take residence upon his dresser and nightstand. Noting the missing photographs of Riley with Rivers gives me a brief pause, and a tingle in my spine, but I continue on.

"What are you doing?" he asks worriedly from just inside the doorway.

I grab the first one I find and shove the plaque toward his face. "What is this?"

"MVP for football."

Crap. That just flusters me more and I toss it aside, ignoring him when he shouts at me to be careful with it.

"This one?"

He looks at it and sighs. "Chemistry award."

"Do you think some dumb jock is going to know anything about *science*?" I am shaking. I have to get through to him. This is important to me in an almost maniacal way. He has to see this. He has to go on.

"Well...biology, at least." He smirks and I come unglued. "

This is not *funny,* Rivers."

"It sort of is. You're cute when you're mad."

I grab the first thing I find—the remote control—and I chuck it at him.

A dangerous spark enters his eyes when it connects with his hip and he storms for me. "The hired help attacking the employer's son? Tsk-tsk."

He doesn't really sound upset. If anything, he sounds like I just turned him on.

He threads his fingers through my hair and tugs my head back, his eyes hungry as they flit across the features of my face. "I'm going to have to reprimand you for that."

My knees go weak. Part of me, a part that is growing on a daily basis, wants to scream: Take me already! But I don't. I haven't reached that desperation quite yet, but if he keeps talking like this and kissing me like he has been, it'll happen. One day soon.

"Do it."

He rubs his nose up and down my neck, his breath warm against my skin. "Oh, I will."

"The papers. School. You know what I mean," I reply raggedly.

He drops his hands from me and steps away. "I will. Same time you register for school. They'll make exceptions for you; you know they will. We can do it together." He crosses his fingers. "We'll be like this at college."

"No."

Frustration twists his features. "I don't understand what your aversion to college is. Is this because of school? It won't be like that; you know it won't."

"It's not about that!" I turn my back to him, forcing my lungs to expand as I fight to breathe. I feel like crying. It was easy to say I didn't want to continue my education when I didn't see the point of it. But I do now. I may have shown Rivers a different way to look at things, but he sure as hell has done the same for me too. I am grateful to him for it, but at the same time, I wish

I could continue on in my bubble of rigidity.

His hand moves to my shoulder, lingering there. "Then what is it about?"

"I can't tell you."

He spins me around. "Why not?"

"It's personal." I avoid his eyes as I tell him this line of bull shit. It *is* personal, but that doesn't justify me shutting him out.

His eyes narrow. "It's *personal*? I've shown you every part of me I could, every part of me I have, whether I wanted to or not—parts of me I didn't even know I *had*, and you won't even tell me why you won't go to school in the fall?"

"Rivers—" I start.

"Look at my face," he demands. He leans close to me, making his features unavoidable. "Look at the scars. You're the only one—" he breaks off, inhaling.

His lips press together. "You're the only one who's never flinched when they looked at them, who never got that look of pity in their eyes as they gazed at me—you're the only one that's touched them, kissed them, acted like they are something good, or even nothing at all, when everyone else has acted like they are something *bad*.

"Even my mom has this sad look on her face every time she looks at me. I can't *stand* it. And you, the girl I never would have considered as anything special, mean more to me than—than...*anything*. More than anything," he breathes. "I have told you so much, so many things, and you won't even tell me this *one* thing."

He's right.

His eyes are lit up with emotion and I am being filleted with the backlash of it as the blackness of conviction trickles from him to me, knowing everything he has said is true. I rub my face, wondering if I can pull another bit of courage out of me.

Do it. Do it for him.

I drop my hands, realizing that, yes, I can. I can do this for him.

I slowly nod. "Okay. If you get your GED and get registered for school, I'll sign up for classes too." My heart is pounding in my chest, both in fear and excitement.

"We'll do it together," he says it, but there is a question in his eyes that makes me want to cry. He's asking about our future—if we have one.

"Yes," I whisper, knowing I will try my hardest to make it so.

The happiness he aims at me in his beaming smile makes my pulse trip and my stomach roll. He grabs me, giving me a hard kiss, and releases me so fast I stumble back.

"I'll call now." He strides from the room, the limp barely noticeable.

I heave a heavy sigh, my shoulders slumping. *Don't make a liar out of yourself, Delilah.*

I PROMISED RIVERS A NEW flavor of ice cream to try every time we went through a pint of the stuff. I think I may have started him down a destructive path of ice cream consumption. Today the selection is cookies and cream.

I peruse the frozen glass for it, unaware of the presence behind me until she purposely bumps into me. I turn, holding a sigh in. Riley stares at me, her pretty features and well-groomed appearance unable to hide the animosity she feels for me. It radiates from her in waves of detestation. I think it's because of Rivers, but I also think it's because of our shared past.

"What's going on with you and Rivers?"

I say, "Nothing," and turn away.

That word, which is the equivalent of emptiness, holds all the weight of insurmountable heartache. Nothing is *so much*.

She grabs my arm and squeezes. "What are you doing? You don't *really* think he likes you, do you?"

I pull my arm out of her grasp. "So what if I did and so what if he does?"

Her face scrunches up, twisting her beauty into something

ugly. "He doesn't. He couldn't *possibly* like you."

"Why?"

She laughs. "Are you for real? I mean, do you really not see? Look at you. Your hair is all a mess and your nose is pierced. You wear ridiculous clothes and you have a smartass mouth. You've *never* been popular. You don't even have any friends. You never have. *Why* would *Rivers* like *you*?"

"You're wrong."

Something in my tone must scare her, because she flinches and takes a step back, but not enough to make her shut up. "I'm wrong? You're a *joke*. He's just using you. He'll use you for the summer, or however long it takes him to get better, and then he'll leave you like you were nothing. Like you are. You're nothing."

Her words hurt, because they're true, in a way—not that she knows that. This, whatever this is, it won't last. It *can't*. Whether Rivers wants our association to be temporary or not, it is. All of this will become nothing one day and I will fade from his memories like I had never been a part of him, his world, or anything to do with him.

I'll be gone, like a fizzled-out spark. Knowing this makes my heart hurt in ways I never thought it could. It won't even matter if he wants it to happen or not; it just will—because there is no outrunning the inevitable.

Taking a deep breath, I decide to say what I have to say and then I'll try to forget her, what she ever was to me, and what she is now to me.

"We used to be friends," I say in a low voice.

She looks around us, as though to assure herself no one heard my words.

My mouth tightens in disgust for her.

"Shut up," she says in a strained voice.

I take a step toward her.

"We used to be friends," I say in a louder voice. "You were just as unpopular as me, or maybe I was as unpopular as you. Either way, it never mattered. It never mattered to me because all I cared about was that we were friends. I know why you stopped being my friend. I felt bad for you at first, and then I felt angry, and now...now I just feel exhausted by it all. News flash, Riley—you aren't perfect. No one is. Stop trying to act like you are."

"You're jealous." The sound of her voice is weak, so like the girl herself. She doesn't have to be. That's the most frustrating thing of all. She doesn't have to be the way she is and yet she thinks she does.

"Jealous? Of you? The girl so obsessed with her looks she has to make herself puke every time she eats?"

Her eyes shift around as she checks for witnesses. She still doesn't get it. No one *cares*.

"No," I continue. "I'm not jealous of you. I never have been."

I take another step toward her. "And when I caught you doing that, part of me felt sick. I wanted to help you. I would have helped you. You didn't let me. Instead, you pretended we had never been friends. And when you
stopped talking to me, I was sad and confused."

Another step.

"And when you turned everyone against me, I hated you. And when you relentlessly picked on me every day because I knew a secret about you, a secret you didn't want anyone to know, not even your best friend, I felt sorry for you. But jealous? Not. Once."

We're at the wall now, Riley's back pressed against it.

"You don't know what you're talking about." Her voice is heavy.

"I think I do."

"You don't know what it's like—you can't imagine—"

"Come off it," I scoff. "We all have issues. We all have shit happen to us we wish didn't. We all want to be a certain way we don't know how to be. Part of life is accepting who you are and being okay with it, instead of trying to change yourself."

"I just wanted to be pretty," she whispers, staring at me with wounded eyes.

"You already were," I tell her, swallowing thickly.

Her eyes lower, covering her shame and remorse from mine. Seconds pass, becoming minutes, and still, she won't raise her head. I suppose there are no words.

I exhale slowly, stepping back, saddened by it all. And this is what we have come to. Once best friends, then enemies, and now we can't even think of anything to say to each other to re- duce the pain of all the years spent hurting one another. Because it wasn't just her.

Sure, she started it every time, but I fought back with words and more. I could have ignored it. I could have tried to talk to her. Instead, I let her go, I stepped away, and watched her turn into something I loathed.

"You've changed," she finally says.

I nod, my chest painfully tight. "Yeah. So have you."

She blinks her eyes, and I pretend I don't see the tears in them. "I had to. I thought I had to for Rivers, but…"

She glances at me, the pain of being replaced in someone's heart evident in the darkening of her eyes. "I realized I had to for me."

I nod again, not sure what to say. I hesitate, and then tell her, "You're more important than anyone else. Try to remember that."

"I'm better now," she tells me in a small voice.

I don't know if she is telling the truth or not, but for her sake, I hope she is.

"I'm glad."

I turn to go, pausing as she says, "I know why he was drawn to you. I understand even."

I don't speak, watching out the window at the traffic zipping up and down the street.

Her voice cracks as she says, "I needed him to need me. You don't. It's messed up, but…I always kind of envied that about you. You were never afraid to be yourself. I was nothing but afraid."

My eyelids slowly close. I inhale deeply, and walk from the store, leaving a piece of my childhood with Riley.

A collage of memories bombards me as I drive to Rivers' home. The first day of kindergarten when Riley smiled at me, her long brown hair in a braid. I thought she was so pretty with her big blue eyes and soft hair. I especially loved her pink flowered dress. I smiled back and we played on the swings together, seeing who could pump their legs the highest.

First grade was a bad year for me. I was only six, but I learned a lot about life and death that year. I can't pretend it didn't change me, because it did. She made me a picture every day for a month. I still have them somewhere in a folder.

Fast forward to second grade when her cat died. She stayed over at my house and my mom made us hot chocolate. We spent the night watching movies and she cried as I rubbed her back.

Third grade we fought over a boy for two weeks until we realized we liked each other better than we liked him. Fourth grade, a girl named Avery moved to our school and Riley started to hang out with her as well as me. We were rotated.

It was the end of sixth grade when I caught her with her finger down her throat. At first, I didn't understand what I was seeing, but I understood her guilt and fury. Eventually, I understood why she stopped talking to me that summer.

And when seventh grade started, I was the school pariah. I even realized why she felt it was necessary to attack me. I had seen her greatest weakness. I had seen that she was flawed just as much as the rest of us. I knew her biggest secret.

Maybe she thought by belittling and ridiculing me, that if I ever did tell anyone what I saw, no one would believe it. It was such a shame, such a waste. It was also clear she never really knew me, not like a best friend should.

I never would have told. I never have.

When I get back to the house, it is like a mountain has broken into pieces from my shoulders and fallen down my back. In the removal of Riley from me, I am raw, shattered, but I am also lighter.

"Funny thing happened at the store," I tell him, watching his back muscles flex and lengthen as he tosses a football in the air and catches it.

He turns to face me, juggling the ball from hand to hand as he waits.

"I forgot the ice cream."

His eyes drop to my empty hands. "I see that. That's sort of unusual, right? Wasn't that the whole purpose of going to the store?"

I wince. "Yeah. I got distracted."

The sudden stillness of his body strikes me as odd. "By what?"

Frowning, I toss the car keys toward him. He catches them, his stance and expression not changing.

"What do you *think* I got distracted by?" I ask slowly.

Did Riley call him or something? Why would she? What would the point of that be? Unless it was to try to wedge a gap between us. If so, I will have to hunt her down and punch her in her pretty face.

He shrugs. "I don't know."

He turns toward the garage, entering through the side door. The garage door rambles up, showing a tense Rivers. "You want to drive the car into the driveway? I need to wash it."

His tone is curt and he won't look at me, which I don't like, but what sets me off is when he chucks the car keys back at me without even glancing my way.

I let them drop to the pavement and cross my arms. "You have two seconds to tell me what is going on."

He snorts, snapping the band of his white athletic shorts as he walks farther into the garage. Kneeling beside a shelving unit, he grabs cleaning supplies and walks back into the sunlight, raising an eyebrow at me. "Are you going to move the car or do I need to?"

Hot anger scorches my veins and I charge him, wrapping my arms around his waist and taking him down without much effort. I think his surprise worked in my favor.

He grunts upon impact. "Damn it, Bana! What the hell was that for?"

I climb over the top of him and glare down at him with

my palms digging into his warm chest. "You tell me what your attitude is for, right now, or I quit."

Wariness creeps into his eyes, but it doesn't remove the belligerence from his expression. "You wouldn't."

"I so would."

"You need this job. You need the money. What about your Amtrak trip?"

"I'll work for my mom. She pays better anyway."

"She does not."

"Okay, so you're right, but at least I wouldn't have to deal with your grumpy ass."

He scowls up at me. Only when I do not budge nor speak another word, does he sigh, closing his eyes. "Jeff Monroe works there. I thought—I thought maybe you'd seen him and talked to him or something," he mutters.

I sit back, becoming blatantly aware of how my body is straddling his, and digest what I just heard. Part of me wants to laugh, part of me wants to demand what is *wrong* with him, and the other part of me—is smiling.

He opens one eye and closes it again. I push against his chest until he looks at me. "Are you jealous?"

"No," he snaps.

I lean down, bringing my face inches from his. I kiss his frown away. "You just made my day," I tell him.

"Glad my stupidity entertains you." His hands rise up to loosely clasp my waist. "You should have tried out for football. That tackle was lethal."

I grin. "Are we going to wash your car or stay like this all day?"

"I'm okay with us like this. Wait—are you going to wear your swim suit?"

"I could be persuaded."

He practically shoves me off of him. "No time for lying around. We've got a car to wash. I'll get you—I mean, *the car*—sudded up."

A twinkle of mischief enters his eyes as he slowly smirks.

I don't mention my encounter with Riley. It has nothing to do with him, not really, and in the letting go of it, I am happier. We end up just as soapy and wet as the car, but we laugh and joke around as we spend the afternoon out-side.

Again, I am reminded of how the simple things are the best things, and that certain people make the difference between being alone and being lonely—and that Rivers fills me with vitality.

EIGHT

I TOOK A FEW HOURS off in the morning, deciding I needed to dye my hair again since the red was fading out. While at the salon, I did something really crazy and went with what the beautician determined was probably the closest shade to my natural hair color, adding some faint blonde highlights throughout to add contrast.

Monica called just as I was leaving, and although I was glad to talk to her, the news she gave me put a layer of sorrow on my time with Rivers. Thomas' mother passed away—that alone being sad enough news—and they are returning in two days. I realize nothing can ever truly go back to the way it was, nor would I want it to, but once they are back, it cannot continue on as it has either.

I smile when I see his long frame sprawled out, stomach down, on a blanket on the wood deck, the sight of him enough to make all my dreary thoughts dissipate. Rivers loves the sun and the sun loves him back, turning his skin an attractive shade of copper as the days go by.

"Are you going to sleep out here too?"

"It isn't like we haven't before." He looks up from the book in his hands and stares. "What did you do to your hair?"

I am unusually nervous as I finger a layered lock of chocolate brown hair, stopping beside him. "I dyed it back to my natural color. Or as close as the beautician could get it."

He pauses. "I like it."

My face heats up and I swallow. "Thanks."

He rolls onto his back, letting the book fall from his fingers to the blanket he lies on. "You're sort of like a chameleon. You're always changing. Your hair, your clothes, your image. Most people are trying to be like someone else, but you seem to be fighting to be known only as you. But how do you know who you really are, if you're always trying to be different from everyone else?"

"I know who I am."

"Who's that?"

"Me." I wink and sit down beside him. "You should go for a walk with me."

"You should lie down with me."

I freeze. The sun comes from behind him, illuminating him like a fireball halo, which sort of makes sense. He is consuming, no matter what his mood. Light and dark play as the sun and Rivers collide. He grabs my arm and tugs. I land on my back beside him, feeling out of breath and it has nothing to do with my short fall.

He smiles a half-smile, and my body tingles. "Can I ask you something?"

I shrug. "Yeah."

"Did you purposely try to be different because you wanted to put distance between yourself and others? I mean, was it a sort of defense mechanism? Because seeing you now, I don't think that image you portrayed in school ever really fit you. You're too..."

He stops, his eyebrows lowering as he searches for the right word. "I don't know, *free*."

"I didn't realize it wasn't okay to be different. I was how I wanted and needed to be. It was other people that had a problem with it." I turn my face to the sky, not wanting to get into any serious conversations. I am free now, yes. I am free because it is all I can be.

"High school is about conformity. You know that. *Everyone* knows that. Be anything other than everyone else and it's like putting a big bullseye on yourself. Did you do it on purpose?"

I sit back, scooting to put distance between us. "I didn't *do* anything. I was just me. That was me then and this is me now. I'm allowed to change, right? Was it so wrong to be the way I was?"

His words are flustering me and I'm becoming agitated. I don't want to talk about high school or how I was then and how I am now and why there is no correlation between the two.

I changed, but would I have if things were different than they are now?

Rivers sits up as well, watching me. "Did I ask something wrong?"

"No. I just…I don't want to talk about it." I look away from the intensity of his eyes.

"I only asked because I want to know more about you. I find everything about you interesting. You sort of rock my world, in an entirely unapologetic way." He smiles and the sun reflects off his face, blinding me with its beauty.

This is not good. This is not what I want. I look at him and realize that, yes, this *is* what I want, but I shouldn't. I *can't*. He can't. Rivers can't care about me. He'll only get hurt if he does. *Too late*, a voice tells me. I draw my knees up and rest my chin on them, closing my eyes against what is glaringly unavoidable.

I'm scared, I realize. I just wanted to help them. I never intended to care about him and I never wanted him to care about me either.

Jumping to my feet, I careen close to the edge of the pool and Rivers steadies me with his hands on my waist.

"Easy." His touch burns me, making me feels things I have never felt before and know I will never feel again. I want to cry. I think I *am* going to cry. "Look, I'm sorry if I upset you."

I pull away from him, hurrying for the house. It isn't my house, so there is nowhere I can really go to get away from him, from my feelings, from my truths. Everything is building and coming at me once—all I have wanted, all I have caught a glimpse of, all I cannot have. I saw it all in Rivers' smile. Tears blind me as I stumble into the cool interior of the house and toward the bathroom, deciding it's as close to my own space as I am going to get.

I lock the door and sink to the floor with my back against the wall, letting the sobs break free. This is the first time I've cried about it since finding out. Somehow, I managed to keep it all in. I was okay with it. I mean, sure, at first, I was devastated, more for my mom than me, but I was dealing with it. But now there's Rivers and there's even Monica, and how can I keep telling myself I am okay with this?

I am *not* okay with this.

Trembles wrack my body and I hug myself, closing my eyes against the pain. The tightness in my throat grows until it is hard to swallow. I hear Rivers on the other side of the door—I can *feel* him on the other side of the door.

He asks me to open it. I know he can't see me, but I shake my head. He is so different from what I really thought. He is...so...good. He is determined, and yes, arrogant, and beautiful. So beautiful. He is strong-willed and stubborn and imperfect and how can I leave him? He is living again. He is smiling and talking and thinking about his future.

And I have his heart clasped between my two hands. If I let it go, it will fall and break. If I squeeze it too tightly, it will hurt. And if I continue to carry it around, I am responsible for it.

I have to quit. July just started and there is August to think about as well, but I can't keep working here. It's going to suck being without the income, but maybe my mom will hire me on at the flower shop, at least part-time. And that isn't even the biggest problem. The problem is Rivers, and what I feel for him. My original intentions got switched around and altered to the point where I should have refused to stay here in Monica's absence. I should have known it was a bad decision.

I never should have asked her about the job to begin with. But she'd looked so sad, and he'd looked so broken, and I figured...I could do this one thing for someone else before I couldn't do anything again. And now look at me—crying in the bathroom of my employer's house with my employer's son pleading with me to come out and tell him what he did wrong.

He did nothing wrong but care about the ghost of a girl.

With the end of my employment at the Young residence set in my mind, I stand on legs that shake, wipe tears from my eyes, and splash water on my face before opening the door. The red eyes and nose can't be hidden. His scent wraps around me and the stinging comes back to my eyes.

I refuse to look at him as I stride for the front door. "I'm going to go for a walk. I'll finish cleaning when I get back."

"I'll go with you."

I stiffen by the door with my back to him. "No."

"Why? I want to go with you. I can keep up."

I whirl around and glare at him, hateful words I don't mean spewing forth. "No. You can't. You're too slow and you'll only slow me down and I want to be alone."

The openness of his face that I've become accustomed to seeing, closes like a door slammed before my eyes. All expression is wiped from his features, but it stays in his eyes. They're hurt and angry. Pain lashes through me like the burning caress of a whip against my heart.

I want to take my words back, but I don't. I tell myself it's better this way, that he has to get used to being without me, but my convictions sound hollow as I walk out the door.

I walk for hours—the sights, smells, and even the temperature are all vague and without form. I walk in a world of gray, my emotions dark and overcast, obliterating anything that could give life to my surroundings. I walk with the hurried steps of a woman who is trying to outrun something she has no control over, trying to escape something complete in its certainty.

I am angry and not even sure who I am angry at. Is it Monica for putting me in a position to stay at her house and fall in love with her son? Is it Rivers for being lovable? Am I angry at myself for thinking I somehow had the right to meddle in their lives and yet had the audacity to think I could stay distanced from it all? Or is the anger at my mom, though I am not even really sure why? I guess because it just pisses me off that she is going to be shattered once again and I am the one to blame.

The house is dark when I return. As I walk up to the front door, I realize dusk has fallen while I was lost in myself. Even before I am fully inside, I know he isn't here. It is devoid of his light. This knowledge causes an ache inside me. I fumble with my phone, staring at his cell phone number when I get to it, and slowly put it back in my pocket. I pace the length of the sunroom, glancing out at the star-filled night, wondering where he is and if he's okay.

And then I stop.

Coldness seeps into me with the knowledge that I do not belong here. This room—with its fire and life—it isn't mine to stand in. This isn't my life. Rivers isn't mine. I've just been pretending. In two days, Monica and Thomas will be back, and what then? Then I'll fade back into the corners of their lives where I should have stayed to begin with. I need to get out, before Rivers returns. Because I know, when he comes back, I won't be able to fool myself into thinking that he cares so little for me as to just let me walk away.

With fingers that tremble, I call my employer. As soon as she answers, I tell her, "I'm quitting."

It's blunt and harsh, but effective. I can *feel* the shock through the phone.

I inhale deeply. "I'm sorry for not giving more notice."

"But...what...why? Did something happen?"

Did something happen? What *didn't* happen? I can't very well tell her I fell in love with her son and that I know, with absolute certainty, that he will end up getting hurt because of it.

Either way, he gets hurt. If I stay, he gets hurt. If I go, he gets hurt. There really is no way around it. But if I put distance between us now, maybe it will hurt him less later.

I respond evasively, "Nothing happened. I just...my mom needs me at the flower shop."

I wince at the lie. I'll have to make it a truth as soon as I can. The wrongness of what I am doing hits me and I feel nauseous. I'm leaving. The fact that I don't want to makes no difference.

Does what I want *ever* matter?

Not lately, not when it counts. My heart feels torn in two, like I know I will be leaving a part of myself with Rivers when I go.

"Is it because I didn't pay you more for staying? Because I had every intention of doing so when we returned. I didn't mean to take advantage of you. I hope you know that. And... I don't know, I thought maybe you and Rivers—I mean, he just seems so much better..." she trails off, clearly hesitant to voice her thoughts.

"It's not that—about the money, I mean. I don't want your money." Getting paid extra for staying here with Rivers would cheapen how much this whole experience has meant to me.

"You're sure?"

"I'm sure."

"There's nothing I can do to get you to change your mind?" Her voice already tells me she knows I will not budge from my decision. I wish she *could* get me to take back my words.

"Positive," I say around a hard lump in my throat.

The pause is heavy with bereavement. "Rivers is going to miss you. *I'm* going to miss you. I want to say he's back to his normal self because of you, but it's more than that. He's more confident, happier, less serious. He's...he's *better* since you came, and I will never be able to thank you enough for that."

"I didn't do anything." A tear slowly makes its way down my cheek. I clutch the phone tighter to my ear and wipe the pain away.

"I think just being you was enough. You're an exceptional young lady." She pauses. "Is it okay if I stop by your mother's shop when I get back into town? A phone call really isn't a proper goodbye."

I nod, realize she can't see me, and in a broken voice, say, "Yes."

"Thank you. For everything."

The sincerity in her tone causes another teardrop to pool in my eyelashes and when I blink, it falls.

I tell her goodbye and end the call, staring woodenly at my tote bag that I need to repack. If only I could pack up the pieces of my heart as well. I decide to wait until Rivers comes back and then I'll go. I owe him that.

I turn around and there he is, standing just inside the doorway, dark and tragic. An aura of pain surrounds him and I am the reason for it. I try to console myself by thinking that if I stay here, that if I continue to live in the present without thinking of the future, he will only be hurt to a catastrophically larger degree.

"Where were you?"

"Walking," he bites out. "I actually know how to do that."

I deserved that. What I said earlier was cruel. And I didn't mean it.

"I'm sorry," I tell him. "For what I said. I didn't mean it. I shouldn't have said it."

He stares at me, not acknowledging my words as he studies my face. "You're leaving."

"I am."

His expression twists with something. "What did I do wrong?"

"Nothing, Rivers. I swear you didn't do anything wrong. You did—you did everything right," I whisper forlornly.

A sound of disbelief leaves him. "Then why are you going?"

"Because I have to."

"Right. I overheard. Your mom needs you to help out at the shop. Must be some floral emergency, right?" His tone says he doesn't believe that.

I turn my back on him and grab whatever I can find of mine to shove into the bag. Sadly, there isn't much. That done, I face him once more.

"Take care of yourself." It sounds so lame, so lacking.

He stands unmoving. "You're hiding things."

I flinch, my breath whooshing out of me. "What?"

"Everything has been fine. You like being here. *I* like you being here. I know you want to be with me, Del. You feel the same for me as I feel for you. Don't try to act like you don't. And now, suddenly, for no reason, you're leaving. Quitting. What happened? What won't you tell me?"

"Nothing. I just...you and me..." I gesture helplessly.

"Me and you *what*?" he asks flatly.

I can't look at him as I say, "You're all sports and I'm all...whatever I am. You're outgoing. I'm not. We grew up in different worlds. We're just—we're too...different." It's a poor answer, a poor excuse, and it isn't even accurate. We are different, and I think that is why we are so compatible.

"You can't be serious."

My face is on fire in shame as I glance at him and away. The stiffness of his jaw is painful to look at. I put that hard edge there and remorse washes over me at my unintentional role in the wounding of him.

"I have to go."

I move toward him and around him. Just as I pass him, his hand shoots out and grabs my arm, halting me. Those dark eyes that see and reveal so much study me. I never understood that about his eyes. In the dark, aren't we supposed to be unable to see? Yet I see everything in them, everything I could ever want or need. My face must reflect my thoughts because his eyebrows lower, like he doesn't understand me and what I am doing.

That makes two of us.

His voice is a rasp when he states, "Instead of thinking of all the reasons why we can't work, why not think of the reasons why we can?"

"You know what I need? I need some space. I need to think." What I am saying is truthful, but I know that doesn't make it any easier for him to hear. It's the best I can tell him right now.

I think he is going to argue with me, refuse to let me go without a fight, but instead he drops his hand from me and backs away. "You got it."

A blade of thin, but lethal anguish slices open my heart. He's letting me go. *This is what you want.* It is and it isn't. It's easiest, yes, but I retract my recent thought that it is best. What is best for me is in this room with me, the room I am walking out of. He lets me walk away. The wound starts with a trickle of an ache and morphs into a steady flow of agony as I walk from the room, out of the house, and away from the boy I cherish.

THE FIRST TEXT COMES THE following morning.

It reads: *I had a nightmare last night. But it wasn't about me drowning this time. It was you. I was in the water next to you and I still couldn't save you. I feel like I'm drowning all over again.*

I type out: *You were never drowning. You never will. You're too strong.*

But I can't send it. I erase the text message and set my phone aside, ready to begin my new job and my new life minus Rivers. I am unbelievably depressed about this. And sleeping without him last night? It was torture and in no way restful, because, yeah, is there such a thing as restful torture?

No.

I shower, brush and then immediately mess up my hair, put a layer of eye makeup on, and dress in a pink and white striped tank top and a purple flowing skirt that hovers at my knees. I grab a lime green scarf from the full-length mirror and loosely wrap it around my neck before stomping down the stairs to start the day. The scarf makes me think of Rivers, which is equal parts soothing and torment.

My mom gives me a quizzical smile when I grab the coffeepot and pour a large amount into my cup. "I'm glad you're home and going to work with me, but are you?"

"Cleaning rooms is my life," I deadpan. "How could I *not* be glad?"

"You quit pretty abruptly. Did Rivers do something?"

Yes. Rivers did something. He was so stinking appealing to me that I found myself falling for him.

"He didn't do anything wrong," I answer tiredly. "And I don't really want to talk about it, okay?"

She watches me for a moment before nodding. "All right. You want to walk to work together?"

I hear the hopeful note in her voice and my first inclination is to push her away, but she is my mom and she is trying so hard, and pushing her away does nothing now but hurt her. I nod and I smile, a pain shooting through me at the way her face lights up when she smiles back. I just made her day and I feel awful about that.

"Will you be around for dinner?" she asks as we walk out the door, everything about her hesitant as she interacts with me.

I never realized how wary my distance made her. I can see that she is afraid anything she says or does may cause me to flee. I rub my face, forcing a smile as I drop my hands.

"You bet. I'll even cook. What sounds good?"

"Hmm. How about spaghetti and meatballs? We can use some of the canned sauce I made from the garden tomatoes last year. Oh, and how about using spaghetti squash for the noodles? Maybe some garlic bread to go with it."

"It wouldn't be a meal without garlic bread."

She laughs. "Exactly. I think we should make some lemon bars.

I've been craving them for *weeks*."

"That all sounds great."

"It does, doesn't it?" She beams at me, lacing her arm through mine as we walk the mile or so it takes to get to her shop.

I return her smile, forcing a lightness to it I do not feel. Seeing how happy my mom is devastates me. Within the cocoon of her joy, I am struggling. I want to mean the smiles I aim her way, I want to laugh with her—to imprint myself upon her mind and heart so deeply there is no chance of her ever forgetting one single detail about me, even though I doubt that is really even a possibility.

You have to tell her.

I promise myself I will, but I cannot promise when.

We get to the flower shop and my mom immediately goes inside to start on her flower orders. I stand outside the small white building, taking it in. There's a large picture window with pink cursive writing that reads 'Flower Appeal' and the surrounding vicinity is bursting with blossoms in vibrant shades of oranges, yellows, and pinks. It's like looking at a sunset in the form of flowers.

I grab the broom from inside the door and sweep the walkway, the sun already attacking me with its hot rays. There is peace in solitude, and there is quiet. And you know what? There is a lot less drama to deal with when the only person you see and talk to is *you*. There was a handful of people I hung around in school, but if

I didn't want to do something with them, I didn't.

They were like a security blanket—a permanent fixture I could rely on to be there. We went to an occasional party together, maybe a movie, bowling. I didn't share secrets with any of them and I never had any inclination to show them who I really was. Just a glance into me was all I allowed and that was all I wanted of them in return.

So began the life of Delilah Bana—the high school years. I guess, in a way, I have Riley to thank. She destroyed me, but she also made me stronger. She made me see that friends are impermanent, but how I choose to be, and how I act, and how it affects who I am, is not.

I experimented with piercings, hair colors, and clothing. I didn't think being different should have made me odd, but I guess I was wrong. The weight of other people's judgment is heavy if you decide to let it be. And you do have that choice. You can care about you, or you can care about everyone else.

I am more important than any label given to me by others who never really knew me.

When school let out, I didn't contact any of the "friends" I'd had throughout my high school years, and it didn't bother me at all. Summer started and I shed the cape that categorized me as one way, and focused on being any way I chose to be. I guess Rivers is right—I sort of am a chameleon. I think we all are. Circumstances in and out of our control are constantly forming us and reforming us. Does it ever end? No. Not until we pass from this life and into whatever lies in wait beyond.

But this, this void where Rivers used to be, is bothering me.

A lot. So now I am thinking maybe it wasn't that I was socially inept or that I would rather be alone than with others, but that there just wasn't anyone I really wanted to be around. I miss him like I think I would miss the sun if it stopped burning in the sky. In fact, he is like the sun to me; glowing, bright, consuming, transcendental.

I set the broom against the side of the building and lift my face to the glowing fireball, inhaling deeply of the summer air, letting the warmth of it wash over my face like a kiss from the sky. I smile, knowing this time apart from Rivers will be short, knowing I have already figured out what I needed. There wasn't anything to figure out, really.

I can't push him away.

I can't live my days knowing he is close to me and yet unavailable because I made it so. I suppose these little hitches of weakness are normal, and still, I wish I could forever remove them from my thoughts. I want to be strong, and being strong means, I can't be scared—or if I am scared, I have to breathe around it and remain centered.

There is a hole inside me. The longer I ignore Rivers, the bigger it grows. I don't want that. Even minutes are adding to the depth of it, widening it. I want to be whole. I can't be unless we are okay. I grab my tote from the pavement and find my phone, my fingers flying over the letters on the mini keyboard.

Me: *I had a dream last night too. You were swimming in the ocean, the blues and greens of the sea like a watery blanket around you. You were alone, but you were okay. You knew the water was all you really needed. You were smiling.*

The responding text shows up immediately: *I was smiling because I knew you were standing on the beach waiting for me.*

I laugh, feeling the prickling of tears in my eyes. I text back: *You were smiling because you were thinking of peanut butter and ice cream and trains.*

His response: *That sounds like you.*

My reply: *You're right. When did you get to be awes me enough to start thinking like me?*

Rivers sends back: *Is that what you're calling it?*

Another text shows up: *I want to see you. Now.*

I want to see him too, but I feel like I should spend time with my mother as well. I just got home and I can't take off already. Plus, I have to work. And I really should be going inside to do exactly that.

I hesitate, then type: *Not yet.*

The answer is fast and one word: *Now.*

I scowl at the phone and quickly text: *No. Working. Need time with Mom. Two days.*

I can feel his incredulity through the phone screen: *Two more days?!?!?!?!?*

I smile. *You'll be okay.*

Rivers: *I will NOT be okay. Just so you know.*

Me: *I know.*

His reply: *Sigh.*

I burst out laughing, pressing the phone to my forehead and closing my eyes. Warmth washes over me, and contentment with it. I send a smiley face back and head inside to do some heavy-duty cleaning.

Today will be a good day, I decide. It feels strange to not be at his house; even sleeping in my own bed didn't feel right. Without his presence I am dimmer than usual, but the atmosphere of the shop is light. Carefree. My mom steps with gaiety I don't recall seeing before, talking to me often, smiling just as frequently. I relax and enjoy what is before me.

I FEEL THE SOFTNESS OF the blanket between my fingers, wanting to wrap it around me and use it as a shield. There were days at the beginning of summer when I fought to get out of bed. There were days where I struggled to do the simplest of things. It all seemed so pointless.

Why pretend everything is okay when it isn't, when I am merely waiting for the imminence that is to befall me? None of those bad days compare to this ache inside me now. It doesn't seem possible that this separation from Rivers should have the capability to block out my darkest days, and yet it does. I don't know if I can stand another day of this, even if I am the one who requested it.

A knock at the bedroom door announces a visitor. I sit up and call out a greeting, bringing my knees to my chin as my mom enters carrying two mugs.

"Yours is hot chocolate," she tells me with a soft smile.

I accept it, murmuring a thank you.

Her movements are hesitant as she sits on the edge of the bed. "As much as I love your company at home and at work, I don't like to see you hurting. I know you said you don't want to talk about it, but I can see that Rivers cares about you a great deal and that you reciprocate his feelings. Maybe you need to go back. Whatever happened between you, you two can talk and work through it."

I blink, surprised by her words, tenderness washing over me that she would sacrifice her happiness for mine. A layer of the sadness falls away and I smile. "I love you, Mom."

It is her turn to blink. She nervously tugs on her blonde ponytail, looking flustered. I don't blame her. I can't re- member the last time I told her I loved her or called her mom.

Looking down, she finally says quietly, "Thank you. I love you too. So much."

I set the untouched hot cocoa on the nightstand and scoot across the bed to her, feeling her warmth, smelling the herbal-flower scent of her skin, and being at peace in her nearness. Wrapping my arm around her shoulders, I press my head to hers and lock my fingers around hers as they clutch the cup between her hands. Her knuckles are white and there is a slight tremble to her body. A sniffle escapes her and I tighten my hold on her.

"I was a brat," I announce.

She laughs, but there is a catch to it. "You were a child."

She knows exactly what I am talking about. It's the conversation we've avoided for years, for far too long. It is time that it was spoken.

"Part of me was guilty that I wasn't there. Even though I was younger and I wouldn't have been able to save him, I thought if I'd *just been there,* he wouldn't have died. That guilt ate me up, made me distance myself. I am sorry. I'm sorry for pulling away when you needed me."

A warm teardrop falls from her eye and onto my hand. Her pain seeps into my skin, becoming a part of me. "You have nothing to apologize for. You were only six, Delilah, and no matter how old you were or weren't, or whether you had been there or not, there was nothing you could have done. It was just Neil's time."

"Is that what you truly think?" I whisper. "That we all have our time to die, and when it comes, everyone should accept it?"

"Accept it? No. Learn to live around the pain, yes. Try to forgive instead of blame? Yes." She leans away to better look at me, her blue eyes lingering on mine. "Every time I look into your pretty eyes, I see Neil. I never understood how the two of you got the same-colored eyes when you didn't have the same father."

"Must be from some awesome part-cat ancestor of yours. What happened to Neil's father?" I ask, something I have always wondered and never had the courage to question.

My mom takes a moment to steady herself by getting up and placing her mug next to mine on the nightstand. She touches the shimmery cream and white floor-length curtains, pushing one back and allowing sunlight in to silhouette her.

Keeping her back to me, she says, "We were high school sweethearts, got married right after graduation, and had no idea what we were getting into or what we were doing. The stress of money and not having enough of it wore us down. We began to fight all the time. We grew apart, realizing we both wanted and needed different things. Our love turned into something ugly, and we came to an agreement that we couldn't keep doing what we were doing to each other. We divorced when Neil was just a baby."

The beating of my heart picks up. "And then?" I prompt.

She glances at me. "And then I made a bad decision that

turned into the second-best thing that ever happened to me."

"The first being?" I tease.

It was Neil. Of course, it was Neil. That boy was adventure and laughter and bullheaded- ness all rolled into one. I miss him still; I miss him always. There is a hole in my childhood that is devoted to the place where he was, and where I wish he could have continued to be.

My mother smiles. "Do you remember Greg Morgan? His father? He picked Neil up every other weekend and on holidays."

"Sort of." I have a vague image of wavy brown hair and eyes in my head for Neil's father. "Why didn't you keep his last name after the divorce?"

"Neil had his father's last name, but you had no one's. I went back to my maiden name for you."

"And you never saw him again, after Neil died?"

Pain, old but no less powerful, flickers over her features and recedes back into her. "Once. I saw him about six years ago. He looked…he looked so sad when he saw me that I just turned away and walked out of the store without even getting what I went there for."

"Does he still live around here?"

"I don't know. I don't know anything about him anymore. Which is probably best," she adds.

"Why is that best?"

Turning away, she begins to pick up my clothes. I protest, but the look she gives me silences me. I guess she needs to keep busy as she talks, and I don't really mind her putting my clothes away. We both know I never will. "Because too much time has passed, too much pain, too much of everything. Sometimes it's good to leave the past in the past."

"Sometimes that's impossible," I mutter.

She pauses, and then folds a pile of shirts. "You're right. You can't escape the past, but you can move on from it. You've done that this summer too. I've noticed. You're more like you used to be, before you turned into a typical teen—happier."

"Happier," I quietly muse. "Yep."

And sadder. Funny how you can't seem to have one without the other.

"Are you going to talk to him? If you ask me, I think you should. He's such a sweet boy. Nothing like what you made him out to be. Who knows, maybe he's the one." She smiles and winks, putting my folded clothes away.

He is the one. The one and only. Even if he wasn't the only one, he'd still be *the* one.

"What did he do to make you so mad anyway?"

I look up at my mom, my eyebrows lowering as I contemplate her question. She waits expectantly, something changing in her expression the longer she waits. And then she exhales slowly and slumps against the dresser. Her mouth opens and closes.

She gives me a helpless look, wordlessly saying she knows. She knows, she wants to help, and there is no way to. Funny how one look at my face can tell her all she needs to know about how I feel about Rivers.

"He didn't do anything," I say when it is apparent she is struggling for words. "He didn't do anything but make it impossible not to love him."

She nods, a touch of sadness in her eyes. Even though she doesn't know the circumstances, she understands how painful it can be to love someone. "You're scared?"

I flop to my back once more, closing my eyes. "Terrified."

"Loving someone is scary, but it's also wonderful."

"I'm scared it can't last," I whisper.

I *know* it can't last.

My mom lies down beside me and strokes my hair. "You know the saying that nothing can last forever? It's partly true. Feelings can stop, people can leave us, but regardless, a piece of them is always with us, in some way. Maybe it's in a song, or a forgotten note, a picture. Even when you no longer love someone or can't be with them, you still remember them, you still remember good parts of them, and you smile.

"Why worry about it lasting or not? Even if it doesn't, you'll still have a part of him. And he'll still have a part of you. And isn't that what's really important? Holding the best pieces of someone in our hearts so that the love never really fades, so that we don't forget that we once knew them, and they were special to us."

My throat tightens. She said exactly what I needed to hear. "Thank you."

"You're welcome. I need help in the garden. Quit moping and get your butt out into the sunshine. Don't forget your sunscreen," she adds as she gets up from the bed. "And call him before he decides to camp out in our front yard."

I get to my feet. "I will. I promise. I'll be right out."

Alone once more in the room, I turn in a slow circle, not seeing what is before me, but what resides in the form of memories. A sleepover with Riley, reading books with Neil, my mom sitting on the bed behind me as she brushed and braided my hair. This room is full of nostalgia. I wonder what it will hold for my mother in months to come. I rub my eyes and sniffle, closing my eyes against my thoughts. An ache forms in my chest and I swallow, wanting it, and what is causing it, to go away. I head into the upstairs bathroom, layer myself in sun protection, and go about helping my mother in the garden.

I tell her about college and she goes still, looking stunned. Then she nods, not saying anything, though the smile on her lips says everything anyway. I pull weeds out on one end of the garden as she tackles the other. The plants rub against my legs, making them red and itchy, but I don't mind.

I go on to tell her about the Brewers game Rivers told me I was going to and she laughs, asking if I know they play baseball. I scowl over that, but it doesn't last long before I am laughing with her. The sun heats my back, dampening my hair and clothing. The bucket fills up with green beans, another with red and yellow tomatoes.

When the garden is weeded and the ripened fruits and vegetables picked, we sit on the outside furniture of the backyard, sipping lemonade and eating chocolate chip cookies. I am exhausted, but in a good way. Sometimes all it takes is some physical work to quiet the chaos of the mind. Birds flitter through the sky overhead, chirping as they go. I watch them dance from limb to limb of the trees in the distance, their innocence and grace causing a smile to swell my chest.

"Where are you going to go to school?"

I push my sunglasses up my nose. "I don't know. Probably the tech school in Fennimore to start. The other day I checked out the classes they offer."

I may have agreed to college, but I am keeping my expectations low.

"For?"

I smile. "Cooking. I wanted a fun class and that's what I decided on. Culinary Art."

"That sounds like a good time. And Rivers?"

"He's okay with it. He gets perks to my scholarly choice. Like...food."

She bumps her shoulder to mine. "What's he taking for classes?"

I mumble, "Business management."

"You don't sound happy about that."

I straighten in my seat, turning to look at my mother as I say in earnest, "Isn't life about following your dreams? Even if they are impossible, you still strive to reach them, right?"

She slowly nods. "Yes. I think so."

I slump back in my seat, picking at a loose thread in the hem of my shirt. "That isn't his dream. He doesn't belong in some stuffy office. He needs to be outside, or at least surrounded by it. And I can't see him running some business, directing people. That isn't him. He needs freedom."

My mouth twists as I tell her, "He's settling."

"What about you? I know you like to cook, but that isn't really what you want to do for the rest of your life, is it? You always wanted to design things, decorate."

Lowering my head, I am thankful for the sunglasses. They hide the pain in my eyes. "I'm not settling. I wasn't even going to go to college."

"I never understood why you made that decision. You're so bright, so creative."

I don't respond.

She finally says, "Maybe this is his starting point. We all have to start somewhere. It's possible he'll change his mind, or go on to some- thing else that fits him better. It's okay to want more for others, Delilah, but you also have to be supportive if they decide they don't want more, not now, and maybe not ever."

I nod, resting my head against the top of the chair. "I should have listened to you sooner. You have amazing advice."

She smiles, reaching over to pat my leg. "That's the thing about kids and parents. Kids don't listen when they should and parents have to realize that and repeat all the words of wisdom once they grow up. It's a tough job and that's why adults do it and not kids."

"Interesting theory."

She pauses. "I'm not sure if that made sense. I had a glass of homemade blueberry wine earlier at Alice's. I brought her over a flower and she wouldn't leave until I had a full glass of it."

I laugh. "It made enough sense."

"Good." She hesitates, and then smiles. "Want to get ice cream at the Ice Cream Shoppe?"

I'm getting to my feet before she is finished talking. "You don't even need to ask."

As we walk, I tell her, "Rivers tried to lure me over to his house today with ice cream."

She laughs, swiping hair behind her ear. "What flavor?"

I swing my arms as I think. "He had a variety. Chocolate chip, strawberry, and butter pecan."

"Why didn't you go?"

"The selection wasn't that great." At her look, I shrug. "I wasn't ready yet. Tomorrow I will be."

"Tomorrow, huh? You have your bravery set to return on a certain day, do you?"

"No. That's just when I told him I would see him again."

"You're still scared after our talk?"

I stop walking, watching the cars and trucks as they move down the street, the sun reflecting off their windows. "I don't think I'll ever *not* be scared. I'll just, you know, work around it. That's what you do, right?"

She puts her arm around my shoulders and touches her head to mine. "That's what you do."

NINE

THE ACIDIC CITRUS FUMES ARE getting to me, causing a pounding behind my temples. I'm hoping it'll stay a dull ache and not turn into something worse. I've spent the last three hours making the small shop as squeaky clean as I possibly can, putting all of my frustration and feeling of ineptitude into the washing of the walls and mopping of the floors.

'I Want You Here' by Plumb really isn't helping me in my quest to ignore reality. I know I need to be fearless. I want to be. I have to remember how to be, from day to day. And Rivers—Rivers makes me fearless. I need his physical presence to remind me that I am not sinking; I am standing.

No, I am *flying*.

I have to use this body, mind, and heart to their maximum potential while I still have the capability. I need to *feel*, not just emotionally but physically as well. And what I want, what I need, what I covet, what I love, is Rivers. I realize caring for someone is painful, I realize opening up to him in all ways will eventually hurt to an unbelievable degree. I know I need to stop being scared of what I feel and just...*feel* it.

I also know he is looking at me right now like his whole existence rests upon my next course of action.

"Hey." He nods, moving just inside the doorway.

I caught a hint of fear, desperation, and hope in that three-lettered word.

His black hair is longer, covering up the scar above his temple. The wounds have faded from pink to a pale tan. If he wanted, he could have his old life back, or some variation of it. Looking at him sends my pulse into a crazy rhythm only my heart can understand. Being so close to him and not touching him is excruciating to me.

I didn't realize how much I truly missed him until he is once again standing before me. I can smell his clean scent; I can feel his eyes devouring me as he tries to replace the recent loss of me by sight alone. My eyes, in turn, rove over him like it is the first time they have been acquainted with beauty.

I set the rag and cleaning solution on the white porcelain of the sink. "Hey."

"Your mom told me you were back here."

"Figured that." When he doesn't reply, I shift my feet and tell him, "I was going to call you. Today, actually."

That was the plan once my shift is done. I was going to go home and call him, or possibly be brave enough to go to his house after work. I hadn't decided which yet, but it doesn't matter now, because here he is.

"I enjoyed your text this morning immensely." He pauses. "'My mom always told me to find something to believe in, so I decided not to like feta cheese. I protest that shit like you wouldn't believe.' Catchy."

I shrug. "Your reply was better. 'I don't like feta cheese, but goat cheese is okay.' *That* should be on a shirt."

A grin teases his lips, but is erased as soon as his eyes lock with mine. "It's been three days."

I lower my gaze, because when I look into his eyes, I see so much, more than I ever thought I'd see in them for me, and it makes me want to cry. I wipe at a speck of dirt on my pink tank top. When it refuses to disappear, I tighten the rubber band around my hair so I have something to do with my fingers. He just keeps watching me, silent and still, and it gets to be too much.

Finally unable to take the quiet any longer, I ask, "Three days since what?"

Three days since I quit, three days since I walked away,

three days since I've felt the way only Rivers can make me feel.

"Since I've had you next to me while I sleep. I miss it. I miss you."

I don't answer. Each night I struggle to sleep, needing his arms and finding only emptiness to hold me during the long hours of nothing and everything. It feels like I am alone in an unending world of disquiet without him. I wonder if this is what death feels likes—this limbo state of black consciousness that you can never awaken from.

"I want to wake up next to you in the morning."

My eyes fill. "I don't think your mother would have the same view on that."

He gives me a half-smile and his eyes light up. "Okay, then I want to wake up every morning knowing I'll see you."

The pain is fast, intense. I rapidly blink my eyes, but it does no good. The tears fall anyway. I avert my face and Rivers quickly tugs me to him, his hands resting on my hips as he stares down at me. We're in this silent showdown as our eyes memorize the features of the face before us.

"Whatever I did to push you away, you have to forgive me—I need you to. I... I can't lose you." He swallows. "I mean, I guess I don't really have you, but I feel like I do. I feel like when you smile at me...my whole body feels it. I've never felt so much so soon for *anyone*. I don't want to lose this feeling. You woke my soul up and the rest of me followed."

"You did absolutely nothing wrong," I tell him in a voice that shakes, his words filling me with emotions too great to try to decipher. I woke up his soul. I *woke up*...his *soul*. Those words are so very precious to me. I mentally wrap my heart around them to keep them near me always.

"Then why did you quit? Why did you avoid me? Why are you *still* avoiding me?"

"I needed some time...to think." The words I speak are true, but it was more than that. I needed to sort it all out, stop feeling sorry for myself, and be thankful for what I get. I tripped and stumbled off the course of my path and now I am back on it.

"And now?"

I meet his eyes. "And now I know what I have to do."

Wariness creeps into his expression. "What's that?"

"Let you wake up knowing you get to see me."

Rivers' fingers slide into my hair, causing the rubber band to fall out. He grips my face and lowers his lips to mine.

His voice is low and full of fervor when he whispers, "I don't know how I missed you all those years. You were there, *right there*, and I never saw you in the way you deserved to be."

"But you do now."

"I do now."

"That's enough," I tell him.

He presses a kiss to my forehead, moving his hands down my arms to my sides. "Don't do that again."

"I won't," I promise, wondering if at some point he and I will both regret these words.

There may come a time, when it will be best to place as much distance between us as possible, for both of our benefits. What will we do then?

"Better not. I don't expect you to come back to work, but I can't go without seeing you. Deal?"

"Deal. I'm sorry I left like I did. I shouldn't have. It was stupid, cowardly."

I blink my eyes against tears. "I didn't want to go."

His fingers tighten around my waist. "Then why did you?"

"I'm scared," I admit. "I'm scared about how I feel about you and what it means."

Rivers moves away and turns his back to me. "You don't think I'm scared? Every day with you scares the piss out me, but every day without you was ten times worse. And yes, what I feel for you—it *terrifies* me. But the alternative is incomprehensible."

He faces me again. "You and me..." He shrugs. "We work."

I grin. "We do, don't we?"

"We really do."

"Who'd your mom get for a replacement?"

Rivers groans, briefly closing his eyes. "A seventy-year-old hag."

"Rivers!"

"She is like the housekeeper from hell, I'm telling you."

I cross my arms. "Really? Why is that?"

"First of all, she isn't *you*." He takes a step toward me.

"Yes, well, sacrifices and all that." I look to the ceiling, hiding a smile.

"And she smells like men's aftershave." He shudders.

"Hmm."

"She won't buy ice cream because it's *fattening*. Trust me, even my mom is having a problem with that one. My mom asked her to pick some up yesterday and she refused. It was kind of funny. The look on my mom's face was anyway, and the fact that she was serious."

"What's her name?"

"Meg. I call her Meg-Hag."

"Charming," I murmur.

He takes another step closer. "She gets a fifteen-minute break every hour and she smokes like a chimney in front of my bedroom windows, so the smell comes inside if the windows are open. She doesn't get the rooms shiny like you do. She should be fired for that alone. She hums *all day long*. Even Thomas is afraid of her.

"The other day he didn't take his shoes off at the door and she yelled at him because she'd just cleaned the floors and he was dirtying them up already. And she doesn't sleep with me at night"" He pauses, tilting his head. "Although, that one I'm okay with."

My face hurts from smiling so hard, but I can't remove the joy from my being.

"She sounds perfect." I grab the front of his shirt and pull him to me.

"She really doesn't," he disagrees, inhaling sharply when I pull the collar of his tee shirt down to kiss the smooth skin beneath.

My lips linger against the warmth of him as my eyelids slide shut and I inhale his scent I have ached for. His nose nudges my cheek and I lift my face, his mouth immediately attaching to mine, bridging them, connecting us. I am awash in heat and love, desire and tenderness.

"You smell like bleach," he whispers close to my ear.

"I wore it especially for you." I smile and feel his smile on my lips before they meet again.

"I FEEL WEIRD PUTTING A name to what we have. I mean, it doesn't feel right—labeling us."

I look up from the flower arrangement I've been studying. I lost track of time letting the frail perfection of them sink in. The softness of the pink petals makes me think of raspberries.

I place my chin in my hand and focus on Rivers. He's wearing a tee shirt the color of the ocean and khaki shorts. Warmth waves through me in gentle strokes of love.

"I agree. No labels."

Frustration takes over his features. "Then what am I supposed to call you?" He nods at Nancy, my mom's full-time assistant, as she sweeps by, immediately turning back to me.

"Del, Delilah, Bana, girl not related to Eric Bana, sexy lady, hey you...It isn't enough." He moves to the counter I'm sitting behind, tapping the fingers of one hand against the top of it.

"You can't just be some girl I know."

"You have no idea how glad I am to just be some girl you know," I tell him thickly.

His expression clears as he looks at me, leaning forward to bring his lips to mine.

"You're *my* girl," he whispers against my mouth.

His words wrap around me like a warm hug and I close my

eyes to better feel the enormity of them.

"What are you thinking?"

I open my eyes to find his directly before me. There are flecks of pale brown and gold within them, even a hint of olive green. "That being your girl is all I want to be. That this —that *we*—are impossible, and yet, we make sense."

Half of his mouth lifts and he nuzzles my neck. "We're almost like peanut butter and bacon on toast, right?"

I perk up. "Did you make one?"

A slow smile takes over my mouth when he won't meet my eyes.

"You did, didn't you? Did you like it? You *loved* it. I can tell. Don't deny it. I see through your lies."

"I only made it to feel closer to you."

I laugh. "I suppose you only ate it to feel even closer to me, right?"

He scowls, but a hint of a grin flirts across his lips. "Are you ready to do this?"

I hop down from the stool. "You bet. I'll make sure Mom is ready to go and meet you outside. Where's your mom?"

"She dropped me off to run an errand. She'll be back any minute. I'll wait outside."

I call for my mom as I walk through the cool interior of the shop, finding her in the small room she calls her office. I thoroughly dislike this room. There is no window and it is cramped to the point of being claustrophobic.

There's just enough room for her desk, two chairs, and a wall of shelving.

I tried to brighten it up when I was ten, drawing hundreds of pictures of different colored flowers for her to hang on the walls. They're still here, faded and wrinkled, turning the walls into a fortress of cartoonish blossoms.

She closes a book and gets to her feet, smiling as she meets me at the door. "All set?"

"Yeah. Nancy is closing up now. Rivers is here. Monica went somewhere and will be back shortly."

She nervously tugs at her dirt-smudged shirt. "I wish I could have changed first. I felt so dingy compared to her the other day when she stopped."

"That's because you were *working* and she was not. She doesn't work. She can do whatever she wants to do and she never gets dirty."

"She seemed sad," she comments.

I bite my lip so I don't tell her it might be because Thomas decided to go back to stay in California indefinitely. Rivers told me in a text last night. It sounds like they are separating. I don't know the full details of their marriage, but I saw a version of what I wouldn't think a happy marriage should be, even though my time with them was short.

Rivers sounded confused, like he didn't know if he should be happy or sad about it. I told him it was okay to be both and he told me to quit shoving my intellect in his face. Then he said he ate all the ice cream so I needed to bring more over. I said I was on to him and he replied that he wished I was on him. I smile as I remember.

"It's because her son keeps eating all of her ice cream."

My mom rolls her eyes. "Come on. Let's not keep them waiting. She seems nice," she adds.

"She is. You'll like her."

Monica kept her promise, coming to talk to me almost as soon as she got back into town. At first, she just looked at me, and then she pulled me into her arms, thanking me, begging me to come back for Rivers, and finally getting herself under enough control to apologize. And then she asked again if I'd come back. I said no.

She offered extra money for my time at her house while she was out of town. I *vehemently* said no. And then she hugged me again, telling me she was so glad we started a conversation that day at the store, and then told me she wanted the four of us to have dinner. I agreed, inviting them to our house for lasagna.

So here we are.

My fondness for Monica grows as I take in her casual outfit of jean shorts and a plain white top. She made sure to dress down so my mom didn't feel out of place in her presence. Or maybe she is just sick of wearing pristinely pressed outfits. I know I would be.

She smiles as our eyes meet, immediately turning to my mom. "Hello. We didn't get a chance to talk the other day. I'm Monica, Rivers' mom, and Delilah's former employer."

The smile my mom bestows upon her is genuine. "Hi. I'm Janet, Delilah's mom, and current employer."

They both laugh and Rivers and I share a look.

"We walked to work today so we don't have a vehicle here. Do you guys want to walk over or take your car?" I ask when the silence draws out.

"Oh, um..." Monica looks at Rivers.

"Rivers has walked farther," I tell her, wanting to make sure any feelings of pity are wiped out before they can begin. Rivers is not the same young man he was when she left for California.

She frowns, but it quickly clears as she searches my stoic features. She nods. "Good. Okay."

My mom takes the lead, Monica quickly falling into step with her; their conversation is at first stilted, but becomes steadier the longer they talk.

Rivers hangs back, snatching my hand up and bringing it to his mouth to place a kiss upon it. He threads his fingers through mine, holding our clasped hands close to him.

"Thank you," he says quietly.

"There's nothing to thank me for."

"There is. There's so much." He inhales deeply, opening his mouth and closing it. After a moment, he shakes his head and begins to move.

My feet fall into step with his as I place a hand on his forearm. When he looks at me, I ask, "What is it?"

He looks torn, unsure of whether or not he should tell me his thoughts. His eyes meet mine and he seems to draw strength from that. With a deep sigh, he tells me in a low voice, "I lost something that day on the river. It isn't something I can get back; it isn't something I *want* to get back. At first, I thought I did, but then I realized losing it was a good thing.

"Do you know what I thought all throughout high school? I thought I was better than everyone. I really did. The conceit of always winning took its dark toll on me. I thought, everyone wants to be like me. I am king of this school and I deserve to be, because I'm good at sports and people like me. People acted like I was something special, and after a while, I believed I was."

He swallows, looking straight ahead. "And then the life I knew was gone. Just like that. I looked in the mirror and saw a scarred person who could barely walk. It was all taken away —everything I had ever had or thought I wanted. Gone. I hated myself, but what I hated more was that I used to think I wasn't anything unless I was something—just like Thomas always told me. Then I was nothing.

"And when I was nothing, I finally *was* better—not better than anyone else, but just...better. Better than I used to be. I lost my old life that day, but I also lost my arrogance. I had to hit the bottom to realize the ground was hard." He grins sardonically.

I smile back, warmed by his words, by his sudden outlook on life and himself. I don't respond; I just take his hand and continue walking. There is a warm breeze to alleviate the glare of the hot sun and I inhale aromas of grilling food and freshly mowed lawns. The scents of summer are some of the best ones.

I watch the people around us in their yards, their cars, their world. "Do you ever think about all the people you see on a daily basis?"

Monica and Janet glance back at us, smiling before facing forward again.

Rivers' grip on my hand tightens. "Yeah. Right now, I'm

thinking about the people ahead of us and I'm wondering what they're saying about us."

"I'm sure only great things."

He glances at me, the scowl disappearing as he takes in my grin. "Well, about me anyway."

"Look at that lady over there." I nod to a woman standing in a yard across the street. She is watching a little boy play catch with a large, fluffy brown dog. "What do you think her life is like? What do you think she is thinking? What's her story?"

"She's laughing," he murmurs. "She's happy. She's wondering how anything could be more amazing than this moment right now."

"I think...she is a stay-at-home mom. Maybe she is active in the community. She looks like a baker. I can see her making cakes, baking cookies. And she likes to decorate them too. She probably gets up in the morning with a smile on her face, knowing she gets to spend the day with her son."

"She takes her son in the stroller as she walks the dog."

I smile. "She loves the sun and muffins."

"She loves her husband."

I nod, wrapped up in our imaginary story. "He's an accountant. The youngest at the firm. He's smart and he's going places, but he loves his wife and son more than any job. He kisses her goodbye and he kisses her hello, thinking he is the luckiest man in the world."

Rivers stares at me, saying softly, "He flies planes. Because he wants to fly and she loves the stars. He flies planes so he can touch them for her, so he can be her personal Superman."

The story shifted, becomes a make-believe tale of Rivers and Delilah; a story of what could be, if that future day is ever to come.

I blink my eyes as tears form, whispering, "She paints every room in the house a different color of the rainbow. He doesn't like it, but he knows she loves it, so he really doesn't mind all that much. Every Friday night, he brings home cheesy movies that he says are scary and makes her watch them, and she does, because when he is happy, she is happy."

He smiles slowly, glancing at me as we cross the street. "He stocks up on peanut butter so there's never a chance she'll run out. He makes her try every sport, just once, and if she doesn't like playing them, he doesn't press her, but she has to at least try them."

"She picks out a random person in the crowd and they form a life around that person. She can tell he thinks it's silly, but he humors her anyway."

"He wakes up beside her every morning, and every morning he is hit with the enormity of how blessed he is. He is thankful for every day he has with her, and all the days in the world will never be enough."

Our steps slow as my house comes into view. My mom and Rivers' mom are already on the porch, quietly watching us, something like delight in each of their faces.

He turns to me, in the middle of the road, and clutches my hands. The smile on his face is beatific, striking, and makes me want to weep.

"Do you know how you make me feel?"

"Slightly insane?" I tease.

"Yes," he answers seriously. "But in the best way. In fact, I feel like doing something really crazy right now."

A flutter of conflicting emotions sweeps through me. Rivers, being spontaneous—it's a little worrisome.

"Please don't."

"I have to," he insists.

"You really don't," I reassure him.

Apparently, he does.

Grinning at me, Rivers spins me around, singing the opening verses of 'It's Time' by Imagine Dragons. We turn in a circle so fast and for so long, I get dizzy, laughter falling from my lips in a waterfall of joy.

He releases me and I stumble to a stop as he steps back, directly into the path of traffic, if any were around, and slides back and forth across the pavement as he continues the song. I imagine the elderly folk in surrounding houses are peeking around their window curtains right about now.

Rivers stops only to ask my mom, "Is this your car?" and when she says yes, he uses it as a prop, causing me to giggle when he slides over the hood and lands on his feet before me.

Air catches in my lungs at that move. He looks at me, grinning so widely I want to grab his cheeks and kiss his smile. But my mom and Monica are watching.

Then I think, *So what?*

And I do exactly that.

When I pull away and see tears in my mom's eyes and that Monica's eyes are suspiciously red, I mutter to Rivers, "I feel like we just exchanged wedding vows or something."

"If we hold hands for too long, they'll probably think we're expecting."

Nodding my agreement, I approach the house. "Come on, the lasagna isn't going to cook itself."

As the four of us sit around the mismatched furniture of our kitchen, I feel serenity with the present, and the slowly growing touch of an inescapable void just beyond us. There is light here, but surrounding us is darkness. We laugh, but there is sorrow nearby. I feel it. It's getting closer.

I am knitting the future together in broken pieces of yarn, tying together loose ends to make a blanket of security for the three people talking with me. I will keep them safe. I will protect them. I will give them each other when I can no longer give them me.

"I know it's probably going to embarrass the two of you, but—" Monica begins.

"But you're going to say it anyway," Rivers guesses.

She hands a breadstick to her son. "You're right. I am. And do you know why? Because it's amazing." She looks from me to Rivers. "Clearly the counseling and physical therapy—"

This time I interrupt. "Have been beyond beneficial. Right, Rivers?"

He frowns at me. "No. Not really. The whole world knows that isn't it, Delilah. It was you."

My face burns as three pairs of eyes focus on me. "It was unconscious, I swear."

"Why don't you want to take credit for a good thing?" my mom quietly asks.

"I don't like attention," I mumble.

Rivers' laughter is incredulous. "You do nothing but draw attention to yourself."

"It isn't like I set out to, or that that is why I act the way I do. I just...I want to live as much as I can. If people are around when I happen to get impulsive, I can't exactly tell them to go away. I can't be like, clear out the grocery store! I feel the impulse to dance."

"I would."

I throw a chunk of a breadstick at him.

What is it with you and throwing things at me?" He pops the bread into his mouth and chews.

"Well, I, for one, am grateful, whether you meant to help Rivers or not. You have. Tremendously. He's so—I've never seen him more content."

Monica pauses, clearing her throat. "Anyway, thank you."

She gets up from the table and begins to clear it.

When my mom starts to wash the dishes with Monica beside her, Rivers leans over to whisper, "I miss you, so much it hurts."

"I'm right here."

"It isn't the same," he insists.

"I know."

"Come outside with me? If I can't sleep with you at night, I at least want to have you next to me in some way, for a little while."

Before I can even offer to help with the cleanup, my mom is nodding me toward Rivers and the back door. I salute her and we head out.

Clouds have taken over the sky—swirling, morphing

masses of gray and white.

"I think it's going to storm."

The wind picks up even as I am saying this, sweeping the tail of my shirt out and causing my skin to pebble. A dew has formed to the grass, strands of it tickling the soles of my bare feet.

"Then I guess we should hurry." He yanks me to him and seals our lips in a heated kiss.

"I have dreamed of your eyes every night," Rivers tells me. "Do you know, every time you look at me, I feel it all the way to the very center of me? And your scent—I lie on the pillow you did just so I can catch a hint of it. Lime and sugar."

His mouth scorches my neck, his fingers biting into my waist. He wraps his arms around me and squeezes me to him, burrowing his face into the crook between my neck and shoulder. I feel the tremor in his body and stroke his back.

"This is torture."

"I have the next two days off. They're yours if you want them."

"I want all of them." He sighs, moving back. "But I'll take what I can get."

"You could always come work at the flower shop with me. I'm sure your flower arrangements would be extraordinary."

"You're really not as funny as you think you are, you know that?"

"I'm *funnier*," I say, poking his stomach.

A tiny light blinks above his shoulder and I grab his arms and whirl him around. "Look! It's a lightning bug."

I bounce on the balls of my feet.

He looks over his shoulder at me. "You act like you've never seen one before."

"I love lightning bugs," I breathe. "I used to spend hours every summer catching and releasing them."

"Like a true fisherman of bugs."

I squint my eyes at him. "Come on—let's catch some."

Without waiting for his answer, I skip forward, turning in

a circle as I catch blips of glowing orbs in that magical time between partial dark and full. I spy one in the grass by my feet and reach a hand down, holding still as the bug lands on my fingers.

"Go on, little buggy, go home before the storm comes." It flies away, lighting up as it goes, and I smile as I straighten.

Rivers' breath tickles the side of my neck as he says, "You are the sweetest version of quirky I have ever had the pleasure of seeing in motion."

I laugh softly. "Thank you. Glad you got to see me in action."

He wraps his arms around my midsection and rests his chin on my shoulder. "Don't ever change."

"I do what I want," I say, just to say it.

Rivers' hold tightens. "That's the exact thing I don't want to ever change about you."

I *feel* those words in my heart.

"Are you two ready for the movie?" Monica calls from the doorway. "We made popcorn!" Her enthusiasm over this detail is puzzling. I prefer potato chips.

I move away and look at him. "What movie?"

"No idea."

"It's a romantic comedy," she supplies and we both groan.

Rivers is into his supposedly scary movies, and I, for the most part, like science-fiction movies. Or rather, anything with superheroes in them—or something out of the ordinary, like thrillers that make you think. Traditional story lines are boring; romantic ones are nauseating, and sad movies just plain suck.

"Why can't it be 'X-Men'?" I grumble as we walk toward the house.

"Why can't it be 'The Grudge'?" he counters.

As we reach the door, I look at him and make the sound the ghost in the movie makes—like a bendable straw being straightened out. His eyes go wide. "What the shit? I didn't know you had it in you."

"Your turn."

He thinks for a minute and then slashes his enclosed hands down at his sides just like Wolverine does and my heart melts.

I pat his cheek. "You're a keeper."

TEN

IT'S STRANGE HOW SUDDEN IT happens. I am standing beside my mother, laughing as we prepare a salad, and then I am falling to my knees on the kitchen floor, the pain in my head relentless, so massive I think my brain will literally explode. I almost want it to, just to relieve the pressure.

I clutch my forehead and squeeze, nausea filling me, and weightlessness descending upon me. I vaguely note my mom calling my name, but I can barely hear her and I can't see around the agony in my head. Lights pulsate behind my eyelids. Hands are on me, a voice is screaming at me, just before it all goes dark.

I wake up in a white room with a beeping monitor and tubes connected to me. Although there is fog around my brain, at least the pain is gone. But the relief is short-lived with me sitting in the middle of the truth, unable to hide anymore. I panic. The stark whiteness of the room is like a stage and I am the spotlight, trembling with all I have tried to deny. I feel naked, exposed. I can't be here. This can't be happening. Not yet. I refuse to let this happen. I need to leave. If I leave, it isn't really happening. This is *not* my destiny. I don't accept this.

No.

A sob escapes me as I grab for the wires and just as I am about to rip them from my skin, a hand stays me. I look up, the shell keeping me together finally shattering as his stricken eyes find mine. My hand goes limp, falling to my lap, as my truth stares back at me from the eyes of the man I healed only to wound again. Tears are streaming down my face and I can't even care about that now.

My heart is breaking. My heart, *my heart* is Rivers, and it is breaking.

He doesn't say anything. What can he say? He just looks at me like I am already gone, like I already left him, and he is unable to accept it. He looks lost. Knowing I am causing him this pain hurts me more than I can deal with.

I didn't want to hurt him. I *don't* want to hurt him, but I am. I am hurting him because I was careless, carefree, and thinking of now instead of farther ahead. I dared to hope. I dared to be selfish. I dared to want a piece of him when he will eventually have nothing of me.

And now look at us, sitting in a hospital room watching one another like we don't know who we are staring at.

It is amazing how steady my voice is as I tell him, "I'm fine."

Rivers slowly closes his eyes. When he opens them, there is raging light in the endless black depths, lightning bolts of fury aimed right at me. "You're *fine*? That's what you have to say to me? You're fine? Well, I'm glad you're fine, because I sure as hell am *not* fine. You can be fine while I am not...*fine*," he grinds out.

"Where's my mom?" I avoid his eyes and his words with my question and the way I fervently search the room. The apprehension is growing—this swirling mass that is called reality is shoving its way into my caricature of a life. I think, if she is just here, this conversation will not happen. I feel sick, so sick. I feel like all of my emotions are building and building and I am going to be ill from them all. They are going to smother me and I will be helpless to stop them.

None of this will happen if my mom would just show up. We won't have to talk about this. This isn't happening. I don't want this to be happening. I am on repeat and I can't shut it off. It is an unbreakable circle of pain and heartache and I am the band keeping it whole. Why can't I keep pretending this isn't happening? I want to go back, even to yesterday, when Rivers was smiling at me, happy, and didn't know I am broken even more than he is.

Everything will be different now. He'll look at me differently.

He'll look at me like people look at him. But I never looked at him like he was anything less than complete, and I cannot *stand* the thought that I will see pity in his eyes after today. I would rather not see him at all.

"She went to get coffee. She's been pacing the floor since we got here and she needed a different scene. My mom's with her." In the next breath, all the anger is gone from his tone and is replaced with overwhelming grief.

Despair, so deep his voice cracks under the pressure of it, shows through when he asks, "Why didn't you *tell* me something was wrong?"

I go still, wondering if he knows any of what is truly going on, or simply that something is wrong. What is doctor/patient confidentiality in a matter like this? I was brought in unconscious. They have my medical history and diagnosis on record here, but I am a legal adult. Did I ever specifically say I did not want anyone to know of my situation if something happened to me?

I can't remember.

Of course, they would want to know what the doctors could tell them about my condition, and what it means for me. Would they tell them everything? Taking a deep breath, I fiddle with the tube sucking oxygen into my nostrils each time I inhale. I don't think I can continue the charade, either way.

And don't I owe him the truth? This once arrogant boy, who is maturing into a decent and good man, who gave me purpose when his life was full of despair, and who gave me something to believe in when I was flailing. He gave me a reason to keep going. This being who was never more unflawed than when he thought he was irreparable.

He only had to fracture to allow me in.

"It's odd, but I think maybe I *was* there for you, but I didn't know it right away. That day was the first day I knew something was wrong. I'd just been released. I was numb, just sitting there, trying to come to terms with it all," I whisper.

I swallow and glance at him. "And then you were brought in,

and when I saw you, everything sort of clarified for me. I knew what I had to do. It was weird how sudden it was. One minute I was hopeless and the next I found hope again."

"What are you talking about?" Slow realization crawls over him like the icy waters of a cold, tumultuous sea of finality. His expression clears and just as quickly is filled with shadows once more.

"Wait a minute." He stares at me, his eyes trailing over my features like he is reminding himself that he knows me, that he has seen my face before, maybe when he wasn't fully aware of it. And he had. "You were there that day—the day of my accident. I remember. You were sitting in a chair in the emergency room when they wheeled me in. You weren't there for me. You couldn't have been. Why were you there?"

I wonder if this is the time for my confession. I've been keeping it inside, refusing to face the truth, denying what is unmistakable even to myself because I don't want it to be real. But it is real and Rivers bringing up the day my world and his world collided and touched in more ways than the obvious, is looking at me with eyes full of unease. He has the right to know, doesn't he?

I turn away from the boy who changed so much because of me; the boy who changed *me.* I look at a painting of the calm waters of the Mississippi River across the room. The waves appear so still, and the picture is so deceptive. Just like me. Just like every breath I am given. What one sees of me is not what truly is.

I lean forward to touch his ravaged cheek, the bumps and dips of it a work of art to me. I smile, but I know sadness seeps into it. "I didn't plan on this."

He grabs my hand and holds it against his face, his brows lowered. "Didn't plan on what?"

I put my finger to his lips. He kisses it and a catch forms in my chest. "Just listen. This isn't easy for me to say. I need to take my time with it."

He nods brusquely, his throat bobbing as he swallows. The

intensity of his gaze singes me. I'm going to miss him looking at me. Although, how will I even know I'm missing it? My expression must reveal something of the pain this knowledge gives me because his hands cup the nape of my neck and he tugs me to him, his mouth hungry and urgent against mine.

I let my mind slip away for a moment, feeling the sensations he evokes in me, feeling joy and happiness and wholeness I have only felt with a damaged boy. There are tears in the kiss, and as I pull away, I see there are tears on his face and feel my own. He knows something. Even if the doctors told him nothing, he knows anyway.

"I had...an episode. I didn't know what it meant. The pain was so intense—the headache was so bad I passed out. When I woke up, I knew whatever had happened to me wasn't normal. Sometimes I wish I hadn't decided to have it checked out. But I was scared, so I did.

"They did scans of my brain. The results weren't good. They wanted to do more testing, but I said no. They told me it was inoperable, so what was the point in taking more pictures and whatever else they wanted to do?

"If I hadn't passed out that day, if I hadn't gone to the emergency room at the exact moment I did, I wouldn't have seen you, broken and bloody, as you were brought into the hospital. I was sitting there, wondering what the hell I was supposed to do now. Your mother and Thomas were in the hallway, crying and holding one another.

"I'm telling you now, Rivers, Thomas loves you. Maybe not in the way you want or need, but he does. He was scared, grieving. Maybe it was partly from guilt, but it was also because he cares for you. You don't cry for someone like that just because you don't want your mistake found out." I inhale, looking away from his vulnerable face.

I want to tell him I love him. I love him *so much*. But I know it will be piercing to hear right now, although it will never truly be one hundred percent received with solace. With love, comes pain. But I do, I love him. And I know he loves me too.

Even if we have not verbally spoken the words to one another, it is so clear to me. Every glance my way, every touch of his skin against mine, the way he responds to me without being aware of it, even the sound of his voice. I can see everything in a way I wasn't able to before all of this.

I love a boy I pulled from the dark and he loves a girl who will return to it.

"I was in the store a month or so later. I didn't realize it was your mom right away, but it didn't take long for me to realize who I was talking to. She offered the job. I accepted. I'd already known I wanted to help you somehow, I just wasn't sure how yet. It was sort of perfect, in a way.

"I made a choice. I could spend the rest of my time feeling sorry for myself, or I could help someone. Your mom...and you. I could live with the past hovering over me or I could step away from it and be the way I always want- ed to be, the way I could have been if I hadn't let everything around me determine who I was. I could choose to be sad, or I could choose to be happy. Life —it's one choice after another. And how our lives are, that's our choice as well.

"Maybe if you hadn't been in that accident, you wouldn't have been able to know the real me. And maybe if I hadn't discovered there was something wrong with me, I wouldn't have been able to *be* the real me. I like to think, it had to happen this way for the two of us to find each other. Because even with all I grieve for, I cannot regret you. I didn't expect to care about you so much. I didn't expect to see past my misconception of you and be rewarded with knowing the real you. I had a goal, Rivers, and you ruined it for me, but I am so glad you did," I whisper.

He is openly crying and I am crying with him. I think the sound of his anguish is even harder to take than seeing it, but both are equally ravaging to me. His tears are wounds to my heart and I am crying blood for him in return. I try to imagine a life without Rivers, and it guts me. And I know what he is feeling. It would be a world cast in gray, without the sun, without light, without warmth.

My mom and Monica find us together on the bed, our arms locked around each other like if we just keep holding on, we won't lose one another. Monica's mouth pulls down and her eyes water as she takes in the sight, quickly looking away as she inhales sharply.

My mom's face crumples and she can't even walk toward us, her legs stiff and immobile. Rivers' mom puts an arm around her to gently prod her forward and they make their way to the bed in a shuffling gait. It makes me think of the first agonizing steps I witnessed Rivers take at the beginning of the summer and my arms tighten around him.

"The doctor will be in soon," Monica says quietly, her eyes touching on me and resting on her son. "Rivers, let's go for a little walk."

Torn between where he wants to be and where he needs to be, he carefully disentangles himself from me, giving my forehead a lingering kiss. He sweeps bangs from my eyes and smiles, his gaze steady and true. That smile tears me apart.

I hear my mother's broken cry behind him and my eyes burn. He leaves with his mom, glancing back at me as he goes. His expression is panicked and desperate, like he is sure he isn't going to find me, but when our eyes meet, the lines fade a little from his face. Monica puts her hand on his arm and unconsciously rubs it as they walk from the room.

I have no choice but to face my mother now.

Looking at her is hard. She no longer resembles the young image I normally procure in my mind when I think of her. Janet Bana looks like all the years of heartache have finally caught up to her and lambasted her into accepting that life is cruel, that life takes more than it gives, and that it is going to steal from her once more. "You know Henry Miller? He lives down the street from us."

She wordlessly nods.

I look down, staring at the stark white of the sheet peeking out from beneath the hospital-issued blanket. "I think about him a lot. All the time, lately. He lost his wife to cancer, his son to a hunting accident, and his daughter was murdered."

I blink and release a set of tears. They slowly trickle down my cheeks. "How can one person be expected to go through so much? It's horrible. And he's so sad. He's in his eighties and it's been years since he lost them all, and he's still just so sad. I see it every time he sits on his porch.

"It radiates from him. Sorrow like that—there is no way to get past it." I wipe the tears from my chin. "I don't want that to be you."

My eyes meet her injured ones. "I don't want you to have to lose everyone you love."

Her lower lip wobbles and she turns her face away, hugging herself against my words. "Did they tell you?"

She wipes at her eyes, finally looking at me. I find it odd that she is standing away from me, like she has to distance herself from the pain being too close to me evokes in her.

"The doctor said he had to talk to you first." The look she gives me is hard-eyed and searching. "He has records, Delilah. Confidential records on you. Records I couldn't see and records he wouldn't say a single word to me about. He's hiding something—something big, something terrible.

"I can see it every time he won't look at me, every time I catch that hint of resigned acceptance he tries to cover up. What is it? What won't he tell me?"

I look at the blanket covering my legs and squeeze it between my hands, then release it. "I—"

"Just tell me this," she interrupts. She straightens her shoulders and looks at me with determination to stay strong in the set of her spine and the directness of her eyes. She wore that look a lot after she lost Neil. I used to think she wore it for herself, but now I wonder if it was for me. And now—as she wears the same look—is it for me as well?

She is so much stronger than I ever gave her credit for. She always reminded me of something frail, but I understand now that I was seeing her wrong, like so many other things.

"Is it..." Her eyelids slide shut and she takes a deep lungful of air. She looks at me, not like I am her daughter, but like I am an equal, and it grieves me that it has come to this. I wanted her to remain oblivious. I wanted to spare her the pain until there was no way around it.

Her voice cracks as she asks, "Is it terminal? Are you dying?"

The tears that fall from my eyes are her answer and I see her sway around the blur of them, fumbling with a chair until she falls into it. She doesn't say another word.

She sits in the chair and she holds her face and weeps; loud, broken, gasping sounds of grief that tighten my throat. I can't watch her, but I can't turn away. My mouth quivers and I stare at the ceiling as she cries, blinking my eyes against my own steady flow of tears.

Pressure forms in my chest and I wonder if this is what it feels like when your heart breaks, when the sorrow be- comes too much and it has to go somewhere, so it flows into your heart and makes it ache, each beat of it agonizing to your soul. Your heart beats to keep you alive, your heart beats so you know you can still hurt. Because to have pain, is to live, and there is no life without it. The pain makes you know you're alive.

I guess as long as my heart keeps aching, I know I am still breathing.

She stands abruptly, moving toward me in hurried steps. Reaching down, she takes my face into her hands and kisses my cheek, pressing her tear-stained one to mine. "I love you, Delilah. You are my gift. You are my heart. And we will get through this."

I try to nod, but I can't move from all the emotions slamming into me and over me. Relief, hope, loss, sadness. I whisper instead.

And what I whisper is, "Yes."

IT SEEMS ODD THAT OUT of all the rooms in the house, the one I feel like I need to be in is Neil's—or maybe that is exactly where I should be. The air is stuffy with the smell of a room shut up too long. I immediately go to the set of windows along the far wall and open the curtains, sliding a window open to let a cool breeze inside. The sun is down and the stars are out. I watch the black and white sky for a moment, and then turn away.

"I miss you, Neil, every day," I quietly tell an empty room. Is this what my mom will do? Sit in my room as she mourns me, talking to the ghost of a memory so she feels closer to me?

Blinking my eyes, I take a stabilizing breath of air. This room reeks of sorrow, of a life taken too soon, of dreams never known, and laughter forever silenced. For weeks after he died, I was in here on a daily basis, sitting on his bed, falling asleep among his blankets at the most random times. I missed his smell—dirt, sweat, and laundry deter- gent—so badly that I went to his room to procure anything that reminded me of him. My mom would find me in his room and quietly pick me up and take me out. It must have hurt her so much to be in here, to find me in here.

I didn't understand that he was truly gone, I couldn't comprehend that I would never see him again. Part of me thought if I waited long enough, he would come back. Because, really, how can someone just be...gone?

The room is still painted sky blue with sports paraphernalia and airplane models on the walls and hanging from the ceiling. His clothes were donated to a secondhand store along with his toys, but there were some things my mother could not bear to part with, like the Spider-Man shirt I hold within my hands, and the trinkets in the room that were dear to him. I found the Spider-Man shirt on my mother's bed after Neil's funeral. She never mentioned me taking it—she never said a single thing about it. I wore it to bed every night until I outgrew it.

And one day I realized that my brother was gone forever, and I never came back in this room after that. I began to call my mom by her first name, and I grew a shield around myself, a shield that was never fully taken down until this summer—until now.

Funny how we all finally decide to start living only when we irrevocably know we are dying.

I carefully lie down on the bed, holding his shirt to my chest, and close my eyes. Contentment flows through me and over me like a warm blanket, filling me and slowing my breaths. I drift away to the sight of golden eyes twinkling like glitter and an infectious laugh, only awakening at the shifting of the mattress as my mom lies beside me, wrapping me in her arms and in the security of her love, before I sink into the darkness once more.

THE BRAIN TUMOR IS INOPERABLE because of its stellar location inside my head. The risk of trying to remove it would be too great to me—there's the tiny matter of major blood vessels that surround it. Basically, chances are I would bleed to death. Radiation was suggested to try to minimize its size, but most benign tumors regrow. Do I want to live for the duration of whatever time I have left of my life sick? No. They said it could be hereditary, but as I have no knowledge of who my father is, that means nothing to me. It was suggested I go to a support group, but I decided to find my own form of therapy. I guess I did that when I saw Rivers and his mother.

When they started talking about experimental surgery, I left. Until yesterday, I never went back.

Maybe I am being unreasonable, but if I can't decide when I get to die, I can at least decide how. Just as I can decide how to live while I still have that option.

I looked it up online, trying to see if there was some way to naturally get rid of it. I knew I was searching for im- possible answers when I did so, but I had to at least try. Maybe my affinity to burn in the sun, and thus stay out of it unless slathered in sunscreen, was to blame. Vitamin D is necessary to remain healthy. Maybe I ultimately killed myself or helped the process along in some way. Maybe it was something I did or didn't eat. Maybe I wasn't active enough, maybe I was too active. Maybe something with my chromosomes changed and messed it all up. Who knows. And really, does it matter?

Each year, more than one hundred thousand Americans are told they have a brain tumor. It is not clear why many of these tumors occur. Those that originate in the brain, primary brain tumors, may be due to genetic or environ- mental factors.

Others, called secondary brain tumors, are the result of cancer that has spread from other parts of the body.

Benign brain tumors, while slow growing and non-cancerous, may be inoperable. And unlike benign tumors in other parts of the body, benign brain tumors often recur. The tumor in my head is benign, but for whatever reason, it is also aggressively growing, and one day, it will be too much for my brain to take—and it will kill me. I know all this because I googled it. Google has helped me these past few months in ways nothing else could.

I'm not saying I just accepted it. I didn't. I mean, when I saw Rivers brought into the emergency room, I found a purpose to not fall into a hole of despair, but I already had it set in my brain that I wanted to fight. Only I didn't know how. I decided that living as much as I could while I had the chance, was the way I could fight it. And I have. I am not sorry for that. But I am sorry for the people I will be leaving, and I am sorry for the pain I will indirectly cause them when I go.

I sit on a threadbare blanket on the porch with my knees up to my chin, staring at the white house with tan shutters across the street, my eyes focused on the sunflowers reaching toward the windows. I feel like that plant right now—proud and strong for months and then wilting and dying before it should be time. It could happen at any moment. Today. Tomorrow. One day, I will have a headache so bad I will lose consciousness, and I just won't wake up.

Pain forms a fissure in my heart, growing as I remember the shattered look in Rivers' eyes yesterday. I put my cheek to my knees and close my eyes. I didn't plan on falling in love with him. It just happened. I wasn't even aware of it until it was too late. He wrapped himself around my heart without me realizing it. I couldn't have stopped it any more than the current beating of my heart.

Rivers shows up with a baseball bat poking out of the top of a red backpack slung over his shoulder. A stillness spreads through me as I take in the sight of him. A dingy white cap is pulled low over his eyes and my pulse speeds up in response to how darkly handsome he is.

He climbs the few steps to reach me and then stands looking down at me. It's the hat, and the look on his face, that affects me the most. His face is determined, his stance telling me to not even bother arguing with what he has planned.

Lips pressed into a firm line, he lifts one eyebrow. That's it. That's all he does. As though he expects me to just blindly follow him without knowing what we're doing or where we're going. Well, I will. Because with him is where I want to be, and he seems to know that.

I get to my feet, fold the blanket up, and set it beside the door. And I wait.

"Hey."

I smile faintly at this adopted form of greeting we seem to have deemed as ours. "Hey."

He hops off the last step of the porch with the ease he used to move with and my heart clenches, but it is a good hurt. His body has always moved with grace, even the disjointed form he had at the beginning of the summer.

"You're getting better," I tell him, nodding to his legs. "You've improved a lot in just one month."

"My legs getting better isn't what's changed me this past month," he replies. He doesn't even pause to ask, "Know what I did last night?"

I swallow, feeling the sting of tears in my eyes. I blink around it. I cried enough yesterday at the hospital. After my discharge, I wasn't sure when I would see or talk to him again or what to expect. I certainly didn't expect this. I was scared he would stay away and I was scared he wouldn't. I'm not even sure how I should act or how he thinks I should. Obviously, he must want me to play ball. He's watching me expectantly.

"Decided to play baseball today?"

"I bawled my eyes out. Pretty much all night." Rivers walks backward down the sidewalk, his eyes never leaving me. "Know what else I did?"

I frown as I slowly follow him, uncomfortable with his behavior, pain going through me at his words. "No."

"I thought, I just found her and she's going to leave me."

I look down at my toenails presently painted pink.

"I cried some more."

My head jerks up and I put a hand across my stomach, hurting from what he is telling me. I open my mouth to tell him to stop, but he narrows his eyes at me, effectively halting me.

"I decided I had two options. I could be angry, I could give up, I could feel sorry for myself."

"That sounds like three options."

Ignoring that, he continues, "*Or...*I could be glad I got to know you, continue to be glad I am knowing you, and make the rest of this summer and whatever time we have, the best you've ever had. Guess which one I chose?"

"Baseball?" I wipe tears from my eyes.

"Yep. Baseball."

He closes the space between us, the bag dropping to the ground, and takes my face into his hands. "I'm going to make the time we have together unforgettable. I'm going to fuse you to me, so that there is no way of knowing where the separation between you and me begins—or even if there is one.

"I'm going to fill this summer with us, so that when you look back on it, all you remember is me, and when I look back on it, all I remember is you. I'm going to put as much life into now as I can. Like you did for me. Now it's my turn."

He presses his forehead to mine, taking slow, deep breaths. After an emotion-charged moment—a moment where I have a hard time breathing and his chest is heaving as he struggles to do the same—he pulls away. "And we're going to play baseball."

"I didn't know you could play with just two people."

He hesitates, then states, "You can't. There are two teams. And they're waiting for us at the park."

My first instinct is to ask who, my second is to say no, and then I decide to just say yes.

"Okay." I take a deep breath. "Let's play baseball."

He lowers the bag, removes a pale pink baseball glove from it, and hands it to me. "You can't catch any balls without a glove."

It's ridiculous how this small gift makes me want to tear up, but it does. It's my first gift from Rivers—the first gift from anyone other than my mother, really. She was an only child and her parents passed away when I was young, so it's always just been us since Neil died. My chest squeezes at the looming day when it will only be her.

"Thank you," I tell him softly, holding it close to me.

He nods, not looking at me. "You need tennis shoes."

I look at my bare feet and grin, wiggling my toes. "I'll be right back."

Rivers explains the basics to me as we walk. He tells me to hit the ball and run, to make it to home base when I get the chance. Anything personal is kept out of the discussion—anything that has to do with yesterday and the future is left unspoken. I know I can't pretend anymore, and I know we will have to talk about it, but right now, I am all right talking about baseball.

I repeatedly catch him watching me as we make our way to the park. I'll glance up and his dark eyes are staring into me with yearning, grief, and pain in them. It is almost as though he is searching for the disease inside of me, and that he wants to find it and sear it from my brain with his eyes alone. The stricken look on his face is easily masked, but I continue to find glimpses of it each time I look up sooner than he gauges I will. And it breaks my heart, but I smile to cover it up. I feel that I will be smiling a lot in months to come.

The park is only a few blocks away from where I live. This is the park I found the dying bird in—this is the park my brother died in. My footsteps slow as I take in the group of people I've been associated with most of my life, but still don't really know. Most of them are tossing a ball back and forth, some are talking, a few are looking our way.

This is the park I will play baseball in.

"Do they—" I start, unable to continue around the lump in my throat.

He shakes his head, shadows flashing across his face. "No. They just know we're playing baseball. No one's going to say anything mean to you either, because if they do, I will pound them so bad into the ground that they will remain flattened there for all eternity," he declares heatedly.

I laugh at the glower on his face. "My hero."

Rivers puffs his chest out. "That's right."

He turns to the crowd. "Let's play ball! Del's on my team. Who else?"

The sun quickly heats my skin, a layer of sweat adding slickness to my hands. I go up to bat, my hands shaking with nervousness. I swing and strike on the first two balls, glance over to see Rivers watching me from the sidelines, and blast the bat into the third ball, sprinting and whooping as I head for first base. Cheers are called as I run and I grin, exhilaration lightening my step and giving me energy to keep going. I make it to first and bounce up and down on my feet, posing to head for second base when permissible.

I get out on third base, and I can't even care. I skip back to the bench, beaming at the congratulations I get from my teammates. I briefly wonder if I could have had more of this if I'd opened up during school. I sit down and open a bottle of water, guzzling it down. Rivers walks up to the plate and my stomach dips. I see the tension in his face and body, and realize how difficult this is for him.

He's doing this for you.

He is too. He's around people he hasn't seen since the beginning of summer, playing a sport he may or may not be able to play, and it's for me. What if he can't run? Can he? I don't know. Sure, he's walking almost as normally as he used to, but that's different than running. He is putting himself directly into a position to publicly fail to prove something to me.

What is it?

I get to my feet, moving to stand behind the fence, fitting my fingers through the brackets of the chain-link as I stare at his back. *You can do this, Rivers. I know you can.* As though he hears my thoughts, he looks over his shoulder at me, the intensity of his gaze stealing my breath. He presses his lips together and turns away, assuming the batting position.

He swings and misses. His form is perfect, but his movements are slower than they need to be to hit the ball. He swings again and I can feel the frustration radiating off him in waves of discord, reaching out to those near, causing an uncomfortable shifting in those around him. I chew on my lip, wanting to help him somehow and not knowing how or even if I can.

"Peanut butter!" I blurt out.

Eyes turn my way, but the only ones I care about are dark brown and slowly find mine. He frowns at me and I shout it again, pumping the air with my fist. He stares at me for a moment in befuddlement and then shakes his head as he laughs, giving me a thumbs up sign as he turns back to the game.

My face burns as I take my seat, not looking at anyone.

"Peanut butter?" George Ronald asks, red eyebrows lifted in his freckled face.

George is short, skinnier than any eighteen-year-old boy should be, and a science nerd. I know he isn't good at sports, but I have to give him respect for being here.

"Yes. He has an unhealthy obsession with it," I lie.

He shrugs. "Okay."

I hold my breath as the ball shoots through the air, squeezing my hands into fists in my lap. "Come on. You can do it. Come on. Hit it. Hit the ball."

He not only hits the ball, he *slams* that ball over the fence located way behind outfield. I jump to my feet, screaming in jubilation. Apparently, my love for sports has finally bloomed. I understand now. I can feel the thrill of winning pulsating through me, the excitement I have for Rivers proves I have now converted into a fan of baseball.

He doesn't even have to run. He can walk and make it. He just hit a homerun. He watches the ball until it lands, and then he looks back and grins at me.

And he runs.

His gait is not as smooth, nor as fast as it once was, but it is still a sight to behold. He makes it home and doesn't stop running until he is to me, sweeping me into his arms and spinning me around. I let my head fall back and laugh, holding my arms out wide.

"We did it," he whispers against my neck, kissing me senseless to the catcalls of the other team members.

We did. We did it. For each other—and we will continue to do so.

This is what it is about; this is why he did this.

He is my tether to this life and I am his.

DEATH DOES NOT DISCRIMINATE.

It takes young and old alike. It takes good people, bad people. It is vicious and it is peaceful. It comes to you in the night, it comes to you in the sunshine of day. It takes you in the form of drugs, murder, disease, and tragedy. It doesn't care what dreams you have, what goals you have set. It doesn't care who you love or who loves you. It doesn't care who you leave behind and it doesn't care who is torn apart when you go. I guess at least it's equally terrible for all.

Death is not kind, to summarize.

I am dying. I say it out loud, feeling my throat tighten. I say it again. I whisper it. I think it. I stare into my eyes through the reflective glass of the mirror and say it once more. I don't think I will ever truly be able to accept it one hundred percent. Until I take my last breath, I think a part of me will continue to hold out for hope. I don't have it in me to just give up.

"I am dying."

Tears burn my eyes and an emptiness floats through me. I touch my face, my hair, I hug myself. It is hard to believe I will be gone one day soon. My voice forever silenced. My eyes forever closed. My heartbeat stilled. How does that happen? How does a person just stop existing? It doesn't seem possible.

No one would ever suspect there is a tumor growing inside my brain, a tumor that is steadily removing my life essence from me. I look like an ordinary, healthy, young woman. Nothing about my features hint at the destructive tumor taking over my brain.

Diseases are like that—they destroy you from the inside out, never showing the inevitability of them until it is too late, until it has gone too far.

Looking at my reflection, it is hard to imagine it is there. There are no signs of it in my visage. A lot of the time I can pretend it isn't true, but then I feel it—a twinge of impermanence, a tug of fatality, a whisper that my time is numbered and that it is running out. More and more I am feeling it.

Death is quietly telling me to prepare those around me, that it will be here for me soon. And that is what I have been doing, or trying to do, even though I have continually mucked it up.

When I was a child, I liked to create. I was told by many I was unique. I liked that word. I liked how it was spelled and I liked how it sounded on my lips. At a young age, I decided I wanted to be that. It helped that I had the right personality for it.

It could be with paint, fabric, Legos, my hair—anything. Colors called to me, clashing designs, and the need to make something original out of something plain and uninteresting. Hence my inclination to dye my hair different colors and wear clothes not generally worn by the students of Prairie du Chien High. Interior design was what called to me the most, when I decided

I needed to be responsible and make a college decision.

I'd decided to attend Milwaukee Institute of Art and Design just a few nights before I ended up in the emergency room. I don't know if I believe in kismet, but it is sort of ironic how life works out, and death. All of my plans altered in one afternoon, all of my goals stamped out, and just as suddenly, another opportunity appeared with a new life and new plans. I do think I was there to see him.

What would I be like now if I hadn't found a ray of hope in a smothering hole of despair? It came in the form of Rivers Young. He was my light and I was his. I pray that light continues to burn long after I have been snuffed out.

Because, all of this, this dying business, it has to be for something. And I have told myself it was him. It is him. I made it be him.

I wonder if I will see my half-brother Neil. When I close my eyes for the last time, will he be waiting? Or will there be nothing at all? I like to think I'll be with him, in some form. He was my best friend, the one I looked up to, until he was abruptly snatched away with a playground fall hard enough and at just the right angle to snap his neck. I went through the pain of losing a loved one. I know how hard it is. I saw my mom go through losing a child.

And now she will lose one more.

Death came for Neil at such a young age—he was only eight. Maybe it felt bad for me so it decided to come a little later. I shake my head, knowing my thoughts aren't making a lot of sense. I wonder if that is from the disease spreading through my brain, or if it's just because I am dying and I know it. I was told it would start to affect my thoughts and motor skills as it grew. It scares me. I don't want to turn into someone I am not. I don't want to lose myself, not until all of me is gone.

When I go, I want to go as me.

Eighteen years. Eighteen years I was given. Did I make the most of them? Of course not. Not until I found out about the tumor. We always think we have more time and that is the wrong way to think, because time is something we never have enough of.

I imagine my death will be uneventful. I'll pass out or fall asleep and I just won't wake up. It won't be too bad for me, but what about the ones I'll be leaving? *What about Rivers? What about him losing you?* The thought is enshrouded in a powerful ache that throbs where my heart is. I turn from the mirror, leave my bedroom, and walk down the stairs of the home I used to avoid and now understand.

One day my ghost will linger here as well.

I find her in the living room, an open photo album in her lap and multiple others sprawled out on the floor around her. Her hair is pulled away from her face in a loose ponytail, cutoff jeans and a pale blue top adding to her seemingly young and vulnerable stature.

She looks up when I enter, and tears are shimmering in her eyes. I pretend I don't see them, smiling brightly as I sit beside her on the floor. She immediately reaches out for my hand and holds it. I can see her struggling to be strong. I tell her she doesn't have to be anymore. "It's okay to cry, Mom."

A broken sob leaves her and the hand clutching my wrist begins to shake.

"If I start, I don't think I will ever stop."

"You'll eventually get tired of it and find something else to do."

She laughs, wiping tears from her eyes. "Want to look at them with me?"

I glance down and see a photograph of a toddler and a chubby baby sitting on a brown couch, both brown-haired and golden-eyed. My heart squeezes. "So we can both become blubbering messes?"

"Do you have better plans?"

I scoot closer to my mom until my arm is resting against hers. "I really don't. Let the waterworks begin."

We start with Neil's baby album. He was an ugly baby—all rollie fat with smashed in facial features and a bald head—and I tell my mom so, which makes us both laugh. We laugh harder when she agrees. I make a comment about mothers supposedly thinking their babies are beautiful no matter what and she says that that is a lie, but they do *love* them no matter what.

"He made up for it as a two-year old," I murmur, staring at a little boy standing in a sandbox with the sun haloing him and dirt covering any piece of skin not clothed. A wide grin shows gaps and teeth. I can't help but smile back.

"He did. He was such a shit though," she muses.

I look at her in surprise and she laughs again, shrugging. "He was. He used to scream every time I bathed him. He liked being dirty. He liked to eat dirt too. I would find dirt in all his orifices."

She pauses. "He refused to eat anything but peaches and peanut butter sandwiches until he was six."

"He loved peanut butter almost as much as I do," I agree, feeling a sweet clenching in my chest—the bittersweet memory of a young boy with a contagious laugh and fierce stubbornness.

I touch the shiny cover of the film, thankful for this moment and the way my mother is opening up to me. She used to keep this part of herself locked away. I am guilty of this as well. I didn't talk about Neil because it hurt and that was wrong. I don't want the same to happen with me after I am gone. I don't want to be thought about, but never spoken of. I want to be remembered, not hidden away like a dark, sad secret. I don't want the ones that love me to hurt when they think of me—I want them to smile.

I take a deep breath and look at my mom. She looks back, silently waiting.

"I don't like to think of myself as a coward, but some things even I shy away from—most notably, the subject of Neil, and the strain between us." I swallow. "I should have talked to you. I shouldn't have pushed you away. I always thought I had forever, that I had time to fix us, but I have realized that none of us have that."

I inhale slowly. "I don't want to go and I am sorry that I am. That sounds so lame, but I don't know how else to say it."

Her lower lip trembles and tears are trailing down her porcelain cheeks. "You make me so proud, Delilah. You always have. Even when I didn't understand you, I admired you. You're so brave, such a brave young woman."

She takes a stuttering inhalation of air. "You're not supposed to be trying to make me feel better, you're not supposed to be comforting me. *I* should be the one to do it. I'm the mother—"

"You're the mother who lost a son and will soon lose a

daughter," I remind her quietly. "I'm not happy about this. In fact, I'm a little hateful, a little depressed, and yes, selfish. I want to have my life. I want to have my wedding and my kids and my career. I want grandchildren. I want ice cream and movies and music. Peanut butter. I want the sun and the stars, sunrises and sunsets. I want the scent of rain around me and the cold of winter, the warmth of a blanket. I want love and laughter. I want to create something amazing and have it be in someone's home. I want to grow old and fat and say whatever the hell I want without caring how others react. I want that sense of entitlement to be bat shit crazy that seems to come with old age.

"I want so many things that I will never have, but..." I wipe tears from my eyes, seeing them mirrored in the blue eyes focused on me. "But I have so much *now*. I have to remember that. You're the one who has to keep living. You...and Monica...and...and...Rivers."

Pain lacerates my heart and I talk around it. "You're going to need each other. You're going to have to be strong for each other. Promise me, okay? When one of you falls, the other two will be there to help them back up."

"I want the same for you. I would give it to you if I could. I promise you. Of course, I promise you," she says, enfolding me in her arms. "You're just starting to live. This isn't the way this is supposed to happen. I'm supposed to go first. I'm not supposed to see my children die." Her voice cracks as she tightens her hold on me, her tears wetting my shoulder.

I am openly crying as I confess, "I always thought you were comparing me to Neil, that you were trying to use me to fill the hole he left within you instead of really seeing *me*, but I realize now that that was never true. You were trying to hold on to me because you couldn't him. You were trying to keep me safe because you weren't able to with him. You can't control the world around you, Mom, but you can take comfort in all that you have. You have me, always. And Neil. You always have us. Don't forget. I'm not really going away."

Her grip on me becomes painful as we both cry, but I don't

mind. We are a mother and a daughter knowing their time together is almost at an end. It hurts. The pain is filling me, pulsating through me. I will cry this night with her and then I will smile for her after today. I will be brave for the ones I love.

I pull away and clasp her hands between mine. Her face is red, her eyes bloodshot, and grief hides the beauty of her features. "Can you promise me one more thing?"

She nods abruptly.

"When you look at your flowers, can you think of me?"

"Oh, Delilah," she weeps, covering her face as her shoulders shake from the force of the sobs leaving her. She grabs me and unceremoniously pulls me to her, brushing hair from my face and kissing my temple. "Yes. Yes. I will do that. I will look at my flowers and think of you."

"Thank you," I whisper.

Not a lot of talking happens after that, both of us too sad to do much of anything except cry and look at memories of lives forever captured within the pages of a photo album. I am seeing myself, knowing this is how I will be soon—just a face in a picture.

"YOU MIGHT AS WELL HAVE a drink with me. It seems silly to make you wait." She blinks as pain filters through her eyes, like she is only now aware of what she just said—I won't be around to drink when I am legally able.

Her face crumples and I pat her hand. "Stop it, Mom. Don't be a sad drunk. No one likes them."

I take the glass from her and try it. "Lemonade and vodka?" I guess.

"Yeah. I decided coffee just wasn't going to cut it tonight." She gets up and mixes another drink, returning to the table and setting it before me.

I sip it, liking the tangy bite it has.

"Do you know what I keep thinking?"

"That drinking and thinking is a bad idea?" I guess.

She shakes her head, swiping tangled hair from her face and behind her ears. "I keep thinking that, if I'd bothered to know who I was sleeping with, maybe none of this would be happening."

"Oh, Mom, don't think that way." I reach across the small table and squeeze her hand.

"I can't help it. What if it's genetic?" She blinks her eyes and tears fall from them. "What if your father has it or someone else in his family? Maybe they could have checked for it sooner. Maybe it could have been operated on be- fore it got to the point where it couldn't be. If we'd only *known*, maybe none of this would be happening."

"And maybe it would have been, regardless. Thinking that way doesn't make a difference in any of this. It is what it is."

She snorts and takes another drink. "Delilah, stop sounding like the adult. You're making me look bad."

I get up with my glass and walk from the room. I come back holding a portable CD player my mom likes to drag into the backyard when she's gardening. It's old school, but effective for what she needs. Drinking to dull the pain is okay and everything, but there has to be a limit, and there has to be music and dancing involved to keep the heaviness out of the room.

"What are you doing?"

I hit play and turn the volume up. 'I Can't Change the World' by Brad Paisley flows from the speakers. My mom is a country music nut. I enjoy certain country songs, but I am more drawn to fast music with unexpected beats and bass, music that physically moves me, although I like anything, as long as it touches my heart or gets my body moving. But this is what my mom likes and tonight is her night, so I pull her up from the table as we sing along with Brad.

It isn't that I've never had alcoholic beverages before, but the times have been infrequent and never with my mother. I suppose all sorts of rules need to be broken in instances like this. Mothers and daughters become drinking buddies, enemies become tolerable, strangers become lovers. One drink becomes two and we dance to Taylor Swift's 'Mean'.

The music and drinks continue to flow as we decide to do makeovers. My mom forms my shoulder-length hair into messy curls, I paint her nails black with pink dots, and we talk about boys. I talk about Rivers and she talks about Neil's father. I wonder where he is. I wonder if he misses his son as much as my mom does. I wonder if he still loves her like she still loves him.

Was the pain of losing Neil the last nail to fall from the woodwork of their connection? Love comes, it fades, it goes, but it always has the power to return. I don't even know if she realizes it, but her eyes light up and her voice softens as she talks about him.

"You know the Willow tree in Mr. Miller's backyard?" I mention at some point during the evening. My eyes are tired and sleep is calling me, but I feel like we need to talk about this. It's important to talk about Henry Miller, his loss, and even his tree.

My mom leans her back against mine, my eyes in one direction and hers in another. "Yes. You and Neil used to love playing on it. I can't count all the times you two would sneak off to it without telling me."

"He never cared. Henry." My voice is soft.

"No."

"He used to sit on his back deck and watch us with a smile on his wrinkly face. He never said anything other than hello and goodbye, but I liked him. There was soundness to him, like he was an unbreakable foundation in an always changing world. Of course, back then I just thought he was neat because he had a Willow tree."

I take a deep breath, closing my eyes. "There's something magical about that particular kind of tree. I wonder if Henry realizes that. I won- der if he had it put there for his family that he lost. Those trees cry for the dead. It's like their branches try to sweep up all the pain and loss in the world and hold it to them so that it does not touch us. I wonder if he thinks the same."

She shifts her position until her side is to my back, placing an arm around me and resting her chin on the top of my head.

"That sounds nice. I'm sure he does."

"I think you should talk to him."

She pauses, and then nods, her chin rubbing against my hair as she does so. "I think I will."

The hours sweep by, turning the evening into late night, and when we finally fall asleep in a pile of blankets and pillows on the living room floor, I feel closer to my mother than I ever have before. I sleep with her herbal scent around me, at peace with tomorrow and whatever it will bring. I awaken to my mother shaking my shoulder and telling me to get up.

"Rivers is here."

Her tone is firm, but I still catch the hint of sorrow in it. She's wondering how many more mornings we have together.

I glance at her as I get to my feet, rubbing my forehead. "He said he wouldn't be over until later today."

"I think he wanted to surprise you." She tries to smooth my curls that have turned into a natty mess. I let her, smiling at her when our eyes meet. Her hand slowly falls away and she gives me a tight hug. "Better hurry. He looked anxious."

I race through the living room and up the stairs to the bathroom where I quickly brush my teeth. I don't even bother to look at my hair because I know if I do, I won't go downstairs until it's into some form of control and that would be wasting time better spent near Rivers.

I sprint back down the stairs, take in the raised eyebrow my mom gives me from the kitchen as she says, "Tick tock," and come to a stop in the small entryway.

Running my fingers through my hair as I move toward the door, I give up trying to detangle the curls when my fingers get caught in the locks. I open the door to sunshine and a gaze immediately set on me. My pulse picks up and flutters form in my stomach.

Dark eyes hold me in place and I put a bright smile on my face. "Hey. I thought you had stuff to do this morning."

"I talked to Thomas last night."

"Oh?" That wasn't what I thought his first words would be

to me. I was thinking something more like a hello, a comment on my bed head, maybe even declarations of love. "Is everything okay with you two?"

He shrugs, looking down. Then he grabs the front of my shirt and pulls me outside and to him. His arms wrap around me as his cheek rests on the top of my head. His heartbeat thunders in his chest and I place my ear to it.

"I missed you," he says into my hair.

That's better.

My smile deepens. "I missed you too."

Rivers pulls away, studying my head. "What did you guys do last night? Exploratory hair fashion?"

"You talked to Thomas about what last night?" I ask, deciding not to answer his question.

"We have a cabin in the woods."

"Isn't that one of those scary movies you made me watch that really wasn't scary?"

"Yeah. Anyway, the cabin is about ten miles outside of Prairie du Chien. We have about a hundred acres of land we inherited from a distant relative of my mom's. Most of it is woods. I guess that's why we originally moved to the area, but Thomas didn't want to build on the land, so instead we found a house in town.

"There's a cabin there that we would stay in every once in a while as I was growing up. We'd hunt the woods and fish in the creek near it. I can't remember when I was there last. It's been a couple years. The point of all of this is that I talked to Thomas last night about me moving out there."

Rivers inhales deeply, his eyes moving away from mine as he says, "I want you there with me. I mean, you don't have to live there, but I'd like you to stay with me for as long as...as long as you want. But if you want to sort of move in, that would be okay with me. I mean, I want you to, but if you don't, I understand. I know you'll love it out there.

"Nothing but trees, green grass—and bugs, but I can't help that. Sleeping without you beside me...it's...reprehensible. I went out there this morning and got it cleaned out. I thought it would take longer than it did. There's running water and electricity. It's small, but it's in good shape. It can be ours, for however long we want or need it to be. And—"

I shut him up with my mouth to his, effectively cutting off his indefinite rambling. A zing goes through me at the touch of his lips to mine, a tremble forms in my legs, and my stomach dips. He ends the kiss only to suck air into his lungs, and then we're kissing again, his hands molding to my back and lower, pulling me against him so all of me touches all of him.

"I'll go pack now." I turn to the door, tugging at his hand when he refuses to move.

"Why aren't you moving?" I ask as I face him.

He opens his mouth, closes it, and opens it again. "I don't know. I just thought that would be harder than it was."

"You underestimate your power over me." I smile as our eyes connect. "Are you apprehensive now? Maybe you don't think you can handle me."

His eyes narrow and he finally moves. "I think I'll be okay finding out." He runs his fingers down my back as we walk through the doorway and I shiver.

"In fact, I think I'll be okay even if I can't handle you." Bringing his mouth close to my ear, he whispers, "I'm sort of counting on it."

I swallow with difficulty, knowing it is beyond time for us to move past the point of what we are to delve into what we need to be. I also know, with absolute clarity, that it will break me, but in the most wonderful of ways.

"One condition," I tell him, lifting my eyebrows.

His answer is swift and firm. "Anything."

I blow out a noisy breath. "You cannot—*cannot*—treat me like an invalid. You do and I go. Promise."

Rivers takes my hands within his and declares, "Delilah Marie Bana, you have too much life in you to ever have me mistake you for being anything other than one hundred percent functional."

I sigh, but it is a sigh of tranquility. Then I grin. "Did you totally just hear me sigh? I'm sighing for you."

"You act like you haven't been doing that all along."

The scent of baking cinnamon hits me as I step into the house and sorrow forms around the edges of my excitement. My mother and I are finally bridging the gap between us and now I am going to blow it apart once more with my distance. This time it is a physical instead of mental distance, but does that really make it any less painful? My mother needs me too. And I need her.

As though Rivers senses my thoughts, he enfolds my hand in his and squeezes, giving me support without saying a single thing. I tell him I need to talk to my mom for a minute and he nods, releasing my hand and moving into the living room.

I watch him, the embodiment of all that I treasure, and I turn away, toward the woman who gave me this gift of life I cannot keep.

Her back is to me, and even so, I can see the stiffness to it that tells me she knows something is up. She wipes her hands on a dish towel and places a pan of dough in the oven, finally turning to look at me. Her smile is brave, but I still catch the hint of melancholy in her eyes. They are darkened by it.

"You're going to stay with Rivers," she states softly.

"I am." I hover by the doorway, looking at the one person I have looked up to, resented, loved as long as I have been alive, and miss even as I am in the same room as her.

"You'll call me?" She blinks her eyes and lowers her head, the trembling of her shoulders betraying her valiant effort to remain dry-eyed.

"I'll do better than call you. I'll visit." I smile as she looks up. "I can't promise every day, but every week. And you'll come see me too. We should plan something now, in fact. How about this weekend? We'll invite Monica over too. I'll cook supper." My smile widens. "Not anything with peanut butter, I promise."

"I would love that."

"I'll have Monica pick you up since she knows the way. I'll tell her four on Saturday?"

The sadness fades as brightness takes over her face in the

form of a smile. "Yes. I look forward to it."

I cross the room to give her a hug, pressing my forehead to hers before letting her go. "Don't worry about calling me or visiting too much. There is no such thing as too much."

Her voice cracks as she replies with, "Right. Like fun and booze."

"Exactly like that."

She moves away, turning back almost immediately. Her eyes trail over my features, as though she is trying to memorize me as I am right now. "It is so hard to let you go, knowing...knowing what we know. But I also know I can't keep you here and I wouldn't want to try. You deserve to be happy and positive and you need to be with Rivers too. I just wanted to tell you that."

I take her hands within mine, squeezing them. "Thank you. I love you."

"I love you too. Go on. I'll see you soon. Oh, and take some cinnamon bread with you before you go."

"I will."

Rivers meets me at the bottom of the stairs and wordlessly lifts his eyebrows. I shrug and head upstairs with him following me. He sits on my bed and examines my room as I find my black and white polka dotted luggage I plan to take on my Amtrak trip.

"The Brewers game is next Sunday."

I fall onto the bed beside him, pulling him down with me. "I can't wait."

"You know, before I would have thought you were speaking with sarcasm, but I know you really can't wait. All it took was one baseball game."

"All it took was one *awesome* baseball game. And you."

"I just made you go."

I shake my head, brushing strands of hair from my face. "No. You played baseball. You ran. You did that for me."

"I did, yeah. I also did it for me. I needed to try it. I needed to prove to myself, and everyone else, that I could do it."

"I know." I touch his cheek. "Thank you for not treating me differently, for not acting like I am about to break."

"How can I do any less than you have done for me?" He faces forward, briefly closing his eyes. "I keep telling myself it isn't real. I keep telling myself it is impossible that one day you won't be here, smiling at me, teasing me, making me feel like I am someone special with just one glance of your golden eyes my way."

"You are someone special."

"I only feel that way with you," he insists.

I partially sit up, resting my chin on my hand as I look down at him. "Then you need to change the way you think about yourself."

He rolls his eyes and pulls me back down, wrapping his arms around me to keep me next to him. "You should have been a motivational speaker, you know that?"

"Well, I *am* multi-talented."

He strokes my hair and my eyelids turn heavy. "I'm not going to treat you like you're helpless. You didn't do that to me and I'm not going to do it to you. But I also refuse to accept what life has decided to give us. It's crap. Pure *crap*."

Sighing, he releases me. "Come on, let's get your stuff ready."

THE MOON IS OUR SPOTLIGHT and we are the performers. Around us is a barrier of tall pine trees, the stars are our blanket, and we are safe within our dark world. Nothing can touch us. Nothing can take me away. The cabin is along the edge of trees to our right, alight with the soft glow of a single lamp in its window, and beyond it is a forest of life.

And we dance.

With our bodies, hands, and mouths, we say what is needed. With every touch, I tell him I love him. With every kiss he places on my lips, he tells me it back. I close my eyes, rest my cheek to his heart, and inhale deeply. It doesn't matter that our movements are a touch uncoordinated. I find the limp in Rivers' gait the purest form of elegance. When his expression shows a hint of frustration, my smile dispels it. He is beautiful to me.

Perfect. I whisper this into his ear and his arms tighten around me.

There comes a point where the sweetness of the moment turns into something more. Our kisses are more urgent, the clothes between us are too heavy, and I step away. The flash of disappointment in his eyes is clear to see, but fades as soon as I grab the hem of my top and tug it off, throwing it as far away from me as I can. I laugh at the look on his face.

"Surprised?" I reach around me and unhook my bra, slowly sliding it down my arms, and let it drop to the cool grass.

He sucks in a sharp breath, his eyes going black.

"I guess so." Next to go are my shorts.

When I reach for my underwear, Rivers says in a harsh voice, "What are—"

I step out of them, whatever he was going to say dying on his lips as he stares at me. I think I catch a curse word, but his lips are on mine before I can ask. The tremble to his hands as they trail over me makes me smile, the ragged- ness of his breathing turns mine just as disjointed. I feel his heart thundering. I feel the way he wants me. I am alive in him, in this moment.

"You won't forget me." I'm telling him, but I am also asking him.

He steps back, his hands falling from me. A minute passes like this, with him wordlessly watching me, and I in turn watching him. Even now, he is forming me into a memory so he cannot.

"I am incapable of that," he solemnly says.

I reach for his shirt, kissing the bare skin it regrettably covered. Within seconds, his clothes are in a pile and he is against me. When the heat of him becomes flush with me, I cannot breathe. Every nerve-ending of mine is standing up, bristling with desire. I need him. I need him in ways I cannot name.

He grabs me and pulls me under him as we fall to the ground, cushioning my landing with his arms beneath my back. My hands are all over him, feeling the corded muscles of his back and chest; my lips tasting his salty skin. His mouth burns a trail over my collarbone and down my stomach and moves on to my neck, my body shivering despite the heat of the night.

He pauses above me, his eyes scalding mine as they ask a silent question. Instead of answering him, I push against him, a low moan leaving him as our bodies connect. My breath hisses through my mouth at the feel of him. I move my hips and he responds. It's fast, frantic, and shatters me.

And it happens again. And again.

Slower each time, but no less passionate. He devours me, he loves me, he ignites my fire and puts me out. It is exquisite torture. And when we are finally sated, we lie in the grass as I silently replay each magnificent detail, a smile of content on my lips. *This* is what it's supposed to be like.

"I want forever with you," he whispers into my ear, his body naked and still wrapped around mine.

Enough time has passed for our breathing to even out and my heart to steady in its beat, but I cannot let him go yet. He apparently has the same idea, his limbs still intertwined with mine, his arms around me, his chin next to my cheek.

I smile into his flat chest, my hand running up and down his arm, liking how his muscles tense and the skin pebbles beneath my fingers. "You'll have me for forever. No matter what, I'll still be in your heart. You know that. That's how I'll live."

I set my palm on the place above his beating heart and feel it pound. "You'll live for me," I whisper, kissing the spot my hand just moved away from.

"Are you afraid? Because I'm terrified."

I move to sit up and he grudgingly allows me to. "I don't want to be afraid. I'm trying really hard not to be. It wasn't exactly easy at first, but now...it is *so hard* knowing this is all temporary. And you know what's really stupid of me?"

I take a shuddering breath and tears form, trailing down my cheeks in rivers of despair. "I still have hope. There is still some part of me that thinks the doctors were wrong and that I am not dying."

I stare at my clasped hands.

Rivers puts on his boxer briefs, handing me his shirt. I put it on, enveloped in the scent of him, and wait until he is sitting before me to continue.

"I was so angry at first, *so angry*. I didn't understand. I couldn't believe it. Why me? That's what I kept thinking. And why my brother? And why...*why*...my mother? She is a good person and she doesn't deserve this—not any of this." I look up with burning eyes and meet his stricken gaze.

"But even in the corner of my mind and heart, there was you. I saw past my pain and saw yours instead. And it helped me. Don't you see? All of this, everything I've experienced with you this summer, has made me able to cope with it. And you, *all of you*, are going to get through this," I tell him in a voice thick with sorrow, but also conviction.

"My accident...the start of the summer—it all feels like it happened a really long time ago. I don't even remember why I was feeling sorry for myself." His eyes dim. "I was feeling sorry for myself, and there you were, with...*this*. I'm such a jerk."

I laugh softly. "You didn't know."

"I don't believe that this is it," he mutters. "That just...it can't be. There has to be another way, there has to be a way to fix this."

"There isn't. Remember what you told me? I couldn't fix you and you can't fix me either. The chance that I would survive an operation of this magnitude is microscopic, and even if I did survive, there is no guarantee I would be *me*."

I press a hand against my beating heart. "I don't want to live half a life. I'd rather live a full one now, while I can."

"You're giving up." His voice is accusatory, but I see the laceration of anguish in his features.

I shake my head. "I'm not giving up. This is my life, for however long it lasts. My life, my choice. Giving up would have been staying in my house for the duration of the summer, for the rest of my life, really. Giving up would have been feeling sorry for myself instead of choosing to help you and your mother, to not decide to take this heartache and make something *good* come out of it. I'm not saying I haven't had my moments.

"There were times when I tried to hide away, but I couldn't do it, not for long. There will be more moments when it gets to be too much and I can't deal. But I refuse to give up. I haven't yet. I won't. I never did, not really. Giving up would have been pushing you away instead of jumping at the chance to love you."

He goes still, his eyes flying to mine.

The smile that touches my lips is large and sad. Joy and sorrow—my two constant emotions lately. "You have to know. I love you, Rivers. Desperately. Undeniably. Wholly. Without regret."

He averts his eyes, standing and turning partially away from me. "I don't—I can't." He grabs his head and spins away, his back lifting and lowering with his breathing.

His eyes are filled with tears when he turns back to me and says, "You love me? I'm going to be the one left behind, still loving you, long after you're gone. I'm going to be the one missing you. I'm going to be the one looking for you, reaching for you, and *never again* finding you.

"I love you, Delilah. I love you to a catastrophic depth that I didn't even know I was possible of having. I am *filled* with you. And..." He tries to speak, but his throat bobs as words fail him.

"I don't want you to regret loving me, or to be sad about it. This is why I didn't tell you sooner, why I didn't know if I *could* tell you. I didn't want my condition to change how people acted around me.

"I didn't want people to feel sorry for me, or themselves. I just...I wanted to live like a normal person while I still could, and you let me. I will forever be grateful that I got the chance to know you, and to love you. I realized you were so much more than I originally thought you were. And I fell in love with you, every part of you. I am *so glad* I got the chance."

I touch his tear-stained face, my heart swelling. "I can't regret this summer, not even if it only happened because of this illness I have. Without this disease and without your accident, we would not be where we are right now. And I can't take it back, not even if it meant living the rest of my life, because that life would have been without knowing you, and *that*, that would be the real tragedy here.

"Can you just love me back? Knowing what you know about me shouldn't change anything, because really, no one knows when their last day will be, right? Let's think of this as both of us having an indefinite number of days, months, or years left on this earth, and let's make the most of what we get."

He crushes me to him and I wrap my arms around his trembling body. I press my ear to his heart, hearing the thundering beat of it. I kiss the spot above it. I kiss his neck. I kiss his lips. They taste of salt and sorrow, love and fear. He breaks away, resting his forehead to mine.

Taking a deep breath, he slowly nods. "Okay. I can do that. I'll love you. I'll keep loving you, for always. I'll love you even when you can't love me back. *I love you*," he murmurs.

"I love you. I love you. I love you, Delilah. Desperately. Undeniably. Wholly. Without regret." Each declaration is marked with a kiss to my forehead, my nose, my cheek, and my lips.

ELEVEN

I FIND HIM NEAR THE window, watching the rain pour down on the grass outside. I have been struggling with myself all morning, with what I need to tell him, with whether or not I can physically say the words to him.

I want to tell him not to mourn me for too long, that it is okay to be sad for a while, but then he has to snap out of it. I want to tell him to smile, to find a way to be happy. I want to tell him so many things and yet all the words in the world seem inadequate in the face of the storm we are approaching.

He feels me behind him, his body straightening. A moment later he is turning to face me. I can tell he is trying to hide his pain, but it seeps out in the lines around his mouth, the darkness beneath his eyes. I hate what this is doing to him, I hate watching him trying to break through the despair that wants to pull him down. He's trying so hard to be strong for me.

"When I..." I trail off, tears burning my eyes. I gather my courage and try again. "When I—"

"Stop," he says in a bleak voice. "Don't even say it."

"I have to. There are things I need to tell you before...just...before."

"No."

A small smile claims my lips. "You're being stubborn."

The fury is swift and potent. "I don't care. I don't want to hear whatever it is you feel the need to tell me. I can believe whatever the hell I want to believe. Who are you to take that away from me? If I want to believe one day you will be miraculously cured, then I get to. You said you had a choice, right? Well, so do I. And

I don't choose to believe I'm going to wake up one day and you won't be there. That's my decision. That's what *I* want."

I nod and the slight motion releases a trail of tears from my eyes. "All right."

He presses his lips to mine and higher yet, warmth spreading through me at the touch of his lips to my forehead. I wrap my arms around his hard frame and hold on tight.

"We're going to be fine," he tells me.

I inhale, nodding. We will be. After it is all over and faded with time, he will be okay as well.

He takes a shuddering breath, his body trembling against mine. "Don't let the future dictate the present. You're stronger than that."

"It's official; I rubbed off on you."

"I know. Don't tell anyone." Rivers stares at me, his eyes shining with wetness as he moves back. His hands forms into fists at his sides. "I don't want you to go," he whispers.

I look down. "I don't want to go either."

I walk to the window and touch the cool pane of glass, watching the sky's tears blur it—or maybe those are mine. I look up just as a tear is released and slides down his scarred cheek. "I hate seeing you so sad. I hate what this is doing to you. I didn't want this. I don't want you to be sad."

He shows me his taut back. I stare at the hard muscles, tense beneath his shirt. I want to ease the strain from them, but keep my distance.

"All of this is bull shit." He whirls around, his features darkened by pain. "This shouldn't be happening. Not to you."

"Rivers—" I begin, but he cuts me off.

"*No.*" His jaw is clenched. "Don't tell me some philosophical crap that's supposed to make this all okay. It *isn't* okay. It will *never* be okay."

He stares at me, his chest rising and lowering faster the longer his eyes are locked with mine. And then his face crumples just before he covers it with his hands.

I move for him, pulling his hands away. He resists me at first, but then it becomes too much and he sinks into me instead of trying to push me away. His fingers cup the back of my neck and he lowers his head to rest against the side of my face, his arms moving up to lock me to him. He pushes us back until I am to the wall and he is pressed against me.

He's trying to meld us together, to give me his strength, his will, to continue to live. He's trying to give me his life. I feel it in the confined darkness trembling through his body with the need to lash out in grief, and my heart swells for him.

"I would trade places with you if I could," he tells me brokenly.

"I know. And I'm sorry I have to leave you."

"What am I supposed to do with you gone?" he whispers against the side of my neck.

"Keep living." I close my eyes and turn my face to kiss the corner of his mouth.

I take a deep breath and say softly, "At the beginning of summer, I asked myself what it all meant, what it was all about—this whole living and dying business. I wanted to know why there was so much pain in life, why others hurt others, why we hurt ourselves. Why we have to die before we've lived a whole life. I wanted to know the point of it all. I know now." I press a kiss to his shoulder.

He tightens his hold on me, quietly listening.

"First of all, you can be eighty years old and not really lived; just as you can be eighteen years old and have lived enough for two. It's all about perspective. And the meaning of it all...it's about not being scared to live, no matter what it brings you. It's about not being scared to love, no matter if you eventually lose it. It's about forgiveness and acceptance.

"And hope—it has to be about hope. It's about knowing, sometimes, there are no answers, and you don't necessarily have to be okay with that, but you have to know that whether you're okay with it or not, that's just the way it is."

We stand like this for an indefinite amount of time, and yet when he pulls away, I miss him immediately. I smile at him, in awe that I am with him, that he is with me. I will hold this love close to me, close to my heart, and I will live in the overwhelming wonder of it.

"I didn't get to choose whether or not I wanted my life this way, but there was one thing I did choose. It was you. I chose you," I whisper.

The breath he takes is stuttering and he tugs me back to him, enclosing me in his arms that make me forget I can be truly okay anywhere outside of them. His arms protect me from the ensuing darkness, from the night that never truly goes away.

He murmurs, "I chose you."

RIVERS IS ON A QUEST to show me all the wondrous moments I have missed while wrongfully looking down on sports. One day, he made me play catch with a football. He decided I'd already showed enough of my prowess with a basketball not to have to endure that again. We went roller skating—I stayed on my feet all of five seconds. He wanted me to try golf, but I argued and argued until he relented and we spent the afternoon playing mini-golf instead. Not that I was any better at that, but at least I had fun hitting the ball up and down the green mat.

I know what he's doing—he's making sure I experience all the things I have not thus far before it is too late. He's forcing me to live; just like I forced him to. And tonight, we're watching baseball.

The stadium is huge. I mean, *massive*. Rows upon rows wrap around the ball field, each filled with an incredible amount of people. The layering of voices is just one loud buzzing. I don't think I have ever been around so many people at once. I find I don't like it all that well. I tighten my grip on Rivers' hand as we take our seats and face the field below us. It's a night game, but you wouldn't be able to tell it's dark out with all the lights ablaze within the vicinity.

"Thomas used to take me to a Brewers game every summer."

I adjust the Brewers cap Rivers got me and look at him from

under the bill of it. "Why'd he stop?"

He shrugs, looking at a man walking up the stairs to the left of us. "I don't know. I guess he decided it wasn't necessary anymore. I think he wanted to love me, but his insecurities wouldn't allow him to, not in the way he should." He nods at the man. "He's a computer programmer and spends his weekends living in a wondrous haze of role-playing video games."

I study the chubby man with balding blond hair and glasses, noting the strain on his face. "He lives at home with his mom and his bedroom is beneath hers. She thumps her cane on the floor when she wants him to turn off the computer."

He grins. "His avatar is a Viking with long, beautiful locks of blond hair and he calls himself Hans."

"His online girlfriend is big and busty and thinks he's sexy in a geeky kind of way."

Giving me a strange look, he tosses a handful of popcorn into his mouth. "Her name is Betsy and she sells make-up."

"They're going to meet this fall."

"And he's going to move in with her, wherever she lives, if for no other reason than to escape his battle-axe mother."

I grin and sip my fruit punch. The air is electric with energy, the crowd alive with anticipation for the game to start. I feel it pulsate through me and even I am anxiously tapping my shoes against the bench.

"You look so cute in that hat," he murmurs, grabbing the bill of the baseball cap, flipping it around to reveal my face, and pressing his lips to mine. He tastes like butter and fruit punch.

"Have you talked to Thomas much since everything? I mean, are you guys all right?" I ask when he releases me, leaning back as three girls shuffle past us to get to their section.

I can tell he doesn't want to talk about it, especially now, but he had to have brought him up for some reason.

"He called me a few nights ago when you were out riding your bike."

"And?" I prompt when he apparently loses his ability to talk.

He glances at me, offering the bag of popcorn. It's a stall tactic and my look tells him I know it is. He knows I don't like popcorn. "We talked about you. We talked about college. My car. That day on the river. He apologized, said he never wanted that to happen. He wants to take me fishing the next time he comes back." He becomes quiet and I patiently wait.

He snorts, shaking his head. "The fact that we talked about anything of significance is monumental. He's trying, I'll give him that. I don't think we'll ever be what I would like us to be; I just don't think it's possible, but maybe we can be something."

"So it was a good talk."

A small smile captures his lips as he nods. "Yeah. I guess it was."

"And you're going fishing." I bump my arm to his.

The crowd shoots to life, droning out his answer. The game is about to start. He gets to his feet, pulling me up with him, and we grin at each other as music blares out of the overheard speakers. The grin turns mischievous, apprehension flashing through me just as the crowd quiets down.

"You can stop thinking you need to be more like me now," I hiss into his ear as I clutch his shoulder to keep him from straightening up and doing whatever it is he is planning on doing.

"You only live once," he counters, tugging away. "And anyway, you imprinted yourself onto my soul, so...you're there, for always. You're a part of me." Half of his mouth lifts. "You're just going to have to deal with it."

And he flings his arms out wide, tilts his head back, and shouts so loudly my ears ring, "I love you, Delilah Marie Bana! Who is *not* related to Eric Bana!"

Bodies turn our way as eyes zero in on us, and Rivers just laughs, tugging me to him and monopolizing my mouth with his. He has such gifted lips. Beautiful mind. Lovely heart.

"I wouldn't be able to do this for anyone else," he whispers into my ear.

"Do what?" I whisper back, my heart pounding.

"Be me."

My being sighs in response and I tighten my hold on him, loving him with all of me, loving him with *everything*. His body may have been fragmented at one point, but his soul has always been indestructible. I smile as we kiss again, thinking of all the many ways we can be torn down and damaged, but where it really counts, we remain impenetrable—a fortress against the onslaught of all the heartache life can bring. *Whole.*

STAYING IN THIS CABIN IS like taking a piece of perfection in a world of heartache and living on it. When I sit in the quiet, and focus on the wood of the walls around me, I can imagine I am safe from it all. If I just stay inside, death won't catch me. It's silly, I know. The cabin has one bedroom, a small kitchen area that opens into a living room, and a bathroom. It's tiny, but cozy. And I love it. I don't think there could be a more fitting place to spend the rest of my days.

My mom fired me. I went to work yesterday and she literally said, "You're fired."

At first, I sputtered incoherently, and then when my brain started to work properly again, I asked why. She said because I don't need to be working when I could be enjoying the rest of the summer. Not that I disagree; it just came as a shock. I told her cleaning is my idea of fun and she said that is exactly what she meant and pushed me out the door.

I thought about her words as I drove to the cabin, and I decided she was right. I did have a trip I meant to take and I can't not do it. That would be like giving up a sliver of joy when all I get are tiny slices of it at a time. In other words, it would be stupid. And Rivers needs to lighten up as well. He's walking around in a fog of gray.

Honestly, I almost feel like *he* is the one with this stupid-ass brain malfunction instead of me. I told him he was a melodramatic punk a couple of nights ago and he stormed out of the cabin. I let him go, knowing not every day is going to be a picture of pretty flowers and rainbows.

There will be thunderstorms, and there will be lightning. There will be downpours.

Sometimes he cries at night. When he thinks I am sleeping, I feel the tremble of his body beside mine, I hear the pain that escapes though he tries so hard to hold it in for me. It isn't every night, but even one night is too much. In the light, he tries to smile. But in the dark his stoic wall crumbles. I cannot stand this. Rivers hurting hurts me. I take his smiles in the daytime and I take his pain in the nighttime, one with joy and one with sorrow.

This has to end.

There are good days and bad days. Days I don't want to get out of bed, days when the pain in my head makes it impossible to get out of bed. There are days when Rivers cannot look at me without tearing up and my mother can- not speak around the grief closing her throat. Days when it takes Monica to forcefully remove Rivers from the cabin and make him do something inconsequential, like fly a kite. I have a list made up of things for him to do when the despondency gets too thick and neither of us can breathe.

I have a similar list for my mother, but hers isn't made up of unimportant events to get her mind off the undeniable truth. Her list is made up of two requests. *Think of me when you look at your flowers*, and, *Call him*.

I truly hope she does. Even if he never cares to speak to her again, even if he has another family and another life, it will be good for her. And maybe he'll be just as happy to hear her voice as I know she will be to hear his.

Monica is my champion. I know it has been hard for her with Thomas gone, but I think the fact that she has me to boss her around actually helps. It keeps her preoccupied. And even after I am gone, she knows I will still be counting on her to hold Rivers and my mother up when they need someone to carry them. And they will be there for her as well. They won't let her fall.

She misses Thomas, I can tell. Or maybe she just misses the idea of him. She is sad, but she also seems like a strain has been removed from her. Her footsteps are lighter, her frown lines are less distinguished. Whether people treat us right or not, or deserve us or not, it is hard to let go of what we know. But I watch her with her son and my mother and I know they are all going to get through this.

They have each other, and in each other, they will always have me.

It is the middle of August. Rivers tested for his GED and passed. School at the tech starts in a few weeks and we will be in attendance. Everything is moving forward as it should, and one day I will too. I sit at the small table in the sparsely furnished cabin, tapping my fingers as I wait for him to get back from the job he started a week ago at the hardware store in town—the job I told him to take because he was driving me insane with his endless hovering and tragic eyes. I can only take so much sorrow before I fall apart and cannot put myself back together.

Two suitcases sit by my feet, my foot occasionally bumping them as my leg nervously jerks back and forth in beat with my foot. I hear the car as the tires meet with gravel and wait. When he opens the door, the frantic pace he moves with turns to a full stop as he takes me in, averting his panicked eyes from me.

I fight the impulse to comment on his obvious distress and then find myself doing it anyway. "Is that what you do every day? Leave with dread only to return with it?"

Rivers swipes a hand through his dark hair. "No. Maybe."

"I want you to stop." I get to my feet, anger causing my whole being to tremble. "I want you to stop being sad all the time. And stop—stop crying, okay? I can't take it anymore""

"Yeah. I'll just flip a switch and it'll all be good. How's that?" He notices the bags at my feet and freezes. "What are those for?"

"I can't keep doing this," I tell him, my throat thick.

His eyebrows furrow as he looks at me with incomprehension.

"What are you telling me? What are you doing, Del?" he demands, fear roughening his voice. He crosses the room to me. "Tell me what you're doing."

I slide a rectangular piece of paper toward him. He picks it up, studying the words. He looks at me, waiting. I pick up the other piece of paper and hand it to him.

"These are two Amtrak tickets," he finally says.

I nod. "We need to leave within an hour. We're escaping. No more sadness. I am drowning in it and I'm going to go insane. I know you are too. I don't want to be crazy on top of everything else when I die."

He glares at me and I shrug.

"Just keeping it real. It's the six-day trip through Memphis and New Orleans. Graceland, baby, and voodoo." I wiggle my eyebrows at him.

Rivers rests the tickets against his lips, slowly nodding. "Yeah. Let's do it. But Delilah—"

I grab the lighter of the suitcases and look up, going still at the darkness of his gaze.

"You don't get to take my sadness away, all right? And sometimes, you're right, it gets to be too much, but I can't feel bad about that, because I just—I love you so much, and... this is shredding me. I'm sorry if that hurts you to hear, but it's true."

His eyes are red-rimmed as they meet mine. "And also...I'll try to stop being such a melodramatic punk."

"Good," I say softly. "Because there can only be one of those in this relationship, and that's already me. You know, fainting and whatnot. Anything to get a little attention."

Rivers smiles faintly. He takes the suitcase from me and picks up the other one as well. "I love you and all your attention-seeking antics."

"That's good. Just wait until the finale. It's going to be epic."

The look he gives me tells me that was too much.

"It's either joke about it or bawl my eyes out," I tell his back.

He swings the door open, calling over his shoulder, "Drama!"

THE INSIDE OF THE TRAIN reminds me of images I've seen of the interiors of commercial planes. There are rows of seats in pairs with an aisle separating another row of the same. It is the middle of the week and I'm glad, because I think a lot more of the seats would be taken if it was on the weekend. It smells like hot synthetic leather mixed with coffee. Rivers is beside me, reading a book.

As the train begins to roll down the tracks, I bounce in my seat. I am so ready for an adventure. Although, this whole summer has sort of already been one. This final trip makes it complete. I realize I made my own bucket list without even knowing it. I think of the people I love, and I think of them years from now, and I really feel that they will be happy, if for no other reason than I have been demanding it of them. Dying has some perks, you know?
People want to fulfill your last requests.

I glance at Rivers and find him watching me with warmth in his eyes.

"I'm excited," I explain.

"I thought you just had to pee."

I laugh.

A teenager walks past with dark makeup, black clothing, and spiky brown hair. "She's in a rebellious faze. She's actually an honor student and wants to be a doctor, but she is struggling to find the real her and experimenting with her exterior in her quest for individuality."

He blinks, setting his book aside to find the girl in question. "She actually wants to be a veterinarian. She loves animals and tries to take home strays any chance she can. Her parents put a stop to that after the third cat, but they don't know about the dog she's keeping at her boyfriend's until she can talk them into letting her bring it home."

"They don't know about the boyfriend either, though, so that is going to make it tricky."

I search the train for another story, settling on an elderly couple. "They fell in love right out of high school. He worked for her dad, helping out on the farm. She brought lemonade out to him one hot day and they smiled at one another and that was it."

"They have two children and seven grandchildren."

As we watch, the man lifts the woman's hand to his lips and places a kiss to it. My heart fills with the soft sigh of watching love in action.

Rivers is quiet for a moment, his voice low and uneven as he says, "There were days when they thought about giving up. He thought being a farmer wasn't good enough for her. She thought getting a job would help out with bills. They both had good intentions, they both had the other in mind, but pride got in the way, putting a strain on them and their love."

"But they always had laughter. They always found a way around the difficult times, because even though they thought about giving up, they never did. They never could."

Rivers pulls his cell phone from his pocket and holds it up to us, turning the camera so we are within its frame. "Tell me their story."

I look at his dark eyes in the screen as I begin. "Their story isn't a fairytale, but that's okay, because fairytales are predictable, and sometimes boring. It's funny how you can be around someone almost all of your life and not know them. That's sort of what it was like for them. They were constantly missing each other."

"Until they were shoved together."

He smiles and I smile. The camera flashes and he puts the phone away.

Under his breath, almost to himself, he says, "It's weird being thankful for something terrible."

I bump my arm to his. "He was such a pain in the ass, but that just made her even more determined to straighten him out."

"She was kind of abusive, forcing him to eat ice cream and grilled peanut butter and jelly sandwiches. He was traumatized for a long time about that."

"He talked about being a pilot and she hoped he never forgot that, no matter what happened."

His fingers interlace with mine. "He wouldn't. I won't. I can't promise I'll do it, but I can promise I won't forget the dream."

My eyes soften. "She thought he had everything, but found he was still searching for that one unnamable thing that makes a person feel like they finally figured out what is most important to them."

"He saw her golden eyes shining like fire and life and knew he'd finally found it."

"Their story isn't over, Rivers—*our* story is not over." I touch his cheek and he turns his face into it.

He nods, swallowing as he looks down. "I know."

"I love you," I whisper, my voice trembling with the depth of my feelings for him.

Smiling sweetly, he wraps his arms around me as the train picks up speed. "I know that too."

WE FIND A PARK NEAR the hotel we're staying at in Memphis. It's small and near a residential part of the city, so it actually doesn't seem that different from where we live. A few swings sway in the distance from the gentle breeze that skims along my skin as well. Although the ride was interesting, it was long and I am glad to be on solid ground. We plan on doing sightseeing tomorrow, but tonight is for relaxing. Sitting in the dewy grass, we recline on our elbows and take in the clash of millions of points of light illuminating the dark.

"Most stars in the Milky Way live for fifty billion years."

Rivers looks at me. "Oh yeah? That's a seriously long time. What determines how long a star will live?"

"The bigger the star, the quicker it dies," I supply, and then go quiet.

"That's not exactly uplifting," he tells me. "What about the sun? Isn't that the biggest star? Your theory doesn't make sense."

"It isn't *my* theory. I read it once. And I don't know why the sun continues to live when it's the biggest star and the smaller stars don't."

"Maybe it isn't as old. It could be a really young star."

"*Or* it isn't the biggest star. Regardless, one day it will die too."

I don't know why this upsets me so much, but it does. It isn't like I will be around for it. I guess because something so beautiful, so infinite, should not have a time limit on it. Like life. Why can't it just go on forever?

"But you know what? Think of that lifetime, Del. It's...*phenomenal*. It goes on and on for such a long time before it ends. Right?"

Smiling, I nod.

He always knows what I need to hear. I am at peace with my time here. I cannot say that I am okay with it, because I am not, and I never will be, but there is no point in fighting a future that will come regardless of whether I am accepting of it or choosing to deny it. I don't think about how much time I have anymore. I don't wonder.

I fall asleep each night thankful to be in Rivers' arms, thankful that I have one more night on this earth. I wake up each morning with a smile on my face because I get one more day.

After a while, he says, "I suppose you read all of this on the internet? What was your source? Facebook?"

I scowl and he laughs. "No."

I did read it online, but not on Facebook. I believe it was Wikipedia.

"You crack me up."

"Ah, my life is complete now."

He reaches over and plays with a lock of my hair. "Mine too. Strange."

I have found, that you can't tiptoe through life, scared of what will or won't happen because of how you choose to live. You have to run at it as fast as you can, without fear, without even pausing to think about what you're doing. If you pause, you fall.

This is my advice: Keep running.

"I can see our life, what it would be like, if we got the chance to grow old together. I already know our story, beginning to end," he says quietly.

I turn my head to find his eyes on me. He puts his hand on

mine and interlocks our fingers.

"What would it be?" I ask him.

Facing forward, he says, "We would finish college—"

"What are we going for?"

"Well, we'd finish the basic stuff and then go on to what we really want to do. I'd fly planes and you'd decorate the insides of homes. In fact, you'd become fairly well-known with your unusual design sense. I'd be your trophy husband."

"Ooooh, I like that. I'd get to dress you up like a doll and parade you around. You could be my visual piece of meat."

"I think you're enjoying the thought of that a little too much. Can I continue?"

I smile, closing my eyes. "Continue."

He plays with a lock of my hair, warmth spreading through my limbs as my body sinks farther into the cool ground. "We'd get married. You'd pick the colors—"

"Pink and black," I supply.

"Pink and black. We'd have one boy and one girl. The boy would have your golden eyes and carefree manner, the girl would be into all things pink and frilly."

"Neil and...Willow." For my brother, and the tree that cries for him—and for all of us that must leave before we are ready.

His hand pauses. "I like those names."

"Me too," I whisper, turning my face into his hand and kissing the palm.

"We'd have family movie night, family game night, take them camping and to ballgames and—"

"Don't forget coloring and drawing...crafts."

"How could I forget those?" he gently mocks.

"We'd grow old and decrepit together and sit out on our porch at night."

"I'd yell at kids to get off the lawn."

I softly laugh, sitting up. I gaze down at him, the shadows formed on his face from a nearby streetlamp heightening the curve of his full mouth, the sharpness of his cheekbones, and evening out the squareness of his jaw. My heart beats with tenderness and it trickles through my veins to fill me with peace.

"We'd live with so much joy in our lives that when our time came to go, we would smile instead of cry."

Like I will.

Rivers scoots behind me and wraps his arms around me. "I like that version. That's our life. Agree?"

"Agree."

And maybe in some alternate world, it would be.

I inhale deeply, wishing I could bottle up this moment right now and wrap it around us so that it never went away. And then I realize, it never does. It won't. This is us, our time, and what we have will never die, not as long as one of us remembers.

He begins slowly, "I think, someway, somehow, we will meet again. I don't know how—I don't know when. But I feel it, here, in my heart."

He touches a hand to the spot above my beating heart and the tempo of it picks up. "This is not our end. There is no end for us."

This might be our story, but this is more his story than mine. It will continue on as his as well—I am merely a character that has a substantial, but small role in the book. The rest is his. All of this, everything I have done this summer, has been for him. In a way, I exchanged my life for his.

I chose him.

We watch the stars as they flicker on with an invisible switch, neither speaking for a long moment.

Then he nuzzles the side of my neck with his nose, whispering into my ear, "I still choose you."

I smile, a star blinking out from the sky as I watch.

That one just went home. My smile deepens.

"I will always choose you," I say back.

EPILOGUE

THE BEST WAY TO DESCRIBE Delilah, and what she meant to me, is to think of two people slowly walking toward one another. There are miles and years between them—an endless tunnel of gray surrounding the encounter—but when they finally connect, a pulsating light forms inside each of them, growing, until it consumes them. They thrive in the burn of it, but it soon fades out, like all brilliant things do, and they are left bereft in the absence of the other half of their soul. That was what we had. That is what I lost. I am not bitter about it, but I continue to grieve that part of my life—the part that belongs to Delilah Bana.

A part of me always will.

I smile. I laugh. And I look at the stars and think of her. I know she would have wanted that, so that's what I do. I miss her smile. It was like a piece of sunshine aimed directly at my heart. I miss her fearlessness and generosity, the sound of her laughter. I miss her eclectic fashion sense and her diversified music addiction. I miss the random things she would say to distract me or to get a reaction out of me. I miss how big and infinite her heart was. It doesn't seem possible that someone who had so much life in them could be reduced to a memory.

Because of her, I healed. Because of her, I loved like I had never loved before. It was a special kind of love; one that cannot be imitated nor replaced. Because of her, I was able to be myself and realized I was fine just the way I was, any way I was.

There are so many 'because of hers'.

We had five months, two weeks, and three days more after the last day of summer, every one of them spent together. On the day she died, the woods were covered in a glittery blanket of snow. Even as Delilah died, she did so with light, smiling as her eyes closed for the final time. A tumor had taken hold of her at some point in her eighteen years, but it was an aneurysm that finally claimed her.

And the tears—I never thought I would stop crying when she left me. I was injured in a way I hadn't thought possible, incomparable to any other pain I'd ever endured, physical or otherwise.

That spring, I planted a Willow tree where she fell. My mom and Janet were with me. My tears helped water the soil around the tree—my tears became part of that tree. I don't go back to the cabin that much anymore, but I know that the tree is still there, growing, mourning, and putting life back into the place where death once was.

Illegal or not, she made me pinky swear to spread her ashes on the Mississippi River—as a way to get me to over- come my fear of the torrential waters and as a way to give them what they sought to find in me and were not allowed. I also think it was her way of giving them the finger. As I did as she requested, I pictured her shaking her fist as she shouted at the river: *You wanted Rivers? Well, you got me instead.* The thought made me cry at first, but now it makes me smile.

Months went by where I barely ate, wanting to be with her, wanting to die so I could see her again. I dropped out of college, slept all day, ignored my mom, Thomas, my friends, and even Janet. It was bad. And then one day I looked up at a dark sky and saw a single star, and felt her. She was telling me to get my ass in gear and live again. That was enough for me to realize I had to get my act together. Not just for me and those around me, but for her.

My mom and Thomas never got back together, but it's strange—we all get along better now than we did as a family. *Now* we are a family; years and misunderstandings later. My mom remarried a guy named Ken. He's a mechanic and covered in grease on a regular basis. He has an easy smile and a laidback manner. As far as materialistic items go, she has so much less than she used to, but you should see the way she shines. She's happy. Life is simple for her and she's happy.

Thomas has remained single, but there is peace to him I never witnessed before. It is like, finally, *finally*, the ghost he was always competing against has been put to rest. I'm not even sure who or what that apparition was, but he knows, and he's overcome it. We see each other a few times a year, each visit spent fishing or hunting without much talking between us. I'm okay with that. Good or bad—he was my father growing up. That can't be forgotten.

Janet listened to her daughter. She called Neil's father. They are now married—for the second time—and I imagine they look how Delilah and I used to look; full of laughter, overflowing with love, and the only thing the other ones sees. Everything good, basically.

We find Delilah in each of us, and that is how we remember her. A flower, a song, ice cream, an ugly scarf—the most random things bring her to mind and we find ourselves smiling at one another, knowing without exchanging words that she is on each other's mind.

I didn't even have a chance to be sad in the months leading up to her death. She never allowed that. How can one being have so much fire, so much positivity, that everyone around her is reflected in her light?

I made a promise to her and I kept it—maybe a little later than she would have liked, but I did. She made me promise *to be happy*, *to live*, and *never regret*. So I did. I went back to college —two years later than originally planned, but I went. I did my required four years and then I went on to flight school. I became a pilot, and each time I fly, I feel her. It's the closest I can get to her. At times it seems as though Delilah is still with me, guiding me with her luminosity, telling me to think of all I have instead of all I don't.

I have so much, I know that now.

The actual time I had with her wasn't enough, would have

never been enough, but each moment was endless in its depth and I wrap my arms around those and I hold them close. I recall her first day of work, I think of the first time she yelled at me, I remember how she pushed me to never give up. She saved me. She saved me just by giving me a piece of her. The injured parts of my life were healed with the parts of her she freely gave, intertwining us in shatterproof ways.

I think of her every day. I think of her and I *live*. I live for me, but I also live for her. I live enough for both of us, just as she once had to.

She was like the sun, the brightest beacon of light in the whole sky, one of the biggest stars out of all the many stars. The thing about the sun is that it can't be contained, it can't be held on this earth, and it is bigger than everything and everyone. She shone for an impermanent length of time, but she burns still in my heart and in my memories. The sun is too beautiful for this world, too *great* for us mere humans, and it must be free. And she is now.

Delilah is free.

And *I* am free *because of her*.

BONUS

My PB and R
BY DELILAH BANA
(Please note: I will never do this again, so you better frame this sucker.)
Peanut butter is good, but Rivers is better.
I smear one on toast, I stare at the latter.
Both go well with bacon, but only one can get a spankin'.
Oh, how I love my glorious PB and R. I could eat it all day, as I drive in his car.
By the spoonful, by the jar— Take it away and I will rawr.
This poem is silly, and Rivers is smelly.
If I were British, maybe I could watch him on the telly?
I love my peanut butter; I love my Rivers.
If you take either away, I will be forced to resort to dithers.
I wrote this for you, just so you know— I guess I can forsake PB, but if it was you, The answer is no.

LINDY ZART

ABOUT THE AUTHOR

Lindy Zart

Lindy Zart is an American USA Today bestselling author who writes across a number of fictional genres such as new adult, contemporary romance, and fantasy. Her rom-com Roomies (2014) was an international bestseller that rose to #1 in Satire Fiction, Romantic Comedy, General Humor, and Humorous, becoming a USA Today bestseller. She currently lives in Wisconsin with her family.

BOOKS BY THIS AUTHOR

Steady As The Snow Falls

Hired by a stranger to write his life story, Beth Lambert arrives at a seemingly abandoned house in the hills near her hometown. She knows the rumors, she knows it is dangerous and unwise. But she needs the money. And she needs to prove that it isn't a mistake to think she can make a career out of a dream.

Inside the house of emptiness and coldness, she finds a man with curt words and haunted eyes. He is eccentric, odd. Brutish, even. He scares her, and he intrigues her. When she learns who he is, she wants to run. But there is the money, and there is the dream, and eventually, there is simply Harrison Caldwell. The haunted man with the black, ugly truth.

Safe And Sound

This is Lola's story.

She has a secret no one can know. Once a safe haven, her home has turned into a prison, and she fears if she doesn't somehow escape, she will lose herself completely. She finds her escape in Jack; a troubled young man with a cynical smile and eyes that see all Lola tries to hide.

But even Jack can't save her from what awaits at home.

Smother

You won't like me.
I am not the nice girl. I am not your friend.
I don't care about you, but most of all, I don't care about me.
Go ahead, hate me.
We all have secrets.
I have them as well—dark, terrible secrets.
The only time I can breathe is when I forget.
I need to be numb. You don't want to know how.
But as long as I can breathe, the past cannot smother me.

Printed in France by Amazon
Brétigny-sur-Orge, FR